CROWD PLEASER

CROWD PLEASER

KAYLEE LOSEY

Smitten Publishing

CHAPTER 1

This guy must be the biggest douchebag I have ever met.

Jett Miller was sitting across the dinner table from the ultimate bro: Mint green long-sleeved polo shirt, khaki Chinos, with a brown belt and matching brown loafers. The guy was wearing loafers. And he was dating Jett's baby sister. What the fuck?

He reminded himself that this was typical. Lizzie was always bringing home dudes who were all wrong for her. They weren't all the same type of wrong, but they were always the worst version of whatever image they were trying to portray. If he was going for the jock look, he never wore anything but basketball shorts or sweatpants, jerseys, and UnderArmor sweatshirts. He'd probably bring a basketball or football *everywhere* and was about as bright as a black hole.

If she brought home a hipster? He'd have skinny jeans, an ironic lumberjack beard, and only drink craft beer. There'd been a few OG wanna-be's with low-sagging pants, oversized shirts, and backwards flat-billed caps, and *several* of these preppy frat bros like the one sitting across from him now.

"Next weekend we're heading up to my parents' ski cabin- beautiful country up there," Brad was saying. *Brad. His name is fucking Brad.*

"Oh, that should be lovely," Jett's mom replied in her airy, friendly, somewhat oblivious tone. Lizzie most definitely got her optimistic attitude about the world and the people in it from their mother.

These monthly family dinners were usually pretty eventful, especially when Lizzie brought home a new man. This was the third new guy this year. The *third* guy she was so infatuated with that she needed to bring him home to meet the whole family.

Sitting around the large dining table were the eldest Miller son, Gavin, and his wife, Rachel, along with their little boy, Grant; the oldest Miller daughter, Allison and her husband, Colin, the parents, the grandparents, Jett, Lizzie, and now Brad. *Fucking Brad.*

Gavin leaned into Jett's space and spoke low so only they could hear. "What do we think, little bro?" Jett noted his older brother's skeptical glance across the table at Brad.

Jett grunted. "Slight improvement over the plus-sized Justin Bieber with a neck tattoo." He took a sip from his bottle of Labatt Blue and winced at Brad's bright white smile as he charmed the parents. "Where does she find these guys?"

"The grocery store, the bookstore, Starbucks...your bar?" Gavin listed, with a sly grin.

"He'd get his ass kicked at my bar," Jett replied, aggressively stabbing a piece of broccoli with his fork.

Gavin snorted loud enough to call attention to their side conversation.

"What are we laughing at, boys?" Jett's dad turned a warning eye on the brothers.

"Jett was just sharing something that happened at the bar last week," said Gavin, innocently.

"Oh?"

Jett nodded. "Yeah, some preppy guy got his ass kicked. Fun to watch." He popped another chunk of broccoli into his mouth as he looked across the table at Brad.

Unfortunately, his attempt to intimidate the guy was unsuccessful. Lizzie gave Jett a warning glare, but Brad beamed. "Lizz told me you own Trojan Horse. That has to be fun work. Got some good stories?"

Jett chewed slowly. There was nothing subtle about his glare as he stared Brad down, who still didn't let up his eager, friendly expression. He swallowed. "I guess."

Lizzie placed her hand on Brad's where it sat next to his plate. She cleared her throat and sat up straighter. "Sorry, Jett's usually more talkative. He's just having a rough time lately."

"Am I?" Jett furrowed his brow.

"Clearly," Lizzie said. "You're lonely. All of your friends have someone now, and that can't be easy for you. Whenever Chris was busy, you and Rae would hang out, but she's in California now, so you notice it more. Why *else* would you be so grumpy?" She narrowed her eyes at him threateningly.

Okay, so his current bad mood didn't entirely have to do with the facts that she'd just pointed out, but they didn't exactly help. Having them pointed out in front of his entire family wasn't doing anything to fix his sour mood either.

Jett was co-owner of Trojan Horse Sports Bar in downtown Traverse City, alongside his best friend Chris Watson- the third. The two of them had been best friends since they were in diapers, and it was a blast working and owning the business together, but Chris was busy outside of the bar. He was married and had a little girl going on three, and his wife, Victoria, was strongly hinting at wanting another baby. While completely supportive of this decision- he *loved* being Uncle Jett to Sophia- it was at times difficult to adjust to the significant differences in their lives.

Still single, with absolutely no immediate prospects, Jett frequently filled his time outside the business playing guitar or piano, playing increasingly graphic video games, and watching increasingly questionable porn. It was more of a hobby at this point, honestly. Some of it just freaked him out, while the rest gave him new creative ideas to...never try out, apparently.

Another one of his best friends, Raelyn DeRose, had recently made the move across the country to Los Angeles upon reuniting with her childhood sweetheart and Major League All-Star, Quinn Casey. Chris, Rae, Quinn, and Jett had been inseparable from middle school through high school. Quinn and Rae had finally- *finally*- figured their shit out enough to get together after years of denial, Chris had met Victoria his freshman year of college, and Jett...well, Jett was still alone.

He'd had a couple of girlfriends throughout college and was lucky enough to meet and hook up with women who came into the bar every now and then, but not very often. He was terrible at talking to women he found attractive, and even worse at keeping their interest. He supposed he came off as too eager or not enough of a bad boy. Quite frankly, Jett was beginning to feel like he was just the type of guy that girls friend-zoned. He was funny, loyal, kind, and would always be there for anyone who asked for his help. Basically, he was the Golden Retriever of men.

"Thank you for that, Lizzie," Jett replied with mock sincerity. "That *must* be it."

"I can't believe you and Raelyn never dated," Allison commented from the other end of the table. "You were actually able to do the platonic male-female friend thing, *even* when she stayed in your apartment last year. I thought for sure that's when something was gonna give in that relationship."

Scrunching up his face, Jett briefly imagined him and Rae in a romantic relationship. *God, that was just wrong.* Rae was attractive, but he'd always felt more big-brotherly feelings toward her- nothing else.

He shook his head. "No...that was never going to happen."

"Have you met *anyone* recently?" his mother pressed. "You're such a handsome boy, I don't see why you can't find someone."

Jett groaned, leaning his elbows on the table as his face fell into his hands. Every family dinner- *every single one-* ended up here. Why is Jett still single? Why can't Jett find someone? Is there something fundamentally undateable about him?

"He *is* a handsome man," Grandpa Ben piped in proudly, "and I'll bet he's got a healthy sex drive. Why settle down when he's got all those twenty-two-year-olds traipsing in and out of that bar of his?" He turned to Jett and pointed a finger at him. "You're only twenty-nine! We Miller men age well and are plenty fertile. You hold out as long as you want. When you're thirty-five maybe you can find a cute twenty-something-year-old sweetie to settle down with and she'll still be in her years to pop out lots of babies for you."

Jett's face reddened and heat filled his cheeks but he couldn't help the quiet laugh that escaped him. "Thanks, Gramps."

Allison scoffed and rolled her eyes. "Jett's not single because he's sowing his wild oats."

"You don't know that," Jett said, defensively.

"Oh please, you were ready to put a ring on Samantha's finger after date number three, and look how that turned out."

Apparently his family was making sure to cover all the bases today: His lack of social life, his non-existent romantic life, *and* his most recent failed relationship. This relationship failed *four years ago*, but they still liked to bring it up for some godforsaken reason.

"This night's really not supposed to be about me," said Jett, scrubbing his hands down his face. He picked his fork back up and looked across the table. "So Brad, you said your parents own a timeshare in Venice Beach?"

Brad perked up, having the attention back on him, and opened his mouth to speak but was cut off abruptly by Jett's mother. "How is Samantha? You two were so cute together. Maybe you should try that again."

Again, Jett groaned. "Mom, I'm not cycling back to my ex. It didn't work out and I'm fine with that. I'm happy being single."

That last statement wasn't entirely true. He *was* fine not being with Samantha anymore but he wouldn't exactly describe his current state as happy. He was content. Kind of. Well, he had been content up until the previous August, but that didn't have anything to do with his friends being in relationships.

"Didn't you meet someone a little while ago?" Allison asked. "Back in September, I think it was, you spent our entire family dinner checking your phone. I remember, because you and Dad are always on us about your 'no phones at the table' rule, and you were completely ignoring it."

"That's right," Lizzie chimed in. "I remember that. You were all cute and smiley. Like a little boy with his first crush."

"It just didn't work out." Jett shrugged. He took a long pull from his beer bottle and tried not to give away too much. He wasn't a good secret keeper. At least with his friends he could put in a valiant effort to keep things to himself, but he usually couldn't handle the stress of holding in information.

Regardless, there was no way he was telling his parents or siblings about his love-at-first-sight moment he'd had at probably the most inopportune time back at the beginning of August.

Don't think about it.

Do not think about Zoey Nunez.

Ope.

That didn't work.

Yes, at the beginning of August he had met the first woman to really catch his interest in a long time. It was the closest thing he'd ever experienced to love at first sight, and the best part was that he hadn't gone completely mute around her. Typically in front of a pretty girl, Jett would clam up and act horrendously awkward. The dumbest shit would just spill out of his mouth and there was no salvaging it.

But with Zoey everything had come naturally. With Zoey...it just felt right.

Three Months Earlier

It was the first Thursday night in August and the bar had been packed. Chris, Jett, the bartenders, and kitchen crew were closing up the bar after it cleared out. Jett had just received a panicky phone call from Quinn about how Rae had never showed up at the hotel like she was supposed to. Trying not to panic and come up with reasonable explanations for this, Jett busied himself restocking the beer coolers.

There was a sharp knock on the front door to the bar and Jett looked up to see his tall, athletically built, messy-haired best friend standing on the other side. He could tell Quinn was a complete wreck and immediately unlocked the door to let him in. Quinn breezed by him, speaking rapidly, going through every single thought he must've had in the past few hours since he failed to locate his girlfriend.

Jett was about to close and lock the front door again when a new figure appeared, running in her heels to the entrance of the bar.

"Oh my God, he moves fast," the woman breathed, straightening herself and brushing the non-existent wrinkles out of her shirt. She looked up and met Jett's gaze as she swept a hand through her long, dark brown waves.

Everything went silent and still.

Jett was vaguely aware of Quinn pacing up and down the bar, and the various staff members just trying to get out of there. All Jett saw was her. Her big hazel eyes, thick black eyelashes, full, bare lips, and smooth, tan skin. She wore a three-quarter length sleeved black blazer over an emerald green shirt, with a black pencil skirt, and black heels. She looked like she'd just gotten off work, but it was three in the morning, so that didn't seem likely.

Her hair fell back over her shoulder almost as soon as she'd pushed it back and she smiled at him.

Her smile made his lungs fill and his heart stutter.

"Hey," she said through her smile. She seemed almost as caught off guard as he felt.

"Hi," Jett said, smiling back. What was happening? He was just standing here staring at her, smiling. He cleared his throat, "Um, we're closed, but if you need-"

"I'm with Quinn," she said, gesturing to the frantic baseball player behind him. "I'm Zoey- his publicist."

"You...work for Quinn?" Jett questioned, trying to comprehend everything. Was that a good thing? Did that mean their relationship was purely professional and always had been? Quinn had a bit of a reputation with the ladies before reconnecting with Rae, and Jett sort of assumed any woman Quinn met, he'd charmed into bed at least once.

"Yeah," Zoey replied, smiling again. "You must be Jett? He's told me all about you guys."

Jett smiled as she said his name, then blinked. She was still standing on the stoop outside the bar and behind her it was beginning to rain. He moved aside. "Sorry, come in." Once he'd closed the door and locked back up, he turned to her again. "Yeah, I'm Jett. Um...he's told you about me?"

"Yes, it only took two years of working for him, but he's opened up a lot in the last month. Seems like being home was good for him," said Zoey. She was looking around the bar, taking in the details before settling her eyes back on Jett. "I'm actually impressed he managed to keep it all such a secret. He's usually thrilled to talk about himself."

"He's always been secretive about his past," Jett said with a small shrug. He eyed Zoey for a minute, thinking, wondering if he should ask. It wasn't his business. But this was the most beautiful woman he'd seen since...maybe ever. She was petite and dainty and feminine and completely perfect. "You're helping him look for his girlfriend, so I'm guessing you and Quinn never...?"

Zoey's eyes went wide as though horrified. "Oh! No. No, no. It's a strictly professional relationship. I'm not interested in...ya know, someone like him."

Interesting. Most women were interested in someone exactly like Quinn Casey.

"Oh, good," Jett sighed, shoulders dropping with his exhale. Abruptly, he straightened his back again. "Not that it matters. Sorry, that really wasn't any of my business- I just-"

"Know your friend well?" Zoey finished with a smirk. "Yeah, I don't blame you." She looked around Jett to where Quinn was still pacing and rattling off every possible bad thing that could have happened to Rae. "Although, this is a whole new side. I've never seen him worry about anyone else before."

Jett couldn't help laughing a little at this woman's attitude toward Quinn and the face she made as she watched him pace. "That's not the reaction he usually gets from girls."

"Yeah, I know," Zoey shook her head. "It's usually more like-" she made her voice high and airy as she played with her hair- "oooh, Quinn

Casey, I know you've hooked up with, like, a dozen girls in the past week, but I'm still going to believe you when you tell me I'm special and different than everyone else." Zoey assumed her normal voice again. "Gag."

Jett couldn't stop the burst of laughter from coming out. "Wow, you really don't like him, do you?"

Zoey shrugged one shoulder. "He's all right. I'm just not a fan of cocky, self-absorbed womanizers."

"And how does your boyfriend feel about you working for a cocky, self-absorbed womanizer?"

"Subtle," Zoey giggled. "But there's no boyfriend."

"Husband?"

She shook her head no.

"Same-sex life partner?"

Giggling again, Zoey shook her head. "No, I'm about as single as it gets. My job keeps me pretty busy."

Jett nodded his head from side to side. "Interesting...she's single, she's super cute, and she's not interested in my best friend. I've never made it this far down the checklist before..."

"Those are some seriously high standards you're setting for yourself," Zoey said sarcastically. "Anything on that list about being a good person? Having a brain? Graduating summa cum laude from UCSD? Being the youngest and most highly regarded publicist in professional athletics? Must love dogs?"

He pressed his lips together and made himself look as though he were thinking particularly hard about this. Humming, he shook his head. "Nope. Just those three: Single, cute, doesn't want to bang my best friend."

They looked at each other for a few moments, both with reserved smiles. Jett was about to break the silence when Quinn swooped in.

"What do you guys think? Can we file a missing persons report yet?"

Zoey broke eye contact from Jett to address Quinn. "It's way too soon for that. It's only been four hours."

Right. Rae was missing. Focus, Jett.

"The bar is about done, we can head upstairs," Jett said. "I'll make coffee and we'll do some brainstorming. I'm sure she's fine, Case." He glanced back at Zoey. The urge to get to know her, to take her on a date, and treat her right was a physical need. He'd never felt this kind of pull toward someone before and he didn't know where to start. His heart wanted to skip through all the basic steps and race to the finish.

One step at a time.

He took a deep, steadying breath before leading the way upstairs into his apartment.

Unfortunately, things had gone downhill later that morning and Zoey had left for Los Angeles with Quinn almost immediately. She came back to Michigan at the end of August, but had been too busy organizing press releases and interviews for Quinn and Rae. They'd texted quite a bit when she'd gone back again and had discussed him flying out to California but their jobs both kept them extremely busy and it just...never panned out.

It was probably stupid to say that he was jealous of his friend for getting to see her every day- their relationship was completely work-related, Zoey had made that much clear- but he couldn't help feeling like it wasn't fair. At all. Quinn got to work with Zoey *and* Rae, while Jett simply had to sit over 2,000 miles away in cold, snowy Michigan and fantasize about the girl he'd probably never have.

And now...

Jett looked up at his family who were all staring at him from around the long dining room table.

"What?" he snapped. Great, now he was cranky *and* sexually frustrated.

Lizzie pressed her lips together and averted her eyes from him. Of his siblings, Jett was closest with Gavin, but he had a particularly protective attitude when it came to his youngest sister and they were still close enough that she could read him like a book. She knew when to stop pushing and quickly change the subject.

"So anyway," Lizzie said brightly, "I'll make sure to take lots of pictures at the ski cabin."

Jett brought his beer bottle to his lips again, but it was empty. Letting out a heavy sigh, he excused himself from the table to get himself another drink. In the kitchen, he reached into the fridge and grabbed another Labatt Blue. He leaned against the fridge after snapping the cap off and pulled his phone out of his pocket to scroll through his messages.

He'd last heard from Zoey on Halloween when she'd sent him a Snapchat of her Little Red Riding Hood costume- it was the most perfect combination of sexy and adorable. The last time he'd texted her for a simple conversation, however, was the first week of October. Over a month ago.

His thumb hovered over the text box for a few hesitant moments. He typed out a brief greeting. Chewing the inside of his cheek, he stared at his message. After another beat, he groaned and shook his head, deleting the text. He shoved his phone back into his pocket and made his way back to the dinner table.

CHAPTER 2

Zoey tugged the hem of her dress down lower on her thighs. She was already regretting the decision to go out dancing with her little sister. It would be a college bar with lots of eighteen to twenty-one-year-olds getting sloppy drunk and grinding on each other until they found someone to take home. It wasn't exactly Zoey's scene. The other option, however, was to let Cassie go by herself, and that was just not happening.

After getting dressed at Cassie's apartment she'd told her little sister that they had one stop to make before heading downtown. Ugh, downtown Los Angeles was going to be a mess, and she was not looking forward to all the lines, the crowded dance floors, or shouting over the loud music to a bartender to get some nasty watered down version of the drink she really wanted. All while trying to keep this unbelievably tight bodycon dress from riding up and flashing everyone in the process.

She'd borrowed the dress from Cassie's closet after being coerced into going out. Zoey really didn't have club outfits. She had work clothes, a few pairs of jeans, and some leisure wear. Cassie had made it absolutely clear that even her tight ankle-skinny dress pants were *not* suitable for going out. So here she was, walking up to Quinn Casey's front door in a teeny-tiny black dress, alongside her nineteen-year-old sister who was sporting a similar red dress. Zoey was sure that even when she was Cassie's age, she'd never worn clothes like this to go out.

Zoey knocked on the front door and waited. Normally she would walk in on her own, but ever since Quinn's fiancé had moved in, she'd seen her client naked and in the heat of passion far too many times to feel comfortable entering *any* room of his house without announcing herself first. About eight too many times, actually. And she really didn't think her baby sister needed to see that.

Quinn's team had just won the World Series- again- and she wanted to give him a run-down of all of his upcoming interviews and press conferences before he went out and celebrated with the team. Quinn wasn't a big drinker, but he always partied hard during these celebrations, and Zoey knew how difficult he was to talk to when he was hungover.

The door swung open to reveal Quinn Casey in nothing but a pair of board shorts.

"Oh my..." Cassie gushed, smiling at the sight of the nearly naked ball player.

Zoey rolled her eyes and put a hand over her sister's wide-eyed stare. "Beach themed party this year?"

"No, I'm not going out," Quinn replied, gesturing for them to come inside. "It's just me and Rae tonight. I've had to share her with the team enough, I figured some alone time would be nice. We're probably just going to relax in the hot tub and have some champagne...work on wedding details."

"Oh, that's...so sweet."

It had been a little over two months since Rae had moved in with Quinn, and Zoey was still adjusting to this new version of him. In one summer he'd gone from having new women in his bed every other night to being a one-woman man. And he was completely obsessed with her. Zoey never thought she'd see what *Quinn Casey* had with a woman and think *If my man doesn't treat me like that, it's not worth it,* but it appears miracles do happen.

Cassie was staring at Quinn again and he was smiling awkwardly back at her.

"Oh, sorry," Zoey said, gesturing toward her sister. "Quinn, this is my little sister, Cassie. Cassie, this is Quinn."

"I know who he is," Cassie said, a dopey grin still on her face. "I just...didn't realize he'd be so much more attractive in person."

"*Cassie*, he's engaged!"

"Yeah, to a complete babe!" Cassie smiled at Quinn. "Your children are going to be gorgeous. You should have lots of them."

"Thank you." Quinn beamed. "I'm trying to get Rae on that same page, but we'll see." He focused his attention back on Zoey, eyeing her evening attire skeptically. "What are you wearing?"

Groaning, she tugged at the hem of the dress again. "I'm going out. Dancing. With my sister."

Quinn brushed a hand through his permanently messy hair and pressed his lips together as he tried to conceal a grin. "That should be...fun."

The jingle of dog tags caught Zoey's attention as the large Bernese Mountain Dog, Harry, entered the room to greet the guests. Keeping her legs pressed together, she squatted down to pet him.

"I can almost see your underwear when you do that," Quinn remarked. "If I were really looking, I'm sure I could."

Zoey glared at him as she stood back up and straightened her dress out. "Don't look then."

"Hey Zoey!" Raelyn entered the room now, wearing a floral patterned purple and white bikini. Her long blonde hair was pulled over one shoulder and she looked like a freaking *Sports Illustrated* swimsuit model. "Cute dress. Are you actually going out tonight?"

"That's the plan," Zoey sighed, then looked back at Quinn. "I was going to go over all your interviews and stuff coming up, but since you won't be hungover tomorrow, I can just do that in the morning. We can get out of your hair and...go dance, I guess."

"Definitely tell me how that goes," said Rae. "I want to know if you meet anybody interesting. Even if they're just interesting enough for the night."

Laughing uncomfortably, she looked down at her feet which were encased in five-inch heels. "I seriously doubt that, but I'll let you know."

"Oh!" Quinn interjected. "Before I forget, we're heading to Michigan for a couple weeks at the end of the month before we head to Paris. Everything should be done by then right? Interviews and stuff like that?"

"Yeah, definitely," Zoey replied. She fidgeted slightly. "Michigan, huh? To visit family?"

"Mhmm." Quinn pulled Rae close to him and wrapped one arm around her. "You should consider taking a vacation. It's the off season, Zo. You work hard...you deserve to have some fun. Travel a bit."

"Change the scenery a little," Rae added. "Michigan can be pretty in the winter."

Zoey narrowed her eyes at the stunning couple in front of her. "I feel like I know where you're going with this..."

"That getting out of California could be good for you?" Quinn offered, innocently. "Northern Michigan has some great places to visit..."

"What's in Northern Michigan?" Cassie asked, her eyes flicking back and forth between Zoey, Quinn, and Rae.

"Nothing," Zoey stated, cutting that conversation off before it could even begin. "I think this is my cue to leave. You guys have fun and I'll see you in the morning."

Cassie didn't look convinced but let it go. She turned to Quinn and Rae and smiled brightly. "You two have a wonderful evening of making beautiful babies together. It was nice to meet you."

Zoey grabbed her sister by her elbow and turned her toward the door. She gave a wave over her shoulder and led Cassie out into the warm Southern California air.

"Ooh, if you're going up to the bar, get me one of those!" Cassie pointed out a bright blue monstrosity in a giant cylindrical cup. The girl drinking it was sucking through a glow-in-the-dark twisty straw and had to grasp the enormous beverage with two hands.

"Seriously?" Zoey looked at her sister, incredulous. "Why can't you just drink a vodka cranberry like all the other underage college girls?"

"Because I want *that!*" Cassie gestured toward the girl walking away with the electric blue drink.

Zoey sighed. "Fine, but if you get bright blue vomit in my car, you're cleaning it up yourself."

Cassie scoffed. "Just pay to have it detailed. Your boss makes like a billion dollars an hour, doesn't he?"

"He's not my *boss.*" Zoey waved a hand dismissively. Okay, well, *technically* he was, but their relationship had never felt like that. She'd always felt more like a single mother trying to take care of her out of control, adult son. "Never mind. Stay here and I'll bring back the neon nightmare."

Up at the bar, she squeezed through the crowd and waited to get a bartender's attention.

I bet the service at Trojan Horse would be better than this.

Ugh, no. Why did my mind go there?

It had been months since she'd stepped into Trojan Horse Sports Bar in Traverse City, Michigan and locked eyes with Jett Miller. Curse Quinn and Rae for bringing up Michigan right before she went to a bar. Even worse, she knew they were actually traveling to Michigan to visit Rae's parents and Quinn's mom, and would no doubt be spending time with the first man in years to make her heart flutter and force her to smile instantly. She'd probably looked like an idiot, standing there on the stoop of the bar, smiling at the hunky, curly-haired bar owner, not even realizing she was about to get rained on.

They'd gotten to know each other in the few hours that they'd spent trying to keep Quinn's panic at bay. She could tell Jett had also started freaking out at some point and really admired the kind of friend he must be. Even when they'd gone out to actually start looking for Rae that morning, Jett hadn't forgotten his manners amid his anxiety and had opened doors for her. It was a small act, but Zoey hadn't seen that kind of basic politeness from a man in ages. Maybe walking around his truck and opening the door for her didn't exactly make him chivalrous on its own, but she'd gotten the feeling he might be.

Zoey was sort of a sucker for classic romantic gestures. A bouquet of flowers just because, offering a jacket when she was chilled, pulling her seat out for her when they went out to eat, dropping her at the door before parking at a restaurant, and yes, holding doors open. She still appreciated the independence of modern relationships, but she couldn't help wanting to feel cared for.

Perhaps it was a result of always being the caregiver, she craved a person who would *just once* do something for her. When she lived at home, she had taken on the role of Mom at the age of nine after her own mother died. Her dad was a Marine Corps veteran with health issues, and immediately after her mother's death he'd been a wreck. Of course, they *all* had, but her parents had been high school sweethearts and her mother was his entire world. He was completely devastated. Taking care of Zoey, her little brother, Ace, and the youngest, Cassie was just too much for him at the time. So Zoey had stepped up to the plate and taken on whatever her mom normally would've done to help out.

Even her job was all about doing everything for someone else. She made all of Quinn's appointments, set up his interviews, she spoke to the press for him, and managed his entire image.

Back when she'd started working for him, he was constantly getting himself in trouble and getting a bad reputation that the league didn't particularly approve of. He slept around a lot, he got in fist fights, and he was photographed in compromising situations on numerous occasions. Zoey knew that forcing him to clean up his act was out of the question, so she'd steered into the skid. Quinn Casey became the Bad Boy of Baseball. He was charming and he photographed well, especially with his shirt off. Once she'd put the spin on his image to make his behavior look intentional rather than delinquent, the media ate it up. People *loved* him.

So, sure, she was great at her job. Maybe the best. For being only twenty-four years old, it was downright impressive. But she'd been taking care of and managing people her entire life. She was ready for someone to take care of her and make her life easier. If she got into a bind, she wanted someone to be there who could pull her out and make her feel as though it was all intentional- a happy accident.

"What can I get for you?" The tatted-up bartender with a bleach-blonde mohawk shouted over the loud music.

"Whatever that giant blue drink is...with the twisty straw?" Zoey shouted back, barely hearing her own voice.

"Blue Balls on a Dragon?" Mohawk said.

Zoey cringed but nodded. "And a gin and tonic- Hendrick's."

The bartender got to work on her and her sister's drinks and Zoey began digging out her wallet when a tall figure sidled up to the bar next to her.

"Those drinks are on me, sweetie."

Zoey looked up to find a tall blonde man smiling down at her. He had floppy surfer-boy hair and a matching tan. He looked young, though she supposed she wasn't old by any means. He just looked younger than her. Not to come across as judgemental or someone who profiles, but she could already tell this guy wasn't her type, whether he was too young for her or not.

"That's okay." Zoey waved her hand with a 20-dollar bill. "I can get them."

"Come on, my treat," the guy pressed.

She still wasn't interested, but free drinks were one of the biggest perks of being a single lady, right? Not to mention, she had a feeling that massive *Blue Balls* drink probably cost at least twenty on its own.

"Can I get your name before you buy me a drink?" Zoey asked. She needed to force herself to relax. Cassie was always telling her how uptight she was most of the time, that she needed to take off the work pants every now and then. Have a drink and engage in a light conversation with someone who was actually interested in *her*, not just her client.

"Zack." He extended out a hand. "And you are?"

Glancing uncertainly at his outstretched hand, she contemplated before letting out an exhale and shaking it. "Zoey."

"Zack and Zoey," he said with a grin. "That's got a nice ring to it."

She bit her lip to try to keep from smiling. "If you're into alliterations."

"I don't know what that means, but I can be into it."

"That'll be eighteen dollars for the gin and tonic and blue balls," the bartender droned, setting the drinks on the bar top.

"That sounds like a lot to pay for blue balls." Zoey struggled to grab both drinks off the bar. "You'd think they'd ask how much more to just finish it." She laughed at her own dirty joke. She didn't typically do dirty jokes or innuendos of any kind. It must just be the immature college-bar atmosphere.

"Was that a dad joke?" Zack asked, looking curiously at her.

"More like a dirty grandpa joke, I think." Zoey laughed at herself yet again.

Zack smiled fondly. "You're funny, Zoey."

"Not as funny as your face!"

Oh no. Why did I say that?

Zoey winced at the look on Zack's face and cringed inwardly at the word-vomit that was likely to come up now.

She didn't necessarily have a hard time talking to guys. Not in general, anyway. But when they were obviously hitting on her and she started enjoying it and trying to flirt back, it usually imploded. It was actually a miracle she'd ever had a boyfriend. Where men were concerned, she could be a little clueless. Oblivious, maybe was the right word. She never knew quite how to interact with them in a non-professional capacity. Typically in a setting such as this, she would go to one extreme or the other: She would make ridiculous comments and jokes- *bad* jokes, like the ones a middle-schooler would make- or she would get all businessy and completely turn them off by acting like a robot. Or a mother. There was no in between.

"Sorry, I didn't mean that," Zoey giggled awkwardly. "You actually have a very nice face. It's not funny at all. It's angular and manly- not funny."

"Don't worry about it-" Zack began before she cut him off.

"You could be like a Superhero. That's sort of what your face looks like. You could be like Captain America's brother. Or Thor's!" She exclaimed. *Oh God, why am I still talking?* "Wait, Thor already has a brother, doesn't he? Loki, that's right. I forgot. Well...obviously I remembered now. You don't really look like Loki though. He's too pale and has dark hair. But wasn't he adopted or something?"

As Zoey continued babbling, she was vaguely aware of the face Zack was making at her. Eyebrows pulled together as though studying some curious, uninterpretable creature. Like an alien.

"So I guess you could be like his *actual* brother. Not like Loki." Zoey paused for breath and wished Zack or the bartender or hell, even Zeus would smite her and stop her right there. "I wonder where they come up with those names. If you were Thor's brother, do you think you would have a weird name, too? I can't imagine having siblings and being like 'Oh, these are my three boys, Thor, Loki, and *Zack*'. It just would be silly. Not that your name is silly-"

"It was nice talking to you, Zoey," Zack said, finally cutting her off. "My friend's waving me over, I gotta go."

"Oh, great. Okay, have fun." Zoey waved awkwardly as he walked in the opposite direction of where his friend was supposedly waving him over. She let out a long exhale and pushed her hands into her long, wavy hair. "What the hell was that?"

"It's still eighteen bucks, hun," the bartender repeated impatiently.

"Right..." Zoey sighed. *Single and dressed up like this, and I still can't get a free drink.* Zoey dropped the twenty dollar bill on the bar top with a couple of ones for a tip before making her way back to her sister's table with the large blue balls drink cradled in her arm and her rocks glass in the other.

Cassie was standing at a high table talking to two men. *Two!* And she looked calm and collected, and was *definitely* not going on a tangent about superheroes. Her eyes went wide at the sight of the monstrous beverage in Zoey's arm and grabbed it from her with two hands.

"Zoey, this is Miles and Jeff," Cassie said with a huge smile, gesturing to each man.

Zoey blinked. "I'm sorry, did you say *Jett?*" She eyed the guy her sister had indicated. He was right around six feet tall and had light brown hair and a short beard.

"Jeff," the man corrected her with a smile. "And you must be Zoey."

"Oh, right, sorry." She shook her head. "Yes, I'm Zoey." *My mind just won't stop going there, will it?*

"Jeff is an accounting major at UCLA!" Cassie shouted over the music, its thumping bass beginning to make Zoey's head throb.

"Accounting? Wow, you must be good at numbers." Zoey groaned inwardly at how stupid she must sound. "I graduated from UCSD three years ago. Are you a senior?"

"Sophomore," Jeff replied. He grinned mischievously at her for a moment. "You know, I've never been with an older woman."

Ugh. Yes, because if there's anything a woman likes to be reminded of it's how much older she is than everyone else in the college bar.

"No kidding," Zoey said, losing her ability to feign interest. "You know, I'm not that much older probably. I graduated early."

"If we head back to our place, do you think you could run into the liquor store and get us some drinks?" Jeff asked, leaning in.

Seriously, kid? That's why you're trying to charm me? Ugh...

Zoey glanced at her sister who was looking hopefully back at her. Clearly Cassie was interested in going to this house party filled with underage college students, but Zoey feared she was going to have to be the bad guy. There was no way her sister was going anywhere with these tools.

"I *could* and I'd love to, *but* I promised my sister a night out dancing!" She smiled brightly. "And she still has about forty ounces of blue balls to consume. So sorry." Zoey grabbed Cassie's hand to pull her away from the table and toward the dance floor.

"What the *hell*, Zo?" Cassie exclaimed. She had the same exact didn't-get-my-way pout that she'd had since she was four.

"All those guys wanted was for me to buy alcohol to get you drunk so you'd sleep with one of them. Not happening."

"Don't forget *you'd* be getting some, too!" Looking away, Cassie took a sip from the swirly-straw before adding, "I don't think I have to remind you how long it's been since you've gotten lucky."

Zoey scoffed. "That's none of your business, and you don't know either! Besides, I'm not going to hook up with some random eighteen-year-old! I'm twenty-four!"

"He's twenty. And why not? Better stamina than whatever old dudes you probably meet setting up interviews."

Old dudes? Zoey felt she could argue by pointing out how frequently and intensely Quinn had sex, and he'd turned thirty in September. He didn't seem to be lacking any stamina. However, remembering the look on Cassie's face when she'd seen Quinn in his swim shorts, she suddenly felt the urge to make sure her baby sister *never* pictured the things Zoey had walked in on in the past couple of months.

"I just don't take sex lightly, okay?" Zoey placed a hand on her sister's shoulder. "It's cool that you can just have fun with it, but that's not how it is for me. So I'm sorry for...cock-blocking you, but you asked me to come out with you tonight. Can we just make it a girls' night?"

Cassie slumped her shoulders before nodding reluctantly. "Okay fine. But if Chris Evans or Michael B. Jordan come in here and start hitting on me, you need to understand there will be *no* cock-blocking!"

Zoey furrowed her eyebrows. "Michael Jordan? The basketball player?"

"No! Michael *B.* Jordan! The hot bad guy from *Black Panther!*"

"Ooh!" Zoey's eyes widened as the image of the hunky non-hero came to mind. "Oh, yeah, I wouldn't cock-block you from him. I might fight you, but I completely understand."

Cassie smiled finally. "Do you realize you whisper bad words? You practically mouthed the word 'cock' both times you just said it."

"I can't help it! It's not a word that comes naturally for me," Zoey half-laughed, taking a sip of her gin and tonic.

"There's a great innuendo there, but I'll leave it alone."

"Cassie!" Zoey gasped. She rolled her eyes at her sister's dirty mind, wondering where she got it from. "Oh my God, just drink your crazy blue-balls drink and let's go dance."

Out on the dance floor, Zoey had turned away several men trying to grind on her, shooed away a few more men trying to grind and maybe even feel-up her sister. Another interesting development was that she couldn't stop picking out each and every man in the place who had a similar build, the same curly hair, or green eyes as the bar-owner-who-shall-not-be-named way on the other side of the country. What kind of sick joke was that?

Usually people from colder states tried traveling south during the winter months, but as the night wore on, Zoey couldn't help the thought that spending December in Michigan might not be such a bad option this year.

The following morning after Zoey had washed all the hairspray and spilled booze off, she headed over to Quinn and Rae's to go over upcoming interviews. She showed up earlier than she'd originally planned, having added another item to the agenda.

"He's going to find it super weird, isn't he? We haven't even spoken in like a month and I'm just supposed to show up and hope he remembers we had chemistry the two times we met?" Zoey had suggested the possibility of traveling to Michigan with the couple when they leave in two weeks.

"Oh, he'll remember," Rae assured her. She swallowed a bite of omelet before continuing, "For one, the dude has no game, so I know you don't have to worry about the possibility that he's found someone else."

"Poor kid," Quinn mumbled, digging into his own breakfast. His hair was especially unruly this morning. Zoey couldn't figure out if it was simply bed-head or if she'd just barely missed their morning sex routine. Probably the latter. *Lord, it must be nice to have regular intercourse like they do.*

"For another," Rae added, "he wouldn't stop talking about you after you and Quinn came back to LA that first time. You guys had spent, what? Eight hours together? He was completely smitten. It was so cute."

"*You're* so cute," Quinn said sweetly, leaning over to kiss Rae on the cheek.

Rae smiled. "Aww, not as cute as you with your freshly-fucked hair."
Called it.

"Sorry, Zo." She gave a somewhat sheepish grin, taking another bite. "Are you sure you don't want any breakfast? I've gotten really good at making these omelets."

"That's okay," Zoey said, sighing. "I've walked in on enough kitchen sex to be hesitant to eat anything here."

"But hey! This time next month, we could be walking in on you having kitchen sex with my best friend!" Quinn exclaimed happily.

"I thought I was your best friend." Rae fake pouted.

Grinning, Quinn shrugged. "I mean, I'd be okay with that, too."

Zoey groaned and rolled her eyes.

"*Quinn!*" Rae threw a pineapple chunk at him. "That's completely inappropriate. She works for you!"

"Sorry, sorry." The way Quinn was still laughing told both women he was *not* sorry. "Okay, well *one* of my best friends, then."

"It's beginning to concern me that he's one of *your* best friends." Zoey eyed Quinn suspiciously.

"Jett is one of the best guys I know," Rae said. "The list goes: My dad, then Quinn- for legal purposes, anyway- and then Jett. And then Chris...and then his little brother, Tyler. Such a cutie."

"I'd argue, but I really can't. In most cases I probably wouldn't make the list, so I'll gladly take second to Charlie." Quinn took another massive bite of omelet, allowing tomatoes and mushrooms to fall out onto his plate.

"You're just a regular Prince Charming, aren't you?" Zoey said, raising an eyebrow at him as he scooped his fallen veggies up with his fingers.

"I've charmed the pants off this one a few times." Quinn gestured to Rae who responded with a bright smile and gave him another kiss on the cheek.

"Ugh, you guys are so gross and cute- *I* want that!" Zoey groaned. "Why do I have to be so weird around guys?"

"You're weird around them?" Quinn questioned.

"Like last night I was fine until this guy was obviously flirting and I thought he was cute so I tried to flirt back..." Zoey rested her chin on her palms. "It was a disaster. He faked having to leave because of a friend."

"Maybe your lack of game and Jett's lack of game cancel each other out, and that's why you hit it off so well," Quinn mused.

"Yeah, that's gotta be it, thanks," Zoey said flatly. Sitting up straight again, she looked across the table at the blissfully happy couple. If Quinn Casey could find love, so could she, right? "You definitely don't think it'll be weird, then?"

"Nope." Rae shook her head. "I think he'll be ecstatic. But maybe shoot him a text or give him a call if you're worried. Just to make sure he doesn't have vacation plans or something."

Zoey took a deep breath and let it out slowly. She stared down at her phone that rested on the table in front of her. There was nothing wrong with a friendly phone call. Just a quick *hey, how's it going?*

It was fine. Totally fine.

It was completely crazy, but everything would be just fine.

CHAPTER 3

"Boom! Oh- sorry, Master Chief! I hope you didn't want to keep your head!" Jett jumped up and pumped his fist, Xbox controller in hand. "I'm still the champion, and you guys can suck it." Thrusting his hips toward the two men still sitting on the couch, he ignored their annoyed expressions and continued a full-scale victory dance.

"This is bullshit." Emerson Yates dropped his controller on the coffee table and leaned back, crossing his arms over his bare chest. "You used cheat codes or something."

"I don't cheat- *you* might be into that, but I'm as honest as good ol' Abe Lincoln, my friend. So pony up, bitches!" After another obscene gesture and hip thrust, Jett finished off his third beer and plopped back down onto the sofa.

Brody Kalahan groaned and reached into his back pocket for his wallet. "Amira's going to kill me if she finds out how much money I lose playing *Halo* with you guys."

"It's your money, you should be able to spend it- or lose it- however you fucking want," Emerson said, reaching for his own wallet off the coffee table.

"Doesn't work like that when you're married, man." Brody shook his head. "Found that out *real* quick."

Emerson let out a low whistle. "Glad I dodged that bullet." He mimed getting shot with a finger-gun to his head and slumped over on the arm of the couch.

With an incredulous glare, Jett scoffed. "I want it known that the only reason I tolerate you is to take your money. That is all."

"Sure it is, Sugar Bear," Emerson replied with a wink. "No one ever wants to admit they want me, but in the end no one can resist this."

Jett hesitantly took the twenty-dollar bill Emerson handed him, eyeing it suspiciously. He wondered for the hundredth time if he should trust anything that came from this guy, but twenty bucks was twenty bucks. Brody handed over his money, too, and Jett slipped it into his wallet.

Chris was usually his go-to guy for spending afternoons and evenings off, but again he'd been busy, having a niece's birthday party to attend.

A few weeks ago, Brody had come into the bar while Jett was helping out up front. He'd just finished up an exhausting case at work in which the family members had fought and bickered over the contents of their deceased relative's will. Jett had made the comment that maybe all they needed was to play some ultra-aggressive video game to simulate shooting each other- maybe in VR. This had resulted in the two of them playing video games in Brody's basement a couple times a week.

Jett had known Brody for several years now, through Rae- he was the husband of Rae's college roommate and *other* best friend, Amira.

The only non-jock in the group, Brody was the resident nerd. Tall and wiry, with flaming red hair and lots of freckles, the guy stood out in their friend circle. He was quiet until he got the right number of drinks in him, upon which he would suddenly turn into some fighting Irish brawler, like Conor McGregor.

It can not be stated enough- Brody is *no* Conor McGregor. Not in the least. Luckily, the times he'd tried to get into fights with random strangers who would have otherwise snapped him in half, his best friend, who could easily body-double for Thor, was there to break it up before it began.

Unfortunately, however, that best friend was Emerson Yates. Jett might have to take back what he'd said about Lizzie's new boyfriend being the biggest douchebag he'd ever met. Emerson Yates was hard to beat in that respect.

Though he was clearly a loyal friend to Brody, he didn't operate that way with everyone.

Emerson had been engaged to Rae just under two years earlier. They'd met shortly after grad school- Emerson had gone to law school at Michigan while Rae finished up her physical therapy degree there. When Rae brought her new man up from Ann Arbor to meet her old friends, they'd actually gotten along well. However, when Emerson had decided to *cheat* on Rae only months after making a marriage proposal, Jett had quickly changed his mind about the smooth-talking corporate lawyer.

As fate would have it, of course, Emerson was almost always at Brody and Amira's when he wasn't at work. He'd nearly moved into the apartment-sized basement until Amira took matters into her own hands and started bagging his stuff up and setting it on the porch. Jett and Amira got along well anyway, but their mutual hatred for the guy who'd cheated on their best friend had really allowed them to bond.

"Next time- *God of War*," said Emerson. "I will fucking destroy you both at that game."

"Isn't that a PS4 game?" Brody asked.

Emerson shrugged. "We can play at my place."

Jett grimaced. "I don't know. Actually going to your apartment seems like a little more effort than a non-friend would make."

"Jett, Jett, Jett..." Emerson sighed, leaning back and sprawling himself on the couch.

"Please don't say my name while you spread your legs like that."

Emerson laughed. "You and I are becoming friends, Jett Miller. It's happening. You just wait."

"Is not." Jett averted his gaze from the cocky dude with a full-tilt, power man-spread going on.

"I give it two weeks," Brody said, putting the Xbox controllers back in their drawer. "I didn't want to be his friend either, but here we are."

"It's true." Emerson smirked. "I'm not only good at putting the moves on the ladies. It's what I do. I make people do what I want. Be what I want. If I want you to be my friend, you will be."

"I'm getting sort of rapey vibes now, so if you wouldn't mind crossing your legs and maybe putting on a shirt, I would appreciate it." Jett grabbed his keys and stretched.

"I've given up on the shirt thing," Brody said, standing up to stretch as well. "Just don't ever let him take his shirt off at your place because that's how you know he's made himself at home and you'll never get rid of him. It's like trying to get rid of fruit flies in the summertime. Or a cockroach infestation. That stray cat Amira keeps feeding…"

"The one she calls Basil?" Emerson asked, one eyebrow raised. "Dude, I think that's just your cat now."

"Oh, so it really is like Emerson." Jett chuckled.

"She *named* it?" Brody groaned. "I'm allergic to cats. I get blotchy and I can't breathe."

"Doesn't that same thing happen when you step into the sun?" Emerson attempted to conceal his grin.

"You're a dick."

"Yeah, but I'm *your* dick." Emerson paused, making a face at his own comment. "Your big dick. Your bigger, better dick."

"On that note, I think I will head home." Jett clapped his hands together and headed for the stairs.

Before his foot was on the first step, his familiar ringtone filled the room. He patted down his jeans pockets and looked around, spotting his phone on the end table. When he grabbed it, he froze at the name lighting up his screen.

He cleared his throat before answering in a lower than usual register, "Hello?"

"Hi Jett, um…it's Zoey."

Her voice made his pulse trip over itself and he struggled to find his voice.

"Yeah…hi. I mean, hey, how's it going?" Jett scrubbed a hand down his face and tried to ignore the curious looks his friend and non-friend were giving him.

"Great!" Zoey replied brightly, "Er...good, I think. Um," she giggled nervously, "sorry, this suddenly feels super weird. I haven't talked to you in like a month."

"No, no, it's not weird," Jett said, his voice now far higher than he'd intended. Clearing his throat again, he found his normal speaking register. "It's good to hear from you. I actually was going to text you a few days ago."

"You were?"

"Yeah, um, I was at dinner with my family...I don't know, I just thought of you." He forced himself to stop there before he said anything weird.

"Oh, that's funny. I went to this club with my little sister and there was this twenty-year-old guy who just wanted me to buy him alcohol. I thought he was hitting on me, but he just thought it was cool that I was older than him-"

"And that made you think of me?" Jett laughed. "Because I'm old?"

"What? No!" Zoey giggled again. *Damn, that's a sweet sound.* "His name was Jeff, but I thought he said Jett- I probably should've led with that."

"That's okay...Besides, I am getting old." Jett sat down in the recliner. Brody and Emerson were both looking at him intently; Brody had his hands out to the side as though asking a question.

"Well, I felt old at this little college dance club that lets in eighteen-year-olds," Zoey replied. "You're only like, what? Twenty-eight? Twenty-nine?"

"I'll be thirty next month. On the twelfth. You know, that's why Case's jersey number is twelve. It's for me. My birthday is 12-12. He didn't want to forget me."

Zoey's bright laugh filled his ears and he couldn't help smiling. "That's not what I heard."

"Well that's because he's a liar. So is Rae. Don't listen to them."

"Actually, that kind of brings me to why I called..." Zoey paused for a beat. "They're heading to Michigan next week, I think they'll be there Wednesday..."

"Yeah?" Jett sat up straighter, excitement buzzing through him.

"Yeah, and well, it's the off season for me too, kind of. I was thinking...I've never spent winter anywhere that actually has a winter season. I thought maybe if you...I mean, I know we talked about you coming to LA a while ago, but...um. If you're not going anywhere on vacation or anything...maybe I could come visit, too."

"Yeah, that would be great!" Jett nearly shrieked, earning him wide-eyed looks of alarm from Brody and Emerson. He cleared his throat. "I mean, yeah...I'd like that."

"Good." Her voice came out in a small breath of laughter. "Okay, well I guess I'll see you Wednesday then."

"Great, yeah, I can't wait. See ya, Zo."

"Bye, Jett."

Jett stared at the phone in his hands for a few silent moments after ending the call before abruptly jumping back into his earlier victory dance.

"What the hell is that?" Emerson reared back, watching Jett's dance with mild disgust.

"*Who* was that?" Brody asked.

"Her name's Zoey. I met her back in August...she's Quinn's publicist."

Emerson snapped his fingers. "Oh, that hot chick he was banging behind Rae's back?"

"*No.*" Jett rolled his eyes. "They were never *banging* or whatever. Rae misinterpreted the situation. It just looked bad."

"But they've banged before," Emerson insisted.

"No they haven't! She told me Quinn's not her type. Their relationship is professional. That's it."

"Here's a new concept for you, Honest Abe," Emerson said, sitting up. "She *lied.*"

"No, she didn't." Jett waved a hand as though batting away Emerson's ridiculous suggestions. "Whatever, I'm not listening to you. She was just calling to tell me she's coming to Michigan to visit."

"Oooh, look at you gettin' All-Star's sloppy seconds." Emerson pumped his fist.

"Seriously?" Jett looked at Brody who simply shrugged.

"I didn't choose this life, it chose me," Brody said, sounding somewhat defeated.

"How long has it been? Aren't you a little out of practice?" Emerson stood up with renewed energy. "We're going out and you're gonna learn how to close the deal."

"That sounds awful, no. No thanks," Jett said flatly.

"Come on! If you knew how to close the deal, you would've already hooked up with this chick by now. Do you really want her coming all the way here just for you to blow it?" Emerson looked pointedly at him. "And who do you know who's a better coach at this than me?"

"He's got a point," Brody chimed in. "I've told him he needs to start a two-week course on this. How else do you think I got such a hot wife? I took his advice."

"That makes no sense," Jett protested. "He's perpetually single and doesn't know the first thing about a relationship. I'm pretty sure *'Don't screw chicks who aren't your fiancé'* has to be in the top three rules of dating."

"Dating? Who's talking about dating?" Emerson winced. "No, I'm talking about making sure she sees you as a sexually appealing person of interest. That *dating* crap is on you. I don't want any part of that."

Jett chewed the inside of his cheek while he considered his options. Okay, so he and Zoey had hit it off and flirted and had some cute back-and-forth exchanges...but was anything about it sexual? Did he want it to be? Well, okay, of course he *wanted* to have sex with her eventually. She was gorgeous and sweet, and he'd be lying if he said the Snapchat he'd received on Halloween hadn't made his dick stiffen. He'd wanted to take a screenshot, but thought she'd find that weird.

There was no way Quinn and Rae could find out that he was seeking this kind of help from Emerson- they would have his nuts. But he couldn't deny that Emerson really did seem to know what he was doing when it came to *closing*.

Reluctantly, Jett groaned and put his arms out in surrender. "Fine. Fine...teach me your ways, Master Chief."

Emerson's wicked grin did nothing to put Jett at ease. "There's my Sugar Bear. I knew you'd come around."

Yep, he was stepping over to the dark side.

Two hours later, Jett was wearing a suit. In a bar. It wasn't his bar, at least. But he was wearing a suit in a bar, and wondering how the hell he'd ended up in this position while Brody had been allowed to stay home.

"I feel ridiculous," Jett murmured. "Why did I have to wear a suit?"

"That's not a real question," said Emerson, taking a bottle of Heineken from the bartender. "Did you look at yourself before you left your place? You clean up good, man. And you're letting all the ladies in here know that you mean *business*. You've got a real job, making real money, and that's all they need to know."

"But I don't really wear a suit to work."

"You own a business. They don't need to know what kind of business. You're a businessman. An entrepreneur." Emerson leaned back against the bar and surveyed the room.

That did sound a lot more impressive, and it wasn't a lie.

Damn...he's teaching me to think like a lawyer.

"Okay, so where do I start?"

"I'm going to be completely honest with you. I've heard you try to speak to women, and it's painful," Emerson stated, eyes still scanning the room.

"Thanks, that's helpful," Jett said sarcastically.

"I'm serious. I would rather watch *The O.C.* from start to finish with my ex-fiancé and *not* get any sex in return than listen to you talk to a woman." He paused, scratching the side of his bearded chin as he contemplated. "Okay, actually that's too far. No, I wouldn't."

"Aw, man! I haven't watched that show since high school!" Jett exclaimed. "Blanket forts, TV drama, and sneaking some wine out of the basement wine fridge- that sounds like a great night!"

Emerson's stare of mild disgust returned. "I would rather be Jabba's gold-bikini-clad prisoner than hear that babbling nonsense you call flirting."

"You'd rock the shit out of that bikini," Jett half-laughed.

"Damn right I would." Emerson gave a curt nod. "But in all seriousness, I would rather watch Spider-Man dissolve into dust on repeat than watch you interact with a woman."

Jett gasped. "You don't mean that. It's not *that* bad."

"I do mean it."

"Harsh," Jett muttered, taking a long pull from his beer bottle.

"Which is why I'm going to advise that you let your body do the talking. There is no substitute for body language. Speak as little as possible, and if you have to wonder if you're talking too much, just stop. Be mysterious." Emerson gestured toward a group of three women walking their way. "Watch and learn."

The women appeared to be in their early to mid-twenties, and they were all attractive enough. Jett observed his broad, Thor-like companion. His mouth turned up slowly into a one-sided grin, his tongue pressed to the inside of his cheek as he swept his eyes from their shoes up to their faces. Making eye contact with the brunette in the middle, his eyebrows twitched up as his grin widened just slightly. He gave a wink.

All three of the women giggled. Like school girls. The one in the middle even blushed severely and bit her bottom lip flirtatiously as she slowed her pace to keep eye contact with him.

Emerson watched as the girls walked away, then whipped his head back around to look at Jett. "See what I did there?"

"That was impressive," he admitted. "Okay, I'll go."

Jett searched for a candidate and eventually spotted two girls, a blonde and a redhead, walking up to the bar. As they approached, he tried to remember the first thing Emerson had done.

Crooked grin. Do the crooked grin.

He pulled up one corner of his mouth. Or at least he thought he did. That's what it felt like. And then he winked. He eyed the girls from head to toe and back up and winked again.

That wasn't right.

He felt one eyebrow arch too far, as if a fish-hook were caught in it before smiling too wide to be considered sexy. At all.

The girls gave him a curious, or more likely concerned, look and made sure to leave lots of space between him and them as they walked up to make their drink orders.

"Well, that wasn't right," Jett stated, refusing to make eye contact with his mentor.

Emerson shook his head. "'Mr. Stark, I'm not feelin' so good…'"

"Dammit! *Infinity War* was so great up until that part!"

"It's fine, it's fine." Emerson grabbed Jett's elbow and pulled him to a different spot near the dance floor. "That was just your first try. Maybe we'll have better luck over here. Girls who are dancing have probably had more to drink, so it can't hurt your game any."

He wanted to be offended, but supposed it was a good point.

"Let's see your crooked grin. You can't pull that creepy-ass *Cheshire Cat* look again. I will literally leave you here."

Emerson made Jett repeat the entire look, from the grin, to the eye-sweep, the tongue-in-the-cheek, to the wink, at least a dozen times. It felt like a full-scale choreographed dance, but he finally got it down. After trying it on about five noticeably drunk girls on their way to the dance floor, he was feeling confident. They'd all smiled back at him, and one had even asked him to come dance with her. He hadn't been pre-pared for that, but before he had the opportunity to respond, Emerson had jumped in and told the girl that Jett was married, and apologized for his lack of self-control.

"Married?" Jett glared at his non-friend. "What the fuck? I'm gonna have to get farther than just *the look.*"

"I'm not about to stand around and watch you white-girl dance to today's best hits," Emerson replied. "Come on, back to the bar. I spot a solid ten. Let's see how you do."

Jett repeated the routine near the bar at least seven more times with women who weren't quite as intoxicated as the ones on the dance floor. He was feeling good about his odds, and for the first time in a long time, he was actually feeling like women found him sexually attractive. Maybe Emerson really should start a crash-course.

At a small high-top table, Jett was chatting up a cute blonde with wavy, shoulder-length hair and bright red lipstick. They'd been making decent conversation for several minutes when Emerson squeezed in next to him.

"How's it goin'? Looks like you've got this one in the bag," he said into Jett's ear.

"Yeah, I guess," Jett said awkwardly, trying to keep a friendly face directed at Hannah.

"You gonna leave with her?" Emerson asked.

"I don't- I..." Jett contemplated. He probably could. He wouldn't be doing anything wrong, really. And he hadn't gotten laid in a long time. Maybe brushing up before the girl who actually mattered got here wasn't the worst idea. But it felt wrong.

Emerson eyed him a few seconds longer. "You made a lot of progress tonight, man. Watch this." He clapped a hand on Jett's back and walked around the small table to Hannah. Jett watched, disbelieving and a little pissed, as Emerson leaned in and whispered into Hannah's ear. She smiled and bit her lip. It was as if Jett suddenly ceased to exist. He watched as the girl's skin flushed and not five seconds later, Emerson's arm was around her waist as he led her toward the door.

What a fucking dick.

Jett gave out a heavy sigh before finishing his last beer of the night. The night hadn't been completely useless. He felt a lot more confident about his ability to be more than just the funny guy when Zoey arrived, and knew he would've felt guilty about leaving with someone else after making plans with Zoey anyway.

He paid his tab and headed out into the cold winter air with two thoughts on his mind:

1. Emerson Yates was definitely *not* his friend.
2. Wednesday could not get here soon enough.

CHAPTER 4

It was significantly colder in Michigan than Zoey had anticipated. She'd been to New York and Massachusetts and various northern states during the early months of spring or late fall during baseball season, but it was almost December. Snow was just around the corner and Zoey was born and raised in Southern California. She didn't have the right kind of blood for this kind of cold.

All the movies she'd seen with girls ice skating outside in cute winter outfits and skirts seemed like a complete sham now. She'd made a list of all the winter activities she wanted to do while she was here, and in the time it took for her to get from the door to the car that pulled up, she realized none of those winter activities were going to be done in adorable winter clothes. She needed a parka, stat!

Zoey slid into the back seat of the car with Harry as Quinn helped Charlie DeRose load all their bags into the trunk. From the front seat, Rae called out the window to her dad, "I told you the Jeep would've been a better option!"

"The Jeep?" Charlie questioned, pulling his door shut. "Rae, I need a damn carriage for all those bags. That big green one was all shoes, I think."

"That's mine," Zoey piped up. "Sorry about that. I'm not familiar with winter, so I just packed everything."

"Oh, that's okay," Charlie said. "Quinn said you're staying at a hotel until they leave for Paris? Smart choice. My daughter is sort of a diva and I don't think living with her for the next two weeks would do any favors for your work relationship."

"Oh, no, I'm sure we'd get along fine, I just-" Zoey paused. How should she finish this sentence? "-really like my privacy."

Charlie laughed lightly. "Yeah, I'm sure it has nothing to do with the fact that Quinn's trying to get my daughter pregnant with a whole baseball team of their own."

Quinn was just slipping into the backseat and his head popped up attentively, eyes wide.

"Well that may be his plan, but I'm still on my birth control," Rae said adamantly. "I will not be a pregnant bride. We've still got about seven months before we even consider that little baseball player."

"Team, Rae," Quinn corrected. "We want a baseball *team.*"

Zoey sat, running her hands through Harry's fur, and watched the back-and-forth argument of how many kids they would or would not have for what felt like the twentieth time this month. A year ago, the thought of Quinn as a father would have been terrifying. Absolutely bat-crap crazy. But now that she'd seen him in this new capacity, she was genuinely curious and beginning to think he'd knock fatherhood out of the park. But she was with Rae on this one- nine kids was a lot to ask for.

Charlie dropped Zoey off at her hotel first, and even helped wheel her bags inside. He gave her a list of contacts if she needed anyone and let her know that their house was always open for guests if she got sick of living in a hotel. She couldn't help smiling at the admittedly handsome older man, and wondered if he just went full dad-mode with everyone he met.

As soon as she got settled in her hotel room, she pulled out her phone and called her own dad as she'd promised when she'd visited him the previous day.

He picked up on the second ring. "Hi sweets!"

"Hi Dad." Zoey plopped down on the queen-sized bed and let out a sigh. "I made it to Michigan. It's cold here."

"I would imagine it is," he chuckled.

Luis- or Lou- Nunez was a tough, rough-around-the-edges kind of guy. He was the type of guy other men avoided in bars because he just gave off the vibe that he wasn't one to be messed with. The only caveat here was with his daughters. He had a soft spot for them, all right, and turned into a jolly Kris Kringle when he spoke to either Zoey or Cassie.

"Are you doing okay? It feels so weird that I'm going to be away for *weeks* and not be able to stop in. You know you can call me if you need me. If I need to come home for anything-"

"Zoey, stop," Lou interrupted. "You don't have to be here all the time. You travel for work and are gone for days at a time, anyway. I'll be fine. I'm not that old yet, I don't need a live-in caregiver."

"I know, I know..." Zoey pinched the bridge of her nose. "Sorry, I just feel weird not knowing exactly how long I'm going to be here. I usually know that I'm going to be in Boston for three nights, and then back home, and then back to Boston. This is just different. It's like-"

"A vacation? One that you desperately need, too."

Zoey heard some sort of beeping sound in the background. "Is that the microwave? Dad, you're not just eating microwave dinners, are you? The doctor said your cholesterol-"

Her dad cut her off, "First of all, Zo, I'm the parent here. Remember? I know you were forced to grow up a little early and I'm sorry about that. It wasn't easy on any of us, least of all you. Second, I am warming up some leftovers that Cindy brought me."

"Cindy's that dentist, right?" Zoey picked her head up off the bed, intrigued. "The cute one with the Australian Shepherd?"

"Dental hygienist," Lou corrected. "Yes, I've been joining her at the dog park with Maximus."

"And she brings you leftovers?"

"She has, yes."

"Are these leftovers from meals that you've shared together?" Zoey pressed.

Her dad never dated when she was growing up. She's not sure exactly how she would have felt about him dating back then, but he'd only recently- in the past five years or so- mentioned other women from time to time. Zoey tried to encourage it, hoping that he would find someone so he didn't have to spend all of his days alone.

Being a Marine veteran, he was active enough. His previous injury had healed up and he'd had enough physical therapy that he could walk without a cane or a walking stick. Zoey had been shocked to come home to find him practicing yoga on their back patio one evening. The exercise did wonders for his joints and mobility, and she tried to join him at least once a week if it was possible.

She knew he visited old buddies for a drink and had a poker night that rotated hosts, so he wasn't *always* alone. Perhaps she was pushing her search for romance onto her dad. The more she failed to find it for herself, the more she wanted at least *someone* to be happy.

"We might be sharing a meal later this evening, actually," Lou replied. Zoey could imagine the way he'd avert his eyes and act interested in something else- his food, his fork, the dying houseplant in the window sill- if they were having this conversation face-to-face.

"Good for you, Dad." Zoey smiled. "I hope it goes well. Cindy is a lucky lady. And even with all the desserts you eat, you can remain cavity-free."

"And I hope it goes well for you, too," Lou added, and she could hear the smile in his voice. "Whoever he is. Must be one hell of a guy to travel two-thousand miles to visit."

"Dad, that's not-" she stopped herself. She was a terrible liar. Most things with words, unless they related to a professional capacity, were not her strong suit. "I feel absolutely crazy, but I hope it goes well, too. I'll tell you about it when there's more to tell. Deal?"

"Okay, sweets. Call me again when you get a chance. Have fun. Go get in a snowball fight or ride a polar bear or whatever they do up there in the arctic."

"Love you, Dad."

"Love you, too, Zo."

Once her call ended, she looked around the room and contemplated her next move. Sure, she'd told people she was coming up here for a vacation. A change of scenery. To see some snow! But reality set in all at once that she'd come up here for the sole purpose of seeing if she could make a relationship happen with the guy that she'd met and spent a grand total of maybe eighteen hours with three months ago.

Well, she was here now and there was no point running from it.

Zoey got up and began unpacking her bags and organizing her clothes into the closets and drawers in her hotel room, setting aside potential outfits. Jett was working tonight but she was still going to stop in and try to make his jaw drop. She hung up possible outfits and lined her shoes along the wall. There had to be something in here.

Her stomach rumbled and she put a hand over it, willing her nerves to get lost. She could sense a headache at the edges of her periphery and closed her eyes, working through breathing exercises. It was just nerves. And maybe she needed to eat something- of course nothing sounded good.

A shower. A shower would fix it. Showers always made her relax and feel renewed with energy.

She grabbed a bath towel from one of her bags- yes, she brought her own towels to hotels- and headed for the shower. Setting the faucet to hot, she breathed in the steam and willed the water to wash her nerves and doubts- basically *any* lingering thought that this was a huge mistake- down the drain.

Jett checked the time on his phone- 4:15. Zoey should have arrived in Michigan about an hour ago. They'd been texting quite a bit since her phone call the other week and he was feeling good about how naturally they'd picked things back up. He couldn't help the nerves he was feeling and had to keep reminding himself how easy things were between them before. It just suddenly seemed like there was a lot riding on this. He was feeling the pressure, and Jett had a tendency to sweat under pressure.

"Hey man, don't overthink it." Chris entered the office and clapped a hand on his back. "She's just another person. There's nothing to worry about. And even if it doesn't work out, at least you'll know."

"Thanks, man." Jett turned to his best friend who was in far more casual clothes than usual. Somehow Chris still managed to make vintage-wash blue jeans, a navy t-shirt, and bright white Nike classics look particularly fashionable. Jett would be perfectly content wearing sweatpants all day if he didn't have to look relatively presentable for work.

"Been hittin' the gym a lot still?" Chris asked, leaning casually against the desk in their office.

"Yeah." Jett couldn't help smiling a little. He'd surpassed his original weight lifting goals and was finally feeling good about himself for the first time since college. It wasn't that he'd ever been over or underweight. He knew he was just built with a little more meat on his bones- it was a distinct advantage back when he'd played hockey- but he couldn't help comparing himself to his naturally lean-muscled best friends. Quinn and Chris had the right bodies to star in Nike commercials or advertisements for exercise equipment, while Jett was more suited for ads featuring outdoorsmen or big trucks.

"I can tell," Chris said, grinning back. "You're lookin' good, man. Zoey would be lucky to have you. You're the best guy I know."

Jett scoffed and rolled his eyes, doing his best teenage girl impression, "Ugh, come on, Chris, you have to say that. You're my boo."

Chris laughed. "Please do not use that voice with her, whatever you do."

"Omigod, Chris, you know you love it when I talk to you like this. Doesn't it just...make you feel special? Give you all the warm fuzzies?"

Chris pointed a finger at him. "Seriously, dude, stop. Nothing will send that girl away faster than making her think she came all this way to hook up with Jack from *Will and Grace*."

Jett cringed. "Oh I really don't wanna do that, do I?" He ran his hands down his face, pulling his mouth into an exaggerated frown. "Why do I get so weird when I'm stressed?"

"It's not just when you're stressed, man. That's just kind of your thing," Chris said simply. Upon seeing Jett's look of mild offense he added, "But you guys hit it off before. You're funny- girls like a guy who can make them laugh."

"You're not funny at all and you're still happily married."

"I don't have to be funny. I'm smooth- that's my thing. Victoria's the funny one in our relationship."

Jett smiled sweetly. "Aw, it figures you'd marry someone who reminds you of me. I'm flattered."

"You know if I swung that way you'd be my first choice, Honey Boo." Chris winked and laughed.

Jett spun around in his desk chair excitedly. "Really? I beat Case?"

Chris considered for a beat. "Yeah…I feel like he's into some weird shit. You know how white people are."

"Fa sho, fa sho," Jett conceded. Although Jett may be about as white as they come, Chris had made him his honorary 'brother' back in middle school, and he carried that badge of honor to this day.

Standing up straight, Chris sighed. "All right, man, well I'm gonna go wait for the truck to get here. I'll unload it so you can stay up front and wait for your future wifey."

Jett hadn't been out of the kitchen for more than five minutes when the door to the bar swung open and Zoey walked in.

Jett stopped what he was doing to take in her appearance. She wore a dark gray peacoat which she held tight around her body, dark blue skinny jeans tucked into tall, light gray heeled boots. He could tell the white sweater she wore beneath her coat had one of those large, swooping collars- he knew his sisters had given him the name for it, but he couldn't remember at the moment- and her long, wavy brown locks fell gracefully over her shoulders. He noted that her hair had gotten longer and maybe a little lighter since the last time he'd seen her.

Her lightly bronzed skin was tinted pink from the bite of the cold weather, and the way she nervously worried her bottom lip with her teeth made his stomach flip excitedly. *God, she was gorgeous.* Her big hazel eyes found him and her nervousness turned into an adorably shy smile.

Okay, yes, he definitely wanted to close the deal this time.

He ran through a brief checklist of everything Emerson had taught him in the last week. *Start with the look. You've mastered that.*

Zoey stood on the other side of the bar in front of him and Jett did his brief eye-swipe from her pointy-heeled boots to her hazel eyes, lined with thick black lashes. His crooked grin was on point and- *yes!* Her smile widened and the pink that filled her cheeks wasn't only from the cold outside.

"Hey there." Zoey's voice was again like music to his ears, but he forced himself to keep his composure.

Don't talk too much. Too much talking leads to babbling. Play it cool.

"Hey girl," Jett kept his one-sided grin.

Hey girl? Who the fuck am I? Ryan Gosling?

Zoey twitched one eyebrow up curiously. "Um...it's good to see you again."

"Yeah, girl, it's good to see you, too."

Girl? Again? What the fuck? And what is this voice I'm using?

"Okay..." Zoey narrowed her eyes at him and looked around briefly. "Michigan...in the winter. It's a lot colder than I'd anticipated for some reason."

"Are you cold?" Jett felt his eyebrow was doing the weird fish-hook thing again, but couldn't stop it. "You know, I actually live right upstairs..."

"I know, I've been there before." Zoey still looked confused.

"Right, right..." He nodded slowly and recovered with a smooth half-laugh. "What I'm saying is, uh...if you're cold, maybe we could head upstairs and I could warm you up." He winked. It was the same wink he'd practiced a hundred times, but *damn* did he get a different reaction.

Zoey reared back and looked at him with disbelief, coupled with significant irritation, "Excuse me?" She shook her head and let out a quick breath, like an incredulous laugh lacking all humor. "Oh my God...This was a mistake."

"What?" Jett's eyes went wide with panic.

"I'm not some fancy, high-brow jet-setter who flies across the country for sex just because I can," Zoey said, narrowing her eyes and taking a step back. "I think I gave you the wrong idea by coming here-"

"No- no, no, no!" Jett ignored everything he'd been coached to do or say and ran around the bar, meeting her only feet from the door. Seriously, two minutes and he'd almost sent her running the other way. "I'm sorry, Zoey. That was stupid. I...I know you're not just coming here for a hookup, I'm sorry."

"I already told you I don't do the one-liners, I don't get charmed by cocky, straight-forward advances, and- maybe I shouldn't say this, but here it is- I don't do casual sex. Maybe that makes me a prude or uptight or whatever, but it's just not me. So if that's what you were looking for-"

"No, it's not." Jett shook his head and placed his hands on her arms so that they were looking directly at one another. "I'm sorry. I just...I got nervous when you said you were coming to visit and a friend offered to *coach* me, I guess. Actually, we're really not friends. I don't know why I took his advice. He's a complete asshole."

Zoey looked skeptically back at Jett but didn't say anything.

"Let me start over, okay? Real Jett Miller here..." He smiled at her, "Hi Zoey, it's great to see you again. You look amazing."

She stared back for a few beats before her mouth finally pulled into a reluctant smile. "Hi Jett. You look good, too."

"About being cold," Jett began, slowing his words to allow a full thought process before speaking, "I have been told that alcoholic beverages can be effective at warming people up. I promise I'm suggesting it as a practicality, not as a move to get you drunk. However, if you *do* get drunk, my apartment is conveniently located upstairs and is equipped with the proper furniture to sleep it off. I even promise to not get weird. Well...I'm always weird, but I promise not to do anything inappropriate."

Zoey let out a small breath of laughter. "Okay, sure. I'll take a gin and tonic with lime then."

"Gin? Oh girl, you fancy!" *And we're back to sounding like Jack!* Chris had given him one piece of advice and he couldn't listen. Jett cleared his throat and laughed it off. "Or, you know, more normal words that don't sound like that."

Zoey laughed- and it actually seemed genuine- as she slid onto a bar stool and Jett got to work on her drink.

Setting the tumbler in front of her, he asked, "So are you staying at a hotel or with Quinn and Rae at their house?"

"Definitely a hotel," she replied. "If I had to listen to two week's worth of Quinn saying 'oh yeah, baby, say my name', I might have an aneurysm."

"He's one of *those* guys." Jett cringed. "Actually that doesn't surprise me at all. You know, I was witness to his first ever hand job. It was over-the-pants...under the table. In public. I had the unfortunate displeasure of making eye contact with him during it."

Zoey nearly spit out her drink as she laughed. "And somehow *that* doesn't surprise me, either."

"Jett!" Chris called out as he made his way to the front. "Did you know we ordered three extra cases of Heineken?" He stopped short as he saw Zoey sitting at the bar, mid-laugh. He smiled wide. "Oh, hey Zoey."

"Hi Chris," she said, returning his smile.

"Three extra cases?" Jett looked back at Chris. "I'll have the servers push Heineken then. If all else fails, I know a guy."

"I know this is profiling, but I always feel like the only guys who drink Heineken are like...the same kind of guys who intentionally wear suits to a bar. They have a sports car as their main mode of transportation, and use a lot of hair gel," Zoey said. "And they have names like Chad or Brad."

"Ugh...*Brad.*" Jett made a face. "My youngest sister just started dating a Brad and he's just like that. Maybe I'll ask him and his bros to come in. Pretend to be nice, but really I just hope I get to watch him get his ass handed to him."

"Is this the little sister who gets infatuated by every guy she meets?" Zoey asked.

"Yep," Jett sighed. "I have to give her credit. She's not afraid to get hurt, but it's like every other month, she's upstairs binge-eating Ben and Jerry's and watching *John Tucker Must Die* on repeat."

"Oh, I love that movie!"

"Good, you can sit upstairs and watch it with her in three weeks." Jett filled up a pint glass with ice and water and took a sip.

"You know who would be a good choice for Lizzie?" Chris asked, carrying a box of bar coasters out and setting them next to Jett. "Tyler."

"Your little brother Tyler?" Jett furrowed his eyebrows. "Dude, they have nothing in common."

Chris shrugged. "We'd officially be brothers though."

"That sounds more important than their individual happiness," Zoey said reasonably, and Chris pointed a finger-gun at her as if to say *exactly!*

"Just something to think about," Chris said before turning to Zoey. "Got a bucket list of things to do while you're here? Jett told me you were born and raised in SoCal. Have you ever seen snow?"

"I've seen it. I travel a lot for work, but it's usually the gross part of winter where everything is melting away into slush. I've never actually done any winter activities."

"Never? No sledding or skiing or ice skating?" Jett asked.

"Nope, never." She shook her head.

"Well, I'll have to fix that," Jett said with a smile. "How about I take you ice skating? I used to play hockey, so even if you're terrible at it, I promise I won't let you fall."

Zoey's smile brightened. "Yeah, I'd like that."

There was a moment of silence in which Jett reveled in his success-he'd asked her on a date and she'd said yes!

He was vaguely aware of Chris standing next to him, grinning as he looked back and forth between him and Zoey. Jett turned and gave his unsubtle friend a look that asked him to kindly leave them alone. Chris nodded and put his hands up, and backed away through the door to the kitchen. It was maybe the only time Jett had ever seen Chris act even remotely awkward, and that made him smile even more.

"It's a date then," Jett said. "Tomorrow night?"

"Tomorrow."

Back in the kitchen, Jett- and everyone in the place- could hear Chris's victorious *whoop* as he shouted in a low, carrying voice, "Yeah, yeah! My boy's got gaaaame!"

Jett laughed and rubbed a hand down his face, embarrassed. "I'm sorry about that."

"Don't be." Zoey grinned. "He's proud of you, it's sweet."

He couldn't help his own winning grin that spread across his face.

Yeah, I'm pretty proud of me, too.

CHAPTER 5

Jett was on the couch in his living room messing around on the guitar, coming up with his own melodies, completely dressed and ready for his date. He still had three hours, and knowing he'd probably get hungry and spill something on himself between now and then, he was mentally picking out a back-up sweater just in case.

"Come on six-thirty, get here...before I go downstairs and have a beer..." Jett sang mindlessly to himself.

There was a sharp knock on the door and Jett called out, "Door's open!"

"Hey Stud Muffin!" Rae called out as she entered the apartment, followed by Quinn and Chris.

"Bonjour, ma petite cherie!" Jett shot back, flourishing his hand in a chef's kiss.

"Are you ready for your daaate?" Rae sang, making her way over to the couch and flopped down next to him.

"I am. I actually feel pretty good. Confident."

"Oh good, confidence is so sexy," Rae replied.

Quinn stretched and let out a satisfied sigh. "Yep, that's why she can't keep her hands to herself. All this confidence drippin' off me."

"I think there's a difference between confidence and a massive ego," Jett countered.

Quinn raised his eyebrows suggestively. "That's not the only thing that's massive."

"Really?" Chris laughed. "You're gonna say that to *him?* Mr. Jett -Big Dick- Miller?"

"Is that what people call me?" Jett gaped, then pumped his fist. "Fuck yes! If you guys came over to give me a pep-talk or boost my confidence before this date, you're doing a great job. Keep going, I wanna hear more of these nicknames."

"You had a name for it in college," Chris said, sitting down in the recliner. "What was it? Deep something?"

Jett chuckled. "My Deep-V Diver?"

"Oh, that's good!" Rae laughed. "You could write a book: *Jett -Big Dick- Miller and his Deep-V Diver.*"

"I would read it." Quinn said. He sat on Rae's other side and began inspecting one of Jett's guitars that was sitting in its stand.

Jett's phone buzzed, vibrating its way along the coffee table. He reached over the guitar in his lap and picked it up. It was Zoey. He swiped to answer.

"Hey!" He greeted her cheerfully.

"Hi Jett…" Zoey's voice sounded strained and quiet. "I'm so sorry, I hate to do this, but I'm sick. I can't make our date tonight."

"Oh…" Jet expression fell. "That sucks." His three best friends all looked concerned as they watched him. "Are you okay? Do you have to go to the doctor or…?"

"I'm really sorry. I should have called sooner, but I just kept hoping I'd feel better. I wasn't feeling great yesterday, but I thought it was just nerves." She coughed several times.

"You're just in your hotel room by yourself?" Jett didn't like the thought of her being sick without anyone around to take care of her.

"Yeah," she rasped through her sore-sounding throat. "I just need to sleep it off, I think."

Jett stood up and ducked out of his guitar strap, setting the instrument back in its stand. "What's your room number?"

"What? Why? Jett, I'm really sick, I don't want you catching it."

"I'll be fine. I just don't like that you're there by yourself. You should have someone there in case it gets worse, or if you need…soup or something."

There was a brief pause before she let out an airy laugh that turned into a coughing fit.

"I'll do my best not to make you laugh while I'm there, but that's sort of my thing, so I can't make any promises."

After she gave him the name of the hotel and room number, he explained the situation to Quinn, Rae, and Chris. They all looked disappointed for him but agreed that going over there was the right thing to do. Rae said to let them know if he needed anything and the three of them left to let him get ready.

This wasn't his ideal way to spend time with Zoey but he was determined to show her that he was one of the good ones.

Zoey winced at the two knocks on the door. She had all the lights off in the hotel room to accommodate her throbbing headache that was concentrating itself right behind her eyes. She rolled herself off the couch where she'd dozed off, pulling the blanket with her and wrapping it tightly around herself.

Slowly, she opened the door and furrowed her brow at the sight before her.

Was she hallucinating now?

There was a tall figure with a giant, block-like head illuminated by the hallway lights. She squinted her eyes.

"It's me!" Jett's voice was slightly muffled.

"Is that...a Stormtrooper helmet?" Zoey asked, her voice hoarse and dry.

"Yeah, I figured I should protect myself from the plague," he replied.

She laughed quietly and erupted into another coughing fit.

He stepped inside and closed the door behind him, placing a hand on her back. "Sorry, it was either this or my...uh...welding helmet."

"Why do you have a welding helmet?"

"For doing...manly things," he replied. "In hindsight I guess that would've been the better option. Give off a better impression so you know I'm not your average hot nerd. I'm also exceedingly handy."

"You said you wouldn't make me laugh," Zoey reminded him through what she hoped was a smile. Her skin felt tight everywhere and she was suddenly aware of how unappealing she must look.

"I said I would try, but that's just something I can't help. I'm the resident funny guy. I'm like a court jester...or a pug."

Zoey laughed and coughed again.

"Sorry," Jett said, and she could hear the smile in his voice. He appeared to be surveying the room through his ridiculous helmet. "You have a couch in here? That's nice...This place is bigger than my apartment," he muttered. He cleared his throat then and asked, "Where do you want to lay down? Bed or couch?"

"Probably the bed," she croaked. "It's closer to the bathroom."

"Have you been puking?"

The alarm in Jett's voice made her laugh again. "A bit."

"Oh, this calls for the strong stuff." He gestured toward the reusable grocery bag slung over his shoulder.

"Did you bring NyQuil?" Zoey asked hopefully.

"Pshh, *NyQuil*." He waved a hand. "I got something better. Come on, let's get you to bed first."

Zoey led the way through the small living room into the adjoining bedroom, and with little grace, she flopped down onto the bed, still wrapped in her blanket.

She stared up at Jett. "Are you seriously going to wear that helmet the whole time?"

He placed the bag on the floor next to the nightstand and pulled the helmet off. "I'm actually sweating under there."

Looking up at him in the low light she studied his face. She noticed it was almost perfectly symmetrical, with a strong, square jaw. His lips...looked completely kissable. They were set into a pout when he wasn't smiling, and when he *was* smiling, his whole face brightened. He had one of those smiles that was completely contagious. His dimples were like parentheses around his laugh lines, making it look as if he were smiling that much wider.

His eyes were some of the greenest eyes she'd ever seen, and they were lined with dark eyelashes, beneath perfectly symmetrical eyebrows. How was this the man who gets teased about being a virgin and having no game? It made absolutely no sense.

Especially with those light brown, boyish curls? He always seemed to leave one lock of curls precisely placed, hanging off-center over his forehead. It was like this wild piece that didn't want to conform with the rest of his hair and just needed to be the center of attention.

Ugh! Why did she have to get sick *now?* Zoey began the mental calculation of how long it had been since she had slept with someone. *How long has it even been since I've kissed someone? Fooled around- even just a little bit?*

"You sure you don't want to get under the covers?" Jett asked.

Oh crap, I'm still just staring at him in silence.

"Here, I'll help you up." He held his hands out and she grasped his forearms- *oh, those are nice, too.*

Zoey felt like Jell-O on her feet and leaned into him to stay standing. He wrapped an arm around her to hold her steady while he threw back the comforter. He unwrapped the blanket that she'd been holding around herself and she let out a violent shiver. Instinctively, he pulled her closer, warming her with his body heat. *Oh mama, he's got strong arms.*

Placing another hand on her upper back, he lowered her onto the pillows and covered her back up. He tossed the extra blanket on top of the comforter and sat next to her on the edge of the bed.

He shifted slightly and cleared his throat. "Okay, and now to unpack the Bag of Wonders." Jett reached for the bag he'd brought and began pulling out its contents. "Saltines...I also brought oyster crackers if that's more your thing. I have chicken noodle soup, I have just noodle soup in chicken broth. I even brought chicken-and-stars in case you wanted to embrace your inner child- I will tell you this in confidence, I *always* go for the chicken-and-stars soup."

"In confidence...so do I," Zoey smiled sleepily at him.

Jett grinned and bit his lip shyly before digging his arm back into the bag. "I also brought bottles of water, vitamin C packets to mix in your water, gummy vitamins, and- drumroll!" he drummed his hands on his knee before pulling out- "Vernors!"

Zoey stared blankly then furrowed her brow as she squinted at the six-pack of soda in his hand. "What?"

"Vernors- it's ginger ale. It's a Michigan thing to drink Vernors when you're sick. I promise it's helpful."

She laughed. "Michigan organic healing."

"That's exactly it." He reached in the bag one more time, "And I *did* bring NyQuil. But go easy on it. Stuff's deadly."

"You really went all out." At a zombie-like pace, Zoey sat up on her fluffed-up pillows and observed the contents of her care package that now littered the bed.

"This is the exact same care package my mom brought to me one weekend when I was sick as hell in college." He unscrewed the lid on a bottle of water and handed it to her. "Stay hydrated."

"Where did you go to college?" Zoey asked, taking the bottle from him and taking a small sip.

"Central Michigan University." He scooted further onto the bed. "It was fun. Not much to do but go to the bar or drink in your yard. There were some good disc golf courses though. And they now have brewing beer as a major, so that's pretty dope."

"How far did your mom have to drive to bring you your care package of Vernors and chicken-and-stars?"

"It's about a two hour drive," he explained. "She really just drove down, dropped the box on the stoop of our townhouse, knocked, and booked it back home. She's pretty great."

"That's so sweet."

"She knew I needed it. I'd been exploding out of both ends for eight hours by then."

Zoey began to giggle, then clamped a hand over her mouth- *uh oh.*

Jett's eyes widened and he acted quickly, running into the bathroom and grabbing the trash can just in time.

She was puking. Yep. She was throwing up in front of this hunky man with strong arms and gorgeous green eyes. What. A. Nightmare.

She felt the weight on the bed shift and he was behind her, holding her hair back.

This was clearly not a romantic moment, but she felt her heart melting regardless.

When the vomiting stopped, he rubbed her back slowly with one solid, warm hand. *Solid and large.*

Okay Zoey, this is really not the time to be thinking about that.

She set the garbage can down on the floor and took another drink of water.

"Here, I almost forgot..." Jett pulled a brand new package of scrunchies out of his jeans pocket.

She felt completely gross and she desperately needed to brush her teeth, but she couldn't help smiling at him. "Who are you, Jett Miller?"

He smirked. "I have many nicknames, though I must admit, none of them are suitable for a first date."

Zoey giggled and leaned back onto her pillows, pulling her hair up into a messy bun, "This is *not* our first date."

"Why not? It's unique and it's a great story to tell the kids- and by kids I mean Quinn, Rae, and Chris, obviously."

Zoey peered curiously at Jett as he organized all the supplies he'd brought into a pile. How was it possible that this insanely sweet, thoughtful, attentive, astonishingly handsome guy was single? Who needs *game* when you're just that perfect?

"Can I ask you something?"

He looked up at her with a "Hm?"

"What kind of non-friend, a-hole told you to use that line on me yesterday?" Her lips curved into a sly grin. "I didn't realize there were actual guys who *coach* other guys like that."

He opened his mouth and paused before responding, "Well, he drinks a lot of Heineken, but that's all I can tell you."

"Does he wear a suit to the bar?"

"He does." Jett nodded. "He even got me to wear one somehow. Not my best moment, but I did look pretty good."

"Does he drive a sports car as his everyday car?" Her grin widened further.

"I...think so. It's not a very practical car anyway."

"Is his name Brad, Chad, or Thad?"

Jett laughed. "No, but I promise it's worse."

After a few more questions and guesses as to who this mysterious not-really-a-friend might be, Zoey insisted on getting up to brush her teeth. Jett helped her up and let her lean on him as he walked her to the bathroom and back to the bed. Once covered back up, she took some NyQuil, popped open a can of Vernors, and asked him to tell her his life story. The whole thing.

Around his third grade adventures, in the middle of a story about how his older brother had shoved a garter snake down his pants during a camping trip, she had interrupted by abruptly sitting up and utilizing the puke bucket.

He told her about a time in sixth grade when he was determined to redeem himself in football with Rae- apparently the first time she'd tackled him twice and really bruised his ego. This time he had succeeded in tackling her, but a group of eighth-grade boys had witnessed it and thought he was being intentionally mean. When they'd stepped in, he'd nearly gotten his butt kicked. Again, Zoey laughed which turned into coughing, which turned into more vomit. Phenomenal.

The final puke incident happened when he told her about a crush he'd had his junior year of high school. She was in his French class, and he'd asked Rae to tutor him in French so that *he* could tutor the girl he liked. Zoey was admiring the extra mile he went, even as a sixteen or seventeen-year-old kid, to do something helpful for this girl he liked, when her stomach started rolling again.

Each time, he helped her get to the bathroom to brush her teeth, and tucked her back in.

She could feel the NyQuil kicking in; her eyelids were heavy and she was feeling liquidy and giggly. If she didn't fall asleep, there was a good chance she would say something embarrassingly honest about how he made her feel.

Scooting herself down into the blankets and sinking deeper into the pillows, she sighed. Before her eyes closed all the way, she spotted Jett's hand resting within reach and slipped her own hand into it.

When her eyes fluttered shut, she felt a small smile appear on her face.

Jett spoke and she couldn't help wishing he were closer, speaking directly into her ear. "I don't want to come on too strong here, but...I think you like me, Zoey Nunez."

Her smile widened as she sunk deeper into the bed. "I think so, too."

CHAPTER 6

The following morning, Zoey had woken up drenched in sweat and feeling a hundred times better. With a long enough shower, she was sure she'd feel back to normal. On her way out of the shower, wrapped in a fuzzy yellow robe, she spotted the stack of soups and crackers on the little desk in her room. She couldn't help the smile that tugged at her lips as she thought about how sweet and thoughtful Jett had been. He'd really taken care of her. It was almost enough to make her forget how embarrassed she felt about puking in front of him so many times.

Looking around for her disgusting puke bucket, she realized it was gone. She remembered getting up once and getting sick in the toilet, but she couldn't remember ever taking care of the garbage can. Furrowing her brow in confusion, she realized her blanket was also missing from the bed. She eyed the contents of Jett's care package again and wondered when he'd left.

After grabbing a can of chicken-and-stars soup, a bottle of water, and a sleeve of saltine crackers, she headed into the living room with its adjoining kitchenette.

Jett was wearing the previous night's clothes as he stood over the stove, stirring what appeared to be a pot of soup. He turned at the sound of the bedroom door opening and smiled.

"Hey, she's alive!" he beamed.

Zoey grinned slowly. "You...stayed all night?"

"Slept on the couch." He gestured toward the sofa where blankets and pillows were folded and stacked neatly. "Feeling any better?"

She found herself feeling overwhelmed at how nice it was that he'd stayed the whole night just in case she needed anything. He really just didn't want her to be alone while she was sick. Again…who was this guy?

"Yeah, much better, actually."

Jett turned the burner off. "I heard the shower running and thought I'd make some soup. You probably should eat something."

Still looking curiously- and maybe a little awe-struck- at him, she walked over to the kitchen counter and emptied her hands. She stared up into his green eyes and another reserved smile crossed her face.

"What?" Jett touched his stubbly jaw. "Do I have something on my face?"

She couldn't wipe the dreamy, dopey grin off her face. "No…I just…I'm usually the one taking care of people. I'm not used to…It was nice being cared for, for a change."

"It was nice to feel needed for a change." He grabbed a bowl out of the cupboard and ladled out some soup. "So, I was thinking for our second date, if you're up for it, we can go ice skating and then to this Mexican restaurant- I *love* tacos. For future reference, I will *never* say no to tacos."

"Good to know, but I think you mean our first date," Zoey said, crushing up saltine crackers into her bowl of soup. "We went over this last night- *that* was not our first date. At best it was a first-date fail."

"Fail?" Jett scrunched his face. "What was such a failure? You got to be taken care of, I got to show off my caregiving skills, you were healed by Vernors, and you admitted that you like me. That's not a fail. That's a first date story for the books."

Zoey protested, "No way."

"Why not? You passed out so hard, you were snoring and drooling a little bit. It was adorable."

"Oh my God, *stop.* You'd better be lying."

Jett took a saltine cracker out of the package. "I'm not a liar. That's one thing you'll learn about me- I don't lie."

"So embarrassing…" Zoey groaned.

"You were also murmuring in your sleep," he continued. "I was cleaning up the room and you would just say random things. Some of it made sense, like when you asked me to stay."

"I asked you to stay?"

"*Told* me is more accurate." He smirked. "I was going to stay anyway, but I think you meant in the bedroom. I would've, but you threw up a little on your blanket and I didn't want to be next."

She let out a mortified groan. "You cleaned up everything in there? Oh my God, I'm even more embarrassed now. You didn't have to do that."

"I didn't mind. You were a cute little comatose patient." He grinned around a bite of saltine. "Especially when you called me Big Papa. Then I knew I had to stay."

"I did *not!*" She laughed. "Now I know you're lying. I would never say that."

Jett put his hands up. "Hey, I heard what I heard. You might've been dreaming about someone a lot hunkier than me, but I took it to heart."

Zoey sighed and shook her head. "What am I going to do with you, Jett Miller?"

His eyebrow twitched mischievously in response and she immediately felt warmth in her lower belly and between her thighs.

"I could think of some things, but…we can save those for the second date."

Grinning into a spoonful of soup, Zoey couldn't help thinking perhaps they *should* count last night as their first date…

Jett took a long shower when he got home, needing to feel both clean and relieved. Was it crazy that he'd gotten so aroused just staying in the same vicinity as Zoey? Even though she'd been puking her guts out all night? Probably. Yes, there was probably something very wrong with him. It was more the way her cheeks and neck flushed when he'd insinuated possible things to do on their next date that had him risking tennis elbow when he jumped in the shower.

It was early and the bar didn't open until two o'clock this afternoon, so he had time to relax a little and check job applications that had come in.

Since July, the bar had gotten busier, and continued to do so even though it was no longer prime bar-hopping season. Chris and Jett had talked about hiring a manager or two if they could afford it, which would help them get a few nights off. As much as Jett loved that he and his best friend had made their dream come true and worked together doing something they truly enjoyed, it would be nice to get more than one night off a week. Maybe get a vacation every now and then. It wasn't rare for Jett to work eleven days straight, get one day off, and jump right back into another week or week-and-a-half work streak.

Chris had tried roping Tyler into it, but the kid had his sights set on law school. Jett had attempted to persuade him that he'd work just as many- if not more- hours as a lawyer as he would managing the bar. Apparently that wasn't the point. Tyler wanted to be one of the "good lawyers," whatever the hell that meant. He was going to use his position to help people in need. He thought being a public defender would be a good way to offer help to those who otherwise couldn't afford it in a corrupt and biased legal system.

Jett sat on the couch with his laptop and went to the job site where he'd posted the manager position. He had six new applicants to look over. Hopefully this batch would be more promising than the past few he'd weeded through.

Maybe it wasn't their fault, but some people really had no idea how to write a resume. They also, he discovered, had no idea who to use as references. It's not hard to figure out if someone's lying on a resume anymore, and it's even easier to find out if the person they put down as a professional reference is really a professional. Though it has its flaws in society, Facebook was a wonderful tool for business owners and employers.

Last week, they had received what looked to be a promising resume. Alexandra Collins, age 28, graduate of Western Michigan University, had put down John Ashby as her first reference. He was listed as a previous business associate. Okay? Well, upon a quick Facebook search, Jett and Chris were staring, dumb-founded at John Ashby's profile picture in which he was smoking a massive blunt and holding up stacks of money in each hand.

A drug dealer.

Her business associate was a drug dealer.

Pass.

Jett printed out the six new resumes to take down to the office later and go through once Chris got there. He suddenly found himself far more interested in planning the next couple of dates with Zoey than going through resumes that may or may not pan out.

He knew he'd have to wait until Zoey was feeling better- Mexican food usually isn't the best thing for an unsettled stomach- but he was itching to take her out as soon as possible.

On his list of potential dates he had:

1. Ice skating
2. Sledding- Group date?
3. Hockey game- she must like sports, right?
4. Frankenmuth Christmas village
5. Pick out Christmas tree- too much??
6. Bake Christmas cookies- Grandma's recipe- fuck yes
7. Christmas movie marathon and chill (wink-wink, nudge-nudge)

Yet another one of Jett's quirks was being completely obsessed with the Christmas season, and having themed activities to rely on was really helping him out. He couldn't help feeling excited that Zoey would be spending her first Christmas with real snow and that she was going to experience a *real* Christmas season. Something about spending the holiday somewhere with palm trees just didn't seem right to him. It never had.

At about 1:15, he pocketed his list, got dressed for work and headed downstairs to get the bar set up. Chris was already there waiting for Jett in the office with a smiling, eager face.

"So...how did it go?" Chris asked through his bright white grin.

"It was good, considering," Jett replied. "She was doped up on NyQuil but she told me she likes me, so I'll call it a win."

"Yeah?" Chris beamed. "She's falling for your goofy ass, huh?"

"I think she might be." Jett looked around as though something were suspicious about this. "But it's early. I have plenty of time to show her what a weirdo I am and send her running away screaming."

"How's she feeling?"

"She seemed like she was feeling better this morning." Jett sat in the desk chair and spun himself around several times.

"This *morning?*" Chris kicked his foot out to stop the chair mid-spin. "You stayed the night?"

"She was throwing up, I wasn't going to just leave her alone. What if it got worse?"

"Did you...rub Vapo-rub on her chest?" Chris winked suggestively.

"No, you sicko. I didn't find excuses to fondle the vulnerable sick chick." *Mostly because that thought hadn't occurred to me. Note to self: Add Vapo-rub to the next care package.*

"Probably for the best. The last thing you want is a hard-on when you can't do anything about it." Chris pulled the back-of-house binder out of the overhead cabinet and began pulling sheets out for the up-coming shift. "When are you going to take her out for real then?"

"Soon I hope." Jett ran his hands down his face. "Between working every night and sleeping all day, it's hard to make time. Oh- speaking of, I printed out six more resumes."

Chris let out an aggravated groan and threw up his hands. "Screw it, let's post them up on the wall and throw darts. We'll call those people for interviews and pick one. I need a night off, too."

It wasn't the worst idea. It would be a hell of a lot easier and less time consuming.

Jett slapped the stack of resumes on the desktop. "Let's do it."

Less than ten minutes later, Chris and Jett were standing in front of a bulletin board covered in resumes. They'd pulled out some older ones just to be fair to everyone but made sure to leave out those who'd listed drug dealers as references.

Chris pulled darts out of the dart board up front and they each had two darts in hand.

"Okay, eyes closed," Jett said. He squeezed his eyes shut and sent his first dart flying.

"Behind the back," Chris announced before sending his trick shot.

"Under the leg- bam! Oh- shit…" The dart missed the board entirely. With a noise of indifference Jett shrugged. "One less call to make."

Laughing, Chris stepped forward and Jett put a hand over his eyes. "Okay, go." Chris threw his second dart and it landed on the same resume as Jett's first dart.

"Well this couldn't have gone worse," Chris said, clapping his hands together. "Let's see who our two lucky winners are." He pulled his first dart out and flipped around the resume. "Simon Barnes, you lucky dog."

Jett pulled the two darts out of the back of the second resume. His eyes went wide when he read the name at the top. "Oof…maybe I should've actually read the resumes I printed this morning."

"You didn't even look at their names?" Chris half-laughed. "Who is it?"

Jett turned the piece of paper around to face Chris who had a similar reaction. "I mean, I'd say we should try again but it feels dishonest. And we hit her resume *twice*. That can't be a coincidence."

"That's exactly what it is. A coincidence. A sick joke." Jett shook the piece of paper aggressively. "No, we can't call her. More trouble than it's worth."

"Oh come on, it was high school. Rae can't still be mad," Chris argued. Of course as soon as his argument was out of his mouth, he cringed at his own words. Rae was sort of the queen of grudge-holding.

"Oh, I think she could."

"Does she even know that she's the one…?" Chris hesitated, cringe still in place.

"Oh yeah, she knows." Jett scratched the stubble on his jaw. "It was like three weeks after graduation and she was finally about to cave and go see Case…and I let it slip."

"Ooooh, so this is about you." Chris snapped his fingers, grinning. "You don't want Quinn to find out *you're* the reason Rae didn't talk to him all summer and therefore didn't talk to him for *years!*"

"I'm not the reason- *he's* the reason. He should've taken our advice!" Jett whisper-yelled defensively. Glancing back at the resume in his hands, he muttered, "But I didn't exactly help the situation, no."

Chris sighed heavily, taking the resume from Jett. "I don't know, man. We went over the terms, I say we call her."

"The terms?" Jett scoffed. "That was dumb. That was just a game and it was dumb and foolish and a completely unprofessional way to choose a new manager."

"When have we ever done things differently?"

Fair point.

"I'll make the calls," Chris offered, taking the piece of paper from Jett. "Who knows? Maybe Alaina Costello could be the answer to our prayers."

Jett groaned somewhat dramatically. Absolutely no good could come of this, he was sure of it.

CHAPTER 7

Zoey had spent all of Friday laying low in her hotel room, alternating between watching *The Office* on Netflix and cheesy Christmas movies on the Hallmark channel. She'd gone through half the six-pack of Vernors and two cans of chicken-and-stars soup. She thought it more likely that the vitamin C packets and NyQuil were to thank for feeling significantly better, but if Jett asked she would tell him it was the ginger ale. It seemed like the nice thing to do.

Saturday morning had come and she'd gotten thirteen solid hours of sleep. That had probably never happened in her entire life. After another shower she felt good as new. She wanted to text Jett right away and tell him that she was feeling up for their date but was interrupted when a phone call from her little sister came through.

"Hey Cass, what's up?"

"Zo- I need to go to the doctor!" Cassie said, sounding urgent and out of breath.

Instant panic-mode set in. "Oh my God, are you okay? Do I need to come home? I can get a flight-"

"No, I'm fine," Cassie cut her off. "I just haven't been to my lady doctor in a while and thought maybe you could call and set up an appointment for me."

Zoey let out a long breath. "Seriously, Cass? Don't do that to me. I thought you found a lump or something."

"So will you call? You know I suck at that kind of stuff."

Deep breath in, two...three. And out, two...three.

"You don't suck at making phone calls, you just don't like making your own appointments."

"Okay? Is that a yes?" Cassie pressed. "Because I know it's not good to let these things go unchecked. You wouldn't want to find out I had cervical cancer that could've been stopped before it was too late."

"Do you think you have cervical cancer?" Zoey asked. Dear Lord, her headache just might come back.

"No. I...okay, don't get mad, but I hooked up with this guy the other night and he sort of put it in before it was wrapped-"

"Cassie! Who was this guy? Are you dating? Was this your first time with him? You guys had just met, hadn't you?" Zoey couldn't help the words from spilling out.

"Hey, I told you not to get mad. And you said it was cool that I could hook up with randos. I don't need your judgment, Big Sis," Cassie shot back.

"Cass, if you're old enough to hook up with *'randos'* and not use pro-tection, I think you're old enough to call and make your own doctor's appointments." Zoey massaged the bridge of her nose with her thumb and index finger.

"We used protection! He just stuck it in like three times without, and then put one on. But I just want to be safe, ya know?"

"Well that's...smart, I guess." Zoey squeezed her eyes shut and tried to focus on something less stressful than her sister's wild behavior. "Fine, I'll call. When are you available?"

Cassie rattled off a few dates and times that would work for her, and Zoey filed them away inside a little mental compartment in her head. Her conversation with her little sister continued for a few min-utes; Cassie went on about how hot the guy was that she'd slept with, another cute boy in her biology class, and all the Christmas parties she was going to over the next week or so. Zoey wasn't surprised that Cassie hadn't asked much about how her trip was going. The girl was so flaky sometimes, Zoey wouldn't be surprised if she'd completely for-gotten she was out of state.

As soon as her call ended with Cassie, she called the doctor's office in California- doing the math on the time change first to make sure it was open already- and made the appointment. She sent Cassie a quick text of the date and time, and received a thumbs up and smiley face emoji in return.

She found Jett's name again and finished her text to him: *All healed thanks to Michigan organics. When's your next night off?*

While she waited for his reply, she went over to the closet and began pulling out cute winter outfits and boots to try on. She knew that even if Jett was working tonight she'd make sure to stop in and see him.

Her phone chimed as she was halfway into a sweater with an odd neckline. She frantically pulled it on over her head, imagining she looked like a cat trying to fight its way out of a knapsack, and rushed over to read her new text.

Jett: Is tonight too soon? I can make it happen.

Zoey smiled wide, despite the fact that her head was definitely in the wrong hole of her sweater, and sent back a reply: *Tonight's perfect.*

Jett: Great. I'll pick you up at 6.

Jett: I assume I can leave the helmet home this time?

Laughing, she sent back: *Unless we're going somewhere with cosplay.*

Jett: Oh God, she knows Cosplay. I think we found us a jeepers.

Jett: Jeepers.

Jett: Jeep

Jett: Jeeper

Jett: K-E-E-P-E-R

Jett: Fml.

Zoey: Omg😆

Jett: See you at 6. Can't wait.

Zoey read through the short thread of messages again. He wasn't even here and he still made her sides hurt from laughing. She looked up from her phone and scanned her closet again. Assuming he was keeping their original plan for ice skating and tacos, she thought she'd better go shopping for some more winter-friendly clothing.

Finding Raelyn's number in her phone, she sent a quick text asking where the best places to shop were. She hadn't expected an almost immediate reply: *I have to go shopping too. I'll pick you up in 20 minutes!*

Well, all right then. She and Rae had gotten along since meeting- at least since Rae had found out that there really was nothing going on between Zoey and Quinn. Zoey was pretty certain she'd done a good job making that abundantly clear. This was the first time they'd be spending time together apart from work. Sure, sometimes it seemed like Zoey was just hanging out at Quinn's house- Quinn and *Rae's* house now, she supposed- but she was always on her phone, making calls or scheduling interviews, responding to emails, or managing Quinn's Twitter account. Yes, she managed that, too.

Zoey had simply assumed they didn't have much in common, and hadn't made the effort to really be friends. Of course, it now occurred to her that Raelyn was one of Jett's best and oldest friends. Several of the stories Jett had told the other night included her, so maybe this was a good thing.

She made an addition to the ongoing checklist/agenda in her brain: Item 232: Become friends with Jett's friends.

An hour later, Zoey was standing on the platform inside a lavish dressing room, looking at herself in the mirror wearing one of the many winter coats she'd picked out. This one was long with faux a fur-lined hood, and while it was super warm and cozy, she had no idea how much mobility it would allow her on her ice skating date.

She pulled the hood up and her vision was completely blocked out by the fuzzy lining when Raelyn stepped out of a nearby dressing room.

"What do you think?" Rae asked as she stepped up next to her on the platform.

Zoey tossed the hood back and her eyebrows shot up into her hairline. "Um...I think you're wearing lingerie..."

"Right. But...what do you think? Is it too cute?" Rae looked down and plucked at the pink bows on the garter belt. "At first I liked that it was cute, but now I'm feeling like if I wear this I have to role play and call him Daddy, ya know?"

Zoey's eyes widened further as her mouth hung open, unsure how to respond.

"Yeah, definitely too cute. Pink is really not my color," Rae said definitively before turning around and heading back into her fitting room.

If she'd known the shopping Rae had to do was picking out lingerie to wear while they were in Paris, Zoey might have gotten a rain check. She knew way too much about Quinn and Rae's sex life as it was, she didn't feel like she needed to take part in planning it. Besides, Rae was tall, tan, crazy-fit, and completely gorgeous. She could wear a pair of boys' Hulk undies down a runway and still turn heads.

Zoey slipped an emerald green winter coat off a hanger and tried it on. She stepped back in front of the mirror and was glad she was wearing heeled boots. She'd look like a little kid in this thing if she hadn't given herself some extra height. Being petite as she was, she'd learned to wear heels as often as possible. She worked around athletes who were all at least six feet tall, and she was frequently the only female among the crowd as well. She had to make sure she wasn't overlooked- literally and figuratively.

"Where is Jett taking you tonight?" Rae called through the closed curtain.

"I don't know exactly," Zoey replied, unzipping the parka-like coat and putting it back on the hanger. "He mentioned ice skating and tacos."

Rae's laugh carried through the thick curtain. "Can't keep Jett away from his tacos. It's the only thing keeping him from his dream bod, I'm pretty sure."

Zoey raised a scrutinous brow in the direction of the changing room. "I think he looks great." It didn't matter to Zoey that Jett didn't look like Quinn or other guys who spent hours a day at the gym. She remembered how strong his arms felt when he'd pulled her close to him after she'd shivered. His body hadn't even felt soft, necessarily. She'd felt muscles beneath his shirt, even if they weren't professionally sculpted.

"Oh, he does," Rae said, stepping out of the fitting room in an ivory and rose gold bustier with matching panties and garters. "I just know he's always compared himself to his friends. Jett's a bit of a jock, all of his friends are athletes, too. He used to make comments all the time about how he was the token 'fat friend,' which is ridiculous because he's never even been fat. He just...likes tacos."

Zoey hummed as she considered this piece of information. "Do you think he's...insecure? I mean, about his appearance or how he looks next to his friends?"

"I know he is," Rae said, inspecting herself in the mirror. "I think that's why he's such a people pleaser. I'm not saying this to talk shit about him- he's one of my absolute best friends and I would do anything for him- but he definitely feels overshadowed."

"How so?"

"Well, for starters," Rae stepped back into her fitting room, "one of his best friends is Quinn Casey. Even before that name really meant anything, it meant something at our school. He was a star athlete, known all over town for his talent, and known with the ladies for...well, you know."

"That wasn't just part of becoming famous?" Zoey asked curiously. "He was always a ladies' man?"

"He came into it late, but he caught on quick." The sounds of shuffling hangers filled the fitting room briefly. "Chris was the star quarterback in high school, and he found the love of his life in his first year of college. I think that threw him a little. It had always been Chris and Jett against the world, and suddenly there was Chris and Jett and *Victoria.*"

"What about you and Quinn? Why would Victoria throw a wrench in things but you and Quinn didn't?" Zoey tried a shorter, puffy coat on.

"We met in middle school and I was just one of the boys. Quinn didn't even think of me like that yet. I played football with them and hockey, I wore athletic clothes all the time and judged their belching contests. Victoria wanted time alone with Chris, and he changed with her and they melded into one unit, kind of." Rae stepped out again in a black and white lingerie set.

"You might have to role play in that, too," Zoey said, becoming slightly more comfortable with her situation. "It's very...French maid."

Rae looked in the mirror and appeared to be considering the pros and cons of this point.

"Is that it? Just Quinn being who he is and Chris...finding someone? Not needing him anymore?" Zoey suddenly remembered what Jett had said about how it had been nice to feel needed for a change. Had he been a member of a duo for so long that he felt left out in the cold without his friend? Or was there more to it?

"His older brother was a big hockey star," said Rae. "Gavin was on all sorts of travel teams and played in college at Ferris State. Jett played, too, but not quite at the same intensity. He'd thought about following in Gavin's footsteps and playing in college, but changed his mind for some reason. Honestly, he might've just followed Chris to the school he wanted to attend, and it didn't have a hockey team."

Zoey looked up, mildly alarmed. "That's a huge decision to make based on someone else."

Then again, was she one to talk? She'd been accepted to a few schools in different states, but had stayed in San Diego to be close to her family. But that was different. Ace was only fifteen at the time, and Cassie was twelve. They'd needed her to be close. She hadn't had much of a choice.

"That's Jett," Rae said, lifting and lowering one shoulder. "He always puts everyone else first. Like I said, he's sort of a people pleaser. It's like he thinks if he doesn't do everything in his power to make everyone else happy, they'll forget he's there."

Putting her last coat back on its hanger, Zoey chewed the inside of her lip. Jett was always so funny and happy it seemed, she never would have guessed he had all these hidden insecurities. Although, maybe that's why he felt the need to be funny. Perhaps he thought if he didn't contribute somehow to their group- in this case, taking on the role as the *resident funny guy*, as he'd put it- that they wouldn't need him around anymore.

"Have you ever told him that you need him? Like...as a friend, just to make him feel appreciated? To let him know he brings something to the table?" Zoey asked.

"More times than I can count." Rae had stepped back behind the curtain and it sounded like she was pulling her jeans back on. "He's helped me get through a lot. He's the most loyal and honest person you'll ever meet, I guarantee it. I don't care if you think your grandma is the sweetest person in the world, Jett's sweeter."

Zoey smiled because she didn't have an ounce of trouble believing it. When Rae stepped out, she was fully clothed again, but honestly didn't look any less attractive or sensual than she had in the lingerie.

Zoey peered at her curiously, and hesitating, she began, "You guys have known each other for a long time...and it seems like you and Jett are really close..." She felt ridiculous for bringing this up, but couldn't help it. Did it even matter? If something had happened between Rae and Jett while they were in college...They'd obviously decided that being just friends suited them.

But curiosity niggled at her like a hard-to-reach itch.

"I know you guys are friends, but…I mean, there was a big gap where Quinn wasn't around but you and Jett obviously stayed in touch…"

"*Oh!* Oh, God no. Nothing has ever happened between me and Jett," Rae said sincerely. "I'd be lying if I told you I never *wished* I was attracted to him in that way, but it was never in the cards for us. My heart's belonged to someone else since I was seven, and that's pretty hard to beat."

Zoey felt the relief loosening the anxious feeling in her chest. She hadn't realized before that she'd been intimidated by the possibility that maybe something had happened between Rae and Jett before. The thought made her feel defensive and insecure, and want to ask all these questions like *how the heck do I compete with that?!* But there was nothing to worry about. Maybe now she could relax and try to get to know Raelyn for real.

Jett slammed the bar phone down on its receiver. "Dammit!"

The bar wasn't busy yet, but people were filing in and he could tell it was about to be a crazy Saturday night. Chris was finishing up his last reports before heading to the kitchen, and Quinn had stopped in to hang out while Rae was out shopping.

"What's wrong, Honey Boo?" Chris asked, looking up from his laptop on the other side of the bar.

"Xander just called off for the night. Said he's puking his guts out. Probably whatever bug Zoey had that's going around. *Fuck*…I won't be able to take her out tonight." Jett fisted his hair with a groan.

Quinn looked up from pint of Two-Hearted Ale. "You don't have another bartender to call in?"

"On this short notice?" Jett shook his head. "I mean, I'll still make some calls, but I doubt it. Nicki asked for the night off a couple weeks ago…Jake, I mean, he's great when he's here, but I can never get ahold of him any other time."

"We...might be able to make it work still," said Chris, though his voice was hesitant and he glanced uncertainly at the door.

"I can't leave you without a front-of-house manager *and* a bartender on a Saturday night." Jett protested. He had already called Corey, the assistant manager, to come in and close for him. He'd get there a little later than usual, but it would make closing easier at least.

"I'll do it."

Jett snapped his head up to see Quinn looking back at him. He gave a shrug. "I tended bar in college during the off season."

"Seriously?" Jett eyed his friend hopefully. "Don't you have plans with Rae?"

Quinn shrugged again. "I've got plans with Rae the rest of my life. She'll understand."

Chris was looking curiously at Quinn. "You know, this could actually be really good for the bar. Everyone knows you're from here, and obviously we've got your jersey and now some childhood photos up on the wall...You bartending might be good for business."

"Hell yeah, it will!" Quinn slammed a fist on the bar top. "Do you have any idea how much I made in tips back in the day? Girls would just come in to see me- in flocks." He gestured to his right. "I had my tip jar over here-" he gestured to his left- "and my phone number jar over here."

Chris and Jett shared exasperated laughs as they looked at each other skeptically.

"Some ground rules," Jett said, holding up a finger. "Number one, no dancing on the bar. This is not that kind of bar. This isn't *Coyote Ugly*, you're not Magic Mike."

Quinn smirked. "You haven't seen my moves. I could be."

"Number two, and I cannot stress this enough, keep your clothes on. All of them. No stripping. Again- not that type of bar." Jett looked intently at Quinn who was now grinning mischievously. "And number three, seriously Case, *seriously*- no starting fights."

Quinn shot Jett two finger guns. "Only finish 'em- got it."

"No!" Jett and Chris replied sternly, in unison.

"What if-"

"No."

Quinn held up a hand. "Okay, but hear me out- what *if*...he's a total d-bag who could really benefit from an ass-beating?"

"No." Jett shook his head.

"How about if he's wearing a San Diego hat?" Quinn asked, narrowing his eyes.

Jett chuckled. "Still pissed about Barrett striking you out twice in one game?"

"Beginner's luck. That fucker. I'll get him next time." Quinn glared as he took another drink from his glass.

"Still no. Not even if Barrett himself comes in, *no fighting,*" Chris stated. "Be on your best behavior, Case. This isn't just a bar, it's our livelihood, okay?"

Quinn spread his arms out to the side with his winning magazine-cover smile on his face. "When have I ever let you guys down? I got this."

Jett looked to Chris who was grinning nervously.

"Fine, okay," Jett sighed. "You got the job."

It was one night. Quinn couldn't possibly do that much damage in one night. Jett silently made the decision to keep his phone on vibrate, maybe even silent, while on his date later that night. Whatever happened, he'd deal with it tomorrow. Tonight he was focused on Zoey. The rest of the world could wait.

CHAPTER 8

Jett knocked on the door to Zoey's hotel room and waited. When she pulled the door open he smiled shyly as a ripple of nerves shivered from his chest into his stomach. She looked beautiful with her long hair down in dark brown waves over her shoulders. Her face had some color back in it, and it wasn't just the subtle make-up she was wearing. He was pleased to see that she was feeling better.

"Hi." Jett cleared his throat and held out the small bouquet of flowers he'd picked up for her. "I got these for you. I don't know if you like roses but Rae said they're a classic."

Zoey beamed as she looked into the arrangement of red and white roses. "They're gorgeous, Jett, thank you." She walked the flowers over to the kitchenette and found a jar to put them in. "I'll have to find something taller, but that'll work for now."

"There's no specific time for ice skating but I thought we'd do that first unless you're hungry now," Jett said, taking a step inside and closing the door behind him.

"We can go skating first." Zoey turned around after filling the jar with water. She set the make-shift vase on the counter with an admiring smile. "Then when I fall on my butt, I can ease the pain with a giant margarita."

"I told you I won't let you fall."

Zoey pulled a cream-colored hat with a giant pom-pom on top over her head. "Just wait until I'm leaning into you with my whole body weight. You're bound to topple over."

Jett raised an eyebrow skeptically. "Yeah, all five feet, ninety pounds of you is going to push me over. I played hockey and had 200 pound guys charging into me. I think I'll be okay."

"Excuse you, I'm five-*four*. That four inches makes a difference, okay?"

"I bet." Jett grinned slyly. "I've never had to worry much about those extra inches though."

Zoey paused to eye him curiously. The corner of her mouth pulled up as she failed to conceal a grin and her cheeks went red. "Was that a penis joke?"

Of course it was.

Jett feigned offense with a gasp. "Zoey Nunez, I was pointing out that I'm six feet tall. That's the goal for every guy. Taller would be nice, but as long as you hit that mark, it's fine." He shook his head slowly as her face reddened further. "I see where your mind's at tonight."

She giggled and looked down at her tall, camel brown boots. "I guess that's what I get for spending my afternoon with Rae." She slipped on her coat and grabbed her purse.

Jett offered his arm as he opened the door. "Guess we better find you a man tonight, huh? Can't have all these wild female hormones buzzing around while I'm trying to teach you to skate."

Zoey shook her head with a laugh, looping her arm through his as he pulled the door shut behind them.

At the skating rink, Jett helped Zoey get her skates laced up, then held her hands in his to walk her out to the ice. In his own hockey skates, Jett stepped backwards onto the ice and braced for her first step onto the smooth surface. One foot, then both feet on the ice and she threatened to slip, but he held her steady.

"Oh my gosh, I didn't realize how slippery it would be." Zoey looked down at her white figure skates as they took their first few timid steps into the rink. She laughed nervously at herself. "That probably sounds dumb. It's ice. Of course it's slippery."

Jett chuckled. "Well, the zamboni smoothes it over to get rid of any tracks that are left, so yes, this is probably the smoothest, flattest surface you'll ever walk on."

"How in the world do people dance and do jumps on this?"

"Try strides instead of those small steps," Jett offered, watching her feet try to get used to the ice. "Like this." He did a few long strides of his own, moving backwards and still holding onto her hands so that he could pull her along with him. "Only you go forward. Here, let's do this." He pulled her toward himself and turned so they were facing the same way, standing side by side. He wrapped an arm around her waist and pulled her arm around his waist.

Zoey's free hand immediately gravitated to where his hand rested on her side. She placed her hand over his, but never took her eyes off her feet.

"Ready? We'll go right...left...right...left." Their strides were in unison as they made progress down the oval-shaped arena. "Look at you! You're a natural."

"I am!" She squealed excitedly. Briefly looking up at him and smiling, she threw herself off balance. "Oh no!" She slipped, but Jett caught her and held her pressed to his body to keep her from falling.

"Told you I wouldn't let you fall."

"I think you planned this well." Zoey ticked up an eyebrow at him. "You knew you'd have to hold onto me the whole time, you get to feel all masculine trying to teach me something athletic, and play the hero by keeping me from busting my buns on the ice."

Jett shrugged. "I'd hate for you to bust your buns. They're kinda cute."

Zoey straightened herself out again and they assumed the position that seemed to be working for them before.

"Do you not want me to hold onto you so much?" Jett questioned, wondering if he should have his arm this tightly wrapped around her on their first date.

"I wasn't complaining," she assured him. "I was giving you a compliment. You really thought this through and I think it's a win for both of us."

Jett's chest filled with warmth as he watched her cheeks redden. He didn't think she was used to saying things that were so forward but it was like she couldn't hold it back. *Good.* He didn't want her to hold back. If he could, he'd like to know every thought going through her head right now.

They continued to make their way around the arena, and Zoey cheered for herself as she made her first full lap without any slips or near-falls.

"Okay, let's try something else." Jett had a firm grip on her right hip and slid his left hand to her left hip, holding her in front of him. "I'm still here so you won't fall, but you have more control, okay?"

"And this is when I bring you down with me."

"Not a chance. You got this."

The whole way around the arena, he had to refrain from pulling her into him. God, he just wanted to wrap her in his arms.

"This feels like that couple's ice dancing," Zoey remarked, and he could tell she was getting more comfortable on the ice, but didn't want to have a reason to let go of her just yet.

"Yeah? Want me to lift you up and skate around with you over my head?"

She gasped. "No way! Can you do that?"

"Sure, just don't flail your feet. I really don't need a blade to the face. A trip to the emergency room might delay those tacos." Jett tightened his grip on her waist, "Ready?"

"Wait, seriously?" Her voice was only tinged with mild panic before Jett lifted her. He could feel the muscles in her petite body flex as she straightened her legs slightly to keep her skates away from his face. After skating around about a third of the oval with her over his head, he brought her down, turning her to face him.

"Impressive." He grinned down at her. "You really are a natural."

"Me? I didn't even do anything!" She smiled back. He loved the sound of adrenaline in her voice and the fact that he'd been the one to give her that rush.

"Sure you did." He brushed a loose wave of her hair back and his gaze focused on her lips for a brief moment before flicking back up to her eyes.

Apprehension and more adrenaline reflected back to him in her hazel eyes. Her tongue swiped her bottom lip. Her hands were resting, just barely grasping his biceps, and his arm was wrapped around her, still holding her steady on the ice. He felt her body go pliant against his with a small sigh and his heart rate kicked up a notch. Or five.

He swallowed and moved his hand to the back of her head and neck, gently tilting her face up toward his. She let him, and he could see her quick, anticipatory intake of breath before leaning into him. He could've taken a picture of this moment. The look on her face that said she was giving into him, letting him have her, that she trusted him. Her full lips were wet and looked so damn kissable. He dipped his head and slanted his lips over hers.

He felt Zoey's chest rise as she inhaled, as if she were breathing him in, and he held her more firmly still against himself. Her lips were soft as they kissed him back and he savored the sweet taste of her mouth on his. They could spend the rest of the evening wrapped up like this and it would be enough.

When he pulled away slowly, Zoey's eyes were still closed and he couldn't help smiling to himself that she looked breathless. Completely gorgeous, and breathless.

Her eyes fluttered open and she smiled up at him, all coy and adorable. So damn cute.

"Do you want to go around a few more times?" Jett asked, unable to wipe his own grin off his face. What he really wanted to do now that he'd kissed her was just take her back to his place and keep kissing her. It didn't have to go farther than that tonight, he just really wanted to feel her mouth pressed against his as much as he could.

"Yeah," she breathed, "then tacos."

"Then tacos," Jett agreed. He took her hand in his and continued around the arena, feeling like he could fly.

Zoey watched Jett dig into the complimentary chips and salsa while she sipped on her mango agave margarita. Her head still felt like it was in the clouds after that first kiss on the ice. He'd kissed her again when they got back into his truck, and there was a part of her that wanted to just stay in there, making out like teenagers. If her traitorous stomach hadn't growled and given her away, they might have. But in true Jett form, he'd heard the sounds of her hunger and insisted they get food ASAP.

Between the bouquet of roses, the way he always held doors open for her, and walked her everywhere with her arm through his, she was slowly becoming obsessed with this man. That wasn't even taking into account how he'd taken care of her the other night when she was sick. She was beginning to think she really needed to meet his parents and find out their secret to raising such a sweet, tender, gentle, yet strong and sexy man.

Men aren't just born that way, right?

"How did you end up being the youngest sports publicist around?" Jett asked after a long pull from his beer bottle. "Is it something you've always wanted to do?"

"No, I sort of just fell into it, actually." Zoey twirled her straw around in her margarita. "I mean, I went into public relations and kind of wanted to be a publicist, but not specifically for athletes."

"No?" Jett smirked. "You didn't just want to be surrounded by muscular, sweaty men all the time? All-access into the locker rooms and all that good stuff?"

Zoey laughed. "No, I'm not much of a sports person. I wanted to do PR for musicians, but I had connections through my college boyfriend. After my internship I got offered the position with Quinn and I kind of couldn't turn it down."

"Your college boyfriend? Was he an athlete?"

"Yeah, and when he was getting scouted all the attention just went to his head. We broke up my junior year, and after that it was like he had a new girl with him every time I saw him on campus. I wasn't jealous- I was annoyed. I thought it was stupid how quickly he'd gone from being in a committed relationship to just sleeping around all the time."

"That explains your attitude toward Quinn," Jett said as he scratched at his beer bottle label. "Did he get drafted then? The ex?"

"Yeah, he plays for Minnesota now." Zoey was completely indifferent toward her ex. Once she'd seen the type of person he'd turned into seemingly overnight, she knew he wasn't the right guy for her.

And yes, it had certainly affected her relationship with Quinn when she'd been hired as his publicist. She could still remember his cocky smirk when they met, as though sizing her up, trying to figure out what it was going to take to get her to sleep with him. She'd drawn that line *real* quickly, and made sure he knew that was not going to happen. She wasn't there to be his friend, or to fool around, she was there to do her job. She didn't love that her job was to try and make him look good- she thought everyone had the right to see him as he was- but she took her job seriously, and knew that if she could handle Quinn Casey, she could get a job as a publicist anywhere.

It hadn't taken long for her to notice an interesting pattern with Quinn, though. He was all charm and one-dimpled smirks in front of people and cameras, but the moment he was in the comfort of his own home, he was quiet. She'd started to wonder early on if three-quarters of his life was just putting on a show, and the real version of him just lived in his own head. There were times she'd try pressing for details; What was his home like? Why didn't his family ever come to games? Where did his fear or refusal of commitment stem from?

Naturally, he'd dodged all of these questions. It was funny in a way; he could be a complete chatterbox and go on and on about himself and how much of a superstar he was on the field, or he could be silent as stone.

"Minnesota?" Jett repeated, snapping her out of her own head. "He plays for the NFL?"

"Mhm." Zoey slurped her margarita again. She saw the look of surprise on Jett's face and remembered instantly what Rae had said about him feeling overshadowed. *Crap. Not my intent.* She shrugged dismissively. "He was a jerk and it didn't work out." When Jett only made a small "huh" sound, she added, "He never would've made me soup or remembered to bring scrunchies."

Finally, he smiled again, and his face went slightly pink at the compliment. "What a loser," he said, and there was an adorable twinkle in his green eyes.

Zoey's phone chirped from inside her purse telling her she had a Twitter notification. "Sorry, I should put that on silent." In the time it took for her to reach into her bag and pull her phone out, she'd received three more notifications. "Twitter is blowing up for some reason."

"You must be popular. Aren't I lucky that I get to take up your highly valuable time?" Jett scooped another chip into the salsa bowl.

"It's actually Quinn's account," Zoey explained, and laughed at Jett's responding expression. "I know it's ridiculous, he can't even manage his own Twitter page without some kind of fallout. Although he's getting better. I might be able to hand this task over to him soon."

"You're making me feel very confident about leaving my bar in his hands on a Saturday night."

"What do you mean?" She flipped her phone on silent and put it back in her purse.

"I almost had to call and cancel our date. I was already leaving Chris without a manager up front, and then a bartender called off. Quinn offered to do it so I didn't have to stay and work."

"If this was last year, he'd already be on the bar dancing with his shirt off," Zoey said. "That was really sweet of him though."

"We went over the ground rules. Although, I think I may have just given him ideas. Case has never been one to follow the rules." He took another swig of beer. "I told myself I'd deal with it tomorrow. Whatever happens...I mean, it can't be *that* bad."

Zoey hesitated as a stream of incidents she'd had to explain away over the past two years flew through her mind: Quinn Casey half-naked, scaling the side of a hotel building. Quinn Casey fighting a college kid in a bar because he knocked Quinn's hat off his head. Quinn

Casey caught having sex on a surveillance camera in the dugout after a game.

She cleared her throat and tried to look reassuring. "Yeah, I'm sure it'll be fine."

Jett's eyebrow twitched up skeptically and he grinned. "Your voice went all high like you were lying."

Busted. "Well, on the bright side, whatever happens, you know someone who's well versed in cleaning up your friend's messes."

The waitress came with two large, steaming plates of food. "Chicken fajitas…" She set the sizzling skillet in front of Zoey. "And the build-your-own taco plate." She set the large platter-like dish in front of Jett with a covered tortilla warmer and he pumped his fist enthusiastically.

"I can't believe you actually just got tacos," Zoey giggled. "It's so basic."

"Basic white girl over here." He snapped his fingers. "I like tacos, and Christmas movies, and peppermint mochas from Starbucks."

"Can I get you two anything else?" The waitress, Celeste, asked as she also laughed at Jett's raw honesty.

"No, thank you," Zoey said, grinning and not taking her eyes off the adorably funny and handsome man across from her.

Celeste walked away and they both began putting their dinners together.

Jett scooped a large helping of guacamole on top of his first taco, and its ingredients were spilling out both ends. "The messier the better. That's how you know it's not missing anything."

"Is that so?" Zoey spooned grilled onions, peppers, and mushrooms into a tortilla.

Jett groaned around his first massive bite, and a mixture of chicken, cheese, tomatoes, and sour cream fell onto his plate. "Mm..oh God...oh God, it's so good." He put a hand to his chest as he finished chewing. "Best taco I've ever had in my life."

"Why do I get the feeling you say that every time you eat tacos?"

He pointed a finger at her. "You got me there. I do. I do say that every time." He looked at her fajita which, in comparison to his fully-loaded creation, looked a little sad. "You need to fill that up more. Just stuff it full. And when you think nothing else can fit, just shove some more meat in there anyway."

Zoey nearly spit, her laugh came out so suddenly. "Just shove some more meat in there? Really?"

"Zoey!" Jett gasped, an expression of mock innocence on his face. "Get your head out of the gutter, woman. You're trying to take an innocent and sacred activity like eating tacos...and turn it into something of one of your sex-crazed fantasies. I had no idea you were like this."

She couldn't stop laughing.

"I don't understand what anyone could even think is sexual about eating a taco. Just...going to town on these tacos." He took another large bite and even more spilled out. "Look at that, it's all juicy, and there's sour cream just dripping out. How is that sexual? Do explain- I beg of you."

Her whole body shook as her face rested in her hands, elbows on the table, laughing. Her sides hurt and her face was starting to get sore, but she was loving it. She hadn't had this much fun with a man, or maybe anyone, in ages. She couldn't believe she'd nearly passed up the opportunity to get to know him better.

"You are way too cute." Zoey smiled at him before taking a bite of fajita. She looked down at her plate and nodded, "You're right, it needs to be fuller."

"See? I'm telling you, if anyone knows proper taco-stuffing technique, it's me."

"You're the guy, huh? You know how to fill 'em up." Zoey tried, and failed, to conceal her mischievous grin.

"All the way. Only way I know how." His green eyes glinted as his smile pulled up just a little farther.

Whether it was the effects of the margarita or just Jett's charm and his goofy, easy way of making her feel comfortable, she nodded her head from side to side. "Hm...guess we'll have to see about that."

Jett froze, halting his chewing as he stared across the table at her. After a few silent beats, he turned abruptly in his seat and shot a hand up in the air. "Check, please!"

She laughed as he turned back to her. Okay, so she didn't really think Jett would try to sleep with her on their first date -or was this their second?- and she wasn't the type to give it away that quickly anyway. But she was quickly realizing she *definitely* wanted to see this man naked.

About an hour later, Jett was dropping her off at her hotel room. He pulled her close and bent low for another breathtaking kiss. This time she felt his tongue swipe at her lips and she opened her mouth to let him inside. She pressed her body against his, grasping at his strong arms, bending back as he bowed over her. It was a little steamier than the average end-of-first-date kiss and it was making her dizzy and warm, with needy sensations concentrating themselves between her thighs.

His phone vibrated in his front pocket where she was pressing her-self- *that didn't help.* She managed to hold back her groan of pleasure, and the small whimper of need that almost escaped when he pulled away.

"I really, *really* want to come in, but I feel like we should take it slow," Jett breathed, his forehead pressed to hers.

"We should," she agreed. She didn't *want* to take it slow. Not now, anyway. But she didn't want the regret of pushing things too fast, either. She was exponentially grateful that he'd spoken the words out loud, because she'd been dangerously close to inviting him inside.

"I had a great time tonight, Zo." He lightly pressed his lips to hers and she smiled into his kiss. "I hope my sexy taco talk didn't scare you off."

Her laugh hummed into his lips. "Not at all. I had a lot of fun. I like spending time with you, Jett Miller."

"Good, because I've got a whole list of dates planned and it's going to take up some of your time." He brushed his fingertips lightly over her cheek and pulled her into another soft, slow kiss. "Goodnight, Zoey."

"Goodnight, Jett."

Back inside her hotel room, she sighed as she leaned against the door. Her eyes found the bouquet of red and white roses on the counter and she smiled to herself.

Perfect. This man was absolutely perfect.

CHAPTER 9

Jett woke up to the glaring sunlight bursting its way through the small gap in the curtain. He stretched with a groan and reached down to adjust his morning wood- *oh shit, can't be leaving that alone today.* Rolling out of bed, he headed straight for the shower, stretching and yawning along the way.

With the shower turned to hot, he stripped down and stepped into the fully-tiled steaming shower, stiffy in hand.

"Oh God, this isn't gonna take long," Jett murmured to himself. He closed his eyes under the hot spray and began pumping his fist slowly over his length. Immediately, he was transported to the previous night. Feeling Zoey pressed up against his body, her soft, full lips under his, the brief taste of her on his tongue before he left her at her door. *Damn,* he'd wanted to follow her inside so badly. But that wasn't the point of taking her out. He liked her. He *really* liked her, and he didn't want to screw it up by pushing her too far too fast.

But that didn't mean he couldn't think about it. He felt a little guilty fantasizing about her like this, but it had to be better than trying to think about someone else while he got off, right?

Jett bit back a groan, bracing his other hand on the shower wall as his release came out in a rush. Chest heaving, he cleaned up and re-focused on getting ready for his day.

Once out of the shower, he toweled himself off and slipped into some fresh clothes. He sat on the edge of his bed and grabbed his phone off the charger on his nightstand.

Holy hell.

199+ Twitter notifications?

99+ Facebook notifications?

He'd left his phone on silent all night and had no idea the social media accounts for his bar had been blowing up. The accounts stayed relatively busy, mostly people checking in from out of town, tagging and saying they'd visited the establishment. But having over 199 notifications was unheard of. What would've made-

Quinn. Right.

It made sense that people would've been excited to see the pro ball player there, especially behind the bar and actually working. Jett imagined all the videos and photos customers would have taken and tagged the bar in.

He flipped his phone's ringer back on and decided to check out some of the notifications. Chris had been right- Bartender Quinn was definitely good for business.

The oldest notifications were what Jett had expected: Photos of Quinn behind the bar, some candid, some posing with customers holding up a glass of beer. There were a few videos of him pouring drinks, tossing and flipping bottles, doing tricks, and putting on a show. Typical.

Jett noticed the tip jar in the background of a picture was stuffed full.

Shit, maybe he'd have to make his friend work for him more often.

Or…Maybe not.

Jett got to the pictures that were posted later in the evening. Around midnight the shirt had come off. Of course it had. His LA cap was flipped backwards as he spun his shirt over his head. There were a *ton* of photos of Quinn shirtless behind the bar. He'd tossed his shirt into the growing crowd, and in one photo an excited college-age girl was holding it up proudly.

"Okay…" Jett sighed. "Please tell me that's as bad as it gets…"

Of course it wasn't. The videos and photos of Quinn going full *Magic Mike* on the top of the bar were next. He'd kept his pants on, but he was still humping the bar.

Jett closed his eyes. *I need to stop looking.*

His phone dinged with a text.

Zoey: I figured out why my Twitter account was going crazy. Looks like the Quinn Casey everyone knows and loves is still in there.

He replied, *Yeah, I'm catching up right now. Please tell me it doesn't get worse than him defiling my bar.*

After watching the dots appear and disappear on the screen a few times Jett braced himself.

Zoey: Quinn may not be your biggest problem…

There was a link attached and Jett furrowed his brow curiously. The headline read *Quinn's Girl Doesn't Play.*

Jett watched in shock as the video played: Quinn on his knees on the bar, as if he'd just slid down it, an excited and notably drunk young woman stretched out and ran her hands down Quinn's chest and abs- and then Rae appeared.

"What the fuck, Rae?" Jett whispered to himself as he watched Rae grab the girl by her arm and swung her around to face her...and punched her in the face. Rae...punched a random chick in the face. At Jett's bar.

"Oh my God," Jett groaned into his hands. He sent Zoey another text: *I bet you thought she'd make your job easier. You must not know her that well yet.*

Once that was sent, he brought Quinn's text conversation up: *You and Rae. Get your asses to my apartment. Now.*

Jett paced back and forth in his living room where Zoey sat in the recliner, and Quinn and Rae sat on the couch. Rae wore one of Quinn's baseball hats pulled low over her eyes, but he could tell she was trying not to laugh. She sat cross-legged with her arms folded over her chest and her body shook with repressed laughter. Quinn did a much better job of hiding his amusement, though there was a slight twitch to the corner of his mouth where he kept fighting a grin. His hair was sticking up in all directions and he tried to smooth it over before attempting to make eye contact with Jett.

"I literally gave you three rules." Jett kept his voice calm even though he wanted to shout. "And you broke *all* of them."

"Technically I only broke two," Quinn said, patting his hair down again. "Rae got in a fight, not me."

"But she wouldn't have gotten in a fight if you'd listened to the first two rules and kept your damn clothes on!" Jett raised his voice then forced himself to take another deep breath. "How do you think this makes my bar look? I told you it's not that kind of place- I don't want people thinking they can come in and start stripping and dancing on the bar."

"I get that," Quinn said, holding his hands up, "but did you see how much we made in tips?"

"I know, Case, I know. You did this in college and had a tip jar and a phone number jar, but that's not how we do shit here!"

"Phone number jar?" Rae snapped her head around to glare at Quinn. "What phone number jar?"

Quinn went wide-eyed before laughing nervously. "Uh…Nothing, baby. It's…nothing…college. Different times."

"Where the hell was Chris when all this was happening anyway?" Jett asked, now pulling his phone out to send Chris a message about this meeting they were currently having.

"I told him I'd match whatever tips I made and give it to you guys to split- well, and the other bartenders that worked last night. He didn't really care once I took the first full tip jar back and grabbed a second."

Jett paused and eyed his friend who was now smirking triumphantly. He narrowed his eyes at Quinn. "How much did you make?"

"Your cut's locked in the office safe. Maybe you should go find out."

Part of him wanted to smack the smug look off Quinn's face, but he was a little caught off guard by the gesture to be too mad. He'd never really talked about money with Quinn, or Rae for that matter, but he didn't think it was a secret that he and Chris didn't have near as much as the other half of their core friend group.

"So...Rae's the only one getting in any real trouble?" Zoey questioned. "Did the girl press charges?"

"She might," Rae said indifferently. "But she needed to learn a lesson."

"A lesson?" Jett repeated flatly.

"Hands. Off." Rae snapped her fingers dramatically with a wave. "Do these women think that because he's a guy they can grope him? It's still sexual assault. That bitch was going for his zipper, I swear."

"And we all know what would've happened if the situation had been reversed," said Quinn. "My ass would be sitting in a jail cell right now."

"But Rae never would've done a strip tease on my bartop..." Jett muttered. He brushed a hand through his hair, refraining from pulling it out as he sat by Zoey on the arm of the recliner.

Zoey sighed and tapped away on her phone. "Well, this should be fairly easy to clean up, especially if we point out that a woman felt him up without his consent. If she tries pressing charges, we'll argue that. No one would try suing either of you with the amount of money you've got in the bank if we have even the slightest defense." Looking up briefly, she added, "Plus, some of your fans were worried that Rae wasn't letting you have fun anymore. So this might actually work in your favor."

Jett rolled his eyes and let out an incredulous breath of laughter. Of course. Only Raelyn DeRose and Quinn Casey could fall into a pile of shit and come out sparkling clean and smelling fresh.

He turned to Zoey and asked, "Does that mean you're not going to be busy today? We could grab lunch before I have to get to work. I'm not going in until around four."

"Hey! That's right! How was your date?" Rae exclaimed brightly. "Did you two...?" She raised her eyebrows three times, suggestively.

"Oh shit, Flower got deflowered, didn't he?" Quinn sat up straight and rubbed his hands together eagerly.

Wow, they could really not make this any less awkward.

"That's not really any of your business," Jett said, standing up. He held his hand out to Zoey and she took it. "We don't have to have tacos again for lunch, but I won't say no if that's what you want."

"Are there any good brunch places around here?" Zoey stood up and put her coat back on.

"I know a few." Jett handed her the pair of gloves she'd set on his coffee table before using yet another voice that he promised never to use in front of a woman he had plans of seducing. "Oooh, girl we 'bout to get our 'mosa on."

To his delight, she shot it right back with a full Z-snap, "Yaaasss, let's do this."

Grabbing his coat, keys, and pocketing his phone, he held the door open for Quinn and Rae to head out in front of them. He wrapped his arm around Zoey's waist, stopping her before they walked out the door and tugged her in close for a kiss. Ahead of them on the stairs, Quinn and Rae ooh'd childishly, but Jett ignored them and pressed a kiss to Zoey's soft lips again.

It was the Tuesday after their first (official) date and Jett was prepping for date number two. Or two-point-five as he'd compromised calling it, since he really believed the night he took care of her should count for something. The assistant manager was working for him that night, but he was still in the bar for the weekday lunch shift.

So far it had been fairly calm, with mostly businessmen and women on their lunch breaks looking for a quick meal. Jett was posted behind the bar, and Quinn was visiting, practicing the French phrases Rae left for him while he nursed his usual Two-Hearted Ale and chowed down on a turkey club.

"*Je m'appelle Quinn,*" Quinn pointed to himself.

"*Enchanté, Quinn. Je m'appelle Jett.*"

Quinn snapped his head up, brows furrowed. "What?"

"I said 'Nice to meet you, Quinn. My name is Jett'." Jett translated slowly as he buffed a wine glass.

"Fuck, talk slower, man." Quinn looked back at the piece of paper and took a sip of beer.

"They're not going to talk any slower in France."

Clearing his throat, Quinn spoke clearly, *"C'est...ma femme. Elle...est...parfaite?"*

Jett tossed his head back in a laugh. "Seriously, she put that on there?"

"Did I say it right?"

"Don't say it like a question. I'm pretty sure she wants you to say that with confidence," Jett offered, still grinning.

"What is it? Not all of these have translations." Quinn flipped the piece of paper around to look at the back.

"You just said 'This is my wife. She is perfect'."

Quinn hummed and shrugged his shoulders, "Not wrong. I mean...she's not my *wife* yet technically. But- wait, what's the French word for fiancé?"

Jett stared at his obnoxiously handsome friend, completely dumbfounded. He paused for a few beats, waiting to see if it would sink in. It did not. "Quinn...fiancé *is* French."

He saw the lightbulb flicker on as Quinn chuckled. "Oh, that's right!"

Oh, what Jett wouldn't give to go through life as blissfully content as that.

Quinn got back to his list as the front door to the bar swung open, catching Jett's attention. He tilted his head curiously at the customer- the *child-* who had just waltzed in. Jett wasn't particularly good at guessing ages of children- or teenagers, or adults, for that matter- but he'd guess the kid who'd just walked in by himself was somewhere between 12 and 14. He was black with light skin, and short, dark brown curls.

The kid sat on the bar stool right next to Quinn and looked directly at Jett.

"Hey, you Jett? Or Chris?"

Jett felt his brow furrow further. "Jett. And who are you? Are your parents coming in?"

"My brother is," the boy replied. "He had to run back to work real quick, but told me to come in here and ask for you guys."

"Why?" Jett crossed his arms, and noted Quinn curiously watching the exchange.

"Because he told me to wait outside and I said- hey, I ain't tryin' to be the next kid on *Taken.* I know in the movies they just take pretty girls, but I know in the real world those creeps take boys, too." The boy was talking and explaining, but Jett only felt this begged more questions.

"Who's your brother?"

"Will. He said you know him." The boy grabbed a menu and opened it up. He looked over at Quinn's sandwich. "That good?"

"Will? Will who?"

"Yeah, it's really good. It's got bacon on it, so," Quinn shrugged. Both he and the boy were ignoring Jett's question.

"I'll get that," the boy said, pointing to Quinn's plate, "and a beer."

Quinn laughed and Jett narrowed his eyes. "I'm gonna have to see some ID."

The boy looked back at him blankly. "I'm thirteen."

"Then I can get you a root beer or a ginger beer, but that's it."

The boy rolled his eyes. "Fine, I'll have a root beer." Leaning back, he muttered, "Will said you were cool…"

Jett filled a pint glass with a scoop of ice and root beer from the soda gun and set it in front of the kid. "What's your name?"

"Kolbe," the boy replied as he shed his coat and hung it on the back of his chair.

"And your older brother's name is Will? And he knows me and says that I know him, too?" Jett still had no idea what the kid was talking about. Luckily, Chris walked up from the kitchen then, so he explained everything he'd learned so far in hopes that he'd know who the kid belonged to.

"Where does your brother work?" Chris asked, eyeing the kid curiously.

"Just like a couple blocks from here, downtown. You guys know him," Kolbe insisted. "He used to date Raelyn DeRose. I know y'all know her, and if you don't, you should because she is *fine.*"

Both Chris and Jett watched for Quinn's reaction. The already-tall baseball player sat up straighter and taller, set his sandwich down and turned to face Kolbe. "Your brother dated her? When?"

"Would *she* recognize you?" Jett was about to call her if it meant solving this mystery.

"Hell yeah, she'd recognize me!" Kolbe exclaimed. He leaned toward Quinn and said in a lowered voice, "Can I tell you something? One time, Raelyn came with me and my brother to the beach...I snagged a pic of that booty." He grinned mischievously and nodded, clearly impressed with himself.

Chris and Jett both did their best to hold in their laughter while Quinn chewed the inside of his cheek. Jett knew exactly how Quinn would handle the situation if he'd been talking to an adult, but he was curious to see how he'd handle a thirteen-year-old making comments about his lifelong love.

After struggling to come up with an appropriate response, Quinn finally tilted his head to the side. He said, "It's a nice booty. I've got a few pics of it myself."

Kolbe's eyes widened. "Can I see 'em?"

"*No!*" Quinn snatched his phone off the bar top where it had been resting. "Those are mine. And I acquired them *consensually,* so maybe you should learn about that."

The kid peered at Quinn curiously. "You sleepin' with her or somethin?"

"We're engaged."

"Naw! For real?" Kolbe exclaimed. He leaned back and appeared to be sizing Quinn up with an incredulous grin. *"You?"*

"Yes, me," Quinn replied, his voice hard as stone.

Kolbe snorted. "Okay, well, my brother was engaged to her, too, so don't get too excited."

Quinn's attention snapped to Chris and Jett behind the bar. "How many ex-fiancés does she have?" he hissed.

"Just the one…that I know of…" Jett said, now confused. He furrowed his brow as he looked at the kid who was now sipping his root beer. Chris merely offered a shrug and a similarly perplexed expression. Jett slipped his phone out of his pocket to text Rae when the front door opened and a familiar deep voice boomed through the bar.

"Hey, All-Star! Long time no see!"

Emerson Yates -tall, blonde-haired, blue-eyed *Emerson Yates*- strode into the bar like he owned the place.

Jett was sure that Quinn and Chris were both doing the same back-and-forth looks between Kolbe and Emerson that he was doing.

"You said your brother's name was Will," Jett said to the kid, watching as Emerson sat down next to him.

"Dude, I told you to tell them my real name or you'd confuse the fuck out of them." Emerson pushed off his winter coat and loosened his necktie. Suited up, as usual.

"Is 'Will' an alias you use when you prey on women?" Quinn glared intently over Kolbe's head at the lawyer.

"My middle name's William. It's just what he calls me."

Kolbe elbowed his brother and gestured toward Quinn. "Hey, he's got booty pics of Raelyn on his phone, too."

Emerson narrowed his eyes at Quinn in disgust. "What the fuck are you doing showing my thirteen-year-old brother naked pictures?"

"I didn't show- He said- and then-" Quinn stammered before resting his palms on the bar. "I didn't show him anything and I'm done talking to you."

Emerson nodded to Jett. "The usual."

Jett froze for a few seconds, sliding his gaze over to Quinn and checking his reaction, but there was none. His friend merely sipped his drink and studied his French notes. Maybe Quinn would just think Emerson came into the bar a lot. Just because Jett knew his drink and food order didn't mean they were friends. They had lots of regular bar customers. And Emerson was *not* his friend anyway. So there was nothing to hide. As long as the video game nights didn't come up.

Jett snapped the cap off a bottle of Heineken and placed it on a bar coaster in front of him. "So...you have a little brother?"

He was expecting to hear that the kid was part of an elaborate plan to get women. Some men used dogs, he'd even heard of guys using their friends' babies. A teenage brother was a new move, but he had to admit he was curious to hear the details.

"Half brother...obviously."

"Oh..." Jett looked back and forth between them again. Okay, he supposed he could see a resemblance. Similar face shape, same mouth, and he even noticed the kid's eyes were blue, though a slightly lighter shade than Emerson's. He tried to remember if Rae had ever mentioned Emerson having a half-brother, but couldn't seem to recall.

"So, how are things going with Zoey?" Emerson asked, leaning on his forearms.

Oh shit.

Quinn's head perked up immediately. "How does he know about Zoey?"

"Um..." Jett froze, wide-eyed, trying not to make eye contact with anyone.

"Because I was here when she called him." Emerson didn't miss a beat. "I was picking up a take-out order and happened to catch the end of the call. Then I got nosey."

Jett stared as the lie sunk in. *Damn, he came up with that quick. And was really chill about it...*

"Yeah, he told me I sounded like an idiot so I must be talking to a girl, so...I explained the situation." *Not technically a lie...just a little misleading, right?*

Quinn seemed satisfied with the explanation. "Oh, yeah, it's always pretty obvious when he's talking to a girl. He gets all...squeaky. Or uses voices and weird accents."

"Ello, puppet! Can I get you a spot a' brandy?" Emerson imitated with a thick British accent.

"Hey pretty lady, you like to go dancing?" Quinn sounded like Gru from *Despicable Me*.

Chris chimed in, "Oooh, girl those shooooes. You look like you ready to rosé all day!"

Jett stood back, glaring at the three men as they carried on.

"Yes, girl, you work that messy bun! Mhmmm!" Quinn Z-snapped.

Emerson went full *Borat*, "You look very nice! How much?"

"You guys are assholes," Jett stated.

"Oh, come on! You know we love you, you weirdo!" Chris put his arm around him and patted his shoulder.

"And Zoey seems to be into it, too," Quinn added.

"Oh yeah?" Emerson raised his eyebrows. "She likes your weird ass? I bet she's kinky."

"It's always the quiet ones," Quinn said over his beer glass.

"Not *always*." Emerson slid his mischievous, antagonizing smirk in Quinn's direction. "Rae's not quiet."

Quinn threw his hands up. "There it is. I thought maybe- *maybe*- we'd get through one exchange without you going there, but I was wrong!"

"Raelyn was kinky?" Kolbe sat up straight and looked to his fair-skinned brother. "How? What kinda stuff did she like? She like being tied up? Handcuffed? She like it in the ass?"

"I can definitely see the resemblance now," Quinn grumbled.

Emerson looked down at Kolbe with mild amusement. "Where do you learn this shit?"

"I have the internet," he explained simply.

"Well..." Quinn crumpled his napkin and tossed it onto his plate. "Kinky or not...where are you taking Zoey tonight?"

"We're going to a hockey game," Jett replied. "I got us some good tickets, and she seemed to like ice skating the other night."

"You guys gonna do it?" Quinn made a subtle hip-thrusting gesture, made less subtle by his double-arm pump.

"I don't know." Jett's voice came out higher than he'd meant. "I don't know. We're just taking things slow."

"Laaaame." Emerson gave a dramatic thumbs-down. "Close the deal. Get in there- and then get *in* there."

"I don't...I don't know what that means. Get in there *twice?*"

"Hopefully it takes more than two pumps, man, but I guess it has been a while for you." Emerson smirked.

Quinn snorted a laugh, then abruptly played it off as a cough and stared down at his notes again.

Kolbe hopped off his stool and looked around before asking, "Where's the bathroom?"

Jett pointed in the general direction and once Kolbe was out of ear-shot, he turned a curious eye on Emerson. "Half-brother? I don't think Rae ever mentioned you having a brother."

He sighed and leaned back. "Yeah, I didn't know for a while. It was...about six months maybe after me and Rae started dating? I found out about him and it was complicated. He lives down state, but some-times his mom lets him come stay with me. One of my dad's many affairs...illegitimate love-child."

"No shit?" Jett looked in the direction Kolbe had headed.

"Mhmm...The great Senator Yates actually blackmailed me and practically threatened Rae if either of us said anything about him," Emerson said. His jaw twitched and he looked pretty pissed off at the memory, not that Jett could blame him. What kind of father did that?

"And not that it's going to come up, but...Kolbe doesn't know why me and Rae broke up. He doesn't need to." Emerson took in a deep breath and his brow furrowed as he looked at his green beer bottle. "My dad didn't...still doesn't want anything to do with him. He hates that I insist on having a relationship with the kid, but...ya know, he's got a single mom who works her ass off for him, and my dad pays her hush-money, but it all goes into savings for his future. I'm trying to be a good influence and he doesn't need to know I'm...not really any better than my dad, okay?"

"Your secret's safe with me." Jett said. He wasn't sure what to make of this version of Emerson. Sure, when he and Rae had been dating they'd gotten along, but ever since the engagement was called off he seemed dead-set on being an arrogant, self-centered, boastful ass hat. This sincere, humbled, big-brother-role-model thing was definitely new.

"Yeah, of course," Chris agreed.

Jett, Chris, and Emerson glanced down the bar at Quinn now, who appeared to be studying his half-empty beer glass pretty intently. He remained silent, but nodded before taking another large gulp of his drink.

There was a brief pause before Quinn changed the subject, "Need another bartender tonight? I can make you another thousand bucks."

When Jett had finally gotten into the safe to see what his cut of Quinn's tips were, he was feeling pretty damn good about letting his friend take over as much as he wanted while he was home. After splitting four ways, they'd all made just over nine-hundred dollars. That was fucking unheard of. Granted, Quinn had matched the tips he'd made with his own money, but still, it was insane. Jett was nine-hundred bucks richer and all he'd done was take an amazing girl out on a date.

"Just keep Rae out of the bar if you're gonna dance on it again," Jett advised. "I could use another couple hundred. It's only a Tuesday night though, so I doubt it'll be anything like the other night."

"Oh shit, I saw that!" Emerson exclaimed with an amused laugh and slapped his hand down on the bar. "That was a solid punch."

Kolbe eventually made his way back from the restroom and resumed his spot between Quinn and Emerson. The guys managed to keep a good conversation going, and Jett was pleased that everyone seemed to be getting along- or that Emerson and Quinn had at least silently agreed to be civil- but he couldn't help the itch in the back of his mind that he'd lied to his friend. It was a small white lie, but that wasn't Jett's style. Emerson had done it so naturally -which really shouldn't surprise anyone, let's be real- and Jett had simply gone along with it.

Shoving down the gnawing feeling that things would only get worse if he didn't tell Quinn the truth, that he really had been hanging out with Emerson outside of work, he reminded himself that Quinn was leaving in a week. He'd forget all about it while he and Rae were shacked up and going at it 24/7 in front of their million dollar view of the Eiffel Tower, right?

Right.

CHAPTER 10

Zoey and Jett stood up to cheer as their team made a goal. She was really getting into the game, and was finding it increasingly difficult to not throw herself at Jett when she imagined him out there on the ice playing. She would love to see him body-checking another player with his strong chest before throwing his gloves on the ice and using his bare fists to show that guy who's boss.

Shows of extreme masculinity weren't usually her thing, but there was something about Jett who was the perfect combination of sweet sensitivity and raw masculinity...*ooh baby*. She wouldn't mind seeing him get sent to the penalty box.

What is wrong with me?

She was still adjusting to the way he made her feel. Just his proximity, his scent, his warm smile, those curls, and those bright green eyes...*argghhh*. She'd been surrounded by California boys her whole life and had no idea there was this entirely different breed of men she had yet to come in contact with.

"Did you ever get in a fight on the ice?" Zoey asked, leaning into him and he put his arm around her.

"Of course. I don't think you're a real hockey player unless you've thrown a punch or two."

She smiled and let the image of him throwing down fuel her fantasy a little.

"Did you ever play against your brother or get in fights with him?" She remembered Rae saying that his older brother had also played hockey.

She felt the low rumble of a laugh through his chest. "We played against each other all the time. Not in real games, but we'd play in the road in front of the house and we'd just straight up brawl sometimes. We get along great, but he'd make a shitty call- he was the big brother so he thought he could be the ref, too- and I'd call him out on it and we'd throw down."

Zoey laughed as she imagined the two brothers rolling around in the street taking shots at one another. "What did your parents do?"

"Mom would ground us, or take our equipment away so we couldn't play anymore." He grabbed his soda- or *pop*, as they called it up here- out of the cup holder and took a sip. "I remember one time when Chris, Quinn, Rae, and Tyler came over, and Gavin was playing, too. They were so used to me being the chill friend of the group- Quinn was the fighter, obviously. But Gavin made that first bullshit call and I just socked him right in the jaw, and we just fought it out. Everyone else was standing back wondering what the hell they were supposed to do. Finally, Gavin stood up, helped me up to my feet, and was like 'fine, no interference' and we just got back to the game."

"How much older is Gavin?" Zoey wondered how much of a size difference there was in these fights when they were kids.

"Three years. Well, just under three years. But yeah, when I was eleven and he was fourteen, he definitely had the advantage on me when we fought like that."

"But that didn't stop you?"

"No." Jett shook his head. "Brothers fight. I've seen Chris and Tyler get after it a few times. It's normal."

"I've never punched my siblings. But I suppose I was too busy taking care of them so that would've been counterproductive."

"I couldn't imagine you punching anyone," Jett spoke into the hat on her head. "You're too sweet. Fierce when you need to be, I'm sure, but...I imagine you'd just strike your opponent down with a look."

"And they'd just know not to mess with me?" She giggled. "Yeah, I'm sure I'm just that intimidating."

"I was intimidated by you."

"Oh yeah?" She couldn't possibly imagine why.

"I asked someone to teach me how to impress you, so yeah, I'd say so," Jett replied. "I went to a bar *in a suit* and practiced talking to girls I wasn't interested in with the hope that when you got here, I wouldn't sound like a complete idiot."

Okay, that was a good point, she supposed. "Did it work?"

Jett's grin was shy, almost nervous, and he shrugged. "A little. I mean, some of the ladies were into it."

Zoey narrowed her eyes at him as jealousy coiled in her chest. "Is that so?"

He must have sensed her jealousy, because he grinned and gave an arrogant sniff with another shrug. "Well, I mean, who wouldn't want a big ol' slab of this premium man meat?"

Zoey burst out laughing. "Yeah, I guess you're pretty hot for an old fart, aren't you?"

"Ouch!" Jett clamped a hand over his chest. "And just before my birthday! I'm already self-conscious about starting my third decade, and here you are making me feel bad about it," he teased. He squeezed his fingers low on her hip and made her squeal and jump with more laughter.

"I'm sorry!" she gasped as he continued tickling her. "Oh my gosh! I'm sorry, I'm sorry! I take it back! You're not old! You're a young, handsome, big ol' slab of man meat and any girl would be lucky to have you!"

Jett stopped tickling her, but kept his hand around her hip as he gazed down at her with an easy smile. "It still hurts a bit," he said, lowering his head, bridging the gap between their lips.

She smiled and her heart fluttered like crazy in her chest. She licked her lips. "Will this make it better?" Closing what was left of the space between them, Zoey touched her lips to his and felt warmth spread through her body. His mouth was firm against hers and she tilted her head to give him better access. When she felt his tongue just slightly peak its way between her lips, there was a zap of electric current flowing through her veins as hot pressure pooled between her thighs.

There was a commotion on the ice, and she and Jett broke apart, sitting up to watch as two of the players started to brawl. One slammed the other into the side of the rink and threw his punches, and the other's teammates skated over to get in on the action.

Hockey was quickly becoming her new favorite sport.

After the game, Jett drove Zoey back to her hotel and walked her to her door again. She was not ready for this night to end. She didn't know exactly where she wanted it to go from here, but she knew she wasn't ready to say goodnight just yet.

Jett leaned down to kiss her, brushing his fingers across her cheek and holding her steady against him. It's a good thing he had a strong grip, because she was ready to melt into the door. The contrast of his soft lips and firm hands made her want to live in his arms.

"It's still early," Zoey breathed as Jett's lips parted from hers. She hadn't thought this through, but the words were out before she could stop them. "If you want to come in...I know your apartment must be loud with the bar open for another few hours."

Jett's eyes flicked back and forth between hers and she watched as they darkened suddenly. He looked down at her lips before sliding his gaze back up to hers.

Butterflies. Definite butterflies in my stomach right now.

He nodded and gave a quiet "Okay", sending her whole body into high alert. Pulse racing. Heart thumping. Loins burning. Check, check, and check.

She swallowed and swiped her key-card, entering her hotel room with Jett close behind. She flipped on the light and suddenly forgot how to speak or move. *Where do I go from here? Do we sit on the couch? Do I lead us to the bedroom? No, no...that's too forward.*

"Um," she turned around to see him taking off his coat and hat. He tousled his curls and kicked off his shoes. *Right. My coat. I can take my coat off without seeming like I just brought him in here for sex.*

Did I bring him in here for sex?

He probably thinks so. But I don't even know.

Zoey unbuttoned her coat and tossed her hat onto the bench by the door. Jett took a step closer to her and bowed his head to kiss her again. Their lips met and her brain went instantly fuzzy. She felt his hands on her hips as he guided her backwards until she felt the hardness of the wall against her back. His hand slid up the side of her body to cup her jaw and his body pressed into her.

Okay, now I am melting. That wasn't melting before. This is.

She was pinned to the wall and the short hair of his beard that he'd let grow was scratching into her skin, completely waking up every inch of her body. His tongue slipped between her lips and she moaned, her body becoming pliant and submissive to his touch.

His hips pressed against her and- *oh...my.* Beneath his jeans and through her sweater she could feel him. His arousal pushed against her stomach and it was...magnificent. And now she was wet. There had been moisture before, but this was different. Her body knew it would take more than a little moisture, more than just a little flexibility to accept *all* of him. And it was preparing itself.

He groaned into her mouth and she bent her head back, urging him to kiss her neck. He caught on, and moved his lips to the slope of her neck, kissing and sucking, his groans making small impressions on her skin. Her breaths were shallow and she couldn't stop the small, needy whimpers from escaping. She rocked her hips into him, feeling his full length against her and bit her lip with a moan.

With his hands, he pulled her arms up so that her hands were pinned just slightly above her head, and he laced his fingers with hers. *Oh. My. God.* So masculine...yet so sweet. *Is this man for real?*

He pressed his lips to hers for a quick, tender kiss. "If this is as far as you want to go, that's fine with me, Zo." He kissed her again. "Just tell me what you want and I'll make it happen."

Relief. Okay. The pressure was off. Of course she *wanted* to go further with him, but she just wasn't sure if she was ready for that. Her body clearly was, but it felt too soon. They'd only kissed a handful of times. What happened to the steamy make-out sessions that led to the sex? Who said being an adult meant skipping that part? That part was fun, too.

"Um, maybe we should go to the couch?" she breathed, grateful that he'd slowed things down. She wasn't sure she'd have been able to on her own.

He gave a short nod before picking her up in his arms as if she weighed nothing. He laid her back on the couch and held himself over her. Looking over at the TV, he found the remote and flipped it on. It was still on the *Hallmark* channel, in the middle of a cheesy Christmas movie.

"Christmas movies and chill?" He grinned down at her, placing a soft kiss to her cheek. He glanced at the TV for a moment. "I've seen this one. It's the one where the girl's a workaholic until she meets the sweet hometown guy and they do the Christmas event and fall in love."

Zoey giggled. "I think that's ninety percent of them."

"Oh yeah..." He sighed. "They should make a new one. The girl is a workaholic, and the guy is also a workaholic, and they meet at a really inopportune moment when said guy's friend has been kidnapped by her ex-fiancé."

"This sounds familiar, but I don't think she was kidnapped." Zoey smiled up at him.

Jett put a finger to her lips. "Shh, it's a movie, it's gotta be more dramatic. So she was kidnapped, and then the guy saves the day and helps his friends realize they should just be together. And then unbeknownst to him, he's completely made the aforementioned workaholic girl fall for him with all his masculinity and charm and not being at all awkward."

"You are very masculine." Zoey touched her fingers to his face and traced his stubbled jaw line. "And you're not *awkward*, you're goofy. And I like it."

"You do?" His eyebrow twitched up and he smirked just slightly.

"Mhmm."

"Yes!" He whispered as he pumped one fist. "Well, I made her like me. My work here is done." He began to get up from the couch but Zoey reached out and snatched his hand.

"Where do you think you're going? You said whatever I wanted, you'd make it happen."

"Ooh, well damn, okay. I guess we're not done here then, my bad." Jett crawled back on top of her and dipped his head to kiss her again. "What do you want then?"

She smiled into his lips. "Just kiss me like you were before and I'll guide you from there."

A small growly sound emitted from him. "Mm, yes ma'am."

The Christmas movies continued to play in the background and they lost track of time as he kissed her, both hard and soft, sweet and steamy. She loved when he kissed her neck and honestly didn't care if he left marks. It was Michigan in the wintertime, she'd wear a scarf if need be. He'd slipped her sweater up and over her head, pressing kisses along her collarbone and chest until she got greedy and wanted to do some exploring of her own.

His shirt came off and she rolled on top of him, straddling his broad frame and running her hands up and down his stomach and chest. He had actual chest hair. Most men back home were pristinely waxed, but Jett was all man. She felt like she could lose herself in him. Kissing, touching, learning his body, and letting him learn hers.

She was acutely aware of his impressive hard length beneath her as she shamelessly rubbed herself against it. He groaned and grabbed her hips, pressing her more firmly onto it and she whimpered. His chest heaved as he looked at her with glazed eyes and he moved his hands to the button of her jeans.

"Let me..." he breathed, and the thick, husky quality to his voice made her want to do whatever it was that he was suggesting. "I just want to feel you...please."

She was soaking wet, and grinding against him through their jeans had her on the edge. The thought of his fingers on her...*dear God.* She nodded. "Okay."

He flipped her onto her back again and lay on top of her. She helped him work her skin-tight skinny jeans down, and he kissed her slowly again as he dipped a hand into the silk of her panties.

"Oh God," she moaned, her head falling back as he barely brushed his fingers over her clit. It was almost embarrassing how quickly she knew she was likely to come undone by his touch. She grasped at his thick, muscular shoulders as he continued touching and petting her there. The feel of his tongue against her neck had her dizzy, wondering what it would feel like elsewhere. His fingers were doing the trick for now, though. Yeah, they were definitely working.

A firm finger slid along her crease and dipped in, and back out. Slowly in...and back out. And back...*in. Oh yes...that's it.*

She bit her lip, trying to hold back her dirty thoughts, her moans that wanted to escape. She clawed at his shoulders when his thumb swiped over her clit, then found a steady rhythm over it.

Her breaths were harsh and getting louder...she was gasping and pushing her hips up into his hand. *Oh God, oh God...yes...yes...there-*

"Oh God, *right* there, Jett," she moaned, pulling him closer, feeling his teeth and hot breath against her neck. His fingers quickened but stayed in the same spot. She gasped as she felt her body reach its peak- and release. *Oh...yes...* There were no words as she arched into him, thighs shaking as they wrapped around him while her orgasm crashed through her. She was vaguely aware of her incomprehensible moans as she squeezed and contracted around his fingers. He buried his face in her neck, and didn't take his hand away until her orgasm had subsided.

"Oh my God..." she sighed, chest heaving as she pushed her hair back. "That was...I needed that."

"I'm here for what you need." Jett's voice was low and husky as he grinned slyly. "Just say the word and I've got you."

She smiled up at him, maybe a little dreamily. She was beginning to think she could get used to having someone care for her for a change. Especially the way Jett Miller did it.

CHAPTER 11

There was an abrupt knock on the door to Jett's apartment as he scrambled around to find all of his interview notes. He and Chris were conducting interviews before the bar opened and he'd done his best to make himself look more presentable than he did on his average work day. Before he got down the hallway to answer the door, he heard it swing open, and footsteps make a straight path for the kitchen.

He sighed. *Lizzie.*

As expected, he peeked his head around the corner of the kitchen to see his little sister digging into the freezer where he always kept at least three different varieties of Ben & Jerry's ice cream for occasions such as these. She had already tossed her coat onto a bar stool and was wearing navy blue sweatpants and a gray hoodie with the hood pulled up onto her head.

"Liz…" he started slowly, tucking his shirt into his black dress pants. "Everything okay?" He knew the answer to this already, but liked to at least offer the benefit of the doubt.

"I'm digging in your freezer for ice cream wearing *sweatpants*, Jett! Do you think I'm okay?" Lizzie snapped back, pulling a pint of *Half-Baked* out of the freezer and grabbing a spoon out of his dish rack.

"What did this one do?" Jett leaned against the wall and watched Lizzie peel the top back off the ice cream and jab her spoon into the smooth surface.

She glared at him, spoon in her mouth. "Do you have to be so condescending? You act like this is something that happens once a week."

Jett forced the derisive and completely condescending laugh down, literally biting his tongue. "I mean, I've noticed a pattern, Liz. I love the crap out of you, but you have horrible taste in men. You need to let me and Chris set you up with someone. Seriously, where do you meet all these *Brads* anyway?"

"I met him at the sporting goods store," Lizzie replied, taking another massive bite of ice cream. "I was looking at skiing equipment and he helped me. I thought he was nice."

"Okay, if a guy helps you pick out equipment, or a book, or food...or whatever, and he doesn't work there, it's because he's trying to sleep with you. He's not just being nice."

Lizzie scoffed. "You would do it just to be nice! It's not my fault I grew up with really good big brothers and that's what I expect men to be like, okay? Really I should be blaming you and Gavin for not being more normal."

Jett considered and realized this was actually quite the compliment, even if it did mean he caused problems for his youngest sister. "Sorry about that, I guess."

"But I can hardly take your advice when it comes to dating." Lizzie walked by him and found her spot in the middle of the couch. "I mean, jeez, how long has it been since you've dated someone? I'd rather just kiss a few frogs and hope I find Prince Charming than reject everyone before they even open their mouths."

"Is that what you think I do?" Jett crossed the living room and grabbed the remote off the end table to hand to Lizzie.

"I figure it must be. I remember coming to visit while you were behind the bar one night and girls were trying to flirt with you and you just completely ignored them. I know Samantha hurt you, but you gotta get back out there. Take a chance, ya know?"

Jett clapped his hands together with a heavy sigh. "I'm not hung up on Samantha. You guys need to get over that. I'm over it, I think my family should be, too."

"So why do you ignore every girl who looks at you?" Lizzie pressed, jabbing her spoon in his direction.

"I...don't. Girls don't hit on me." Jett looked at his sister as though she'd hit her head. "Do they?"

She laughed and gave him an incredulous look. "Seriously, Jett? *All the time!* And then you just say something nice and they get all swoony, and then you leave it at that. Are you just oblivious to it?"

Furrowing his brow, he tried to remember a time someone at his bar had hit on him. Or someone anywhere had hit on him, and he hadn't immediately gotten awkward and started using weird accents and scared them away.

"Well, that's not important anyway because as it just so happens, I'm seeing someone."

Lizzie gasped and threw off the blanket she was wrapping around herself. "You are? Omigod, tell me everything! How'd you meet? Where'd you meet? Have you taken her on a date? Where'd you go? Oh my gosh! Is she spending Christmas with us?" She gasped again and clapped her hands together. "Is she coming to your birthday dinner at Mom and Dad's? She needs to meet everyone- Jett! This is so exciting! I'm so happy for you!"

Even in the midst of her own heartbreak, Lizzie was absolutely ecstatic at the idea that her brother had found someone, and he really had to appreciate that.

Jett smiled at his sister, then looked at his phone for the time. "I really don't have time to answer all these questions right now. I have an interview downstairs in a couple minutes, but I'll come back up and fill you in, okay?"

"Just tell me her name!" Lizzie smiled brightly.

"Zoey...Zoey Nunez."

"Oh perfect!" Lizzie pulled her phone out from under her. "I'm going to Facebook stalk her!"

"No, you're not!"

"I am, actually. Oh look! I already found her!" Lizzie stared down at her phone, holding it with both hands. "Oooh, Jett, she's cute!"

He rolled his eyes. "Okay, I have an interview to go do, so...happy stalking, you weirdo." Jett grabbed the folder with his interview materials and headed out the door and downstairs to the bar.

Chris was waiting for him in the office, studying the two resumes that had been picked in that chance game of darts. He gave Jett a brief rundown of their work experience and qualifications. While it didn't feel right, Jett couldn't help the instinct to instantly write off Alaina's interview. He didn't have anything against her personally. Back in high school, she'd actually been pretty cool and he remembered enjoying talking to her when they had classes together. It was childish, of course, to hold anything that happened in high school against someone, especially when it had absolutely nothing to do with him, but he couldn't help feeling like bringing her in would only create unnecessary drama with two of his closest friends.

The other applicant, Simon Barnes, sounded promising enough. They'd checked his references on Facebook and none of them seemed to be falsified. His resume wasn't any more or less impressive than Alaina's, which was unfortunate. This meant he really had to rely on Alaina completely bombing the interview to keep his friends happy.

Simon came in at 11:20, which was ten minutes early. He gave decent answers and was friendly enough. He didn't completely wow them, but it was a management position for a bar. Jett wasn't entirely sure how impressive the candidates for this role would be anyway.

He and Chris talked positive and negative points until Alaina walked in a few minutes early for her interview as well.

Neither Jett nor Chris had seen her since high school, and she still looked like herself, but no longer sported her long, loose curls. Alaina's hair was done in a choppy, medium-length bob, with a mixture of dark brown and caramel-colored highlights. She had three earrings in each ear, and a bar up top in one ear. Her style perfectly reflected the attitude Jett remembered, and it just worked. She looked edgy, but completely professional in her black ankle-length skinny dress pants, burgundy blouse, and black blazer. She wore several bangles on one wrist, and her nails were manicured in a gunmetal gray. She looked like she could easily go from manager to bartender in a second's notice.

"Hey Alaina," Chris greeted and smiled easily at her as she approached. "Been a while, huh?"

Alaina smiled back. "Yeah, it's good to see you guys. I'd heard a while ago that you had opened this place, but I just came back to town a couple months ago."

The three of them sat down and caught up briefly before starting the interview. Jett was wondering if they were being completely fair to Simon, given that they knew Alaina and already had a relatively easy-going rapport. It was slightly less professional than the previous interview, but somehow Alaina was coming off as far more impressive than any of their other candidates.

She'd gone to college for art and business, and had tried opening her own studio in Grand Rapids. After years of saving up, she'd finally got the money to put down on a space, but it fell through when the owner sold it out from under her. She was still painting and doing photography on the side, and said that it might be better that way. Turning your passion into the thing you do every single day can take away from the joy of it, and this way, she said, she could do as much or as little art as she wanted.

In college, she'd tended bar at a restaurant and was moved up to shift leader, then assistant manager. She had done that for several years, and her last job in Grand Rapids before moving back home was bartending at a swanky little bar downtown that Jett and Chris had both heard of.

They'd just about closed the interview when Jett caught Alaina's eyes wandering behind him to the spot on the wall reserved for Quinn's accomplishments. His jerseys, a poster, some magazine covers, and now a signed ball along with a few childhood photos of him on their local baseball field adorned the wall next to the liquor display.

Alaina noticed that Jett was watching her and she let out a small breath of laughter. "I, uh...didn't realize you guys let him work here until the other day. He's changed a bit, huh?"

Chris chuckled. "Yeah, imagine that. Who knew a multi-million dollar contract and being labeled as one of the best players in professional athletics could make someone so carefree and easy-going?"

"He's not the quiet, angry kid we all knew once upon a time." Jett eyed Alaina curiously for a reaction. He wasn't sure exactly what kind of relationship she'd had with Quinn years ago. When it was going on, he'd assumed it was purely physical, but was aware of their similar home situations being a source of bonding between them.

"Good for him. He worked hard for it...he should enjoy it." Alaina's casual response put Jett at ease. Of course it would be silly to think she had lingering feelings for him, but then again, Quinn's feelings for Rae had withstood the test of time, and *lots* of one-night-stands.

Wrapping up the interview, they shook hands and let her know they'd be in touch. Once she was out the door Chris turned to look intently at Jett.

"I know you think it's going to be problematic," Chris began slowly, "but...she's kind of our best option, don't you think?"

Jett groaned and put his head in his hands, resting his elbows on the table in front of them, "Don't *you* think it's going to be problematic?"

"Not at all. Sometimes I forget how long ago high school was until I see someone I haven't seen since then, and everything just seems so trivial. Besides, Quinn and Rae are together now. They're happy and completely in love. I really don't think either of them are going to take issue with it. And if they do, we can kindly remind them that it's our business, not theirs, and we're the ones who make the hiring decisions."

Jett rubbed his brow a few times, considering. "She's obviously the best option. I just don't want to cause problems."

"It won't," Chris insisted. "Give your friends more credit. They'll be fine. And they're only going to be here like once a year anyway."

Jett met Chris's gaze for a moment. They probably would only be there once or twice a year. That meant *Zoey* would probably only be there once or twice a year.

What the hell was he doing? He knew it wasn't Chris's intent to make him think about how he was possibly going to make things work long term with Zoey, but that's exactly where his head went.

Chris seemed to make the connection and exhaled, looking guilty for putting the thought in his friend's head. "Dude, I'm sorry, I didn't mean to…"

Jett shook his head and waved him off. "No, it's okay. I'm going to have to figure it out eventually anyway. We'll have to decide how to make it work. If we think it's going to work."

"And you do."

Jett scratched his stubbly beard that he really needed to shave. "We've only had a few dates."

"That doesn't mean anything. You can just know." Chris stacked the papers in front of him and slid them into a folder. "I think you know. I think you knew when you met her. You guys will figure it out."

Remaining silent, he nodded, looking down at the table.

"Cool, now you've got your own problem to deal with, so you can stop worrying about the one that may or may not arise when we hire Alaina." Chris gave Jett a pat on the back and stood up, making his way to the back of the bar and into the office.

He wished it was that simple. Jett wasn't one to just put his friends' issues on the back burner to deal with his own problems. He was the fixer, the guy everyone went to when something was wrong. If he couldn't fix the problem, he would listen to his friends vent until three in the morning. He was the guy who'd give his friends a place to stay when they weren't in a state to go home, he was the guy whose door was open every time his sister's heart was broken, he was the guy who remembered scrunchies so no one he loved would ever have to worry about throwing up in their own hair.

Jett was the loyal friend. And he couldn't help feeling like he'd been making several decisions that would challenge that label. He was also beginning to wonder if he was going to have to, for the first time in his life, be the selfish friend, when it came to the woman he was undeniably falling for.

It was still early and the bar didn't open for another hour, so Jett trudged back upstairs to get bombarded with questions from his sister.

At the top step, he paused, certain he heard a low male voice inside his apartment. He hadn't expected Quinn to stop by, but thought maybe he wanted some extra help translating Rae's French phrases that she'd left for him.

He pushed the door open and froze, ice crystalizing in his veins at the sight on his couch.

Lizzie was still sitting on his couch on the middle cushion as he'd left her. But now she was accompanied by none other than Emerson. *Oh hell no.*

"What the hell are you doing here?" Jett slammed the door behind himself and stomped into the living room. Emerson was the very last person his sister needed to meet. Good God, the guy was all the bad things about every one of her ex-boyfriends rolled into a sugary eye-candy coating.

"Oh, hey man!" Emerson grinned up at him, leaning back and spreading his arms on the back of the couch. "I was just on my way back to work from lunch and I thought I'd stop in to see if you were coming to my place tonight for some *God of War.*"

"Oh, right." Jett flopped down in the recliner. "I'm not gonna be able to make this one."

"Spending time with Zoey?" Emerson raised a curious eyebrow in his direction.

"We were just Facebook stalking her together," Lizzie interjected proudly. "You didn't tell me she lives in LA! But anyway, *Emerson* here explained how you guys met. So cute."

Jett furrowed his brow at Emerson. "Do you actually know how we met?"

The suited-up lawyer shrugged. "I know enough. You guys couldn't find Rae, Quinn was panicking, and I saved the day letting you know she'd been safe with me."

"Christ," Jett muttered under his breath.

Emerson was already putting on a show for his sister, playing the hero, making it look like he'd swooped in and saved Rae from a terrible fate. Jett leaned his elbows to his knees and looked sternly at the man sitting far too close to his sister for his comfort.

"Listen, this is my little sister, and she just got out of a relationship. She just came over to eat some ice cream, wallow a little, and probably watch *John Tucker Must Die*, so I really don't need you coming in here and putting the moves on her. *She* doesn't need you coming in here and putting moves on her."

"I'm not wallowing!" Lizzie gasped. "And that's really not your place to say. Besides, he wasn't putting *moves* on me. He was just being friendly. And you should be more appreciative of your friends, Jett. It sounds like he's really helped you with this Zoey girl."

"Oh does it?" Jett arched an eyebrow and aimed his gaze again at the smooth-talker who had clearly already worked some kind of voo-doo on his youngest sister. "How's that?"

"He told me all about how he encouraged you to go take care of her when she wasn't feeling well. He said you were just going to stay home and wait around for her to feel better, and he told you to get up and go show this girl you mean business!" Lizzie sat up straight on the edge of the couch cushion. She glanced briefly -adoringly- at Emerson, before looking back at her brother, "That's what girls really want. A man who's going to just step up and show her how much he cares. And I bet she loved it. *And* I bet you never thanked him for the suggestion."

Emerson was biting back a grin as he shrugged at Jett's incredulous glare. He took a deep breath and counted to three, completely unsure of the words that were about to escape him.

"Well, first of all...that's a fucking lie, Lizzie. He is lying to you. He wasn't here when Zoey called to cancel the date and, seriously? You were just talking about how you have the best big brothers in the world, and you didn't think that was my idea to go take care of her? This guy-" he gestured to Emerson with a nod of his head- "would never do something like that. He would, however, lie to make himself look good. He would also take credit for the good deeds of others- turns out he is capable of distinguishing right from wrong, he just doesn't care when it comes to his own actions."

Lizzie peeked sideways at Emerson whose grin had yet to falter.

"He will say and do whatever it takes to sleep with you or any woman he finds remotely attractive," Jett continued. "He sleeps with random women all the time. I wouldn't even want to know his number-"

"Actually that's not entirely true," Emerson interjected as he held up a finger. "I have like six regulars on a rotation. They don't know about each other, but I can't just be sleeping with new women all the time. Gotta stay clean."

"A rotation?" Lizzie questioned hesitantly, scooting away from him slightly.

"Yeah, one for almost every night of the week. And then I get a night to myself," he explained, as though it were the most obvious thing in the world.

"What about the night you took home the girl I was talking to?" Jett wasn't sure if he should be completely disgusted by this new information or a little impressed. Probably both. A guy who could work a schedule like that had to know what the hell he was doing.

"Olivia canceled," Emerson said. "Something about her boyfriend coming home early."

"Oh. My. God." Jett and Lizzie blurted in unison.

"What the fuck is wrong with you, man?" Jett dragged a hand down his face.

"You don't care that she has a boyfriend?" Lizzie seemed to be completely in shock that someone could be so blunt about his nefarious nighttime activities. She'd dated plenty of guys like him, they just weren't like this around *her*.

"What did I tell you, Lizz?" Jett looked at his sister almost apologetically, "He was lying to you. He's just really good at it."

"So, you weren't really the one to find Rae and let them all know she was safe, either?" She eyed Emerson now as though he might suddenly shed the suit and charm and reveal his devil horns and pitchfork.

"Well, I was there. And I did help her calm down. I told her to go talk to All-Star before she jumped to conclusions." He scratched his beard and looked proud of himself.

"Oh please," Jett snorted. "You were all about making it seem like you two had hooked up."

"Uh, yeah, when *he* showed up. I *like* Rae. I can be nice to her just fine. I don't like All-Star's smug, arrogant ass."

Jett rolled his eyes, but he found that he actually believed him for some reason. It wasn't completely inconceivable that he'd actually been decent toward Rae and decided to flip a switch when Quinn showed up. Ironically, Quinn hated Emerson for the exact same reasons. He thought he was smug and arrogant, and never deserved Rae in the first place. Also, the whole cheating bit. That didn't sit well with Quinn, either.

"So you just lie to make yourself look good? Like...all the time?" Lizzie glared at Emerson, surely thinking of all the men who had done exactly that to her.

The lawyer shrugged, indifferently. "More or less."

Lizzie slid to the empty couch cushion, furthest from Emerson and muttered *pig* under her breath.

"See? He's just like all the other guys you date." Jett leaned back in his chair, satisfied that he seemed to have broken the illusion Emerson had created.

"Hey!"

"Why did you and Brad break up? We hadn't got there yet before I left..." He looked knowingly at Lizzie and she deflated, sinking back into the couch.

"I'm not telling you." Lizzie crossed her arms and looked toward the window near the fire escape.

"Why not? You tell me about all the other Brads and Chads and Bretts."

Emerson laughed and looked back and forth between the siblings. "Oh this should be a good one then."

"Because...you're my big brother and it's weird to talk to you about this stuff."

Jett rolled his eyes. "Liz, you're twenty-two and you date. A lot. Not like Emerson, exactly, but you have boyfriends all the time. I know you have sex. Just please don't give me the details. Any of them."

"I wouldn't mind-" Emerson was cut off by Jett throwing a coaster at him.

Lizzie still refused to make eye contact with her brother.

Jett paused for a beat while his heart nearly stopped at the thought. "You'd tell me if he, like...forced himself on you, right?"

Even Emerson's eyes went wide with concern as he looked at Lizzie.

Luckily, she immediately shook her head. "No, no, nothing like that. Well...I guess there was some lack of consent, but..." Now looking back and forth between Jett's and Emerson's concerned stares, she sighed. "He tried to film us. Without asking me. And I would've said no anyway, but...I saw the camera's light before anything really happened and then I got out of there."

"Are you fucking serious?" Jett's eyebrows shot upward. "Does he still have the recording? What do you mean 'before anything really happened'? You still...had clothes on or what?"

"I'm not going into detail about this with you!" Lizzie wrapped the blanket around herself again. "I wasn't naked or anything and I doubt he kept it. I can't imagine it got very exciting after I stormed out."

"Did you slap him?" Emerson asked. "Because you should've slapped him. I know that shit happens all the time, but it's messed up."

Jett eyed him skeptically. "Honestly, I wouldn't be surprised if you'd done that before."

Looking mildly offended, Emerson reared back. "Hey, everyone has a line. I make sure all

the women I film are completely informed about what's going on."

"Oh yeah? Go full lawyer on them and draw up a little contract to sign?" Jett asked, somewhat amused.

"If that was a stipulation, I would, yes. Actually, I have one written up just in case of that very situation, though it hasn't happened yet."

Emerson checked his expensive-looking watch before heaving himself off the couch. "Future reference: Always ask to see a contract. I put in mine that I won't sell or mass-produce anything, or post it online. But no one signs, so I can actually do whatever I want."

"But you keep it to yourself, right?" Lizzie asked, looking a little frightened to discover the answer.

"Of course I do. *I'm* in it. I don't need that shit getting out and destroying my career." He stretched and straightened his suit jacket. "Speaking of, I need to get back to the office." Turning to Lizzie, he pointed a finger at her. "Make better choices." And turning to Jett, he said, "Good luck with Zoey. I can't believe you haven't fucked her yet, but I wanna hear all about it when you finally do."

"My God, you're charming," Jett said sarcastically.

Emerson smirked in response and started out the door. He poked his head back in. "And Lizzie, if you ever want, I can make a spot for you in the rotation." The bastard winked before Jett stood back up and yelled at him to get out, swiftly closing the door behind him.

"You have some interesting friends, big bro," Lizzie said, attention still focused on the closed front door.

Jett fell back into his chair, rubbing his temples. "He's not my friend."

Lizzie didn't look too convinced, but shrugged and lay across the couch. She pointed the remote at the TV and pulled up a streaming network and settled on her usual post-break-up movie.

Nope. He couldn't hire his best friend's old arch-enemy *and* become friends with her ex. That wasn't the type of friend he was. Needing to escape the sudden onset of guilt, he pulled out his phone and texted Zoey about getting together later that evening. If anyone could put his mind at ease, or at the very least, help him get out of his head for a few hours, it was her.

CHAPTER 12

The previous evening, Zoey had come over to Jett's apartment shortly after his sister left. He wasn't scheduled to work, but was on call in case things got busy downstairs. They'd spent the majority of the evening on his couch, making out and fooling around while Christmas movies again played in the background. He could check 'Christmas movies and chill' off the date list now.

There was something fun about all the build-up between him and Zoey. They hadn't jumped right into sex, and he was fine with that. The way they'd lay tangled, side by side on the couch all evening was reminiscent of high school make-out sessions and he kind of loved it. There was a fun, daring kind of mystery about it. He didn't know how far they'd get or what they'd do, but he was excited for whatever happened.

It was late Thursday morning and Jett was pulling into the hotel parking lot to pick Zoey up. His head was swimming with scenes from the previous night's hot and heavy lip-lock session on the couch and he couldn't help grinning to himself, remembering the way she'd gasped at the feel of his full, hard length in her hand for the first time. Warmth spread through his chest and down to his cock, abruptly waking it up. Her hand had felt so small and soft in contrast to him. He took a slow breath, but still couldn't wipe the grin off his face as he turned off his truck and hopped out.

In the interest of marking things off his list of date ideas, today they were going sledding. They were driving over to Chris and Victoria's and then they'd all drive up to Timberlee Hills together. Sophia was coming along, of course, and she had been completely ecstatic over the phone when Jett had called to suggest it.

When Jett knocked on Zoey's hotel room door, it didn't take long for her to swing it open. She beamed up at him, and grabbed the collar of his ski jacket to pull him down so she could kiss him. His arms instantly wrapped around her waist. Feeling her tongue against his lips, he pressed into her and groaned. Damn, if he thought his cock had woken up before...

"Good morning," Zoey breathed as she parted just enough to speak into his lips.

"Now it is," he growled as he kissed her back. Sliding his arms around her bottom, he pulled her up onto him and she wrapped her legs around his waist. He kicked the door shut behind him with one foot and carried her into the living room, laying her down on the couch.

"How many layers do you have on?" She unzipped and pushed his jacket off his shoulders as he kissed her neck.

"Too many." He slid a hand beneath her sweater and palmed one of her full breasts. He couldn't help himself. A completely selfish, ravenous urge had taken over and he suddenly wanted her all at once. The way she grasped at him and undressed him did nothing to curb his craving for her.

Her back arched into him as she moaned, "Oh my God, I can feel you through all these layers."

His body was fully awake now, and he wasn't surprised at all. Even if he was

wearing jeans and snow pants, he knew how hard he was. There was no concealing that. And fuck, if her saying that didn't make it that much harder.

"I can't stop thinking about your hands on me," Jett groaned into the spot just below her jaw. "The sounds you made when you felt what you did to me... saw how big it was."

A small whimper escaped her lips and he watched her skin flush, felt the heat of it on his mouth. "Let me..." She tugged at the waistband of his snow pants. "I want to feel it again."

Fuck. Yes. Didn't have to tell him twice.

Jett sat up and began shedding his extra layers. Having kicked his snow pants and blue jeans off, Zoey straddled him where he sat on the couch, seating herself in his lap. Chest heaving, eyes glazed and heavy with need, he looked up at her and practically hissed when she palmed him through the thin fabric of his boxers. She stroked his length up and down, in a slow, measured rhythm, gazing back into his eyes with the same dark, heavy look he could feel in his own.

Zoey leaned forward to kiss him, and took his bottom lip between her teeth before pulling away. "I couldn't stop thinking about my hands on you either."

Jett's eyes closed as he leaned back with a groan. Fuck, he loved hearing that. The thought that she might be as hungry for him as he felt for her...his cock throbbed, pulsing under her small hand.

She slipped her fingers beneath the waistband of his boxers now and pushed them down. He raised his hips to help her and watched as her eyes lit up at the sight of him. Bare, hard, and standing at perfect attention. She began working her hand up and down his thick shaft, rolling her hips with the motion.

He lifted his hips in rhythm with hers and imagined moving inside her. His head rested on the back of the couch as he savored the feel of her small hand sliding up and down his cock. *Fuck* he was hard. Veins pulsing, blood pumping. Imagining how wet she might be getting from feeling him, he reached for the button of her jeans and undid them, slipping them as low on her hips as her position would allow.

Today her panties were a light pink cotton fabric and he could feel her wetness through them. He grunted with pleasure as he began rubbing her through the thin layer, his cock throbbing harder as he felt her getting wetter. She picked up the pace, leaning over him, head bowed next to his so she could watch. He felt pre-cum beading at the head of his dick and knew he was close. So fucking close.

"Oh God, that feels so good," she whispered into his ear before letting out a moan and bucking into his hand. "Yes...oh please, yes...don't stop, *please.*"

Jett groaned and slipped a finger into her panties, along her slick crease and back up to her swollen clit. She hissed into his ear and pressed her teeth to his skin. When she rocked into his hand again, he slid another finger into her, and continued working her sensitive clit with the swipe of his thumb. He wanted to feel her contracting around his fingers, tensing and shaking before showering him in soft, praising kisses.

"Faster," Jett panted greedily. "Mm, fuck that's so good."

*"Jett...*yes, yes- oh *God!"* Zoey's nails dug into his back, her teeth pressed into his neck with a drawn out moan and her body shook and quivered around him.

"Mmm...*yes,* baby, oh fuck." Feeling Zoey wrapped tight around him sent him over the edge. His cock throbbed and ached right up until that final release. "Oooh...God...yes..." His voice was a low groan as he spilled over Zoey's hand. His chest heaved with shallow breaths, and he melted into the couch with the light touches of her lips to his skin that he'd grown accustomed to. She kissed his forehead, his cheek, his jaw, his lips, and he fucking lived for it.

Zoey slid off his lap and disappeared for a few moments before coming back with damp towels from the bathroom. After cleaning up, Jett wrapped a hand behind her head and pulled her lips to his, swiping his tongue through her mouth, tasting her and savoring every second he was near her.

"We might be a little late," Jett said with a smirk as he zipped his coat back on.

"I'll blame you for that." Zoey pulled her winter hat with the large pom-pom ball on. "If you weren't so irresistible, maybe we would've made it on time."

His smile grew as the warm and fuzzy feeling spread through his chest again. "Who me? *I'm* irresistible?"

She tilted her head to the side as she looked at him. "Yeah, you kind of are."

"Can I get that in writing?"

"I have a feeling you can probably get whatever you want from me." She threw a mischievous grin over her shoulder as she headed for the door.

His already wide grin doubled and he rubbed the side of his now bearded jaw, lost in the words she gave him. He couldn't remember the last time someone praised and complimented him so openly, but he was starting to think he could really get used to it.

In a few strides, he caught up to Zoey and held the door open for her. She beamed and reached up on her tip-toes to plant a kiss to his cheek before they walked together out the door.

Standing at the top of a massive sledding hill, Zoey looked to the bottom to see where the ground leveled out. It seemed like a long way down, and she had never exactly been a thrill seeker. Then again, there were small children all over the sledding hill, so it couldn't possibly be that dangerous. Jett promised to hang onto her and, in the event that the sled did tip over, break her fall. After their ice skating adventure, she didn't see any reason not to believe him this time around.

"Ready?" Jett sat down on the long sled, legs wide. He gestured for her to sit in front, so she settled herself between his legs, scooting her butt up to his crotch. Yep, she was already liking sledding so far. "Be good, my niece is here," he whispered softly into her ear.

She looked over her shoulder innocently. "What was I doing?" She gave her butt another wiggle, rubbing against where she knew that magnificent cock of his was. "Oh, you mean that?"

Jett groaned into her hair, "God, you're killing me." He pressed his lips to the small bit of exposed skin on her neck. "All right, let's go."

He pushed off the hill and their sled slowly crept near the edge. Closer and closer until...*woosh!* Like the top peak of a roller coaster, the sled went flying over the hill. It was so much faster than Zoey had expected, and she found herself laughing with delight from the rush of it.

It was over so fast, and at the end of the hill she let herself lay back on Jett, still smiling from the surge of adrenaline. She felt like she got the same amount of joy out of it as a little kid. Finally, she stood up, and Jett stood next to her holding the sled at his side. They waited and watched as Chris and Sophia flew down the hill, listening to the little girl's jubilant shrieks and giggles all the way down.

When they reached the bottom, Sophia hopped up quickly and ran over to grab Jett's hand. "I go with Uncle Jett next!"

Chris got up and picked up their sled. "Of course, because we all know Daddy's chopped liver when Uncle Jett's around."

Jett swung Sophia up into the air and caught her, holding her with one arm and the sled in the other. He looked at Zoey with a grin. "Now is the hard part...we have to walk back up."

She looked at the roped off side of the hill where people were making their way back up with various sleds and saucers.

"At least this place has stairs so it's not like mountain climbing," Chris said, leading the way to the stairway.

Jett was absolutely right. The trek back up the hill was definitely the hard part. Zoey was nearly winded by the time they got back up and needed to pause to catch her breath.

"You okay?" Jett put a gentle hand on her back.

"Oh yeah," she panted. "I'm just wishing I was a more active participant in gym class."

"Really? You don't run or anything?" Jett's gaze swept her from head to toe.

"No, just yoga. Which is great, but maybe I should do more cardio."

"Ooh, bendy, are we?" Jett raised his eyebrows suggestively.

She poked his side playfully. "Guess you'll have to find out."

"Come on, Uncle Jett!" Sophia's little voice called from where she stood next to her pink princess sled.

"I don't think Uncle Jett's gonna fit on that sled, sweetie," Jett said hesitantly. "Uncle Jett might break it. Why don't we use mine?"

"Princess Tiana sled!" Sophia insisted, shaking the rope of the little pink sled. "Pleeeease?"

Jett sighed. Turning to Zoey he said in a low voice, "Guess I'm gonna go sit on Princess Tiana's face. Hope I don't break it."

Zoey looked down as she laughed into her hand. "Oh, I can't wait to watch this." She stood next to Victoria as Jett and Sophia got situated on the small sled.

"Why didn't Daddy have to use the little sled? He used the big green one," she heard Jett say as Sophia sat in his lap.

"This might be the cutest thing I have ever seen," Zoey said with a wide grin, not taking her eyes off of Jett.

"Oh, she's got that man wrapped around her little finger," Victoria replied, watching with amusement, too. She wore her hair in her natural curls with a pair of earmuffs working simultaneously as a headband. Victoria's dark skin obviously wasn't reddening from the cold, but Zoey could still tell she was still freezing with each sniffle. Apparently living in the cold didn't make you completely immune to it.

"Everything is about Uncle Jett. It frustrates Tyler to no end. He'll come to visit and she'll just go on about how 'this is how Uncle Jett plays this game', 'Uncle Jett makes me chocolate chip pancakes for dinner', 'Uncle Jett wears the big hat when we have tea parties'."

Zoey let out a burst of laughter. "Oh my God, please invite me over next time there's a tea party."

"He does accents, too." Victoria smiled fondly. "A horrible British one, usually. But Sophia loves it."

Zoey watched as Jett and Sophia went over the peak of the hill and heard the little girl squealing and giggling the whole way down again. They must've hit a small bump near the bottom of the hill, because the sled went sideways. Victoria gasped, then relaxed when she saw that Jett had held onto her young daughter and she was perfectly unharmed.

"I hope you're able to make it work." Victoria said, readjusting her scarf and holding her coat tight to herself as a gust of wind blew over them. "I know with you being in California and him being here, it's complicated, but he completely adores you."

Zoey was caught somewhere between feeling warm at the nice words and halted by having the issue of distance being pointed out.

Of course she'd thought of it. That was the whole reason she was just going to let it be back in September when they'd stopped communicating regularly. But then she had been hit by the sudden urge to see if this thing would work, made a rash decision to come here, and things were great. But then what? It was possible that Zoey could do her job over the phone and stay in Michigan most of the time, but did she really want to be attached to her phone constantly? She'd have to be one of those people who wore a bluetooth earpiece everywhere just in case something came up. Her job required her to be reachable at all times.

"He's an amazing guy. Of course I'm sure you've figured that out by now. It doesn't take long to see it," Victoria continued, clearly oblivious to the minor panic her comment had caused. "I've known him since my freshman year of college, and he was just a goof. But a loyal goof. I couldn't tell you how many times Chris and I, or even me and my girlfriends would call Jett for a ride somewhere or to come pick us up from a party that was about to get broken up. He's always there for you, and will literally ask for nothing in return."

She had no trouble believing any of that. She had a hard time wondering how he hadn't been snatched up already, but wasn't about to complain about that.

"I hope we can make it work, too." It was all she could say without getting on a tangent. Without letting her brain spiral out of control with a million questions about how they were going to make it work long term.

Jett and Sophia made their way back up the hill, Sophia riding piggyback on her beloved uncle. As soon as he set her back on the snow, she was jumping up and down, wanting to go again.

"Uncle Jett! Let's *go!* Let's go again!" Sophia cheered, grabbing onto his hand.

"All right, but I say we race." Jett met Zoey's eyes and they brightened, "Me and Zoey against you and your dad."

Sophia squealed with excitement and hopped over to Chris, grabbing his hand and pulling him toward the edge of the hill.

Jett pulled Zoey close and kissed her forehead. He kept his lips on her and spoke low, "Don't be scared to wiggle that cute booty on me again."

She grinned and felt her cheeks redden just as her phone began ringing in her pocket. Pulling her gloves off, she unzipped her coat pocket and took her phone out with a quick apology to Jett. "Hi Quinn, what's up?"

"Did you see the new article that came out?" Quinn's voice was a combination of panic and anger. "People are printing shit about my *mom* now. Her condition, and digging into my past- I'm not doing a fucking exposeé about my tragic childhood. I don't care how much it makes me seem more real or relatable or understandable- it's no one's business."

"Whoa, whoa, slow down…" Zoey turned away from Jett and walked a few paces. "There's an article out about your mom's health?"

"Yes. They're talking about how she was seen going to a clinic for her dialysis treatments and now people are fucking speculating about what put her there. Somehow they know she has kidney disease, and it's not just articles online. There was a goddamn talk show of all these gossiping assholes going on about how 'Quinn Casey must've come from a troubled home' and how that *explains* me somehow."

"Don't you guys leave for Paris tomorrow?" Zoey caught Jett's curious gaze and responded with an apologetic look.

"Yeah, and I don't need people fucking snooping around my mom's house. This shit's none of their goddamn business."

She'd never heard him so fired up about something. He rarely cared what was printed about him in the press, what people said about his sex life or aggressive behavior. This was new. She supposed he really had worked to keep his past a secret for years. Clearly it was important that people remain ignorant about it- even *she* still didn't know all the details.

"Quinn, it'll be fine. With you leaving for a couple of weeks, it'll give people time to settle down about it. If no one can contact you for a comment-"

"Yeah, I'll give them a fucking comment: Back the fuck off. It's none of your goddamn business...*fuck*."

"Quinn, listen to me. I'll handle it, but you're leaving at the right time. By the time you get back, they'll move onto something else."

"And if they don't?" he asked. She could hear the nervous tension in his voice.

Zoey hesitated. Quinn always avoided questions about his past. She tried pushing every now and then, but never too hard. He had the ability to cut off the interrogation with a look. Quinn might be baseball's sexy, fun-loving playboy, but there was another side to him. A darkness that he kept tucked away.

"You're going to have to tell me, Quinn," she said finally. She closed her eyes with a wince, anticipating his angry response. "If I know everything that you want to keep hidden, I'll be able to redirect their attention. Come up with a cover story. But...you need to talk to me."

Stony silence met her on the other end. It was uncomfortable and she could practically feel the tension radiating through the phone, but she remained quiet, waiting for him to break the silence.

"Things at home, Zo...growing up like that..." Quinn let out a heavy breath. "It was bad, okay? I don't want to dig it up again. I'm trying to start over with my mom and this is all just bringing it back."

Chewing the inside of her lip, she debated pushing for more or respecting his privacy. She opted for the latter. For now.

"Consider it handled, Quinn. We'll ask people to respect you and your mother's privacy and if they can't do that, then we'll come up with a plan B, okay?"

He let out another breath and Zoey was sure she'd heard Rae's voice in the background. "Sorry, Zo. I don't mean to be yelling at you, I just...fuck, I don't like people knowing about this shit."

"I know. I've got this, okay? Go to Paris, have fun, relax, have a ridiculous amount of sex with your fiancé, and everything will be fine when you get back. Trust me."

"Yeah, okay. Thanks, Zo. You're the best."

Tucking her phone back into her pocket and making her way back to Jett and Chris, she offered a half-hearted smile. "Work stuff."

"Was that Case?"

She nodded. "Yeah, could you hear him? I've never heard him so worked up before."

"Everything okay?" Jett furrowed his brow. "He wasn't yelling at *you*, was he? Because I'll have to talk to him about that."

"No," Zoey nearly laughed. "Some media outlets are digging into his past, trying to figure out his...issues with his mom."

Chris grimaced. "Ugh...yeah, that's always been a touchy subject."

"So does that mean you have to work or...?" Jett asked.

"No. Or, not right now. It can wait. Let's race." She reached up on her toes and kissed Jett's cheek. He was so cute when he was concerned like that.

"What about me?" Victoria asked, grabbing the green sled out of Chris's hands. "I think I can beat all of you."

Giggling, Sophia jumped up and down with excitement watching her mom join in.

They lined up their sleds and got ready. Sophia had the honor of shouting 'on your mark, get set- go!' before all three sleds were sent down the hill in a blur. It was hard to tell who won the race, but they let Sophia decide the winner- Victoria. The group went back up and down the hill at least six more times until everyone was cold and exhausted. Sophia protested, but fell asleep almost instantly on the drive home.

In the back seat of Chris and Victoria's SUV, Zoey took the middle seat next to Sophia's car seat and leaned on Jett who kept his arm wrapped around her shoulders. She felt like she could fall asleep in his arms like this, even though she was shivering. She had no idea the snow could make her feel chilled to the bone, and couldn't wait to get back to the hotel and get into some fresh, dry clothes.

For now, though, Jett's fingers laced with hers as his other hand traced lightly up and down her arm. She rested her head on his shoulder and breathed him in.

She didn't want this to end. This time with him, with them together. She didn't know how she was supposed to go back to California and just leave him behind. But that phone call had been a swift reminder of just how much of her time and attention was required to do her job.

There was no going back to how things were, that was for sure. She just had no idea what a future with Jett looked like. She only knew that she really hoped there was one.

CHAPTER 13

At the apartment, Jett was getting the shower set up for Zoey so she could warm up. He hadn't realized how cold she was until an intense shiver ripped through her in his truck. Instead of taking her back to the hotel, he drove them both back to his place to ensure she warmed up properly. Okay, she was probably capable of doing that by herself, but he really liked taking care of her.

"This thing's kind of messed up. I've been meaning to fix it, but haven't had the time." Jett wiggled the diverter on the shower faucet and it finally switched to the overhead spray. "There. It's set on hot." He leaned back out of the shower and turned toward Zoey who was smiling at him, lips pressed together. "What?"

"Nothing...I just...could get used to you taking care of me like this. I feel like I should return the favor."

"I enjoy it," he replied simply. "You don't have to do anything special for me." He lingered for what was probably too long before realizing the shower was steaming up and she was still shivering. "I'll let you shower and, uh...pick out some clothes for you to wear. Hope you're okay with sweatpants." Kissing her on the cheek, he then dipped out of the bathroom and headed down the hall to his room.

The sound of the shower curtain being drawn shut caught his attention and he couldn't help the image that took shape in his head. Zoey in his shower. Naked. Standing under the hot spray of water with steam billowing around her.

Fuck, man. Control yourself.

He focused on finding her some clothes to wear and trying his best to busy his mind with thoughts other than the fact that she was fully naked, in his apartment. Just through the door, down the hall, and through another door. And a curtain. Zoey. Was naked.

Yeah, that worked really well, guy. Good job.

Settling on a pair of black sweatpants, an old t-shirt, and a hoodie with his gym's logo, he folded them neatly and took them back into the bathroom- yes, where Zoey was naked and bathing herself. He left the stack of clothes on the counter and, thinking quickly, grabbed the towel that was hung up next to the shower for her. Down the hall, he tossed the towel in the dryer on high heat for a few minutes before taking it back to hang up for her.

In the kitchen, he got out different selections for hot beverages: Coffee, decaf, tea, hot cocoa. Realizing he didn't know which of these she preferred to drink, he made a mental note to ask some of the simpler questions: What's your favorite beverage? Are you a coffee drinker? Are you a morning person or a night owl? Do you sleep in complete silence or do you need white noise? Or music? What's your favorite movie? Television show?

They were things that were likely acquired over time by observations or casual conversation, but he found himself wanting to know everything about her. He knew she had siblings and that as the oldest she'd taken care of them a lot, but what about her parents? What were they like? Were they together? Separated? Did they get along?

Lost in thought with his finger tracing the ridge on his coffee mug, he didn't realize right away that Zoey was standing just outside the kitchen, watching him curiously.

"You okay?" She took a step closer to him. "You seem...deep in thought."

Jett blinked. Her wavy hair was wet and tousled to one side, and she stood in front of him only wrapped in the gray and white striped towel that he'd warmed for her.

His throat was suddenly dry and he had to clear it to speak. "I, uh...I put some clothes on the counter for you in there."

"Yeah, I saw them." She took another step closer. "You warmed my towel."

"I did."

A smile curved up her lips and her hazel eyes brightened as they looked up at him. She inhaled and looked down at her bare feet. Jett followed and noticed her toes were painted red. Taking one step closer, she was only inches from him when she let her towel fall to the floor.

Jett's eyes did a slow scan from her red toenails, up her lean legs. She was bare between her legs, which he'd known from feeling her, but he'd yet to see it. Her stomach was flat, her waist narrow, and her breasts were full and round. They weren't overly large, but seemed big on her small frame. His eyes lingered there for several long seconds before continuing up to her collarbone and neck, which he'd already kiss and licked and sucked at so many times. He knew exactly how that skin felt on his mouth and tongue.

When he reached her eyes again, her gaze was heated. The desire that lit her eyes acted like a hook, reeling him in with no hope of escape. Not that he wanted to anyway.

It was sudden and urgent, the way he dipped his head to cover her mouth with his. The way he pulled her body into his, instinctively. Possessively. He hitched her up onto his waist and carried her through the apartment, down the hall and to his bedroom. Shutting the door behind them, he swept over to the bed and lay her gently on the covers.

He hovered over her now, appreciating the view of her beneath him. Forcing himself to slow down because he wanted to savor this moment, this whole thing that had been built up over the past week and was now here. Right in front of him. Her fingers reached up to trace his jawline and those hazel eyes flickered back and forth between his own gaze.

Jett dipped his head to brush his lips against hers, letting his hands explore. Over the curve of her hips, her small waist, her ribs, palming her breasts and massaging them gently. A moan escaped her lips as he brushed the pad of his thumb over her nipples. He trailed his mouth down her jaw, her neck, tracing his tongue along her collarbone. The need to explore, to touch and feel and taste every inch of her was combatting with the urge to just take all of her now. All at once.

Zoey's fingers grasped at the hem of his shirt and pulled it over his head. Splaying her hands across his chest, she let them slide down and feel him, too. Unbuttoning and unzipping his jeans, her finger tips played around the band of his boxers.

His heart was pounding, veins pulsing, blood rushing. It felt like he'd waited a lifetime to be with her. With this one woman. He wanted to savor everything. Use his gentle kisses and touches to draw out her moans and gasps of pleasure. Move inside her, feel himself fill her up over and over until she was quivering around him. He needed to know she was as desperate for him as he was.

His lips moved down, brushing lightly across her soft golden skin. He kissed the soft skin of her breast, trailed a tongue around her nipple before sucking it into his mouth. She arched into him and he groaned. Every little response of her body, he was storing in his mind. He needed to memorize everything she liked, the things that made her moan, what made her gasp or grab needily at his shoulders so he could repeat them on a loop.

Her hands ran up his sides and over his shoulders, to the back of his neck. Fingers pushed into his hair and pulled him closer as he moved to give the same attention to her other breast. She was always quiet, as if holding in her thoughts, her wants, her needs. Jett was determined to bring those out. No more holding back, he wanted it all.

He rutted against her, pressing his length into her bare skin and she gasped. There was something about her being completely naked beneath him while he was still clothed that made him want to be that much gentler with her. Was the roughness of his jeans too harsh against her bare skin? Or did she enjoy it?

Zoey's hands reached down to his hips and pulled them, forcing him to grind into her again. He let her guide him, and watched as her hips rose to meet his. She arched her neck back, eyes closed, looking completely lost in the sensation.

He was hard. So fucking hard. Rock solid. But he wasn't making this about him yet. He needed to hear her let go, feel her give over to him.

His lips continued their path down her body, pressing kisses along her ribs, her stomach, sucking at her sharp hip bones. He was laying between her legs, kissing her thighs, trailing his teeth up and down her smooth skin. Looking up, he saw that she was studying him. Without breaking eye contact, he traced a finger down her crease where she was glistening and wet. He asked the question with his eyes- *is this okay?*- and felt her body relax with an exhale as she tangled her fingers in his hair again.

She was warm between her thighs, heat radiating off her, and he could tell she was struggling to keep her hips still. They wanted to move, thrust upward in a greedy, demanding motion. He kissed her sex lightly and she gasped and whimpered. He couldn't see it, but knew she was biting her lip to restrain herself from telling him exactly what she wanted. He kissed her again, this time sliding a finger between her glistening lips.

She let out a quick breath and rocked her hips up. "Please...Jett, *please.*"

He flicked his tongue around her clit, licking and sucking. She responded instantly, moving her hips into him, setting the pace she wanted. Wrapping an arm under and around her thigh, he used it to anchor her. He could pull her into him like this, or just rub smooth circles against her skin with his palm while his mouth and other hand worked to drive her wild.

He was lost in her. Tongue and teeth and fingers against her soft wet skin. Her sounds, finally letting loose. Finally giving over to him. Trusting him with her body. He wanted to hear her, wanted those words of encouragement with each touch, each kiss.

Oh God...yes, please...please, Jett, more. Don't stop...oh yes, don't stop.

Each little praise fueled him. Sparked a fire, completely desperate to please her. Her cries for more were everything he needed. Knowing she was enjoying his touch, feeling her get wetter for him on his lips made his dick throb and ache. It was a fucking miracle it was still tucked inside his boxers and hadn't completely unleashed itself.

He reached down and pushed his boxers and jeans down farther so he could stroke himself. Pleasing her had him hard beyond belief and he felt like he'd fucking explode if he didn't touch himself to this. Groaning into her skin as he wrapped a fist around his cock, he felt a pull at his heart in his chest. He wasn't sure if he was going to implode or burst or pass out, but there was absolutely nothing more erotic than this. At least that, he knew.

Curling a finger inside her, she lifted her hips off the mattress with a drawn out moan of pleasure. He flicked his tongue against her clit again and slid another finger inside her.

"Yes!" Zoey was crying out, "Oh God, yes! There...*there*...Oh God, don't you stop, Jett, *please!*"

She gasped and shuddered and he watched as her body covered in goosebumps, watched the pink color spread up her body as she continued to cry out. She contracted tight around his two fingers for what seemed like several minutes, keeping his mouth latched onto her pulsing clit. He felt her body relax around him and she sighed, sinking into the mattress. Her fingers were still fisted in his hair, but she relaxed her grip and began massaging his scalp gently.

Jett moved back up her body, leaving a trail of kisses on the way. Her hips, ribs, between her breasts. He kissed her neck, jaw, and temple, sweeping a hand into her hair and watching as her eyes peered up at him.

"That okay?" He ticked an eyebrow up and pressed his lips to her jaw again.

She sighed with a breathy, incredulous laugh. *"Okay?"* Zoey's hands skated up and down his sides, down his chest, over his stomach, before she took him in her hand again. Her eyes broke from his as she gazed between their bodies.

He took a slow breath through his nose as he watched her stroke his length. His eyes closed and he let out a low groan as she cupped his balls in her hand before sliding her hand back up his cock. Her thumb brushed over the head where pre-cum was accumulating.

"If you keep touching me like that, we're going to have a mess to clean up," he warned, but moved his hips, sliding his cock through her hands.

"You're so thick," she breathed, not taking her eyes off where she was feeling him. "So long...*God*, it's a wonder you can keep this thing hidden."

Jett groaned again, feeling his chest and stomach do flips at her praising words. "Think we can make it work for you?"

"We'll make it work." Zoey reached behind his neck and pulled his mouth to hers.

Their kiss became fervent, demanding, as she continued rolling her hips up to him, and he rocked in and out of her hand that still held him. Jett kicked his jeans and boxers off the rest of the way. He moved his hand down their bodies and between her legs again, feeling, circling her clit, sliding fingers into her until she was grasping, begging for him.

He reached over to his nightstand and grabbed a condom out of the drawer. He sat back to roll the latex over his full length. Zoey bit her lip as she watched, and he felt his heart pounding again. His dick was harder than it had ever been and was aching for release *now*, but he was going to take it slow. Make sure it felt good and that she adjusted to his size before thrusting too greedily.

Settling between her legs, he held himself at the base and traced the head of his cock along her slick skin. It was a chore to not dive right into her. Laying so vulnerable beneath him, with those gorgeous tits rising and falling with her bracing, steady breaths. Legs spread for him, inviting him in. He'd imagined this a time or two, but he'd forgotten about how frenzied he'd feel, how impatient.

Slowly he dipped the head in. And out. Back in, pushing just a little further. Back out. He placed a hand on the side of her head, looking into her eyes as he pushed in again. She gasped as he held himself back.

"Shh, just relax, baby. We'll go slow," he assured her.

Her body relaxed beneath him and he inched in slowly...*torturously* slow. Jett couldn't believe his willpower to hold back, but he knew she needed to adjust. Zoey gasped again before it turned into a moan and she began pushing her hips into him, asking for more.

"Please, Jett," she panted. "Please, I want to feel all of you."

He groaned, nearly letting out a growl as he finished pushing into her, seating himself deep. She let out a moan that made his cock stiffen even more and as she wrapped her legs around his waist. Holding himself there, he breathed through the overwhelming pleasure of her heat, squeezing him so tight. Too damn good.

"Holy hell," he groaned. "Goddamn, baby, you feel like heaven."

Zoey whimpered, her short, panting breaths puffing against his neck as she adjusted to him. Then she curled her fingers in his hair and pulled his mouth down to hers, slowly moving her hips and making him groan against her as they moved together.

Moving slowly over her, out, and back in, slowly out, even slower back inside, she gasped and pushed her hips into him again. He kissed her neck, sucked at the spot just below her jaw, feeling how tightly she was wrapped around him. He'd have to go slow. Goddamn, she was so tight, there was no way he'd last if he thrusted too hard, too fast.

"So...good..." she moaned. "You feel...so good."

He moaned into her neck, still rocking slowly into her. He was tempted to pick up pace, but he needed to make this last. He needed to enjoy the feel of her skin against his, her nipples brushing against him as he moved over her. "Does it hurt, baby?"

Zoey shook her head and hummed. "It's really...really good. So full..."

With a grunt, he increased the pace just slightly. She began to unravel. Clawing at his shoulders, scratching his back, whispering into his ear as he sucked on her neck. They were pressed together in a tangle of limbs, wet kisses and tongues. She fisted his hair, pulled him closer, urged him to move faster. He studied every response of her body, savored each gasp, each whimper of pleasure.

"Faster, Jett...oh God, you're so deep, oh my-" Her pleas were panting and desperate. The most beautiful sounds he'd ever heard.

He sat back on his heels and watched himself entering her. Hands wrapped around her hips, he pulled her into his lap as he sent his thrusts just a little harder. He watched her tits move with each movement of his hips, and it made his mouth water, wanting to suck on them.

"Zo, you're so fucking beautiful. Fucking gorgeous. You have...the most perfect tits." Jett continued to watch them with a heavy-lidded gaze, obsessed with this view.

"Your mouth," she reached for him, "I want your mouth on them."

Instantly, he leaned over her again, laying his weight on her as his mouth came over one breast, then the other. She arched against him. Moaned, pleaded, and praised him. *Oh yes, Jett...please, yes. That's so good...oh God, you feel so good.*

If it were possible to touch and kiss and lick her everywhere, all at once, he would. He wanted to devour her, claim her, please her. He wanted everything for her. He wanted to hear his name on her lips as she came, wanted her to whisper all her thoughts in his ear, to hear how he made her feel.

"You're so tight around me, baby," he breathed against her skin, "You feel so perfect...It's so good. *Too* good." He adjusted his thrusts so that he was rubbing against her clit as he moved into her and she gasped, digging her nails into the back of his neck from the pleasure.

"Oh yes, Jett...just like that. Oh my God..." She threw her head back and let him continue his work on her body. Drawing out that perfect orgasm by feeling, kissing, and rubbing all those perfect spots.

He felt when her body reached its peak. Opening his eyes to watch her unwind beneath him, he saw the flush of her skin, the tightening of her muscles. She grasped his hair and pressed her hips into him, nearly screaming as she squeezed even tighter around his cock.

And that was it for him. She was so small, so tight, and now tighter, wrapping and contracting around his throbbing shaft. He picked her hips up again and sent his final frenzied thrusts into her, no longer worrying about going too hard or too fast. He couldn't help himself from the rare moment of greed, taking what he needed from her body.

Sweat dripped off of him as he bit out a slur of deep, shaky praises. "Oh my God... fuck...*yes...*" He collapsed over her, breathing heavily as he felt his cock still pulsating inside her.

Jett's forehead rested against her shoulder as they both caught their breath, and she took his face in her hands. She kissed his temples, his cheeks, his jaw, the corner of his mouth. He loved that she did this. It was her way of thanking him or saying he did a good job. Maybe it was silly to like it so much, but he'd come to look forward to the reassurance she gave him.

"That was so good..." Zoey whispered into his ear. She pressed her lips just below his ear before whispering again, "So...so good, Jett."

Zoey watched over the counter as Jett finished making two cups of hot cocoa for them. He brought the steaming mugs over to the couch and sat next to her. She was wearing his clothes while her own were in the dryer, and she loved being surrounded by his scent. She leaned her back into his chest and he draped his arm lazily around her, kissing the side of her head sweetly.

"Do you watch anything besides Christmas movies?" She asked, eyes on the TV screen where *Christmas Vacation* played.

"Not in December, no."

"Is it safe to assume that Christmas is your favorite holiday then?" She took a sip of her hot cocoa and sighed as she felt it warm her from the inside.

"Definitely. And yours?"

"Also Christmas," she replied. "I thought I'd like it more with snow, but I had no idea it makes you cold to the bone after being out in it all day. I have no idea how you do it."

Jett hummed with a laugh. "You get used to it. I thought I did a pretty good job warming you up."

Heat flared in her cheeks as she smiled. "You did a great job."

"Oh yeah?"

She took another sip from her mug before leaning forward and setting it on a coaster on the coffee table. "Actually, you did such a great job…" she turned around to face him, sitting in his lap with her legs straddling his, "I might just have to return the favor."

Jett's eyes went wide before grinning and setting his own mug on the end table behind him. "And how would you do that?"

She began kissing him. His temple, his cheeks, his jaw, his lips. Her tongue found his and she melted into the taste of him, savoring and moaning against his lips as they kissed deeper. Her hands curled behind his neck and she rolled her hips in his lap. It wasn't long before she could feel him again beneath his sweatpants.

Less than an hour ago he was inside her, and the memory of him was imprinted between her legs. She could still feel him, the dull ache he'd left behind, but she suddenly felt that it wasn't enough. She wasn't sure it would ever be enough. He was full, thick, and long, and so, *so* big. But she didn't think she could ever stop wanting him. The way his body drew hers in was unstoppable, and it was unlike anything she'd experienced with anyone else.

She wasn't quite as experienced in the sexual sense as some of the other girls her age, but already she didn't have to guide Jett. She didn't have to speak or move his hands or adjust her body under his. He listened. His body listened to hers and gave her exactly what she wanted.

He lifted the oversized t-shirt over her head and his mouth covered a nipple while his hand teased the other. She felt both frantic and at ease when she pulled his shirt off, watching her fingernails scratch lightly down his chest and stomach. Stuck between wanting to savor him and wanting to feel him moving hard and fast inside her, she felt her way down his body, grasping him over his pants.

Her eyes drank him in; broad chest peppered with dark hair, the ripple of strong abs, and a trail that led from his navel down into his sweatpants where she knew that amazing cock was ready for her again. She'd never felt like she could just stare at someone's naked body, but she wanted to with him. She wanted to study him, feel him, watch him as he moved under her. Over her. She couldn't fathom why he'd ever be self-conscious or want to look more like his friends. His body was manly and strong and powerful.

He switched sides and sucked her other nipple into his mouth and she bowed her back, pressing her chest into him. She wanted him to bury his face in her breasts, worship them. And so he did.

One hand stroked the length of him, hard and eager, beneath the fabric of his sweatpants, while the other hand felt his shoulders, his chest, his stomach, before skating back up to start over. "I love how you feel, Jett," she whispered. "I love feeling your body."

He groaned into her skin as though she'd said exactly what he'd wanted to hear. What he'd needed to hear.

She began working his pants back down and he paused. "Hang on," he breathed, "hang on." He reached into the pocket and pulled out a condom before helping her with the task of getting him out of his pants. She lifted an eyebrow at him and he grinned. "Thought I should be prepared."

"Good call." She smiled into his lips. He then helped her undress and dipped his hand down to feel her. Zoey hissed at his touch, still swollen and sensitive, but she was wet and willing to push through just to be full of him again.

"You okay?"

She nodded, grinding herself against him. She wanted him to know how badly she craved him, to feel how much she needed him.

"Don't lie to me," he growled into her neck. "I don't want to hurt you."

"You won't." She ran her hands over him again, and danced her fingers on his tip before sliding down his shaft, cupping his balls, and coming back up. "Please, Jett...I want it."

Another groan came from deep inside his chest, telling her she'd won this battle. She sensed she could always win with him. That he would always give her what she wanted as long as she asked.

He ripped open the condom wrapper and slid it over his hard flesh as she watched. He grabbed her hips and pulled her forward with a whisper, "Come here."

She hovered over him and fisted the base of his cock, staring into his blazing green eyes as she lowered herself onto him slowly... slowly... *right...there.* She sighed, pressing her forehead to his and they both watched as she began riding him. Slowly. Deliberately. Feeling inch by thick inch of him slide out...and back in.

There were no words between them, just breathing. Steady and controlled at first. Biting back a whimper, she began rolling her hips more smoothly, a little faster. She felt right where her clit was rubbing itself on him. *So...good.*

As she increased her pace, he began lifting his hips to meet hers. He was no longer watching himself enter her, but he was studying her face. Watching for her expression to tell him what she liked, what she needed.

Zoey leaned over him, letting her nipples brush against his skin, letting her body slide against his and- *oh God..there. Right there.*

She gasped and curled her fingers into Jett's hair, letting the explosion go off from deep inside, spreading like wildfire, flaring heat all over her skin as she cried out.

Jett groaned and his breathing came in rasps, getting off on her pleasure. "Don't hold back, Zo. Ride it, baby, ride that cock."

His voice was thick with need and she was desperate to please him, to do exactly as he said because she already trusted that he knew what her body needed. She rode out her orgasm, taking everything she needed from having him inside her until she finally relaxed with a long, shuddering, sigh into his neck.

Jett wrapped his arms around her and rolled, pulling her down onto the floor beneath him. He grabbed the blanket off the couch and threw it over them before dipping his head to her neck where he began sucking, kissing, and licking. Still inside her, he moved slowly, his weight pressing her down. She liked it best with their bodies pressed together, feeling his skin move with hers.

Watching him move over her, she saw his face was set in concentration. He was still studying her, listening and responding to her body's every need. God, he was so attentive. So determined to give her everything. His hands moved over her breasts, down her sides, her hips, traced down and back up her thighs. Back up her sides, he pushed her hands over her head and laced his fingers with hers as he held her down.

Mouth and tongue traced her neck and collarbone, finding her breasts, before working back to her neck. Just below the jaw, beneath the ear where she loved it the most. The man left no surface untouched.

"*So* good...oh God, it's so good," she panted as she felt him move inside her. He filled her completely. So deep, he pressed right where she needed him. She'd never felt so full, she was sure her body would never have room for anything but him ever again. Butterflies danced around in her stomach when she realized she would still feel him inside her long after their bodies parted.

He moved faster, harder, *deeper*, as if that were somehow possible. His grunts and breaths became hungry, ravenous. He needed her as much as she needed him. This wasn't just sex. And it wasn't just *fucking*. But it was way too soon to call it anything else, wasn't it?

They were connected, and it was so much more than physical. She was lost in him and he was lost in her and she couldn't imagine ever wanting anything else. As satisfying and amazing and unworldly as he felt, she couldn't get enough. Enough of his touch, his mouth, his movements.

She came undone beneath him, coming and screaming, letting loose anything that she'd normally hold back. It felt impossible that it could be that good. But it was.

He turned wild over her, frantic and frenzied, hard and fast. He was groaning and calling out, *Oh fuck, that's it, baby...* He shook, his muscles tightening, his body shuddering, sweating, twitching, before he collapsed over her again.

He breathed into her neck, and they were both hot and sticky with sweat. He kissed down her neck and shoulders and propped himself up to look at her.

"Was that...okay?"

She almost wanted to laugh at the question. The sex was obviously more than okay. What was happening between them was more, too. More than okay. More than what she'd expected. And happening so much faster than she knew was possible. She wasn't entirely sure how to answer the question with words, so instead she put a hand on the side of his face and brought him down to her for a kiss.

Jett pulled her back up to the couch, and they kept their clothes off, letting their arms and legs tangle around each other beneath the blanket. Her head rested on his chest and he continued a steady trail of his fingers up and down her arm as they turned their attention back to the movie. Every now and then Jett would press his lips to the top of her head in a sweet kiss, and she couldn't imagine ever wanting to be in someone else's arms.

CHAPTER 14

Jett stirred at the faint knocking sound on the front door. His arm squeezed tighter around warm, soft skin and his eyes opened. He let out a satisfied sigh at the sight of Zoey in his arms, pressed against him, face buried in his chest. He placed a kiss on the top of her head and relaxed back into his spot on the couch.

Another knock on the door reminded him what woke him in the first place.

As he tried to figure out the best way to get out from under Zoey without waking her, the door to his apartment flew open.

"Is Zoey here?" Quinn let himself into the apartment, and his eyes went wide at the sight on the couch. "Oh..." His face twisted into a knowing grin. "Ooh..."

"What do you want, Case?" Jett whisper-yelled to his friend. Quinn was wearing a black leather jacket over a gray team hoodie, and distressed blue jeans with a pair of black and white Converse. Jett couldn't help wondering how much the guy paid for blue jeans that looked like they'd been dragged behind a car for five miles.

"I've been trying to call her all night. She's always got her phone on her."

Glancing at the still-sleeping woman on his chest and back up at Quinn, he gave him an annoyed glare. "Well, she's been here, so..."

"I see...she's been otherwise occupied. Good job, buddy." Quinn winked and gave him a thumbs up. "But seriously, I need to talk to her and I don't have a lot of time."

"Aren't you leaving this morning?"

"Yeah, that's why I need to talk to her now."

"I'm not waking her up," Jett was still whispering. "Dude, Case...we're *naked*. Can you like...call her when you land or something?"

Ignoring Jett completely, Quinn shouted into the room, "Zoey!"

Jett jumped and wrapped his arms around her tighter. *Jesus*, Case. You fucking psycho." Zoey stirred in his arms and groaned, burying her face further into Jett's chest. "Could you let her sleep? I'll take a damn message and she'll call you later."

Quinn smirked. "Damn, Jett. You wore her out with that deep-V diver, huh?" When Jett's glare didn't falter, Quinn checked his watch and sighed. "Fine. Tell her that Rae's not getting charged for punching that chick in the face *and* there are about four networks trying to get an interview with me about my childhood, and that's not fucking happening. No questions, no stipulations, no negotiations. I'm not doing it."

"That could've been in a text, Case. Or an email," Jett said, incredulous. It was hard to believe this was the same guy who was always so insistent on doing things for himself, and only ever reluctantly accepted help. Jett was beginning to wonder how much Quinn relied on Zoey and how much of her time he took up.

Quinn took a step toward the door. "I'm proud of you, kid!"

"Have fun in Paris with your future wife," Jett said, waving him out the door.

"Oh, that's right. Rae has something for you..." Quinn reached into his jacket pocket and threw what looked like large chunks of pink and red confetti into the room. "Congrats on becoming a man! We knew you had it in you!" Quinn's sly grin was plastered to his face as he slipped out the door.

Squinting in confusion at what had just been littered all over the floor, he realized what they were.

"Fucking flower petals..." Yeah, that had Rae written all over it. Jett laughed in spite of himself and settled back into the couch.

"I have to ask…" Jett began, pouring Zoey a cup of coffee. She sat on one of the bar stools at the half bar of his kitchen. "Exactly how much do you do for Quinn? Because it seems like there's a lot of shit he could do for himself that he just pushes onto you."

After waking up, she'd been so cute and shy about having fallen asleep on the couch. She'd asked why he hadn't woken her up to move to the bed, and also if she'd dreamt that Quinn had walked into the apartment and been absurdly loud.

Zoey's mouth tugged up in a shy, almost embarrassed grin. "Honestly, there's a chance I go above and beyond the duties of a publicist. I'm more like a publicist *slash* personal assistant *slash* personal secretary. But he hired me directly rather than from a firm. It's got its benefits, though. I schedule his interviews and conferences, I tell him where he needs to be and when, I manage his image, I speak to the press for him a lot. Sometimes I have to coordinate with the team's PR team and their rules." She chuckled. "I swear the people in that department hate him sometimes. Baseball is supposed to be a wholesome, family fun event, and I don't think I have to tell you most of Quinn's photoshoots aren't exactly family-friendly."

Jett smirked as he sipped his coffee.

Zoey continued, "I probably don't have to make his doctor appointments, but I do. I'm sure he could communicate with his personal trainer, but it goes in the calendar and I manage his calendar, so it's just easier sometimes so he doesn't schedule a session over a press conference or something."

Jett slid her mug over to her and took the seat next to her. "That sounds insane. I wonder…" he paused, hesitating for a beat, "I wonder if he takes advantage of you doing all that for him because he had to do everything for himself as a kid."

Zoey glanced up from her mug curiously. "How do you mean?"

"Well, you know about his mom and how he grew up," he replied. "The kid was on his own except when the DeRoses stepped in. And even then it was a fight. He pushed back when my parents tried to do stuff for him, too."

"Honestly," she sighed and wrapped her hands around the warm mug, "he only told me the bare minimum about his home situation. So I guess, no, I really don't know about that. I sort of just figured he enjoyed having people do stuff for him so he could mess around, and I've been playing the 'mom' role since I was nine, so it just worked."

"Since you were nine? Why nine?"

"Oh, well…" Jett watched her chew on her bottom lip. She tucked a piece of hair behind her ear and got fidgety, spinning her coffee mug and scratching at a speck on the countertop. Finally she cleared her throat and said, "My mom died from ovarian cancer when I was nine."

Jett stared, frozen in place. He was completely baffled that he hadn't already learned this about her. It was huge. This was the type of thing that defined a person. Just last night they'd been engaged in some of the most intimate love making he'd ever experienced. He'd thought that was huge, but this…this seemed like the kind of thing you know about a girl before you completely lose yourself inside her, fall to pieces on top of her, beneath her, and have to will your heart to not explode.

"Zoey, I'm…so sorry. How…I feel like a jerk. Like I should've asked about this before."

She gave a one-shouldered shrug. "It's fine…It's just not the type of thing that comes up naturally in conversation."

Jett studied her, brows furrowed in concentration, hoping she'd tell him more.

"It was…tough. My dad is a Marine Corps veteran and he was still recovering from an injury he got overseas. He was battling that, PTSD, and mental illness, and then mom got diagnosed. They were high school sweethearts. Dad put everything on hold to take care of her, but it had already spread too far. She died just over a year after the diagnosis, and Dad wasn't exactly in a state to take care of three kids on his own. So, I stepped up and did what I could."

She only looked up at him when she'd finished speaking and Jett held her gaze, staring in amazement at the things she'd been through. Suddenly the insecurities that had been itching at him over the past few weeks seemed to disappear. So what if he didn't have a multi-million dollar salary or trust fund like his friends? He had a family. A big one that liked to meddle in each and every part of his life, but he never had to give up his childhood for them.

"How old were your siblings?" Jett asked.

"Ace was six, and Cassie was four. Old enough to recognize Mom's absence. I had to sort of explain why she wasn't there a lot. Especially to Cassie." Zoey swirled her spoon around in her coffee cup. "I taught myself to cook, I got really organized and made sure Ace and Cassie had all their school things ready. That's probably why I'm so good at keeping up with crazy schedules. I had everything written out on the fridge and kept up with it. Dad's doctor's appointments, therapy, Ace's baseball practice, Cassie's dance lessons. I was the one who got after them about grades and reminded my dad about parent-teacher conferences. He got better and was able to help more eventually, but he was pretty distraught the first couple of years."

Not wanting to judge of course, Jett couldn't help thinking Zoey and her siblings must've been distraught, too. It seemed like a lot to put on a nine-year-old to take care of the family like that when she was also grieving.

"Do you guys still have a good relationship?"

"Yeah," she said, smiling fondly. "I talk to Dad on the phone almost every day. And I go visit him a couple times a week. We do yoga together on the back patio and eat ice cream- it's a good balance."

"That's good you still make time for family even with Case trying to take up all your time."

"I keep a pretty tight schedule of everything and everyone in my life." She drank deeply from her mug and sighed. "Sometimes it feels like there's not a second of my time that's not accounted for."

"Sounds kind of exhausting," Jett said, placing a hand on her arm. "Don't you ever want a break? Sounds like you could use some time to just worry about yourself for a change."

Zoey grinned, glancing sideways at him. "That's a little ironic coming from you, isn't it? Are you Pot or Kettle?"

He laughed quietly. "Okay, true. But it's different. I didn't have to do all that for my siblings. I choose to do things for my friends and people I care about, but I never had to. When I do it it's just a weird compulsion. A character flaw. I can't help it."

"It's definitely not a character flaw," she said with a laugh. "Maybe that's why I like you so much. You actually take care of me for a change instead of the other way around."

"Well, like I said, I enjoy taking care of you." Jett gently pushed his fingers back into her hair, holding the side of her face and letting his thumb trace her cheekbone. "I also enjoy learning about you. I want to know everything."

"Everything?" she asked, eyebrows raised.

"You asked for my entire life story on our first date," he pointed out. "You also interrupted me several times by puking, and then fell asleep during it. A little rude, but I got past it."

Zoey giggled, and he loved the way her whole body shook with her laugh. "You're a far better storyteller than I am though."

"I've got until four o'clock."

She aimed a quick glance at the clock on the stove then let out a defeated sigh, "Fine…"

She began with a story about when she was five and her little sister was born. She had apparently gotten up in the middle of the night when Cassie was crying, found her mother in the nursery, and, with her hands over both her ears, shouted at her mom, "Can't we take it back?!" She described it as one of the most selfish moments of her life.

Unlike when Jett was telling his stories, he never interrupted her to throw up. When they moved to the couch, however, he did interrupt her by taking his clothes off. She paused, having lost track of what story she was telling, but pushed through, opting to finish telling the story straddling and riding him on the couch.

About a half an hour later, she was in the middle of a story about playing hair salon at her friend's house. The friend had used real scissors instead of play ones and ended up giving her the worst haircut of all time. Jett chose this moment to slide down her body, between her legs, and kiss and lick her pink, swollen pussy until she was pulling his hair, bringing him closer, screaming and coming on his lips. He had to give her credit for being able to focus enough to tell the story up until her gasping and pleading made the words inaudible.

They'd moved to his bedroom at some point, and he moved over her, kissing and licking, exploring her whole body with his mouth while she told him about coming home from college to find that Ace and Cassie had thrown a complete rager and trashed their house. She was describing how furious she'd been when Jett reached into his nightstand for another condom.

"You don't *sound* furious," he said, playfully eyeing her as he rolled the condom on.

Her eyes glazed over as she watched him situate himself between her legs. "Well, I was…"

Jett smoothed a hand up her thigh and down before hitching her leg up onto his shoulder. He kissed her ankle, up to her calf and gazed down at her. "This okay?"

She responded with a nod, and he saw the rise and fall of her chest become more distinct. He pushed his thick length into her slowly, and she took in a sharp breath, the slightest furrow creasing her brow.

"You okay?" He brushed his fingers over her clit in a V-shape and she moaned with a shudder.

She nodded again and whispered, "More."

He pushed in again, rubbed her again, and her head fell back, eyes closed. She looked so gorgeous like this, giving over to him. He reached behind her and grabbed a pillow to place under her hips, then leaned into her, over her. He braced one hand on the bed next to her head and the other held her leg up on his shoulder. God, this was a good angle. He felt like he could reach all the way inside her, everywhere.

"Then what happened?" Jett asked, smirking at the way she bit her lip and smiled at his question.

"I…kicked everyone out," she began, "Oh *God*…and made them clean up- mmm, yes, I love how your fingers feel on me."

"Did they get in trouble?" He moved over her, rocked into her, quickening his pace. He wanted her to keep talking, to hear the transition where it became too much to form coherent words.

"Yes...*yes, God yes.*" Her back bowed off the mattress and he sent his thrusts deeper and faster. She moaned and whimpered, grasped at his ass to pull him closer, urging him to go harder. "You're so hard, Jett...*oh God, I love it*, you feel *so* good."

"Did they ever do it again?" Jett could tell she was getting close to losing herself, to making him want to fall into her.

"Yeah..." She let out a sigh. "Jett, *please*, you feel so good...your cock is so good."

Jett groaned into her ankle. He hadn't heard her say dirty words yet. She urged him on, told him *more, harder, faster*, but he'd never heard her say words like *cock* or *fuck*. He loved her innocence, but loved even more that he could make her shed it. Just for him.

He pumped into her, eliciting those gasps and moans from her sweet mouth. Her tits moved with each snap of his hips and his mouth was watering as he watched them. Fuck, he could watch them all day.

She was begging now, lost and wild, and it was all just for him. He relished being able to turn someone so cute and sweet into this writhing, sexy, insatiable being beneath him.

Yes, Jett...yes, ohmigod, yes!

He bent lower, folding her, kissing her mouth, her cheek, her jaw. He sucked at her bottom lip and felt her groan vibrate into him.

Small, sharp gasps came in fast as her body tightened around him, squeezing his cock, fisting his hair, hot breath against his lips.

She cried out, "Oh God, oh God, *ohmyfuckinggod!*"

His chest nearly exploded as he came with her. Sweat dripping, breath, hot and heavy as he pressed his teeth to her jaw with his shuddering, guttural groan. His sounds were so animalistic, he wasn't sure it was really him. He came so hard he saw stars and his body shook, thrusting into her over and over until he was completely empty.

This time he was the one showering her in kisses. Her face, her jaw, her neck, back to her mouth where their tongues connected and wrestled until their breathing settled.

There were only the sounds of their collected breaths, slowing and steadying. He could hear his own pulse thrumming in his ears and wondered if she could feel his heart beating as they lay chest-to-chest.

He slid out of her, tied off the condom and threw it away before collapsing back on the bed with her. He pulled her onto his chest and she curled into him. His body felt like gelatin, and he was hot all over, as if sparks had just been ignited on every inch of his skin.

"Hey Zo," he spoke into her hair and she hummed, "I think you're a way better storyteller than me."

He felt her body shake the way it did when she laughed. The feel of her body against his made his chest tug again. He knew he had a tendency to fall too hard too fast when he got into a relationship, but this felt different.

He *was* falling, and fast. And he thought she might be falling, too. But he feared that neither of them was prepared to talk about how to make a safe landing.

"Everything is going great, Dad. How are things with you and Cindy?"

Zoey was hanging up a bundle of clothes on hangers inside the closet of Rae's spare room. Since Quinn and Rae were vacationing in Paris for the next two weeks, Zoey was taking up residence at Raelyn's house and saving herself some serious hotel room expenses. Rae had even left her the Jeep to drive so she didn't have to catch a ride with an Uber if she wasn't with Jett. After the other night, she just wanted to fall asleep with Jett at his place again, and wasn't sure how much time she'd really be spending at Rae's house. Unfortunately, he'd been working closing shifts all week, so she'd been seeing him during the day before his shifts began instead.

"Oh no, Sweets," her dad said, and she could practically hear the shake of his head. "We're not focusing on me and Cindy right now. You promised to tell me more about this *Jett* guy when there was more to tell. It's been over two weeks now, so...tell me."

Somehow Zoey had managed to get around talking to her dad about Jett in their almost daily phone calls. Mostly she would tell him "It's still new" or "I'm seeing him again tonight" but had left out any finer details.

She let out a long sigh. "I suppose there's not much more I can do to stall." Then sitting back on the plush queen-size bed, she smiled dreamily. "Honestly, Dad, he's...pretty amazing."

"Amazing?" Lou repeated. "Wow, that's high praise from you. So you're saying it was worth the trip across the country into the arctic?"

Laying back on the pillows, she went on to tell her dad all about Jett Miller. How he'd taken care of her when she had to cancel their first date, and the carepackage he'd brought her. About the gorgeous bouquet of roses he brought for their actual first date, ice skating lessons, and watching him devour an entire platter of chicken tacos. She told him about meeting his friends and spending time with them on their sledding date, how he always opened doors for her and was a complete gentleman. His obsession with Christmas and Christmas movies, their frequent lunch dates, and she even gushed over his beautiful green eyes.

She left out all the couch make-out sessions, their sex marathon, and anything else that involved his wonderfully enormous penis. That particular detail was one she intended to keep entirely to herself.

"Wow, Zo, he sounds like quite the catch," said Lou. "Any idea why he's still single? Or have you not uncovered that piece of the puzzle yet?"

"Dad." She rolled her eyes. "Why do you have to assume there's something bad? Or that he's hiding something?"

"I never said he was hiding something. Do *you* think he's hiding something?"

Another eye roll. "Dad, he's a really good guy. He works a lot, and I think that might be part of what makes it hard to date. But I work a lot, too, so we both get it."

"Where does he work again? Some bar?" Lou questioned, voice dripping with skepticism.

"He *owns* a sports bar, Dad. And it's a very successful one. They just hired a new manager, I guess, so he's hoping to have more nights off."

"Does he drink a lot?" Lou pressed.

And here's the interrogation...

"He has a beer or two with meals every now and then."

"He's friends with that baseball player you work for, isn't he?" Her dad continued, "What does that say about him? All I've heard for the last two years is how arrogant Quinn is, how he sleeps around and treats women like disposable paper products- good for one use, and then throws 'em away. Your words, sweets, not mine."

Zoey threw her head back into the pillows and stifled her annoyed groan. "They've known each other since they were, like, eleven. And Quinn's really not that bad. He's completely obsessed with his fiancé and has been for years. Besides, that has nothing to do with Jett. You can have friends who have different views on what romance should look like."

She heard the "hmph" her dad let out before his next query. "What about his family? Does he have a good relationship with them? Does he have siblings? Are his parents good people?"

"Actually, he is very close with his family," Zoey said confidently. "He has two little sisters who he's very protective of, and an older brother who he's really close with. His parents are still together, and I will be able to tell you more after tomorrow night because I'm going to meet them."

"You are?" The cynical tone seemed to disappear on these two syllables.

"Yes. It's Jett's birthday this weekend and his family is hosting a dinner for him tomorrow night. He says they'll all be there. Parents, siblings, even his grandparents."

"Oh...well, good," said Lou, the familiar firm tone back in his voice. "You can tell a lot about a man by meeting his parents. I'm glad he's taking you to meet them."

Zoey grinned triumphantly, but tried not to point out that he sounded like he was actually giving Jett a chance. "I will let you know how it goes."

They talked a little more about Jett and Michigan before covering their other usual bases; his health, what he's been eating, how Cindy's doing, and of course Ace and Cassie. By the end of the call she felt pretty satisfied that her insanely protective father wasn't able to reasonably complain about her new man.

She looked at the clock after ending her call and felt a tug in her chest at the thought that Jett was working all night. It was only eleven o'clock, so he still had three more hours until closing time. Even though they spent time together before he had to work, she still wished he was in bed next to her.

Tempted to go to the bar and visit him, she reminded herself that he would be busy, they wouldn't be able to make out, and he had insisted she get some sleep. He didn't want her staying up all night just because he had to. And of course at this request, her chest had swelled with warmth knowing that he just wanted to make sure she was taken care of.

So, instead of booking it across town in the dark, in the snow, which, even with the four-wheel drive of the Jeep, she was still nervous to drive in, she snuggled into bed in her pajamas, and turned the bedroom TV onto the *Hallmark* channel. She got out her phone and sent Jett a quick Snap of her screen with the message *These movies are always so much better when I watch them with you.*

Only seconds later he responded: *I'm not sure how I'm supposed to explain to my family why Christmas movies give me hard-ons now.*

She smiled and blushed as she wrote back, *I'd say you'll have to just learn to disguise it better, but come on.*

He responded, *Snow pants?*

Again, she giggled and typed back *Yeah, because that won't be suspicious.*

His response came quickly again, *Ah, it's a blessing and a curse. What can I say?*

The fact that Jett was not a cocky guy by any means, but still could brag about his undeniable assets was a complete turn on. Every time she thought back to him asking if she could 'make it work', her stomach did happy flips and she felt butterflies deep below her belly.

They exchanged a few more messages back and forth until Zoey caught herself falling asleep between his responses. She sent him one last message telling him goodnight and slipped off into dreams of Jett above her, beneath her, between her legs, and oddly enough, wearing nothing but snow pants on the couch as they watched Christmas movies. Everything she loved about her sweet, sexy, goofy man.

They pulled up in Jett's truck behind a group of cars in the driveway of a large white colonial style home with black shutters. The house was bigger than Zoey had expected, but she supposed with four kids it likely had to be a decent size to be comfortable. There was a walkway that led up to a small covered front porch with large white pillars on either side. The pillars were wrapped in thick garland and the door had a wreath filled with poinsettias, frosted pine cones, and shimmery gold leaf accents.

It was dark enough already to see the white Christmas lights that had been strung all over the house, outlining the roof, throughout the trees, and in the bushes lining the front of the house.

"This house looks like it belongs in a *Hallmark* movie," Zoey said, eyes traveling over all the decorations.

"I know." Jett smiled as he looked down at her. He pointed over their heads. "Careful who you get caught on the porch with."

Zoey looked up to see a mistletoe hanging directly above them. "Wow, your parents really go all out," she said as she leaned into his kiss.

The kiss lasted longer than she intended, and they must have had someone inside watching them because the front door burst open suddenly. They broke apart, but Jett kept a hand on her waist as they looked to see an old man, presumably Jett's grandfather, standing in the doorway. He was tall with lots of gray hair and glasses. He wore a dark green sweater and a huge smile on his face.

"So! You took my advice and went for a younger one!" The old man beamed, looking from Jett to Zoey and keeping his wide grin on her.

"Oh my God..." Jett muttered, looking down and covering his eyes in embarrassment. He glanced up apologetically at her, then looked at his grandpa. "Hi, Gramps."

"Happy birthday, my boy! And who is this?"

"Gramps, this is Zoey." Jett gestured to her and she grinned somewhat shyly at him.

"See? I told you to go for a younger gal. How old are you- twenty-two? Twenty-three?"

Zoey gave a sideways glance to Jett who still looked as if he wanted to crawl under a rock. She laughed quietly to herself, then looked back at Jett's grandpa. "Twenty-four, actually, but I think you're right. It's still worth bragging about for an old man like this guy over here." She nudged Jett and he narrowed his eyes playfully at her.

Jett's grandpa laughed gleefully and ushered them inside, offering to take her coat.

"Old man, huh?" Jett asked, one eyebrow raised.

She lifted a shoulder. "You're officially six years older than me now. I mean, you're in a completely different decade."

"Everyone is here and they're excited to meet you, Zoey," Jett's grandpa said, smile still not fading from his face as he led her and Jett into the living room where several people were gathered.

The living room was spacious, but still cozy with its many personal touches. There were family photos on one wall and along the mantel above the fireplace. A Christmas tree that had to be at least ten feet tall stood in front of a large bay window, decorated with white lights, various gold and red ornaments, and several homemade-looking ornaments that Zoey suspected were made by Jett and his siblings when they were in school. A long sectional encircled the space on dark cherry wood floors, there was an area rug beneath the coffee table, two reclining chairs on either end of the sectional, and several throw blankets and pillows on each piece of furniture.

There were two women who looked to be about Zoey's age, each of whom had brown curly hair and green eyes. She knew instantly that they must be Jett's sisters. The one with the darker brown hair sat with her foot curled beneath her on one end of the sectional, while the one with lighter, caramel-brown colored hair sat on the floor playing a card game with a little boy. Gavin was easy enough to spot, because he looked like a slightly older version of Jett with a fuller beard.

She expected to spot Jett's dad immediately, assuming he would also have the curly brown hair and green eyes, but was instead surprised to see that his hair was a much darker shade of brown and straight. All the Miller siblings seemed to have gotten his eyes, and their mother's curls.

An older woman sitting in one of the recliners had white hair and was the epitome of the word *grandma.* She sat quietly and watched the room with a small smile on her face, admiring what her family had grown into.

The little boy on the floor looked up and his eyes brightened, his face lighting up with a smile. "Uncle Jett's here!"

The room's attention seemed to shift all at once to where Jett and Zoey were standing under the archway that separated the entryway from the living room. There were various greetings, but everyone seemed to stop and wait for Jett to address the obvious new member of the group.

"Everyone, this is Zoey, which I'm sure you've figured out by now," Jett said, finally breaking the attentive silence of the room. "Zoey, this is...everyone."

The man she had guessed was his dad approached with a friendly smile. "Hi Zoey, I'm Drew, Jett's dad. We're all really happy you could make it. We heard you're from Los Angeles? How are you liking the cold?"

Zoey returned his smile. "It's definitely an adjustment, but the snow is beautiful. It feels like I'm in a Christmas movie."

Jett's mom, Shelly, introduced herself and offered to get her a glass of wine, and when she came back from the kitchen with the large goblet-sized glass of Pinot Noir, she began introducing the rest of the family.

Lizzie was the sister who'd been playing with her nephew, Grant, and she was particularly enthusiastic about meeting Zoey finally. Allison and her husband, Colin, were friendly and asked several questions about how they met and how long she was staying in Michigan.

The small itch she'd been trying to ignore returned again at the thought of leaving Michigan without Jett. And how would she leave *with* him? He had all of this here. His business, his friends. Her job was feeling more and more like she could do it from a distance, but she couldn't leave her dad. And her brother and sister still needed her. *God,* who knew what kind of trouble Cassie would get into if she was gone for long periods of time?

She immediately knew she liked Gavin; he was essentially Jett's twin, but three years older. His wife, Rachel was quiet but friendly, and their son, Grant was absolutely adorable. At about five years old, he had the signature Miller curls, but in his mother's white-blond hair color. He also seemed to adore Jett, asking him right away if they could go outside and play hockey.

"Sorry, little dude, it's already dark out," Jett replied, sounding truly bummed. "Last I checked your mom said no playing hockey in the street after dark."

"You say that like it's an unreasonable request," Rachel said. She held a glass of white wine in one hand and a Christmas cookie in the other.

"Did Grams make cookies already?" Jett asked, eyes wide as he spotted the frosted, star-shaped treat in Rachel's hand.

"There's a whole tray in the kitchen."

Jett groaned and put a hand to his stomach. "Fair warning," he said with a glance to Zoey, "this is where my winter weight comes from."

"So, what exactly do you do for a living?" Lizzie asked, sliding up next to her once Jett made his exit to the kitchen.

"I'm a publicist," she answered vaguely. "I basically manage and maintain the image of my client. Set up interviews, talk to the press sometimes. A lot of public relations kind of stuff."

"And your client is Quinn?"

"Yeah. He keeps it interesting."

"So you just get to follow him around all the time?" Allison cut in. "Oh my God, nine-year-old me is so jealous of you. He was my first crush."

"Mine too," Lizzie agreed with a dreamy sigh. "Of course that was way before every other girl in the world fantasized about him. I think I was seven when I realized I was in love with him."

"We were going to share him," said Allison. "We even made an agreement that I would have him for certain months and holidays, and Lizzie had the others. It was the perfect plan."

"Sounds like you had it all figured out," Zoey laughed lightly. "I'm starting to think I'm the only girl in the world who's never had a thing for him."

"Well *that's* a relief," Allison said. "Jett's been competing with Quinn on every other level since they were kids. I can't imagine how he'd feel if he thought he had to compete for your attention, too."

Zoey wasn't entirely sure what to say. Allison was the second person who had implied that Jett felt overshadowed by others or was maybe a little jealous, but she had yet to see that side of him at all.

"Turn the game on!" A male voice cut through Zoey's thoughts. "Who are they playing tonight?"

"Minnesota," Gavin replied. "They're going to get destroyed."

Zoey's eyes snapped up to the television that had just been turned on, just as Jett returned with three Christmas cookies in one hand, and one with a bite taken out of it in the other.

"Cookie?" he asked, offering her one of the three in his left hand.

She blinked away from the TV screen and looked at his handful of sweets and smiled. "Thanks." Taking a frosted Santa cookie from him, she asked, "Tacos or your grandma's Christmas cookies?"

"No. You can't do that to me." He shook his head vigorously. "I can't choose. I *want* to say Grams's cookies because they're special, and we only get them once a year. I can get tacos all year. But...I feel I'm betraying my love for tacos. But if I say tacos, then I'm betraying Grams. So, I just can't choose."

"Betraying tacos is equal to betraying your grandmother?"

"That's about the jist of it, yeah." He smiled and gave her a peck on the cheek before taking another bite of his cookie.

"Jett, are you putting money in?" Gavin called out from where he sat on the couch. There was a jar with dollar bills in it on the coffee table and pieces of paper where it looked like bets were being placed on the football game.

"Who is it?" Jett's eyes slid to the TV screen and saw the team names displayed: Minnesota at Detroit. Zoey knew next to nothing about sports, except for what she was required to know for her work, and even she felt like this wasn't a completely fair pairing. He looked back to Zoey for a moment and gave what she thought might have been a forced smile before nodding back to Gavin, "Sure, put me in for Detroit."

"Seriously?" Gavin asked, eyebrows raised.

"Seriously." Jett pulled his wallet out and walked over to the coffee table where they wrote down their bets. Zoey assumed there was something regarding the score in their bet, otherwise it looked like Jett was the only one betting on the home team.

"You're gonna lose your money on your birthday, man." Gavin shook his head as he took Jett's folded piece of paper and put it inside an envelope.

Jett found his spot next to Zoey again and she asked, "Do you do this often? Bet on sporting events?"

"All the time. This might be one of the worst bets I've made in a while, but it's on principle. I can't root for them anymore."

"Well, I hope their luck turns around for this game then." Zoey reached up on her tip-toes and kissed the corner of his mouth.

Later at the dinner table, the entire family's focus was completely on Zoey. They asked about living in California, what it was like having Christmas with palm trees instead of pine trees, about her family. They asked about her work, how much she traveled, how often she got to be at the baseball games.

She had been a complete champ about answering all their questions and Jett could tell they were loving her already when they turned their attention on him. He was certain they had been waiting with embarrassing stories from his youth to tell her, and therefore had been completely prepared. He was pretty much an open book and there wasn't a whole lot that embarrassed him, so he was ready to watch them try.

"When I was six and Jett had to babysit me and Allison, I made him be the butler for my tea parties," said Lizzie with a wide grin. "I always insisted he use a British accent, and there was a uniform Allison created."

"Yes, it was one of Mom's cooking aprons paired with a top hat off of one of my teddy bears," Allison said, holding up a finger. "The top hat was way too small, but we bugged him so much, he just wore the uniform to make us shut up."

Jett shrugged as the table around him erupted in giggles and laughs. "And now I do the same thing for Sophia. Ask her who her favorite uncle is- I'll give you a hint: It's not Tyler."

"Victoria told me all about that," Zoey said, smiling at him. "Apparently when Tyler comes to visit, Sophia has to constantly tell him how *Uncle Jett* does everything, including tea parties."

"I'm a seasoned veteran of girlish torture." He took a bite of mashed potatoes then waved his fork at his family sitting around the table. "Who's next?"

"I remember having him convinced that hockey was a good exercise for his penis," said Gavin, leaning forward in his chair. "He came into my room one morning after we'd spent the whole previous day playing street hockey, and he thought he overdid it. He just had his first wet dream and his erection wouldn't go away."

Everyone burst into fits of laughter, though his sisters made disgusted faces.

Jett laughed and felt his face turn slightly pink at that one. "Okay, okay, but to be fair, it was pretty impressive. Anyone would've been alarmed."

He noticed Zoey glancing sideways at him with a grin, as though she didn't want to give away exactly how impressive she thought they still were. He gave her hand a brief squeeze before taking another large bite of his dinner.

"That's just a Miller trait," Gramps chimed in between bites of pot roast. "Well endowed, every single one of us."

"Ew, Gramps." Allison scrunched up her face.

"I did *not* need to hear that about my brothers and my dad," Lizzie said, placing her knife and fork down on the table.

"It's true," Shelly said with a shrug. "How else do you think I ended up with four children?"

Jett nearly spit his drink out with laughter at that admission. "Jesus, Mom. What the hell kind of dinner topic is this?"

"I mean," Rachel began from next to Gavin, "from what I've seen...he's not wrong."

Allison and Lizzie again erupted in groans of disgust while the family- even Grams- laughed. Gavin held his beer glass up in cheers to no one in particular.

Jett turned his attention to Zoey, giving her a not-so-subtle stare, daring her to say anything to her family about the matter. Her face turned bright red as she looked back at him, grinning.

"Oh my God, Jett, they *just* met me," she whispered, though the whole table had now turned their eyes on the two of them. Jett shrugged and couldn't keep back his shit-eating grin. Finally Zoey sighed and held up her wine glass. "Can confirm."

Jett clinked his beer bottle on the edge of her wine glass and they both took large swills of their drinks.

"This is the most appalling dinner conversation we have ever had," Lizzie stated, still not touching the remaining food on her plate.

"Even more appalling than that time you brought that Dane guy home and he explained in detail how pierced his own nipples *and* his dick?" Jett asked skeptically. "I think not."

Lizzie rolled her eyes and reached for the bottle of white wine in the middle of the table to fill up her glass.

Dinner finished up, and Jett's parents cleared the table with help from Grams and Lizzie. His mom brought out a birthday cake, and although it felt completely childish that they all still sat around and sang *happy birthday*, he loved it. He loved their family traditions and that when he came here everything was how it had always been. Perhaps he was traditional, but he couldn't imagine things any other way, and he couldn't wait to share more of these moments with Zoey.

"Oh! No fucking way!" Gavin shouted from the other room while Shelly cut cake and passed it around. He came back into the dining room, "Detroit's winning. What the hell?"

"Really?" Jett looked up with a grin.

"Fucking Alex Hillsborough is out after a wicked tackle," his brother explained, reaching over for a plate of chocolate cake.

"Gavin- watch your language!" Rachel scolded.

Zoey made a small coughing noise next to Jett and took a quick sip of wine as her eyes slid from the television down to the table.

"Hillsborough joined the team- what? Two years ago?" Jett asked, brow furrowed.

"Yeah, but still, the guy can run. They don't have another runner like him on their team."

Zoey suddenly seemed very interested in the piece of cake in front of her. Finally she looked up at Jett, holding her fork with a small bite of cake on it. "I feel like it shouldn't surprise me that you're a double chocolate kind of guy."

His eyes flicked back to what he could see of the television screen from where he sat. There was a small segment being played about Alex Hillsborough's career in the NFL and how he'd graduated from...yep, the same school Zoey went to.

Obviously he knew Zoey had dated a guy who now played for the NFL, but seeing the guy on screen and knowing who it was some-how made it more real. Hillsborough was a six-foot-five dude with dark brown, nearly black hair, bright blue eyes lined with thick black lashes. Jett remembered overhearing conversations in the bar about how *dreamy* he was from several women, especially college-age girls who came into the bar during football season.

He was...well, he was sort of the Quinn Casey of the NFL. Posed for magazines, was featured in at least one sports drink commercial, and was even rumored to be making an appearance in a new football movie that was set to come out the next year.

That's Zoey's ex? How the hell was he supposed to compete with that?

It's fine, Jett. She's with you now. She told you he was a jerk to her. Don't make this a competition.

Of course that was easier said than done when he'd grown up treating nearly every facet of his life as a competition. He competed against his brother, Chris, Tyler, Quinn, even Rae sometimes. Everything they did together involved some sort of winner and loser situation. It was friendly competition most of the time, sure, but that mind-set was ingrained in him.

"Wait, Zoey, didn't you say you went to UCSD?" Gavin asked, still standing with his piece of cake so he could watch the game better.

"Oh, um, yeah." She nodded and cleared her throat.

Gavin raised his eyebrows. "Did you ever have classes with him?"

She shrugged, clearly uncomfortable talking about her ex-boyfriend with Jett's family. "I saw him around campus."

"Remember, Gav, she's around professional athletes all the time. It's probably nothing to see a dream boat like Alex Hillsborough strutting around," Allison reminded him. "That's a tough call though. I don't know who I'd want to follow around more...him or Quinn Casey."

Jett eyed Zoey for a moment, not sure exactly what reaction he was looking for. He wasn't sure what made him say it, but suddenly he announced, "They dated, actually."

Zoey's eyes went wide as she stared back at him, likely wondering what had compelled him to tell his whole family. He was fairly certain she didn't want them all to know, and maybe now she was a little annoyed, but there it was. He clenched his jaw briefly, turned away from her and focused on the chocolatey dessert in front of him. Of course the sugar was getting to him already and he wasn't particularly in the mood for birthday cake. Maybe another beer.

"You guys *dated?*" Allison stared, awe-struck, and sat down in the chair on Zoey's opposite side. "What was that like? He's totally gorgeous."

Zoey laughed uncomfortably and Jett could feel her eyes on him still. "Um, it was...I don't know, he's just another guy, I guess. He turned into a jerk later on when he started getting famous and that was it."

"Well, shit," Gavin said. "I'll remember that. No longer rooting for them. I may lose twenty bucks tonight, but it's worth it."

Jett had to appreciate his brother's support. As competitive as they were, Gavin would always have his back when it mattered. Not that this was a competition. Zoey wasn't dating that guy and clearly had no interest in getting back with him, but it still poked and prodded his pride a little bit.

He glanced up and across the table where Lizzie was watching him. Again, she knew his moods and read him well. At first she looked a little sad for him, but then shifted her gaze to Zoey and back with the tilt of her head.

Looking at Zoey next to him, she was poking at her cake with her fork. She looked upset and he immediately felt the kick to his stomach when he realized he'd put her on the spot and not only had himself pissed off, but it looked like she might be, too.

Dammit, and things had been going so well. Fucking jealousy is a bitch.

He took her hand and stood up. "Hey, come with me." He tilted his head toward the living room. She looked up at him with curious, hazel eyes and stood and followed him. They went through the living room, back into the entryway where the stairs led to the second floor. He walked into his old bedroom which was almost exactly how he'd left it before leaving for college.

"Me and Rae are the only two people I know whose childhood bedrooms are like a time capsule," Jett said, pulling Zoey into the room. "Chris's parents turned his into Sophia's second room for when she stays, and I guess I don't know what Quinn's looks like now, but I'm sure it's different. But my parents haven't touched my room."

Zoey looked around the room with its poster-covered walls, his full-size bed, still with the same green plaid comforter, the small desk and wheeled desk chair with its broken spring. Anyone who sits in it has to be ready to balance if they don't want to fall backward onto the floor.

The posters ranged from cars he'd fantasized about owning, to Red Wings, Lions, and Tigers, to swimsuit models. There was a whiteboard on one wall next to the window that had several initials and numbers on it: QC, RD, CW, TW, GM, and JM. It looked like quite the intricate chart, but was just a scoreboard of the various games they'd played.

Zoey was studying the whiteboard and he saw her lips curve into a grin. "So Chris won the most football games, Rae beat you all at swimming? What's 'HRD'?"

"Home Run Derby," Jett said, sliding behind her and letting his arm curl around her waist. "No surprise Case kicked all our asses at that."

"No, I guess not." She studied the board some more. "You beat Gavin in hockey."

"He likes to point out that he didn't always play, so I had more opportunities to win, but I still won."

"This is really cool that you have all this in here." She paused, still reading and deciphering the chart. "Wow, Quinn really sucks at volleyball."

Jett laughed. "Yeah, you'd think his height would help him out there, but he's terrible."

"You guys had pole-vaulting contests?" Zoey asked, pointing to the smallest chart on the board.

"Uh, just the one time." Jett scratched his jaw, laughing slightly at the memory. "It wasn't a real set up. We sort of created our own and it was just a bad idea overall. I won because I was the only one who ended up without an injury."

"You guys must've had so much fun growing up together. I wish I would've had close friends like that."

"You didn't have any best friends?"

"Carley Martinez was my best friend through middle school," she explained. "But they moved north right before we started high school. I had friends, and I got along with most people, but I always felt like I was the floater friend. Like I could hang out with this group, or that, but never really stuck close or quite fit with one or two others."

"I can't imagine what I would've done without my friends." Jett pressed his lips to the side of her head. "I probably would've been less competitive."

"Is that what that was downstairs?" Zoey asked. "You, feeling competitive with my ex who I told you I have absolutely no interest in?"

Jett spoke into her hair again and breathed in the sweet scent of fresh berries, "Yes. And I'm sorry for putting you on the spot like that...I don't know what I expected you to say. Maybe...that he might be rich and famous and a fucking giant, but you'd take me over him any day."

"Well, I would take you over him any day." She tilted her head up to face him and kissed his jaw. "Seriously, there's no competition."

He gave a half-hearted smile and gestured toward the board. "It's hard to remember that when my entire life has been about competing. I'm constantly competing with my brother and it's usually over the dumbest stuff. Last November, we had a beard-growing competition." She laughed and so did he at the ridiculousness of it.

"Allison is younger than me but she got married first, Gavin's already got a kid. Lizzie...well, I'm not really jealous of her relationships, but my parents always seem hopeful when she brings a new guy around and then grill me on why I won't just meet someone already." He rattled on, "And then there's Chris who always seems to be one or two steps ahead of me. Quinn, obviously...being a pro-ball player and all. And then there's Rae who has always just been..." he paused to let out a small puff of laughter, "Well, Rae. Everything about her life has always been so easy and beyond perfect."

"I'm sure it's not as perfect as it looks from the outside. It never is. I mean, she's on her second engagement because she got cheated on, didn't she? That had to leave a mark. That's probably why she was so quick to assume what she did when she saw me at Quinn's hotel room back in August."

"True," Jett sighed.

He thought of how hurt Rae had been when she showed up at the bar after catching Emerson with that legal intern and a sudden wave of guilt crashed over him. He'd been hanging out with the guy who did that to her. Acting like they were friends. Sure, he could say over and over that they weren't, but the fact of the matter was that he'd at least been enduring and tolerating Emerson's presence. And it bothered him less and less each time.

"You don't need to compete with everyone," Zoey said. "I know this is going to sound cheesy, but everyone is on their own timeline. I mean, if we'd met in your freshman year of college, I would've been twelve or thirteen, so…"

Jett snorted. "Shit, that's right. Wow, thanks for putting that into perspective, I feel like such a cradle-robber now. Six years doesn't seem like a lot until you look at it that way."

"Well, lucky for you I'm an old soul." She turned to face him and their lips met.

Eyes closed, he sighed when they parted. "We should probably get downstairs before they assume I'm defiling my old bedroom."

Her hazel eyes gleamed up at him. "We should get downstairs before we *start* defiling your old bedroom." Jett let out a playful growl and Zoey grabbed his hands, pulling him toward the door.

Downstairs, the family was back in the living room and Allison was standing in front of the Christmas tree facing everyone. Colin stood next to her with his arm around her. Allison met Jett's eyes and smiled.

"Oh good, everyone's in here!" she said, beaming. She leaned into her husband, and Jett knew immediately what was going on. "So, Colin and I have a little announcement…" Allison pulled a card out and opened it. "Colin and I are expecting a little one in May!" Inside the card was an ultrasound photo of their baby.

Everyone erupted into cheers and squeals of excitement, rushing to hug Allison.

Jett let out a sigh, knowing his family would forget all about how this was supposed to be his night. Yes, he was excited for his sister and maybe he was being selfish, but come on. His birthday dinner, his new girlfriend that they'd all been pestering him about, *his* birthday traditions. And Allison just had to go and steal his thunder.

Happy birthday to me.

Zoey kind of couldn't believe how Allison had swooped in and stolen Jett's night away from him. By the sounds of it, he doesn't get to be the center of attention often unless they're grilling him about settling down. She wondered if all the Miller siblings were competitive with each other and if on some level, Allison had done that specifically to one-up Jett.

No matter. Zoey knew how she could make him feel special and like all the attention was on him. She'd been waiting, planning to put the focus on him since it was his birthday.

She pulled him through the door to Rae's house, having opted to go there since the bar was still open and his apartment would be loud for a few more hours. Down the hall and into the guest room, she dragged him by the arms and pushed the door closed.

She pushed his back against the door and wrapped her arms around the back of his neck to pull him down to her, kissing him hard, sweeping her tongue into his mouth to taste him.

"What's your favorite position?" Zoey breathed between kisses, working to get his belt and pants off.

"I don't know, whatever you want." He pulled her sweater dress over her head and she had to press her body against him to stifle the goosebumps that rose on her skin.

"We always do what I want. It's your birthday. You tell me."

After pulling off his sweater, Jett lifted her up and she wrapped her legs around his waist. He turned them around and backed her against the door.

"I want to taste you," he rasped into her neck and slid a hand up her thigh, a finger finding its way inside her panties. "Here."

"Something for *you*, Jett," Zoey said, arching her neck for him.

"That is for me. I like doing it. I *love* doing it. I love feeling you come against my lips. You get so wild from it, and it's all for me." He slid his finger inside her and she gasped.

"Fine, but after, you let me."

"Let you, what?"

"Use my mouth on you." She bit his lip and felt his body still for a beat.

"You...don't have to."

"I know I don't *have* to. I want to." She kissed him again. "Do you not like it?"

"Uh, no, I fucking love it."

"Good." She kissed him hard again and he moved her over to the bed, setting her down gently and lying on top of her.

He began his slow slide down her body, kissing her neck, trailing his tongue across her collarbone, dipping his head to her breasts as he unhooked her bra. He paid special attention to each breast before continuing down, over her ribs, kissing her hip bones, and looping his fingers through her silky red panties and pulling them down her legs.

Then moving up, he took his time, kissing her ankle, her calf, the insides of each thigh, scraping his teeth lightly across her skin.

He slid a finger into her again and groaned with her. "Wrap your legs around me. I want to feel you grabbing my hair, or fucking my face. Whatever feels good to you, that's what I want."

Zoey's heart fluttered and the butterflies in her stomach might have passed out. She sighed shakily and nodded, giving a breathless "Okay."

She felt two fingers petting her, spreading her open before his tongue flicked around her clit. And *oh God*...it was so good. He'd done this several times, and each time had given her an amazing, earth-shattering, mind-blowing orgasm. But tonight he felt different. Unhinged. Not his usual calm, careful self.

His tongue worked her clit as his finger slid back in, pumping slowly in and out of her. Then adding another finger, he pressed deep inside her and she arched her back off the mattress with a long moan of pleasure.

She buried a hand in his tangle of curls and pushed her hips into him, demanding more. He sucked and licked, lightly teasing with his teeth as his fingers still pumped slowly.

She was crying out as he increased his pace. He had one arm curled around her thigh and pulled her into him over and over, in a steady rhythm. He groaned against her slick skin as he flicked his tongue around her, pulled his fingers out to rub either side of her clit before sliding them back inside.

He released her leg and she looked down to see him fisting his length, sliding his hand up and down his shaft with the rhythm of his mouth against her.

What was it about this that was so goddamn sexy? Was it the way the muscles in his shoulders moved as he pleasured himself? Was it the fact that he was so turned on by turning her on that he just had to touch himself? Was it just that it was all so filthy and taboo, and seeing him like this made her feel like this unbelievably confident, sexy woman that she had certainly never felt like before him?

She reveled in everything he did to her. All the things he made her feel, all the things he made her want and need and crave and beg for. *Holy hell*, he was the sexiest man alive. And he was...hers, wasn't he?

"Yes...yes...Jett, *God*, it feels so...good," she panted, still grasping his hair and rocking her hips into him.

She was so close.

Right.

There.

Don't...stop.

A tight, tingling sensation began in her core and burst outward, down to her toes that curled hard, her legs wrapped around him and she screamed praises, his name, and some unintelligible sounds and whimpers.

Her body was still coming down, settling from the massive explosion that had her nearly in tears with how good it was, when she glanced down at Jett between her legs. She met his bright green eyes as he kissed the inside of her thigh, still stroking himself, but slower now.

She reached for him. "Come up here."

Slowly but surely, he obliged, sliding back up her body, pressing kisses to every inch along the way. He sat up straddling her, cock still in hand and she reached to take over.

"I love doing that to you," Jett said, his voice a low growl. "The way you respond to my mouth, and I can see it up close..."

"You're the first one who's ever...well, I've never been able to orgasm that way before you," Zoey admitted. "You have a very talented mouth."

Jett's eyes brightened and he smirked a little, knowing he was the only one who could do that to her. He traced her bottom lip with a finger and she dipped slightly to suck it into her mouth, making him groan deeply.

She mimicked what she wanted to do to his cock on his finger, sucking and wrapping her tongue around him, all while feeling him grow harder in her hands.

"Do you want to lay down, or do you just want to fuck my mouth?"

Where had that come from? God, he made her say and do and think things she'd never imagined. But she couldn't help what he did to her, and she certainly wasn't complaining.

"What?" Jett furrowed his brow, then one side of his mouth twitched up the slightest bit. "What do you mean?"

Grinning mischievously, she made up her mind. She'd never done it like this before, and she wouldn't be surprised if polite, always-pleasing Jett hadn't either. "Get up here."

Jett moved up so he was straddling her chest and his eyes were dark and hooded as he looked down at her. With pillows propping her up, she grasped his cock again and guided him to her mouth. Her tongue swirled around the head before she brought him in fully. Or at least as much of him as she could take.

He groaned loudly and leaned over her, bracing a forearm on the headboard.

Her mouth worked around him, tasting, sucking, sliding him in and out, and she urged him to move his hips, set the pace.

"Baby," he breathed, watching as he slid himself in and out of her. "Fuck…I've never…god, you're so sexy. Look so good like this."

She moaned and whimpered around him, gasping and guiding him with her hand when he pushed just a little too far.

He reached down with one hand and held the side of her head, sweeping his thumb across her jaw. "That as far as you can go, baby?" She moaned and nodded, loving him watching her like this. She could feel him holding back, wanting it to last because she was making it so good for him. He made her feel so sexy, so desirable, like a goddess.

He pushed in and pulled back out, and she licked his entire length before wrapping her lips back around him. She used her mouth, her hands, pumping with one and feeling his balls with the other. He was so hard in her mouth, and she felt when his slow thrusts started to lose control. They became less fluid, a little more jerky.

"Fuck, baby," he panted. "Oh God, I'm gonna come. Where should I-" Zoey met his gaze with a look that she hoped conveyed that it was his choice and he groaned again, loudly. She felt it inside her chest and felt liquid with pleasure, knowing she was driving him absolutely wild.

His breathing was heavy and ragged as he moved between her lips, and with what seemed like much effort, he pulled out at the last second, pumping his fist over his dick, releasing himself all over her chest and stomach.

"Fuuuck…" he groaned, long and drawn out as he came. She felt the warm wetness as most of it landed on her chest, and again was overcome with the feeling of being completely desirable, irresistible, and *his*.

Jett leaned against the headboard, catching his breath for a few beats before landing on his back next to her. His chest rose and fell with his deep breaths and his hand found hers, lacing their fingers. He brought her hand to his lips and kept them there, pressing light kisses to her fingers and palm.

"I've never done it like that before," Jett said between breaths.

Zoey let out an airy laugh. "Me neither."

"Good," he sighed. "Does it make me a caveman that I like that I can be your first for some things?"

"No. I like it, too."

He propped himself up on one elbow and did a slow scan of her body. "How about that I like seeing you like this? Like I'm marking my territory? Does that make me a caveman?"

Zoey met his eyes and flicked her gaze back and forth between them. She wanted him to say it. To say *why* he liked it. So that she could know they were on the same page.

It's because it makes you feel like I'm yours. All yours.

It hit her suddenly how much she wanted to be his. And she wanted him to be hers. Was it too soon for those kinds of declarations?

Finally she forced a small smile. "Maybe a little." She watched him look her over again and felt warm and tingly at the way his eyes lingered on her breasts that were still covered in him. "But I'm okay with it."

He smiled and kissed her lips before rolling the other way to get off the bed. "I suppose I should clean you up before round two." She watched him walk, naked and confident, into the hallway to find the towels across the hall in the bathroom.

She had plenty of time to catch her breath and for her heart rate to go back to normal, but suddenly her heart was pounding in her chest. She was in a complete free-fall for this man and she needed to figure out how to land. They'd been together only a few weeks, but already she felt as though her life back in LA would be completely empty without him. They needed to talk about this together. Where they were going, what exactly they wanted out of this.

Slow down, Zo.

We don't know if he's there yet.

Jett returned with damp towels and cleaned her off before lying on top of her and goofily blowing a raspberry into her neck, making her laugh.

He looked down at her and kissed her nose. "I like you, Zoey Nunez."

"I like you, too, Jett Miller."

He shrugged, feigning arrogance. "I know." She laughed and swatted playfully at him. He looked more meaningfully at her this time, the trace of his laugh still on his lips, but full sincerity in his gaze. "I mean...I *really* like you."

Her heart leapt, both overjoyed and relieved because she knew exactly what he meant. He was falling for her, too. Maybe he wasn't in love yet, but he was on his way.

The small knot of panic loosened in her chest and she relaxed beneath him. Reaching for the TV remote on the nightstand, she asked, "Christmas movies and chill?"

He smiled and nodded, then pulled the corner of the comforter back for them to get under. She slipped under the covers and he flipped the light off before squeezing in next to her. And then it was all skin against skin, his mouth on hers, sliding against each other, feeling and moving together.

Nothing else existed. No crazy, time-consuming jobs, no California, no distance, no giant life-altering decisions. At least for that night, her life was right there in that bed.

CHAPTER 16

The following morning, Zoey went with Jett to the bar, having packed an overnight bag since she planned to stay with him after his day shift. He'd told her she could hang out upstairs and watch movies, but she opted to stay at the bar, watching him work.

He was training a new manager, Alaina, and Zoey thought she seemed cool enough. They exchanged brief conversation while Zoey sipped on a ginger ale and caught up on some emails for work.

Quinn wasn't kidding; there were *a ton* of news outlets trying to get interviews with him. All because his mom was seen leaving her dialysis treatment? There were plenty of reasons someone might need dialysis other than drug use. The more Zoey read her emails and found articles with such accusations, the more she thought something else must have leaked somehow.

"Quinn's mom is on dialysis because she has kidney disease, right?" Zoey asked, scrolling through her inbox. She had typed up a brief response to address any emails that had come in requesting a comment or interviews and was hoping it would fit to copy and paste it to reply to each one.

"Yeah," Jett replied from behind the bar's point-of-sale screen. "Stage five, I think."

"And all these people are just assuming she's a drug addict?" Zoey didn't take her eyes off her laptop as she read yet another email from a trashy gossip site asking for comments or confirmation.

"Well, she is. But I think it's shitty that they're just assuming it."

Zoey lifted her gaze to Jett abruptly. "She is?"

"Seriously? He hasn't even told you that much?"

"I suspected, but he's never actually confirmed it. He just said that he was raised by a single mom, was really poor, and didn't have a good relationship with her," she explained, somewhat stunned at this new information.

"Yeah, she was really into heroin when we were in high school."

Zoey looked wide-eyed from Jett to the woman he was training. That was exactly how stuff got leaked. Jett seemed to notice her alarm and shifted his gaze to Alaina. "Oh, she went to high school with us. She knows."

"Oh." She let out a relieved breath. "Did you know Quinn and Rae and their group really well, too?"

Alaina smirked a little with her laugh. "I knew them, yeah. Raelyn and I weren't exactly tight, but I did get to know Quinn pretty well our junior year."

The uncomfortable stare Jett gave the screen didn't go unnoticed. His eyes were as big as saucers and he looked to be trapping something in his mouth, lips pressed tight together. Zoey narrowed her eyes at him curiously and tried to decipher the meaning behind it.

In June when Quinn had called her saying he'd reunited with Rae and was taking her out on a date, he'd given her a lengthy run-down of his childhood and every big moment they'd shared. As though a bright white light bulb flickered on, she gasped, "Oh! You're *that* Alaina! Oh my God, Quinn told me about you."

"He did?" Alaina and Jett asked in unison.

"Yeah, I made him tell me everything. I wanted to know about each time he screwed up in the past and why he and Rae couldn't make it work back then."

"Aw, and remembering his mistakes made him think of me? I'm flattered," Alaina said.

Zoey's immediate reaction was to apologize, but Alaina's tone sounded playful and teasing. She must have noticed the expression on Zoey's face because she laughed. "It's fine, seriously. It's just funny remembering how dramatic high school was."

Relieved she hadn't offended her, Zoey relaxed. "Yeah, it's four years and it feels like your entire life depends on how those four years go," said Zoey. "Well that's cool that everyone can put that stuff behind them anyway."

"Super cool," Jett said awkwardly. Zoey couldn't help the feeling he was intentionally avoiding eye contact with both women.

"Raelyn's not mad that you hired me, is she?" Alaina asked. "Is that why she hasn't been in the bar since I started?"

"No, no…" Jett scratched the side of his face. He'd trimmed this morning, but not completely shaved his beard off and Zoey loved the scruff. "She doesn't know that I hired you. But like you said, high school was dramatic. And it was a long time ago. I'm sure she'll be fine."

Zoey couldn't help the laugh that bubbled out of her. "Oh my God, you're scared to tell her. You're afraid she's going to get mad at you."

Jett looked back and forth between her and Alaina, a new defensive set to his posture. "No! No, I'm not *scared* of Rae. It's my bar, my decisions. And she…she'll be fine with it anyway. She's super chill." His voice went weirdly high at the last two words.

Zoey raised a skeptical eyebrow and looked from Alaina to Jett and back. He looked to be forcing nonchalance as he suggested, "Who knows, maybe you guys will become friends now."

Alaina let out a high, derisive laugh. "Okay, Jett. Yeah, I'm sure the princess and I will become the best of friends."

"Princess?" A low voice boomed from the door as a gust of cold wind blew in. "I only know one person by that name and sadly I don't see her here."

Zoey moved her attention to the somewhat familiar figure making his way toward her. She could've sworn she'd seen him before but couldn't place where. He sat on the barstool next to her and gave her a quick sweep from her boots to her face and smirked the cockiest, most self-assured smirk she had ever seen.

"Nope," Jett interjected firmly.

The man looked at Jett curiously, and his blue eyes twinkled mischievously. This guy was setting her *danger* meter off on high. Red flashing lights, buzzers, sirens- all of it. He was extremely handsome and he knew it. He was probably ridiculously charming, overly confident, and very sexually experienced. But he was dangerous. She could just sense it.

"What? Is this another one of your sisters?" the guy in his perfectly tailored suit asked. Zoey felt like she was being X-rayed when he eyed her again.

"It's Zoey, you jackass," Jett replied, staring daggers at the man. Clearly Jett knew he was bad news, too.

"No shit?" The man's eyebrows went up. "Damn, Jett, she's way too hot for you. No wonder you guys haven't fucked yet."

"What we have or haven't done is none of your business."

Completely undeterred by Jett's obvious unfriendly tone, the man continued, "Okay, but you told me you would tell me all about it when it happened and I haven't heard from you since last week."

Jett rolled his eyes, exasperated. "And I told you we're not friends. I'm not sharing that shit with you." He moved his attention to Zoey. "You might want to just head upstairs, baby. He's an asshole and you shouldn't have to endure him."

"Baby?" The man repeated, grinning. He flicked his gaze back and forth between her and Jett. "Oh, she's *baby* now. Okay, so you've definitely fucked. All right. Let's hear the details." He lifted his chin in her direction. "How was it? Disappointing? Did it seem like he needed a lot of practice? Did you fake it?"

"Emerson, for fuck's sake, will you stop talking?" Jett groaned.

"Are we allowed to kick him out?" Alaina whispered to Jett.

"I don't think there's much point in it. He'll just keep coming back with more bro-power."

"Emerson," Zoey repeated with a nod, the name clicking into place. "You're Raelyn's ex-fiancé."

"Correct," he said with a wink. "Ex as in former, no longer attached, single, and if you're interested I can-"

"She's not interested," Jett cut him off. He set a bottle of Heineken on a bar coaster. "Now shove this in your mouth and shut up."

Emerson let out a low whistle. "I hope he doesn't talk to you like that. I'd treat you better."

Zoey laughed dryly. "You cheated on your fiancé, but you'd treat *me* better?"

"Only once." Emerson waved a dismissive hand before taking his first long pull of beer.

"Three times," Jett said, now leaning his forearms on the bar. "You told Rae you cheated three times."

"Did I?" Emerson's eyebrows pulled together. "I say a lot of things." He took another swig of beer and faced Zoey again. "So how about those details? Was it that bad? Can't share?"

Jett muttered something under his breath and Zoey turned confidently toward the suited-up player. "Actually, it was the best sex I've ever had. We had sex for probably six hours. Multiple orgasms. And his penis is huge, so, kind of hard to top all that."

Emerson stared back in stunned silence.

Zoey grinned, satisfied he'd finally stopped talking.

Jett's face was turning red but he smiled nonetheless before giving an appreciative nod.

They all waited in silence for Emerson to process her response, simply enjoying the facial expressions he went through as he contemplated how to proceed.

Finally, after what felt like several minutes, he opened his mouth. Then closed it. Then opened it again. "So, what's *huge,* exactly?"

"Oh, I'm not sharing that." She shook her head. "No, that knowledge is all for me. I will tell you, though, that it took some adjusting."

Another stretch of silence engulfed them and she and Jett were trying not to laugh.

"You have rendered him speechless," Jett said out of the corner of his mouth. "That is a superpower if I ever saw one."

Emerson was staring generally beyond Zoey, not looking at anything in particular when his hand went to his tie, he looked down briefly. "I...just realized I need to- I'm wearing the wrong...suit." He appeared slightly dazed as he slid off his barstool and tossed a ten-dollar bill on the bar.

Only making it three steps toward the door, he turned around and looked at Zoey again and pointed to Jett. "Seriously? *This* guy?"

"Seriously."

Emerson peered skeptically at her, then continued his path toward the door. Again, he turned around and came back to the bar, this time with his attention on Jett. "*God of War* tonight at my place again if you want to join. Just me, Brody, and this new kid at my office. Intern."

"We've got plans," Jett said, tilting his head toward Zoey.

"You can impale her on your massive cock when you get home, dude. Come on."

Ignoring the unnecessarily crass comment, Zoey chimed in, "I used to play that game with my little brother all the time. Got pretty good at it, actually."

"Really?" Jett grinned. She loved how his face seemed to light up every time he learned a new piece of information about her. A new piece of her history.

"Then you can both come," Emerson said. "Honestly, playing video games with a girl sounds...like a fucking nightmare, but I'll give it a try."

"All right," Jett sighed, giving in. "We'll see you tonight I guess. *Your* place..."

Once the door to the bar closed and Emerson was gone, Zoey gave Jett an amused grin. "This should be fun."

Jett groaned and leaned forward, landing his face in his arms on the bar top. Zoey massaged his scalp through his thick head of curls as he mumbled into the bar, "I'm a bad friend."

"No, you're not," she assured him. "Have you guys been hanging out?"

"Sort of. I lied to Quinn about it. I don't lie."

"So, tell him the truth. You can hang out with whomever you want. You can also *hire* whomever you want."

"Are you saying '*whomever*' just to sound more wise? Because it's working," Jett lifted his head and peered up at her.

Her lips curved into a smile. "Maybe I am."

Jett stood outside the door to Emerson's apartment, Zoey at his side. They stared at the enormously imposing door for what felt like ages. Emerson's apartment complex was situated just off the main strip and had views of the lake and the city. It gave the impression of a New York high rise that had somehow been airdropped into their small town. The door man- yes, this place had a door man, and security- had let them up to his sixth floor apartment after making a call up to him and giving their names.

"Do we knock, or do we just turn around?" Jett asked quietly, still staring at the gold-colored number 6A on the door.

"I mean, he knows we're here already. And I kind of feel like making it up here was an accomplishment, I sort of want to see what's on the other side," Zoey replied.

Letting out a long sigh, Jett held his hand up and knocked three times.

The door swung open and Emerson grinned- or maybe smirked is more accurate- when he saw them standing there. Jett wondered if he looked intimidated or freaked out, and urged himself to relax.

He realized he'd never seen Emerson in anything other than a suit and tie or his far more casual bare chest and sweatpants. Or perhaps he had back when he and Rae were dating, but had since forgotten. He wore dark blue jeans and an open black and white plaid flannel shirt, with a plain white t-shirt under it.

"This is the most normal I've seen you look," Jett said, caught off guard by his appearance. Seriously, he looked like...just another guy.

"Yeah, well, I knew you were bringing your girl with you so I thought I'd tone it down a bit," he said, and winked at Zoey as he held the door open for them to enter.

The door closed behind them and Jett looked around the space which he could only describe as the most bachelor-pad looking bachelor pad he had ever seen. The apartment was spacious, with an open floor plan. From where he stood he could see into the kitchen, which had black cabinets with black quartz countertops, brushed nickel accents, and a backsplash that was varying shades of gray. One wall had large windows that overlooked the lake and there was a black brick partition wall separating the kitchen from the living room.

Dark hardwood floors spread throughout the apartment, and the area rug in the living room looked like faux gray-wolf fur. A large black leather sofa and matching loveseat were angled toward the opposite wall with a 60-inch television set into it, and beneath it was a long, electric fireplace. There were dark wood beams across the ceiling, and the shelves built into the walls all had back-lit displays, showing off various books, a sleek stainless steel clock, vinyl records, and other decorative items.

"Nice place," Jett said, still looking around and catching small details here and there. He noticed the hallway past the living room and assumed that's where his bedroom was, and probably a bathroom, maybe a guest room.

"Thanks. Just had it remodeled this summer." Emerson wandered over to the fridge which, like Jett's place, was black stainless steel. "Either of you want something to drink?"

"I'll take a beer. Zoey?"

Zoey took a few steps toward the kitchen and peered into the fridge, "How old are you? You have Snack Packs and Go-Gurt."

"They're for my little brother when he comes to visit," Emerson said defensively. "He'll be up again next weekend. I also have pizza rolls and Hot Pockets."

"Okay, but other than that, you have Heineken, Labatt Blue, a partial bottle of red wine, and ranch dressing," she pointed out, looking more closely into the open refrigerator. "You're not a real grown-up."

"I am, too," Emerson scoffed. "I have a job that requires me to wear a suit, I pay all my bills on time- sometimes ahead of time- and I even wipe my own ass."

Jett laughed and rolled his eyes. So much for toning it down because his girl was here. Emerson was obviously flirting with Zoey, just in a far less direct way. Luckily, Jett knew there was no way Zoey would ever go for a guy like him. If she hadn't been interested in Quinn because he was too much of a player, there was no way anything Emerson said or did was going to work.

"Was that a *Big Daddy* reference?" Zoey asked, smiling.

"It was," Emerson confirmed. "I was sort of hoping you'd just call me Big Daddy in response, but I suppose you've already got one of those."

Zoey looked over her shoulder at Jett and shook her head. The "*can you believe this guy?*" was written all over her face.

Jett heard male voices growing closer and looked past the living room down the hallway. Brody's flaming red hair was easily recognized, but he hadn't expected to see the tall, dark man with hair cropped short just like his brother's.

"Tyler?" Jett blinked and made sure he was seeing correctly.

"Jett?" Tyler looked somewhat alarmed to see his brother's best friend standing there. "What's up? What are you doing here?"

"Game night, I guess," Jett replied, then looked back at Emerson who was watching the interaction closely. "How do you know each other?"

"I..." Tyler began. His eyes flashed to Emerson, then back to Jett, and he let out a sigh. "Okay, you can't tell Chris-"

"Nope!" Jett put his hands up. "No, I'm not keeping secrets from your brother. I'm not lying to your brother. I don't want to know. Just make something up that I can tell him."

"You would still be lying, wouldn't you?" Tyler countered. "It's not that big of a deal, I just don't want him giving me shit."

"Chris?" Emerson questioned, handing Jett a bottle of Labatt. "Like *your* Chris?"

"Yeah, Tyler's his little brother. How the hell do you guys know each other?"

"He's the new intern at my office. The new office bitch," Emerson replied.

Jett furrowed his brow. "Ty, that's a *corporate* law office. Emerson's a bank lawyer. He helps banks sue people who already don't have enough money to fill their accounts. You said you wanted to be 'one of the good ones'."

"And that's why I don't want Chris to know. Or my parents," Tyler said. "It's just an internship, and it's a *paid* internship. Law school isn't cheap. I can't afford to not get paid for the next few months."

"So just tell them that," said Jett. "They've gotta understand you need to make money."

"He'll be getting paid even more when he drops the *good guy* dream and just comes to work for us after his internship is done, too," Emerson interjected. Tyler rolled his eyes, and Jett assumed this was a frequent discussion the two of them had.

"Just don't say anything to Chris, okay?" Tyler pleaded. "I'll tell them eventually, I just don't feel like taking shit about it."

Jett let out a heavy sigh-slash-groan. He supposed simply not saying anything wasn't the same as lying. And it wasn't as if Chris was going to ask him about it.

He nodded and conceded reluctantly, "Okay, fine."

Now that everyone had a drink in hand, they made their way into the living room. Zoey and Jett took a spot on the soft leather loveseat while the other three men sat on the extra-long sofa.

Jett introduced Zoey to everyone and Tyler smiled. "I heard you took my niece sledding."

"Your niece who loves me more?" Jett said smugly.

"Yeah, okay," Tyler snorted. "Just because I've been away at school doesn't mean she loves you more."

The large TV screen appeared to be booting up the game when the prompt asking for the WiFi password popped up.

"*Brody,*" Emerson practically growled. "Did you fucking change my WiFi password again?"

"I did," Brody said, straight-faced as he picked up a game controller. "It's now *chlamydiaking88*. No spaces."

"Jesus Christ," Emerson muttered, typing in the ridiculous password. Next to Jett, Zoey shook with quiet laughter. "He does this all the fucking time. *GimmeCock69, PickleTickler3000.* One time it was just *'mmmdicks'* and he couldn't remember how many m's he used."

"Yeah, well, when your Xbox Live name is KingDong88, you're kind of asking for it," Brody reasoned.

"Hard to argue with that," Tyler muttered.

Finally, the game screen loaded and Emerson explained the game. They were all on the same team and had various quests to complete with seemingly impossible obstacles placed in front of them. Each character had a set of special skills to contribute to the team, and if all else failed, they simply had to try not to get killed.

After two hours of playing, it was clear that Jett was *not* the pro at this game like he was with *Halo,* and the competition was really between Zoey and Emerson. She wasn't kidding about being pretty good at it. They made it through three quests and Jett felt like he, Brody, and Tyler could have set their controllers down and it would've gone just as well.

"Well, you guys all suck at this," said Emerson, going back to the main screen at the end of their last quest. "Next time I'm just inviting Zoey. The rest of you are going to get me killed."

"Or we can just go back to *Halo.* Or *Call of Duty,*" Brody suggested. "This might be the nerdiest game I've ever played and I used to play *World of Warcraft.*"

"Emerson's a closet nerd," Jett sang delightedly.

"There's nothing closeted about it," Brody said. "Have you seen him on Halloween or any time a new *Marvel* movie comes out? He has Thor costumes for each movie and an authentic hammer replica that he bought at a comic book store."

"Okay, but ask me how many times my *Ragnarok* costume has gotten me laid. Do you have any idea how many women I've fucked while wearing that thing?"

"At the same time?" Brody asked. "Or different times?"

Zoey coughed and set her beer bottle down, looking at Jett with wide eyes.

"Oh, different times," Emerson replied. "Don't get me wrong, the threesome is every guy's fantasy, but I actually like to take my time with a woman. Make her feel special."

Jett quirked an eyebrow curiously. "Really?"

"Absolutely," Emerson confirmed. "Give a woman just a little extra attention and she'll be begging to suck your cock."

Zoey made a disgusted kind of sound and Jett rolled his eyes. "On that note…" Jett said, standing and stretching, "Time to head out."

"Good idea," Emerson said with a smirk in Zoey's direction. "She's as good as I am at that game. Bet she'd want to see how I put the hammer down if I dressed the part."

Zoey pushed her hair back as she stood up and gave him a friendly smile. "Pass."

"I don't think your hammer's got anything on Jett- *Big Dick*- Miller over there," Tyler chuckled. "Sorry man."

Emerson's eyes widened as he looked back and forth between Jett and Tyler. "That's real? That's a real thing? And people know about it?" He scrubbed a hand down his face. "Shit, and you're black and you think he's got a big dick. What the fuck?"

"God, I just love having this over you." Jett smiled, puffing his chest out as he pulled his winter coat back on. Zoey wrapped her arms around his waist and reached up for a kiss.

"All right, get out. I get it. You win this one. I'm out. Go have sex with your enormous penis, you fucking mutant." Emerson was waving his hands, shooing them away.

Tyler met them at the door, glancing over his shoulder at their host. "Got any useful tips on how to handle this guy at work?"

Jett laughed and shook his head, scrubbing a hand over his beard. "Not a clue. Best of luck to you on that, though."

"He's almost too much of a stereotype to be real," Tyler said. He looked down at his feet, and Jett could sense he was uncomfortable. "Listen, I…it's not just that I haven't told Chris about the internship. I sort of…made one up. I told him I was doing something else completely."

Jett groaned. "Man, why did you have to tell me that? Just tell him about this one. You know I don't do secrets."

"I will...eventually. I promise. Just don't mention anything about it to Chris. Please. I'm not asking you to lie, I'm just asking you to not say anything."

"You'll make a great lawyer, Ty," said Jett, patting him on the shoulder. "I won't say anything though. Promise."

Tyler nodded and a look of relief washed over him before shifting his gaze to Zoey. "It was nice to meet you, Zoey. You've got a good guy here. Maybe the best."

Zoey smiled and tightened the grip of her arm around Jett as they walked out. He felt the knot in his chest tug again as he felt the weight of yet another secret adding to the list. It really shouldn't be that big of a deal. This one at least had nothing to do with him but he couldn't help the gnawing feeling that he was still doing something wrong.

He held onto Zoey now, focusing his attention on the one thing he was sure he was doing right.

CHAPTER 17

"No, he is not interested in an interview," Zoey said robotically into the phone. "He's not even in the country at the moment, but assured me he has nothing to say on the matter."

She threw her head back in exasperation and waited, only half-listening to the woman on the other end. Jett was just ahead of her at the Christmas tree farm, and she was getting sick of having to answer these calls. He picked her up just before noon after having worked a closing shift at the bar and he looked absolutely exhausted, but was still his cheerful, goofy self when he opened his truck door for her. And now this was the third phone call to interrupt them since they'd arrived at the tree farm fifteen minutes ago.

"Well, I don't know where those rumors are coming from. His mother has chronic kidney disease and is seeking treatment which, yes, happens to include dialysis."

She watched as Jett checked out a tall fir tree and suspected he was trying very hard to look like he wasn't already over these phone calls, too. He had to be getting annoyed with her phone going off every five minutes. The memory of Quinn telling her that it was her off-season, too, made her want to laugh. If anything, his off-season meant more work for her.

Finally wrapping up the call, she shoved her phone in her pocket and caught up with Jett. "I am so sorry. I can't believe how crazy people are being about this right now."

"It's okay," he said, smiling half-heartedly and looking at the massive tree in front of him. "What do you think?"

She craned her neck slightly, looking to the top. "I think...it's way too tall for your apartment. You'd have to cut a hole in the ceiling."

"Damn, you're probably right." He sighed. "Maybe we could put it in Rae's house. She has high ceilings."

"You wouldn't have to worry about dragging it up your narrow stairwell, either. But I still think it's too tall for her house. Quinn's place back in LA would work. He's got vaulted ceilings."

Jett hummed. "Of course he does. Well, I'm not taking it on a plane. Moving on."

There was a thick layer of powder to trudge through after a heavy snowfall the previous night. It was gorgeous, and all the trees looked like they belonged in a winter wonderland. Zoey could almost ignore how cold her nose was as she admired the scenery.

She looped her arm through Jett's and leaned into him as they walked through the snow. Spotting a small, almost bare pine tree, she stopped and pointed it out. "Aw, it's a Charlie Brown tree!"

"I have way too many decorations and ornaments for a Charlie Brown tree."

"You could put it in the bar," she suggested.

"So it can get knocked over by drunks? Poor thing looks like one shove will strip it of all its needles." He ushered her forward. "How about this one?"

"It's very green. And fluffy," she replied. She reached out to feel it and felt a sharp poke through the knitted pattern of her gloves. "Ouch! Prickly, not fluffy."

Jett chuckled. "Yeah, that's why we call them needles."

"Okay, but after stringing on lights and hanging ornaments, I think I'll be all scratched up. Or bleeding."

"We can't have that," Jett said, kissing the side of her head. "All right, I'm sure there's a softer one around here somewhere."

Zoey spotted a small cabin-like house that was dressed up to look like a gingerbread house and brought Jett to a halt next to her. "What is that?"

"That's Santa's cabin. They usually put it out front when it's in use, and there are a bunch of lights and it's a whole thing."

"It looks empty. Come here," she wrapped both hands around his forearm and pulled him toward the small house. She stood up on her tip-toes, looking around before grabbing the door knob and pulling it open, dragging Jett behind her.

It was a very small space, with just one room. It was really more the size of a shed than a cabin, and it was only partially decorated on the inside. A large red and white chair sat in the middle, with a high back and ornamental candy canes.

Grinning wickedly at Jett, she asked, "Have you ever had sex in Santa's cabin?"

He arched an eyebrow as he looked down at her and returned her grin. "That sounds like a really good way to get on the naughty list."

"That's okay. I don't think there's anything I really want for Christmas that I'm not already getting."

Jett tugged at the top button of her peacoat and worked his way down. Grabbing her by the hips, he backed up to the chair and sat down, pulling her into his lap. "Why don't you sit on my lap and tell me what you want anyway."

She straddled his lap and curled her hands behind his neck as she kissed him. Despite the cold, his hands were still warm as he slid them beneath her sweater and palmed both her breasts.

"*God*, these are perfect. I swear, I just want to bury my face in them."

"Oh my God," Zoey moaned. "*Please*, do it."

He shoved her sweater up and let his mouth go straight for her breasts. His head was inside her sweater as he folded the cups of her bra down so his mouth could cover a nipple, licking and swirling his tongue around it, sucking at her skin. A hand massaged the other, squeezing almost desperately, as if he couldn't get enough. Couldn't gain control. He kissed between her breasts before switching his mouth to the other side and she shivered at the feel of his tongue on her skin there.

Zoey slid her hands to his jeans and began undoing them, wanting to feel his warm, thick length filling her hands. She reached into his jeans and groaned when she found him hard and full. She wanted to ride it. To feel herself stretch to accompany his size as he slid in and out from beneath her.

"Jett, let me..." she breathed, stroking his cock through his boxers as it lay pressed against his stomach. Already, her thoughts were coming out scattered, chopped into half-phrases as she tried to process exactly what she wanted. All of him. Any piece he would give her. Any way he would please her. "Inside me...please."

"You wanna ride it?" he rasped. His hands pressed her tits together and he was sucking between them, licking the swells, like he was trying to consume them.

"Yes...God...I don't care," she panted. His beard scratched at her skin and contrasted with the soft, wet kisses he was showering her with, and his cock was growing harder with each touch, each stroke. "Just *need* it."

Her phone rang.

She blew out a long exhale and Jett groaned, teeth to her skin. "Baby, don't answer it."

"Jett, it's work." Her voice was breathless but filled with frustration. She shoved her hand in her coat pocket and checked the screen.

"Just let it go to voicemail. You're going to tell them no anyway."

"I know, I'm sorry. I'll make it quick, I promise." She gave Jett a pained, apologetic expression before swiping to answer, "Zoey Nunez."

"Hi, Miss Nunez? This is Carla Wright," a female voice said. The woman sounded like she belonged in a news anchor chair, not behind a computer writing the stories. "I write for SoCal Tea with a Twist."

Zoey rolled her eyes. Tea with a Twist was a trashy gossip column that was aptly named. It certainly threw a twist in its stories. "Okay, now isn't a good time. You can email me-"

Carla cut her off, speaking slowly and clearly, "I was wondering if you'd like to comment, or if Mr. Casey would like to comment on the interesting pieces of information we found regarding his mother."

"He's not interested in any interviews or comments-"

"This isn't about his mother leaving a clinic, Miss Nunez. This is about her arrest record as well as a drunk driving incident from 2009. It would appear Ms. Casey was in jail several times from 1993 through 2010. It's all making for a very interesting story..."

Zoey sat up straight, feeling as though she'd been doused in freezing cold water. "She *what?*" Jett looked at her curiously, obviously sensing the shift in her demeanor. He let her sweater drop back down and rested his hands on her thighs.

"Quite the record, really. Drunk and disorderly conduct, possession of drugs, child endangerment, neglect, more drug possession, more drunk and disorderly. She's got charges of being under the influence of illegal substances as well as alleged prostitution." Carla paused, likely for dramatic effect, but Zoey was grateful for the chance to process everything. Unfortunately, the list didn't stop there. "There's a really interesting one from 2006. Apparently she and another man were arrested on drug charges. But the man, while intoxicated, was also charged for assaulting a minor at her residence."

What the hell?

Zoey cleared her throat and did her best to not sound completely blind-sided, "Mr. Casey is not currently in the country, but I'm sure he will have a comment regarding...this new information."

"Do *you* have a comment, Miss Nunez?" Carla asked. She sounded friendly, but for some reason Zoey imagined her smile would look more like a dog bearing its teeth.

"Not at this time."

"Wonderful, Miss Nunez. We'll be in touch then."

Zoey heard the three beeps that signaled Carla had hung up and she stared at her phone for several long moments.

"What's wrong?" Jett tilted his head adorably, reminding her of a concerned puppy.

"Um...Somehow this...trashy gossip column got its hands on Quinn's mother's arrest record?" She replied in a question. Of course she had no knowledge of this. Any of it. She felt her brow crease as she wondered why the hell Quinn wouldn't have given her a heads up about any of it. "Is that...I mean, does that sound possible? Does she have a lengthy criminal record?"

Jett sighed and leaned back. "Probably. I don't know all of it."

"She said it contained incidents from 1993 through 2010."

He looked up, seeming to be thinking or trying to remember something. "Well, I met him in 2002. In sixth grade. I know about a few times she was arrested. Probably not all of them. Rae might be the only person who knows about all of them. But I was there for one."

"The one in 2006?" Zoey's eyebrows shot up. "She said a guy was arrested for assaulting a minor?"

"Yeah, I was there. All four of us were."

The four of them. Quinn, Rae, Jett, and Chris. Zoey had thought she had their friendship figured out when she'd gone to Jett's house on his birthday. The scoreboard, all the small details that were left in his bedroom. She'd just assumed their bond was a normal one. Close, but otherwise just typical kid and teenager stuff. She had no idea the kinds of things they'd been through and seen together. Of course Quinn would have to talk to someone about it for her to know.

Zoey liked their group. She liked their dynamic and that she might get to become a part of it in time. But this suddenly had her feeling like an outsider. There was no way she would be able to develop the same bond with all of them that they had developed over so much time.

"Who...?" She almost felt indecent asking too much about something Quinn clearly wanted kept a secret. But this wasn't just his story, it was all of theirs. And Jett could tell her about it if he wanted.

"Quinn. He took a few hits. Gave a couple, too." Jett shrugged. "I mean, he can throw a punch, but we were only fifteen or sixteen. This was a grown man who was on...something. I don't know what. Cocaine...maybe meth."

She was silent for a few beats as she imagined what that must have been like. Blowing out a humorless laugh, she shook her head. "The mystery of Quinn Casey just keeps piecing itself together."

Suddenly she looked back down into her lap. *His* lap, where she still straddled him. "I'm sorry. We were…" she gestured between them, "and now we're…"

"Talking about Case?" Jett asked, eyebrow flicking up just a bit.

"Exactly."

Jett brought a hand up to cup her face and pulled her lips to his. "I think we can get the sparks flying again."

She smiled into his kiss and let herself melt back into him.

And that's when the door to the cabin opened.

"Hey! You can't be in here!" A man with a bushy gray mustache snapped through the tension.

Zoey felt Jett's body deflate beneath her and she reluctantly slid out of his lap.

"Just…testing the chair's durability. I hear Santa's a big dude," Jett said. When he stood up, he was not particularly subtle about zipping and buttoning his jeans back up, and Zoey had to stifle a laugh. They passed by the man awkwardly and continued their quest to find the perfect tree.

One hour and one-thousand phone calls later- okay, maybe like seven phone calls, but still, seven? Seven phone calls in *one hour?*- they were on their way back to Jett's apartment with a tree in the bed of his truck.

He talked to her the whole way back, though her head was down, staring at her phone as she answered emails. Apparently that gossip column wasn't the only news source digging up dirt. Zoey still responded to his comments and laughed when he made jokes, but he felt like there was some other presence in the cab of his truck. It was as if Quinn was sitting there in the middle seat, separating them and talking over him the entire time.

He reminded himself several times that this was just her job. She didn't have an office or a building to go to. Her phone *was* her office.

And that was a good thing, even if it didn't seem like it right now. It meant she could work anywhere most of the time. Like...Traverse City, Michigan instead of Los Angeles, California. Maybe.

But the shitty thing about her phone being her office was that it followed them everywhere. Her work and people who wanted to get in touch with her to create work could be there. Everywhere. Constantly.

Chris was at the bar getting ready to work and stopped to help them haul the tree up the stairs. The stairwell was narrow, but they managed. They set the tree in its stand, got the tree skirt around it, and Jett and Chris both lugged the giant storage tote of ornaments and lights out of his storage closet.

In the living room, Zoey was sitting on the couch...phone to her ear. Again.

Chris gave Jett a knowing glance and lowered his voice, "Been like this all day?"

"She literally got twelve phone calls- *twelve*- in the time we were at the tree farm. All of them asking about Quinn. Good God, I love the guy, you know that, but it's like high school all over again after he figured out he had game. I liked a girl, and she only had eyes for Quinn Casey."

"Yeah, man, I remember." Chris nodded with a grimace. "Well, at least it's not like he's making out with her in front of you or...asking to borrow your car so he can take out the girl you were crushing on."

"It feels like it, and he's not even here." Jett fisted his hair and leaned his elbows on the counter. Of course, even then it hadn't been on purpose. Jett remembered the third time Quinn mentioned having a date with a girl Jett liked in high school. He finally told him that he kept asking out the girls he was interested in and Quinn immediately canceled because, obviously, if she wasn't Rae, he didn't really care.

"Don't take it too personally, man," Chris said, giving him a pat on the back. "Besides, if she didn't work for Case, you never would've met her."

Chris made a quick exit, waving to Zoey on his way out. She returned the gesture with a smile and a wave of her own before getting back to her phone call.

Jett got started opening the box of ornaments and decorations, pulling the strings of lights out to check if they were all still good. He was on his third string of lights when he heard a heavy, exasperated sigh behind him.

"This is nuts. Quinn gets home in a few days and I told him I'd have it handled. It's completely blowing up," Zoey said, slouching into the back of the couch. "I never thought it would get this crazy."

"Yeah, well maybe he'll have to deal with it for a change," Jett said. He could hear the impatience and annoyance in his voice, but didn't know how much he could control it at the moment. "He never told you about any of it, so I don't see how he expects you to handle it."

Zoey considered for a few beats before getting up to join him next to the big red bin of decorations. "I think the more he denies it, the harder they're going to come at him. I think he's going to have to just admit it, don't you?"

"I think...this tree is going to be the best one yet once it's decorated," Jett replied, looking up at the tree before glancing at Zoey with a small grin.

"Oh my God, I'm sorry. I'm going on about your friend and we're supposed to be..." She pushed her hair out of her face with both hands. "Right. Okay. Decorating the tree. I think you're lucky I came with you because you almost ended up with one that would've made you bleed."

"You have proven yourself to be a great tree-picker-outer. I'm impressed," he said. "Now we'll see how good your decorating skills are."

"Oh, well I assure you, if there's anything I excel at, it's ornament placement. It's an underrated skill, but I might be the best." Zoey picked up a strand of lights, ready to get started.

Jett eyed her playfully. "I'll believe it when I see it."

The tree took four strands of lights, several long pieces of silver tinsel garland, at least a dozen extra-large bulb ornaments, and countless other decorations. Doves, frosted pine cones, icicles, snowflakes, red, gold, and green bulbs, and some deer. There were sprigs of holly with berries, and a few hockey themed decorations. By the time they were finished, it looked like it belonged in a department store display. Only better. Jett definitely thought it looked better.

They stood together, admiring their teamwork and Jett pulled the final piece out of the bin.

"Would you like the honor of putting the star on the tree?" He held the shining gold star out to her.

"I think I'm going to need some assistance," she replied with a smile, taking it from him.

Jett squatted down and let her get on his shoulders so he could lift her to the top of the tree. "I'm liking this position we've got going." He smirked and playfully nipped at the inside of her thigh. "I think we need to make it a new tradition."

Zoey giggled and reached the star out to place on the very top. Finding the end of the last string of lights, she plugged it into the star and watched it light up. Jett brought her back down, helping her get back to the floor next to him and they stood back again to really appreciate their handywork.

And then, as fate would have it, her phone rang...*again.*

Jett was unable to conceal his disappointed groan and even saw Zoey's shoulders sag at the now annoyingly familiar tone.

"Well, we got the whole tree done without interruption," Zoey said, turning and bending to pick her phone up off the coffee table. "I wasn't even counting on that."

He watched as she swiped to answer, and she barely had her greeting out when he made the decision. Jett swiftly grabbed the phone out of her hands and spoke into it, "She's busy right now." He pushed the button to end the call, then turned her phone off.

"Jett, I-"

"You're taking the night off." He tossed her phone into the recliner behind him then slipped a hand around her waist, pulling her in and pressing their bodies together. "I'm done sharing you today."

Zoey's eyes flicked up to his and she looked surprised. Finally, she nodded and he felt her body go pliant against his as she gave into him. He tilted her chin up with one finger and covered her mouth with his.

The heat they'd felt in Santa's cabin at the tree farm immediately returned, and it was as if his body wanted to pick up where they left off. He tore her sweater off and bent his head low to her breasts, showering them in rough kisses, wanting to scrape his teeth at her soft skin. Hands on her hips, he led her toward the couch and sat down, pulling her back on top of him. She straddled his lap and bowed her back, allowing him to devour her perfect tits.

He nearly ripped her bra off and couldn't remember the last time he'd felt this wild. This desperate for someone. Maybe never. He needed to feel like she was all his. He needed to feel her, touch her, taste her everywhere. He wasn't just trying to make love to her. He was trying to claim her as his own. God, he just needed to have her here with him and have no other interruptions. Know that there was nothing else on her mind, no one else she was thinking about.

Her black leggings slid off easily with her thong, and she was sitting in his lap completely naked while he was fully dressed. He wondered if it made her feel vulnerable, or if she trusted him enough that she was comfortable like this. His eyes made a slow, sweeping path down her body and he saw her skin prickle with goosebumps, saw her nipples go taut under his gaze.

"I love looking at you like this," he said, watching his hands slide down her sides to her hips. He just barely dipped a hand to where she was spread over him, teasing, and making her gasp before slowly sliding his hands back to her breasts. "Does it make you wet? Watching me drink you in like this?"

Zoey swallowed then whispered, "Yes." She leaned forward, brushing her lips against his. Slipping her tongue out to taste his mouth.

"Show me," Jett growled into her mouth. She whimpered and rocked her hips into him, as though his words had taken control of her body.

He looked down between their bodies and watched as she slid her own hand between her legs, touching herself. Making herself gasp and moan with pleasure.

"Jett, please," she whispered, "Touch me. Feel how wet you've got me. Just from undressing me...looking at me."

Jett shook his head. "Show me."

Zoey let out a shaky breath and whimpered again, pulling her hand away and bringing her fingers to his lips. His tongue swiped out, licking and sucking her fingers, tasting her. He groaned around her fingers, and picked her up, laying her on the floor in front of their tree.

"God, you *are* wet for me, baby," he rasped into her neck. Making a trail downward, he licked the long line of her collar bone, kissed between her breasts and sucked a nipple into his mouth. Still dressed, he pressed his hips into hers, pushing her down, grinding his length against her, knowing how she'd love the rough sensation of his jeans where he was hard against where she was bare, soft, and wet.

"Please, Jett...I need it. Need you," Zoey panted harshly.

He kissed down her ribs, her stomach, sucked at her hip bones, and settled himself between her thighs. His favorite place to be. He lightly traced a finger up and down her slick skin where she was glistening and ready for him. Waiting to be devoured. Conquered. But he took his time kissing the insides of her thighs until she was rolling into him. Her body was begging him for release, but he wanted to hear it on her lips.

"Jett...please," Zoey whimpered. Her body was getting so impatient. By now it knew what was coming and didn't want to wait. Her body knew what he did to her, what he made her feel, and needed it now.

"Please, what?" His eyes flicked up and he saw her chest heaving, hips rolling, body squirming. *So* impatient. He loved it.

"*Jett*, please, I need you." She tangled her fingers in his hair and tried pulling him closer to her core. Heat was radiating off of her and he moved so that his mouth was hovering just over her pussy.

"And what exactly do you need?" He pressed a soft kiss to her bare skin, just above where she needed it.

She moaned, her hips lifting off the ground, searching desperately for him. "You. Your mouth, your tongue. *Please*, I just...*God*, Jett, I need you to make me come."

Finally, he obliged. Without warning, he slid a finger inside her and his tongue found her clit. Circling, licking, sucking, pumping his finger in and out. Adding another, she moaned loudly and arched her back. Already so wet, she wasn't going to take long to come undone. She grabbed his hair and pulled him deeper, fucking his face, going completely wild for him.

Her body shook and jerked. She gasped and moaned and whimpered, her breathing came in loud rasps as he pleased her. His cock was hard as a brick in his pants and he couldn't wait to plunge into her. He might not even wait for her to come down all the way. His cock throbbed, his balls ached for release, and he didn't want to take his time anymore.

Zoey was screaming now. Screaming his name and praises and *yes, yes! Oh my God, Jett, yes!* She shoved her hips upward and into him, begging and pleading through her orgasm for him not to stop, telling him it felt so good.

Undressing himself in record time, he grabbed the condom out of his pocket and slipped it over himself. Zoey was still gasping and catching her breath when he slid into her, sending his first thrusts slow, slow...giving her time to adjust, before picking up his pace.

He sat back on his heels and wrapped her legs around him, sending deep, snapping thrusts hard into her. He watched her body's reaction to him. Her tits bounced with each movement, she was flushed and sweating, her head thrown back, mouth open in silent cries of pleasure. So fucking sexy.

"Fuck, Zo...your mouth wide open like that makes me want to fuck it again. You're so goddamn sexy, baby," Jett moved over her, leaning forward to kiss her mouth, taste her tongue, suck on her neck. She kept her legs wrapped around him and slipped her hands behind his neck, plunging her fingers into his thick curls.

Moving into her over and over, he felt the slow build to his climax take shape. It was so good, but he wanted to hear her scream again. Wanted to feel her contracting around him, squeezing him. "I can't get enough of you, Zo. *Goddamn,* you're so perfect. I just want all of you." His hands grasped her breasts and he moved faster.

"Jett...oh god...Jett, I'm so close," she panted. "Fingers...please, touch me."

He slipped a hand down to her clit and rubbed her in circles, feeling the way it made her clench around him when he touched her. "Like that, baby?"

Unable to give an audible response, Zoey gasped and whimpered, hips pushed off the floor, pressing hard against his body as she squeezed him so tight. Her whole body quivered and shook as she came around him.

He collapsed onto her, and they were chest-to-chest, feeling the slick slide of their skin, feeling her nipples poke into him. He grabbed her hips and snapped into her. Again and again. She was still shaking and panting, breathing heavy and desperate.

"Come on me," she breathed. "Please, Jett, make me yours."

Her words sent a shock to his dick and he barely had enough time to pull out and slip the condom off. He pumped his fist around his cock and her small hand reached down to help him finish. He released himself on her, over her tits, on her stomach, across her ribs and hips.

Hovering over her, he dipped his head to kiss her. He smiled down at her, sweeping his gaze down her body, sticky and covered with his release. "You don't mind me making a claim on you like that?"

She shook her head no. "I want to be yours." Lightly brushing her fingertips along his jawline, she pulled him down for another kiss.

"I want that, too."

"And even though you might have to share me sometimes," she began, and his eyes flicked up attentively, "I promise, you're the only one I want- the only one I've *ever* wanted- to have me like this."

He swallowed and pressed his forehead to hers. "And I want to be yours, Zoey. You can have all of me, okay?"

She smiled playfully at him. "I guess being on the naughty list this year paid off. That's all I wanted anyway."

Jett rolled onto his back and tangled his fingers with hers and they stared up at their tree in silence. No phones ringing, no one barging in demanding their attention. For the moment at least, everything was perfect.

CHAPTER 18

The next few nights, Jett stayed with Zoey at Rae's house, enjoying his daytime shifts now that Alaina and Corey were taking on the bulk of the night shifts. Zoey had made the executive decision to assign herself working hours in which she would answer calls from news outlets and reporters, and Jett had taken to turning her phone off at night so they weren't woken up by the sound of her phone ringing. It was also nice falling asleep to the silence of Rae's neighborhood rather than the noise of the bar booming downstairs until two in the morning.

The night before Quinn and Rae were due back, Jett helped Zoey pack and move her things over to his apartment. She had only mentioned checking out hotels to stay at a few times. He really didn't want her to check into a hotel, hoping she'd simply stay with him, but he supposed it would be nice to have a quiet place to go where people weren't constantly storming in and out. At least three times now, they'd been fooling around in the living room or back in his bedroom and someone had walked in. Lizzie, Chris, even Emerson on one of his lunch breaks. Jett supposed that's what he got for being so reliable.

Regardless, they stayed at his apartment that night, unsure if Quinn and Rae would get back early or late.

Communication with Quinn had been difficult for Zoey with the six hour time difference. Jett could tell she was nervous for Quinn to get back and find out that things hadn't blown over- actually, the media was far more interested in the new leaks that had come out about his troubled past- and was really hoping she'd get to tell him about it in person rather than worry him while he was on vacation with his fiancé.

He made space for her clothes in his closet and a dresser drawer, making note to clean out the closet in the spare room so he could feel like he was making more of an effort to accommodate her staying with him.

Once her bags were unpacked, they'd showered together and taken the heat that had started there back to the bedroom.

Again, they made love for hours. Jett couldn't stop touching her and memorizing each curve of her body. He had never been so insatiable. As hard as he came each time, he thought for sure it would've been enough to satisfy his craving for her, but they would catch their breath and he'd feel her skin against his, her leg draped over him while she slid her hand along his chest and he'd be hard all over again.

He thought he was dreaming about making love to her, feeling wet heat around his cock, when he groaned and lifted his hips, feeling the tickle of her long, wavy hair brush against his thighs.

It was dark in his room, except for the moonlight reflecting off the snow outside, creating shadows. There was no more noise downstairs or outside, so he knew all the bars were closed, and downtown was asleep for the night.

He looked down his body and growled at the realization that Zoey was between his legs, getting him off with her mouth. He reached beneath the sheets and cupped the side of her face, tracing his fingers along her jaw that he could feel was opened wide to allow him in fully.

"Trying to wake me up, baby?" Jett's voice was groggy with sleep, but he grunted with a slow thrust into her mouth as he felt her tongue swirl around the head of his cock. "Because I'm fine with it...*fuck.*"

She continued working him, with her mouth, her tongue, her hands, until he wasn't sure he could hold back. He wanted to come in her mouth, but he wanted to watch her body shake with an orgasm again even more.

"Baby, come up here," Jett whispered, reaching for her.

She gave one more deep swallow before coming up for air, straddling him and looking down at him with sleepy but eager eyes. Holding onto him, she rubbed against his length, feeling it along her clit and letting her eyes flutter closed and her head fall back. He could feel how wet she was, grinding against him for her pleasure, and he wanted to give her more.

"I woke up and my hand was wrapped around your cock," she whispered. "You were getting hard already and I just...needed you."

"I'm not complaining." Jett bit his lip with a grunt as he watched her get off on using his body like a tool. "You wanna ride it or just get off like that?" He moved his hips, increasing the friction against her clit and nearly coming at the way her back arched and her tits pressed forward.

"Haven't decided yet," she replied, a playful smile on her lips.

"Whatever you want, baby. I could watch you like this all night."

She leaned forward, finding his mouth with hers and tasting him, their tongues wrestling, breathing hot and heavy on each other's lips. He pushed his fingers through her hair and held on tight, and they were moving together. She was over him and his dick was hot and wet, slick skin squeezing all around it.

Moving in and out.

Deep and slow.

Losing himself beneath her.

His heart pumped hard and fast in his chest, tugging, feeling like it was about to burst. He craved her. Needed her. Couldn't fucking control himself with her.

He was absolutely wrecked for her.

"Jett," she whispered his name in a desperate plea. "Jett, please."

Reaching a hand between them, he felt how swollen her clit was and she hissed, begging him for more. Begging him not to stop.

She panted and slid her hands up her sides, grabbing her breasts that completely filled out her hands.

"Oh *fuck* yes," Jett groaned, watching the moonlit silhouette on top of him. Petting her clit with one hand, he grasped her hip with the other, pulling her down on him. "So fucking sexy."

A shiver ripped through her and he knew her skin was hot and flushed when she gasped and began to shake, throwing her head back as she came. He felt her orgasm all around him. Felt hot, wet skin, squeezing tight inside her.

He grabbed her hips with both hands and pushed himself into her, harder...faster. Wanting to take it all, to feel everything. Part of him hoped he could finally feel completely relieved this time, but another part of him wanted to hold onto the insatiable, never-ending desire for her. It was too good to ever have enough.

He felt the build reach its peak and- *oh fuck, oh fuck- fuck, I'm coming...coming so fucking hard.* The explosion went off like a nuclear bomb. He felt his chest expand, the heat spread from deep inside and ignite every part of his body. Breath coming in heavy rasps, he kept her hips firmly on top of him, challenging himself to relax while he was seated deep inside her.

Zoey bent forward and kissed from his chest, up his neck, and to his lips, her long hair brushing soft along his skin.

It took several moments of catching his breath for his head to clear before he realized how wet everything felt between his legs. It wasn't just sweat, and it wasn't just from Zoey.

"Zo..." he began, then cleared his throat, "Zo, I'm not wearing a condom."

"Shhh..." she whispered against his mouth and kissed him, "It's okay. We'll be okay."

The weight of her words hit him like a heart-reviving shock to the chest. She wasn't worried because whatever happened, they'd be fine. She wanted it to work. She wanted to be with him, *only* him, and she wasn't afraid of having to rearrange her life to make the commitment.

"We can...I can go to the store and get Plan B or...whatever you want, okay?"

She nestled her face into his neck and he felt her body relax into his. "We'll worry about it tomorrow."

But for now, he understood, she just wanted to enjoy this. Being with him, nothing between them.

"Zoey," he whispered into her hair, and she made a faint, sleepy sound of acknowledgement, "I'm completely falling for you."

Jett felt a puff of air against his neck as she let out a small sound. "Jett, I've already fallen."

He closed his eyes and let the words sink in. He played them on a loop in his head. His arms held her close, face buried in her hair, breathing in her scent.

She's already fallen. She's mine. She...loves me.

They slept until ten and lounged around in bed for a while before deciding to get up. They showered before getting into bed, but after several rounds of steamy love-making sessions the night before, their bodies were sticky with sweat and...*other* stuff.

Washing her hair, Zoey blushed, biting her lip as she remembered their spontaneous middle-of-the-night sex. She wasn't sure who this new Zoey was who'd overtaken her body, but she kind of loved her. She was bold and sexy and did things like wake her boyfriend up with blow jobs. She made time to have a life and wasn't letting work dictate everything she did.

Granted, she felt a little bad about not keeping everything under control while Quinn was away. She knew he'd be upset. Maybe furious. But there wasn't a whole lot she could do. If people were set on digging into his past and there were demons to find, someone would find them and drag them to the surface. Reporters were relentless. They didn't care what kind of trauma they might be rekindling. They just wanted the story. She just hoped she got a chance to talk to him about it before he saw any of the new articles that had been printed- particularly the one she'd seen by *Tea with a Twist.*

But for now, she was giddy and happy and...*in love.* She'd been half-way back to sleep when he told her he was falling for her- *completely* falling for her- but it hadn't impacted her any less. She'd gotten a great night's sleep and was ready for another day with the most perfect man she had ever met.

In true Jett Miller fashion, when she walked out into the kitchen in her bathrobe, he already had her coffee set out for her. He had figured out exactly how to make it with just a splash of hazelnut creamer, and had been making it for her every morning for the past week.

She took in his appearance as he stood over a griddle pan, making eggs, bacon, and French toast, wearing black basketball shorts and a maroon hoodie. He had apparently also felt the need for a shower and had fully shaved for the first time since her arrival. Really, he could pull off either look; clean-cut or scruffy, but she couldn't deny how much she loved the feel of his stubble between her legs.

"You shaved," Zoey said, taking her usual seat at the counter.

"Yeah…" He rubbed a hand along the side of his jaw. "There was…something in it. Sticky. We got sort of acrobatic last night, I wasn't sure if it was yours or mine so I just…figured I'd be safe."

Zoey giggled, peering at him admiringly over her coffee mug. "Well it looks good. I like the beard, too, but you've got a great jawline. Seems a shame to cover it up too much."

He grinned shyly, the way he does when he doesn't know exactly how to take a compliment, and made up two plates. His plate had about twice as much food as hers and she snuck a crispy piece of bacon off of it.

"Excuse me, Miss Nunez, but what makes you think you can steal bacon off my plate?" Jett asked, reaching over and snagging a piece from hers.

"I *did* wake you up with my mouth last night."

He paused and seemed to consider for a moment before giving her back the slice of bacon. "Fine. But that's the only time you can use that today. If you want to use it for something else, you have to do it again."

"I feel like it should cover at least two free passes."

"I'll consider it," he replied, pouring maple syrup on his French toast.

After breakfast, or brunch at this point, Jett got dressed and ready to head downstairs for work. She kind of loved that he worked right below his own apartment, though she could do without all the noise until two in the morning.

As usual, she thought she'd fill her time while he was working to do some work of her own, but first she wanted to call home and make some arrangements.

There were only a few days until Christmas and she really wanted to spend it with her family. She hadn't seen them in over a month, and she also really wanted them to meet Jett. Even though her dad was ridiculously protective and liked to come across as intimidating, she knew there was no way he could dislike Jett.

She found her phone and turned it back on, ready to see just how many emails and voicemails she had- a lot. A ridiculous amount, actually. She groaned and plopped down on the couch, flipping open her laptop so it was ready to go when she got off the phone with her dad.

Work could wait. She needed to get Jett a spot at the family table for Christmas.

"What's up with you?" Chris asked, eyeing Jett with a curious smirk. "You look like a sixteen-year-old boy who just got his first blowie."

Jett laughed. "Well, I won't go into detail, but last night was...pretty fucking great."

"Up all night, huh?" Chris nodded his approval. "Okay. Get it, man. Good for you."

Jett's dopey grin returned as he mindlessly grabbed a box of empty beer bottles to set out with the returns. He was sure he looked dazed and absolutely stupid, but he didn't care. He was flying high, enjoying the sensations of this blissfully happy feeling that completely encompassed him. Nothing could get him down. Not a damn thing. Hell, he'd probably even find a visit from Emerson enjoyable and his bro-like tendencies endearing.

He didn't say anything when Xander showed up ten minutes late for his shift at the bar. Instead he gave him a high-five and told him it was good to see him. When Chris mentioned they were out of fry-seasoning for their beer-battered fish, he happily improvised and made a new seasoning mix that was barely distinguishable from their usual.

Today was fucking phenomenal.

He was only working until seven and had a whole evening ahead of him baking Christmas cookies with Zoey. And he really did intend to bake cookies. It wasn't just a ploy to get her in a sexy little apron for spontaneous kitchen sex. Not that he would be opposed to that as a consequence, of course.

It was going on five o'clock when another gust of cold wind entered the bar. The place was filling up and the snow was really coming down heavily outside. Jett was on the customer side of the bar, talking to one of the bartenders about the previous night's Red Wings game when he looked up and saw Quinn storming up to the bar with purpose.

"Hey Case, how was Paris?" Jett lifted his chin in greeting and gave him a friendly smile.

Quinn's returning glare was...not so friendly. "Are you fucking kidding me? Jett, have you watched *any* fucking sports channel recently? Jesus Christ, Zoey *knows* about this, right?"

Right...Quinn's tragic childhood was being exploited as a topic of interest on every news outlet that gave a shit about sports or celebrities. So...most of them.

"Yeah, she knows," Jett replied, finding himself puff up in defense of his new girlfriend. "She's been on the phone non-stop, telling everyone you don't want interviews, you don't have a comment. Basically doing what you asked."

Quinn narrowed his eyes, looking almost menacing as he stared incredulously at Jett. "She told me it would be handled by the time I got back. She said it would blow over and I wouldn't have to worry about it."

Jett stood up straighter and furrowed his brow at his friend. "And she thought it would. Dude, it's out of her control what people are able to dig up about you. All she can do is talk to them for you and tell her what you wanted her to say. Not to mention, it's a little difficult for her to handle this when you've never told her about any of it. She's fucking overwhelmed and doesn't know where to start."

"This isn't her first time coming up with a cover story," Quinn snapped. "Her job is to manage my image, not know everything about me. She doesn't have to know what's true to make something up that people can believe."

Jett laughed humorlessly. "Yeah, you're right. We'd all hate for you to lose your *perfect* image. Jesus, Case, if you admitted to even half of this shit it would probably help your image. People might think you're more than just some asshole who can fuck whoever he wants because he's got talent."

Quinn reared back and his eyebrows shot up. "Excuse me?"

Fuck. I didn't mean to say that...out loud.

Yes, Quinn was one of his oldest friends. They had been through a lot together, but it was hard for Jett to ignore how much he'd changed. He wasn't the same guy he'd been back when they were kids. Even when they were teenagers and all the girls in school wanted Quinn, he'd been relatively quiet about it. Humble even, at times. But the Quinn Casey who'd been on TV and in the news and on *SportsCenter* and *ESPN* over the past six years was someone else entirely. Didn't he realize that?

Jett rolled his eyes. "Act like you don't know that's how people see you. And you know what? It works for you. People still love you. Of course they do- Quinn Casey can do no wrong, right? He falls down, he stands back up with a smile because he found a fucking hundred-dollar bill on the ground. It must be so fucking nice to have someone there to make sure everything is taken care of for you."

"Is that what you think?" Quinn sneered. "You think my life is *perfect* because I worked my ass off to get out of that fucking house? To go somewhere? To not end up like my mom or, hell, even my dad, whoever the fuck that is?"

Jett became aware they were drawing a crowd. The music wasn't too loud yet; they kept it at a lower volume through the usual dinner shift and cranked it later on. Quinn was shouting, and honestly, he looked like he wanted to hit someone.

"What I'm saying is that you ask too much of Zoey," Jett replied, in a more even tone. "She works her ass off to schedule all your shit, she talks to all these obnoxious reporters so you don't have to-"

"It's her *fucking* job, Jett! If she's sick of it, I'm sure she'll let me know, but she can't just stop doing it."

"It's not her job to schedule your doctor appointments. It's not her job to make sure you go to your personal training sessions. It's not her job to make sure you get up on time in case you sleep through your alarm," Jett rattled off, feeling himself stand up straighter, pulling his shoulders back as he took a step closer. "She's your *publicist*, Case, not your mommy. Maybe you should try picking up your own messes for a change."

"What the fuck's your problem?"

"What's *my* problem?" Jett pressed. "Case, you have no fucking idea how much you've changed, do you? You used to hate having people do shit for you. You used to have some semblance of humility, but now look at you! You've spent the past six years fucking around with any girl who'd look your way, completely ignoring how you got there in the first place. Pretending you're this cool, smooth-talking ladies man, refusing to acknowledge your past and anything that actually made you a somewhat decent human to begin with."

Quinn laughed, low and humorless. "I should've seen this coming. You've always been jealous of the attention I got. You were always jealous when the girls you liked were more interested in me, and you were jealous that I got recognized for baseball more than you did for hockey. It's starting to sound like the only reason you could stand being friends with me back then was *because* of my home situation. I might've been better at everything else, but at least my home life sucked, and that meant you were winning at *something*."

Jett fumed, letting out heavy, heated breaths as he clenched his fists at his sides. God, Quinn could be a dick sometimes.

Quinn still looked like he could have punched Jett, but instead he threw his hands up and tried to walk around him. "Whatever, I don't fucking need this right now. I need to talk to Zoey. Is she upstairs?"

Jett stepped in front of him again and halted him with a hand to his chest. "You're not going up there."

"I'm not?" Quinn stared down at him, arching a cocky eyebrow.

Jett couldn't believe how quickly he heated up. That cocky, self-assured look, like Quinn was going to do whatever the hell he wanted regardless of what Jett said, put his blood on boil.

"No, you're not. Not when you're like this."

Quinn smirked and nodded, and of course it pissed Jett off even further. "She still works for me, Jett. Just because you're fucking her now doesn't change that."

It didn't matter that Quinn was a few inches taller. It didn't matter that he was like a wall of solid muscle. And it suddenly didn't matter that they'd been friends since they were eleven years old. Jett charged and shoved Quinn, hard.

Quinn stumbled back and caught himself on a table. He got his bearings and instinct took over, coming back ready to take a swing. Jett wasn't going to wait to either dodge or get hit, so he put his fists up, ready to go, too.

The only contact Jett was met with, however, was Chris's shoulder, shoving him back as he and another much smaller form got between him and Quinn before either one could strike.

"What the hell is going on? Why are *you two* fighting each other?" Chris shouted. His voice carried over everything; the music, the excited sounds of onlookers. He looked at Jett as though he were a complete stranger and said much quieter, "What the fuck, man? We talked about this. It's not personal."

Jett glared over Chris's shoulder at Quinn. "He made it personal," Jett growled.

Rae was with Quinn now, wrapped around one of his arms and looking back and forth between Jett and her fiancé in horror. Jett realized with alarm that she must've been the other person to get between them. Jesus, what if he'd hit her?

Quinn glared back and there was a twitch in his jaw where he was clenching his teeth. When he looked down at Rae, he wrapped his arm around her waist and nodded toward the door.

Looking back one more time, Jett saw Quinn's eyes travel behind him and he spun around to see Zoey looking horrified at the scene that had just unfolded before her. Instantly, Jett wanted to know how much she'd heard, and hoped she understood he was just sticking up for her.

"I'm glad you're having fun, Zo," Quinn said, his voice slicing through the thick tension, "but I think your work is slipping a bit." He looked back at Jett one more time but still spoke to Zoey, "Your phone was off all morning. Call me back when you get through my messages. *If* your boyfriend's okay with you doing your job."

Jett was shaking with fury. Ready to explode. Ready to hit something. Someone. Goddamn, he was pissed. He couldn't believe his friend was being such a dick. He blew out a hot breath through his nose and stared Quinn down until he turned with Rae and walked out the door.

CHAPTER 19

Upstairs in Jett's apartment, Zoey was hastily throwing together an overnight bag. She had just looked at her phone and saw that, buried beneath all the reporter calls and voicemails, Quinn had been trying to reach her since the previous evening. He must have seen something on the news or online about all the new information that had come out and wanted to know how that had all happened. Her last text from him simply read *A head's up would've been nice.*

A sinking feeling in her gut told her that he was absolutely right. It was ridiculous for her to expect that she could talk to him before it reached his ears. Apparently he and Rae had been met outside the airport with a herd of reporters, shouting questions at them as they ducked into Charlie's car.

She hoped he would understand that she just wanted to talk to him about it in person. She had no idea what kind of statement to make, no idea what would cover up all this evidence that was being brought to the surface. Honestly, she thought his best option was to tell everyone, "Yes, that's exactly what my life was like growing up. I don't have further comments, and would appreciate it if everyone could respectfully leave it alone."

But getting him to agree to that would take a lot more than a quick text or a phone call.

She heaved a bag onto her shoulder and made her way out to the living room just as Jett walked through the door.

He glanced at the bag on her shoulder and the boots on her feet. "Zoey, where are you- You know I was just trying to defend you, right? He was way out of line coming in here like that."

"I know, Jett, but Quinn was right. I've been completely slacking on my work. There's no reason I shouldn't have at least given him a head's up about what he was coming home to."

"So...you're leaving?" He eyed the bag, looking alarmed, but she could tell he was trying to hold back.

"Not for good," she assured him. "I just need to go talk to Quinn and figure out what we're going to do about this. Hopefully it won't take long, but he's stubborn and he's not going to like what I have to say, so...I might end up having to stay late."

Chewing the inside of his cheek, he nodded quietly.

"I sort of put off checking all my emails and messages this morning. I guess Quinn had been trying to get in touch with me since last night, right before they got on their flight. I can't believe I didn't see all his messages." Zoey pushed a hand through her hair, thinking for the hundredth time that she could consider herself lucky if she didn't get fired. "But anyway, I booked a flight back home-"

"He's making you go back home?" Jett snapped. "Back to California? Why? Things aren't going to be any different there than they are here. He can't just run off and take you along with him because he doesn't want to face the truth."

Completely taken aback by his tone, she put up a hand to stop him right there. "Okay, first of all, this is my job, Jett. I had no idea it bothered you so much that I worked for him. I thought you guys were friends."

"Maybe we were," he muttered.

"And second, I'm not going back to California because Quinn wants me to. Before I started checking my emails this morning, I called my dad. I wanted to take you back with me...to meet my family. I thought it would be nice to spend Christmas with them."

Jett's chest deflated and his eyes closed. He pinched the bridge of his nose. "Shit, I'm sorry, Zo. I'm just...still amped up from what happened downstairs. I guess I'm a little on edge. Quinn was really pushing some buttons."

"I heard."

Jett winced. "How much did you hear, exactly?"

"Just the last part before you shoved him." She looked meaningfully at him, setting her bag down and grabbing her coat off the hook. "I don't know what history you guys have. I don't know if fighting is just something you two do, like brothers or something, but I really hope you can figure out a way to be okay with it. I might be able to work this out so I can...do my job long distance."

His eyes finally met hers and he looked a little more relaxed. Like a wave of calm had washed over him. He nodded and gave a half-hearted smile, "We'll make it work. And I would *love* to spend Christmas with your family. Even if it means palm trees instead of real trees."

"Palm trees *are* real trees."

Jett shrugged and made a sort of skeptical noise.

She laughed and, once her coat was buttoned, grabbed his shirt to draw him in with a kiss.

"Hey," he mumbled into her lips.

"Hey?"

"Are you sure you have to leave tonight?" Jett asked, pulling back just enough to speak. "It's crazy out there. Why don't you just wait until morning?"

She shook her head, both hands resting on his broad chest. "I can't put it off, I really need to take care of it tonight." Jett was the most perfect, spectacular distraction but right now she needed to work first, play later.

Jett made her promise to text him when she got to Rae's house before his mouth came over hers again and she sunk into it, letting him take control of the kiss, control of her heart. Then she left in a happy, dazed rush, ready to go clean up this new mess.

Zoey hopped into Rae's Jeep Wrangler and started it up. The snow was coming down in thick flakes, and the wind was blowing, creating drifts in the streets. Having to use the massive snowbrush in the back seat, she had never been more appreciative of simple, innovative technology. Things no Southern Californian would have considered.

The roads downtown weren't bad, and it seemed a lot of people had opted to stay in rather than risk the bars in this weather. If it weren't for the sick feeling she still felt at having let Jett completely distract her from her work- a welcome distraction, but a distraction nonetheless- and if he hadn't just nearly punched Quinn, she would have asked him to drive her to Rae's house. She struggled with driving in the snow in the daylight when it was clear. By the time she hit M-37, the snow was thick and her entire windshield was a complete white-out.

Her heart pounded in her chest, unsure of what to do. Should she pull off to the side of the road and wait for the snow to stop? Should she just inch along at a snail's pace and accept that it would take an hour to get there?

She let out a long breath and made the decision to pull off and call Jett. Surely he could hold off on fighting with Quinn if her life was in danger. Flipping on her turn signal, she slowly inched to the side- or what she at least hoped was the side of the road. She reached into her purse and dug out her cell phone.

When she sat back up, there was a flash of bright lights in her rear-view mirror.

A loud crunch.

The Jeep lurched forward with a hard jerk.

A sharp pain in her head made her unable to distinguish if the Jeep was falling forward, or if it was just her.

And then it was dark.

Jett's leg wouldn't stop bouncing up and down as he stared absently at the television screen, waiting for Zoey's text that she'd made it to Rae's safely. He glanced out the window at the snow coming down in a thick white sheet. Chewing the inside of his cheek he couldn't help mentally kicking himself for letting Zoey go out in this weather. She didn't like driving in the snow when it was barely dusting the roads, let alone a blizzard.

Looking back to the television, he flipped through channels until landing on a sports network. There were three men and one woman at a large semi-circle table having what appeared to be a rather intense discussion.

Then a photo of Quinn in his blue and white uniform popped up in the corner of the screen. Jett groaned and rolled his eyes, only catching the tail-end of a comment made by one of the men at the table- "...met him, and I never would've thought he had these kinds of demons tucked away"- before turning the TV off.

"Fucking Quinn..." Jett muttered, slouching back into the couch. He flopped his head to the side and looked down at his phone again. Still nothing from Zoey.

She left about forty-five minutes ago, and he expected her to take the roads slowly, but was honestly hoping she'd call for him to come get her and bring her back.

Jett stood and slunk over to the piano that was now pushed in front of the window to accommodate the Christmas tree in the small living room. He sat on the bench and began playing a slow holiday tune when his phone started ringing.

He swiped to answer without looking at the screen, "Hey baby, did you make it to Rae's okay?"

"Jett, it's Rae."

Furrowing his brow, he pulled the phone away from his ear and glanced at the screen. Yep, it was indeed Rae's contact picture that lit up his phone. "Oh, hey. Did Zoey make it to your place okay? I knew it would take her a while."

"Actually, no. She's okay, but we just got a call...she's at the hospital. She was in an accident on her way here," Rae spoke hesitantly and slowly. "It sounds like someone rear-ended her when she pulled off to the side of the road."

Everything around Jett seemed to stop and he stared off as he processed what he was hearing. It felt like the happy bubble that had been making his heart float blissfully inside his chest every time he thought about her had popped, and his stomach sank with a sick, gnawing feeling. He *knew* he should've pushed more. Should've made her stay.

"Jett?" Rae's voice intruded his dizzying spiral of panic.

He shook his head, wondering why he was still sitting there on the phone with Rae. Clearing his throat he mumbled a quick "I'm on my way" into the phone and shoved himself away from the piano.

Keys, wallet, phone. Coat, gloves, boots. And he was out the door.

The roads were absolute shit, and he couldn't believe he hadn't at least offered to drive Zoey to the house. Rae said she was okay, but she was still at the hospital. What's okay? Still stable? Does she have any cuts or bruises or sprains? Any broken bones?

Jett drove as quickly as the conditions would allow, booking it to the hospital in record time for anyone who ever had to drive in a snowstorm.

He rushed to the reception desk and gave Zoey's name, and the woman working nodded and sent him in the right direction. There wasn't anyone trying to keep him out of her room, and he appeared to be the only one there so far.

In the hospital room, she was sitting up in the bed with a small bandage on her forehead, above her left eyebrow. Jett jogged over to the side of the bed and reached for her, holding her face in his hands.

"I'm so sorry, baby. I should've driven you or made you wait or-"

She smiled, looking relieved to see him there. "I promise I'm fine, it's just a cut. My head hit the window pretty hard."

"What happened? Rae said you got rear-ended."

Nodding with a wince, she replied, "Yeah, I was pulling over to call you, and the car behind me had already lost control and slid into me. It came out of nowhere. I didn't even see them until they were right behind me, the snow was so thick."

Jett brushed his thumb over the small white bandage on her forehead. "Did they check you for a concussion?"

"Not yet, but they're going to. I'm waiting for them to take me for a scan."

He leaned over her and kissed the top of her head. "I shouldn't have let you go out in this. I should've taken you. I know you hate driving in the snow, I don't know what I was thinking."

"It's okay," Zoey insisted. "I was pretty persistent about going tonight." She tilted her head curiously for a beat. "How did you get here so fast? They called Quinn in the ambulance and he's not even here yet."

"Why did they call Quinn first?"

"He's my emergency contact since we're on the road together all the time."

Jett nodded and swallowed down the itch of irrational annoyance he felt at this. "Well, there's no need for them to risk coming out in this. I'll just take you back to my place and I can drive you over there in the morning. I have years of experience driving in this stuff, so you'll be safe with me."

It wasn't long before a nurse came in to take Zoey away in a wheelchair to be scanned for a concussion. Jett made himself comfortable in the chair closest to the hospital bed while he waited.

At the sound of voices and the shuffling of feet just outside the door he looked up to see Quinn and Rae through the large glass doors looking like they were arguing. Their voices were hushed and Quinn was shaking his head no, gesturing into the room. Finally, Jett saw Quinn walk away from the door and Rae entered the room.

"This fight between you two is ridiculous," Rae stated firmly as she pulled the sliding door shut behind her.

"You don't need to be here. I can take her back with me," Jett said, choosing to ignore her comment.

Rae's stare was steely as she narrowed her eyes at him. "Jett Miller, you guys are best friends. What the hell is your problem?"

"They took Zoey back for a scan to see if she has a concussion, so I'm just waiting for them to bring her back." Jett leaned back and sprawled out in the chair, not meeting Rae's gaze now.

She let out an exasperated sigh, taking a seat in the chair next to him. "Fine. Stay mad. But I'll be the first to tell you that making up with Quinn is always an enjoyable experience."

Jett made a face. "Gross."

"I'm glad things with you and Zoey are going well. Wanna tell me all about it?"

He couldn't help the small smile that tugged up his lips. "Things are really good."

"And how was your first time?" she teased with a nudge.

"My first time *with Zoey*, you mean?"

"Whatever." Rae shrugged, grinning playfully.

Jett laughed lightly and smirked. "Well, let's just say my deep-V diver didn't fail to impress."

"Oooh, look at you," she giggled then high-fived him like the bro she'd always been to him. "Get it, Big D."

The glass door slid open again and Zoey was wheeled back into the room.

The nurse, a tall, thin man with short brown hair, gave them all a reassuring smile. "No concussion, luckily. But we still want her to take it easy. She'll probably get a headache or two over the next couple of days, but as far as we can see, there's nothing to be alarmed about."

Jett breathed a sigh of relief. The nurse told them they were free to go, and Jett helped Zoey get her coat back on and walked back up toward the lobby with Rae.

"Rae, I'm so sorry about your Jeep. I don't even know what shape it's in," Zoey began as they walked through the double-doors that separated the ER from the waiting room.

"Don't worry about it." Rae waved dismissively. "It's probably lucky you were in that anyway. I'm sure the damage can't be that bad."

In the waiting room, Quinn stood up from his chair and walked over, avoiding any eye contact with Jett as he stood next to Rae. He was fairly certain Quinn was just planning on ignoring his presence all together.

"How ya doin', Zo?" Quinn asked. His posture was stiff and uncomfortable, and Jett saw that signature muscle twitch in his jaw where he clenched, likely holding back some sort of rage reaction.

"I'm good. No concussion, no major injuries."

"Good." Quinn nodded curtly then gestured toward the front doors. "Uh, well, we've got a car pulled up just out front. I can take your bag and-"

Jett snorted derisively. "Seriously, Case? I think you've done enough for one night. She can come home with me and I'll drive her over tomorrow. You can put her to work then."

Quinn's jaw twitched again and he glared at Jett. "What do you mean 'I've done enough'?"

"I mean, if you hadn't been such a dick to her and made her feel bad about not handling *your* problems that you didn't even prepare her for, we wouldn't even be in a hospital in the first place."

"So it's *my* fault she got in a car accident?" Quinn asked, glare not faltering. "How about the guy who sent his girlfriend out in a blizzard when she's barely seen two inches of snow? I figured you were more of a gentleman than that."

"*Quinn*, stop it," Zoey said sharply. "I didn't want him dropping me off because I figured you two needed some time to cool off."

"I am cooled off. He's the one that shoved me," Quinn argued.

"Because you needed to snap the fuck out of it," Jett interjected. "You disrespected Zoey and came into *my* bar looking for a fight. You fucking found one."

"Jett, please," Zoey's voice cut through whatever Quinn was about to say and she grabbed him by the arm, steering him away from another confrontation. "Honestly, enough is enough. You said you'd find a way to be fine with me working for him. He's your *friend.* I know you're pissed at him right now, but this is my job. I need to get this handled."

"You want to go with him?" Jett felt the stab to his pride hit him square in the chest. "Zo, I can drive you in the morning. Take the night off. You've had a rough day."

"I've been taking a lot of nights off lately," she said, dropping her gaze. "It's not hard to see I've sort of dropped the ball on this whole thing. Sure, it's not all my fault- I was completely blind-sided and unprepared, but I still could have dealt with it better."

Jett felt like he was just waiting for her to change her mind. Make the rational decision and come back to his place. Work could wait. She didn't need to handle all of it tonight.

Come home with me. Pick me.

He couldn't say anything though, so he just waited.

Finally, her hazel eyes met his and she went up on her tip-toes to place a soft kiss to his lips. "I appreciate you standing up for me and everything you're trying to do. Just please let me get this under control, okay? And you can have me after."

He could only nod as she stepped away from him and walked back over to where Quinn and Rae were waiting. His chest felt as though it was going to cave in on itself as he watched her walk out the door and stood back wondering what the hell he'd done wrong.

CHAPTER 20

Quinn held the door open for Rae and Zoey and shoved it closed behind them against another large gust of wind and snow. It had been a fairly quiet ride to the house, though Zoey wasn't entirely unfamiliar with Quinn's brooding moods. He was clearly upset about his fight with Jett, and honestly, Zoey wasn't feeling that great about leaving him at the hospital looking like a sad puppy either.

After peeling off their extra layers, Quinn found his way into the living room and plopped down on the couch with a dramatic sigh. Harry greeted Zoey and Rae, wagging his tail with excitement- clearly he'd missed the memo about everyone's sour mood. Rae led the big dog downstairs to let him out into the backyard, and Zoey followed Quinn, sitting herself down in a chair adjacent to him and wondered where to begin.

Just as she was getting her thoughts put together, organizing them in the neat way they had been before her accident when she knew exactly how to present the issue to Quinn, his voice came out gravelly as he said, "You hated me when you first started working for me."

It wasn't a question, and she really didn't know how to respond. However, something in his tone, his posture, this new defeated sort of demeanor told her that he needed honesty.

"Yeah, I kind of did. You weren't easy to like."

"Because...I'm arrogant? I'm just some asshole who thinks he can fuck around and get whoever I want because I've got talent?"

Zoey's eyebrows shot up in surprise. Well, okay, yes, that was the general first impression she'd gotten of him and why she hadn't liked him, but since when did he care about that? Since when did he recognize the person he'd made himself into as anything less than exactly what he wanted people to see? He had always been so content with it. Sure, she had suspected it was just a show, just a front to cover up something more genuine, but he'd played the part so well and seemed to enjoy it.

"Well, I know there's more to you now, but yeah. That was the initial impression," Zoey admitted.

He let out another heavy sigh before sitting up and leaning forward to rest his forearms on his knees. "Maybe...maybe it's time I retire that image."

"You're off to a good start," Zoey said with a shrug. "I mean, you're engaged and you're almost never photographed without Rae anymore. People know you've changed. They can see that you're happy and it's not just some act you're putting on to get better attention."

"Yeah, well, apparently I still look like an arrogant asshole to some people."

Zoey chewed her bottom lip. "Did Jett say something to you?"

Quinn ran a hand through his hair and kept his gaze down at his feet. "I don't really care what most people think, or what they see or the assumptions they make. But when one of my best friends thinks that's the real me..."

She nodded and was actually grateful for this conversation. That he was actually being honest with her and not just brushing off the things that got to him so he could just act moody for days without explanation. "So...does this mean no more fist fights or bar top strip teases?"

Quinn half-laughed. "Let's not get carried away, Zo. Not everything I do in public is just for show." He ran a hand through his hair again. "I've always gotten into fights. I was angry. I get angry fast and I don't have what some people would call *impulse control.* I think my first fist fight was in kindergarten when a kid took my spot on the storytime mat."

Zoey couldn't help laughing at the image, but still hesitated before asking, "And are you ready to tell me *why* you were so angry all the time?"

His eyes shifted over to her. "I think you've figured out why by now."

"Quinn, you know I would've been able to give some sort of statement if I'd been a little more prepared. And it was easy enough deflecting people who were just making assumptions about your mom, but then I got the calls about her arrest history and I had no idea where to go with it. I mean, I can't make something up that contradicts actual records."

"I know…" He sighed again. "I guess I've been covering that stuff up for so long that it's just second nature. Someone asks me about it, and I deny it. I tell them they don't know what they're talking about…or I punch them in the face."

"I'm not saying you have to give a long speech and tell a big inspirational story of how you overcame the odds- although that might be nice for some kids in similar situations to hear- but I think we both know you're going to have to at least admit that it happened. That your home life wasn't great, you're healing your relationship with your mother after all this time, and you'd like to just leave it in the past."

Quinn eyed her skeptically. "What, you think I should do a special feature on my childhood so I can be all inspirational?"

"If you want to retire the playboy image, you might consider focusing on being someone kids could look up to. It wouldn't hurt."

"I'm not someone kids should look up to."

"You want to have kids of your own, right? Aren't you going to be a role model to them?"

Quinn's brow creased, and she couldn't tell if he was considering her point or just thought she was crazy. "Dammit, Zoey. You had to go and make sense on me."

Rae came back upstairs with Harry, who now looked like the abominable snowman. Rae sat on the couch next to Quinn and began absently rubbing his back in a consoling way that just seemed to come so naturally.

Quinn leaned into her touch and relaxed. "Zoey thinks I need to be a role model…for children. Not college dudes."

"Great, so she's going to make you even more irresistible to women," Rae said, giving him a peck on the cheek.

"I don't think there's any toning this down, babe," Quinn replied, sensually rubbing his hands down his sides.

Zoey rolled her eyes. "Okay, well if we're going to change your whole image, we've got some work to do. It's going to take baby steps...we'll issue a statement, set up interviews on different sports networks. I'll make sure they don't dive into anything you're uncomfortable with."

Quinn nodded and they got to work. It felt good to work like this, to have something in front of her that she actually knew how to solve. Having Quinn's cooperation on these types of things always made her job so much easier.

They flipped through different sports and news channels to see what was being said about him now and came up with their own ways of addressing it. Zoey began sending out emails to the more reputable networks that had contacted her over the past several days, and researched different youth events Quinn might be able to get involved with to get him some good press.

It was about three in the morning before she finally got into bed. Of course she knew Jett wasn't closing, but couldn't help the image of him crawling into bed sleepy after a long night of work that popped into her head. She tried not to think too hard about how sad and defeated he'd looked when she left the hospital as she shot off a quick *goodnight* text that hopefully wouldn't wake him up.

Closing her eyes, she reminded herself that she would see him tomorrow and it would be like tonight never even happened.

Jett spent the morning laying in bed until he absolutely had to get up for work. He'd spent too much time staring at the text from Zoey that had come in a little after three in the morning.

Goodnight, Jett. Sleep well, rest up, and I'll see you tomorrow when this is all taken care of.

The message was little comfort to him for how awful he felt about the previous evening. Awful because he was in such a great mood before it all happened. Before Quinn, before the accident, before she left him alone at the hospital.

It was Chris's day off, so he couldn't even vent to someone about everything, though Chris had sent him a few texts the previous evening to check in. Jett had told him about the accident and that Zoey had still left with Quinn rather than come back with him and let him take care of her. Maybe it was an addiction at this point, but it had really been nagging at him all night that she had gotten hurt and he couldn't take care of her.

He remained silent throughout most of his shift and had barely come out of the office unless he was needed for something. Even when Alaina came in for her shift, he didn't have much to say to her comment about missing the show the previous evening.

Someone at the bar had taken a clear video of the argument between him and Quinn, and it was now trending on Twitter and Facebook. There were even reaction videos being posted on TikTok, which Jett thought was a bit much. It's not like they'd actually punched each other. And it's not like it was anyone's business, either.

Checking his phone for what felt like the five-hundredth time that day, he was again disappointed to see that he didn't have any new messages from Zoey. She was taking care of stuff. Getting work done. But how long was that going to take?

Around three o'clock, he received a text from Emerson telling him that he might have to take Brody's place as his new best friend, but he really wasn't in the mood for that conversation. He was still mad at Quinn, and felt like he had a right to be, but their fight had left him with a sour taste in his mouth and an unsettled feeling in his gut.

It was about six-thirty when Jett finally felt like he could leave the bar in Alaina's hands and checked out to have a drink at the bar.

Of course, their bar primarily aired sports channels, so he wasn't surprised to see Quinn's picture pop up a few times. Even the video that had been making its way around the internet was played on one channel.

Great, now people were talking about him, too. Some people were calling him a dick for attacking Quinn while he was clearly going through a rough time, while others were applauding him, saying it was about time someone took a shot at Quinn's massive ego.

Neither of these critiques made him feel any better about it. The only thing that would make him feel better, he was certain, was seeing Zoey walk through the door.

After his third beer sitting at the bar, he paid his tab and headed upstairs, thinking he might mess around on the guitar or piano for a while. He knew he didn't want to just sit on the couch and wait for Zoey to text him, or to watch Christmas movies and have to jack himself off because that was a new weird thing that happened now. He was tempted to text Zoey himself, but didn't think that was something she needed. She'd made it clear she needed to focus on work and he didn't want to distract her.

In his apartment, he played guitar, he played piano, he tried to play some *Fortnite*, but couldn't get into it. He avoided the TV, because he knew all the channels he watched would either be talking about Quinn or showing Christmas movies. He cleaned the kitchen, caught up on laundry, and fixed the diverter in the shower. Finally, at about eleven-thirty, he resigned himself to the couch and checked his phone again.

Still nothing new from Zoey. Emerson and Brody had each texted him asking about the next video game night, and Chris had sent another 'checking in' text. Jett was lying on his back on the couch, staring up at his phone, trying to figure out what and if he should text Zoey.

They weren't fighting. Were they? There was no reason he couldn't send her a message. At least to say goodnight. He sent her a quick, and hopefully not too needy, *Goodnight, Zo. Will I see you tomorrow?* And with a heavy sigh, he dropped his phone to his chest and waited.

He was on edge and couldn't for the life of him figure out how he was supposed to fall asleep without hearing from her. He didn't want to fall asleep without her next to him again. He'd tossed and turned the entire previous night, wondering if he had done something wrong. Wondering if he'd been too pushy or if she was upset with him for distracting her from work. Was she upset with him for the fight in the bar? Maybe seeing that side of him had her questioning things. Questioning *him.*

The lights were off except for the glow of the Christmas tree and he thought he might have better luck trying to sleep on the couch.

Just as he allowed his eyes to close, there was a knock on the door.

His eyes snapped open and he rushed to pull the door open. Zoey stood with her gray peacoat, heeled boots, and gorgeous hazel eyes staring up at him.

"I'm sorry it's so late...I didn't want to wait until tomorrow."

Relief washed over him and he pulled her inside, covering her mouth with his, claiming her lips with a long, demanding kiss. His tongue parted her lips, wanting to consume her. She was the first refreshing gulp of water after a long walk in the desert. The first gasping breath of air after being held under water. He needed her now more than ever.

They were pulling at each other's clothes, peeling layers, letting it all drop to the floor leading a short trail to the countertop that separated the kitchen and living room. Zoey was stripped down to her bra and panties, and Jett lifted her onto the counter, pulling her legs around his waist. She pushed his sweatpants down and slid her hand into his boxers, palming him with a desperate moan.

Jett pushed into her hand, feeling his length slide along her soft palm as he kissed her neck. He was frantic and wanted her now. Wanted to make her come. Wanted her to make him come. On her, inside her mouth, bent over and plunged deep. Dammit, he didn't know where to start or where he wanted to end, but he knew he needed it now.

Next time they could take their time and go slow and feel and touch every inch of each other's skin, but right now he needed to take. He wanted to be greedy and come first so that she'd have to get him hard again. So that she'd have to beg him to keep going.

He shoved his boxers down and Zoey halted him with a hand to his chest. "Wait, wait, get my bag." Jett bent down and grabbed her purse that had been dropped to the floor and handed it to her. She grabbed a large box of condoms from the top and smiled. "Thought we might need more."

Jett ripped the box open impatiently, tore into the first foil package, and slid the condom over himself. He was so hard and so fucking ready to explode he could just about go at his own touch. Somehow a day without Zoey had felt like a year without her touch and he didn't know how to handle it, but knew he couldn't go without it.

He pulled her to the edge of the counter, slipped his fingers into the band of her panties to slide them down, and sunk in. She gasped and curled her hands around his neck, pressing her forehead to his. Their lips touched, but her mouth was open in a silent cry. She exhaled and relaxed around him, hot and wet and tight. He wanted to slam into her hard, bodies crashing together until he completely fell apart.

Hands on her thighs, he watched himself slide in and pull out. Their heads were still together when he whispered, "Zo, I don't want to go easy on you tonight. I won't be able to. I missed you. One day without you and I can't believe how much I fucking missed you."

"I missed you, too." She moaned when he added fingers, lightly petting her clit. "Whatever you want, Jett. Please..." Her head fell back and her eyes closed, as if waiting for him to be unleashed.

Jett gripped her hips and pulled her body onto him, hard and fast. Harder...faster. She was gripping the counter with white knuckles, cries coming out in short gasps. He pounded into her and dug in his fingers. He was sure he'd leave a mark on that perfect, golden-olive skin of hers. He'd hate to mark it up, but relished the idea of leaving behind something that said she was his. That this was something only they shared.

He pumped harder into her, frantic, animalistic, grunting and feeling sweat start to bead up and run a trail down his chest. He watched himself enter her over and over, feeling her get wetter, listening to her moans and cries and desperate pleas for more. Her nails scratched into his shoulders now and she was holding onto him. They'd both leave marks. He thrusted faster, snapped his hips harder, urging her to dig in, make her claim.

Oh God, he was going to come. He was going to lose himself and she hadn't got there yet. He shoved her bra straps down and dipped his head to her breasts, licking and tasting, feeling them on his lips. It sent him over the edge. Her perfect round tits on his mouth, *fuck*, there was nothing like it. He fucking loved them.

"Mmm, god*damn*...Baby, yes...*yes, oh god...*" He growled into her skin and pressed his teeth to the smooth skin of her breast as he felt the climax. The tension and tightening deep inside, followed by euphoric, dizzying release.

His breath was hot and heavy on her neck as he leaned into her, her body still wrapped around him. Her arms around his shoulders felt momentarily tense as she realized he'd gone without her.

Jett kissed his way up her neck to her lips. "Don't worry, baby, we're not done yet." He pulled her off the counter and she kept her legs wrapped tightly around him as he moved her to the chair, also snagging the new box of condoms off the counter for good measure.

Sitting with her straddling his lap, he pulled out so he could tie off the condom and start fresh. Jett pushed his hand through her hair and brought her mouth to his, kissing, demanding, conquering her lips. Owning her taste. Her kiss sent a lightning bolt straight to his cock and he felt like he was already woken up, already revived for another round.

He finished taking her bra off and gestured for her to lean into him, to bring her perfect tits to his mouth. Zoey held them up and he dipped his head, licking around the nipple, scraping at the soft skin with his teeth before sucking into his mouth. He swirled his tongue in circles around her breast, licked and sucked her cleavage before taking the other nipple into his mouth.

His hand was wrapped around his cock and he stroked up and down slowly, feeling himself get harder as he tasted her. He was always such a giver, always got off on giving orgasms and pleasing her, but he was someone else tonight. *He* wanted to be pleased. *He* wanted to get off over and over and take her any way he wanted.

Looking into Zoey's eyes, she seemed to understand that he needed this. That he needed to be the center of attention just this once. That feeling of her choosing someone else over him was still there, nagging at him all day. He needed to be reminded that she would pick him, please him, be with him over anyone else when it counted.

Jett felt Zoey's hand grasp his cock and moved his own hand away, letting her take over. She worked him with two hands, massaging his balls, sliding her soft, delicate hands along his shaft, feeling every thick inch of him, and reveling in it. She kissed him and caught his bottom lip between her teeth, sucking gently before sliding herself off his lap and onto the floor in front of him.

His sigh came out shaky as he willed his body to relax. She was on her knees for him. *Holy fuck.* Her hands skated up his thighs. She grasped his cock and licked the entire length from base to tip, swirling her tongue around the head before covering him with her mouth. Sucking him in and slowly out. Her hand held him steady and pumped where her mouth couldn't reach. She brought him in as far as she could and he let out a long groan.

"Oh...*God...*" His breath was slow and steady, maintaining control and wanting this feeling, this image to last. He watched her head move up and down in his lap, felt the warm, wet heat of her mouth all around him, the tickle of her long hair on his thighs.

Reaching forward, he gathered her hair and pulled it back so he could see more. Watch her mouth stretch as it wrapped around him, see her sweep her sexy hazel-eyed gaze up to him with a deep moan.

"Fuck, Zoey...I love watching you like this, holy fuck," Jett breathed. "Your mouth feels so goddamn good, baby."

His hips began to move, sending slow, gentle thrusts into her mouth. Wanting more. Needing more.

So good.

Fuck, it's so good.

He didn't know if he should come like this or give her something first. He *loved* her sounds when he pleasured her. Making her let loose all those dirty thoughts he knew she hid from everyone else. He was the only one who could make her feel that way. He was the only one who she could truly be wild for.

Zoey was moving quicker now, her mouth sliding along his slippery, thick cock. Her hand working him, making him want to blow.

Fuck. Not yet.

With his free hand, he grabbed another condom out of the box and then motioned for her to get back in his lap. "Dammit, baby, that mouth of yours almost made me come before I was ready."

She leaned into him and kissed him. "I love it. I love that I can make you feel so good you have to hold back."

Jett reached out and rubbed her clit with two fingers and dipped another inside. "You like being on your knees in front of me, don't you? You're so wet for me and I've barely touched you." He watched as the blush crept up her skin at his words. She closed her eyes and enjoyed his touch, moving with him as he pushed two fingers inside.

"I do," she breathed. "I want to make you feel the way you make me feel. The way you make me go crazy and do and say things I never thought I would."

Jett's breath escaped him like a gust of wind. He knew he had that effect on her and loved it, but hearing it spoken on her lips made him even more needy. He rolled the new condom on and pulled her on top of him. She slowly slid down with a whimper and a shaky exhale before rocking her hips into him, moving over him.

"Feels so good," she whispered, lips to his ear. "So good...so big. Oh *god*, I can't believe it's mine."

He groaned as a new fire ignited in his chest. With a new sense of urgency, he lifted them both from the chair and headed for the hallway. He pressed her against the wall, pushing into her, frantic and frenzied. Her legs were wrapped tight around his waist and her arms around his shoulders, clinging to him as though he was the only thing holding her together.

They fell to the floor and he moved over her, sweaty, hard, and desperate. She came beneath him with a loud cry of his name surrounded by panting and whimpers and moans.

He still needed more.

Back off the floor, they crashed into the wall again, stumbled into his bedroom. He pushed her against his door as he closed it and pinned her hands over her head before sliding down her body and pulling one leg over his shoulder. She came again against his mouth, and he could feel the muscles in her thighs shaking, wanting to give out.

He scooped her up and carried her to the bed, climbing over her and plunging into her again. And again. Fast, hard...so *fucking* good.

Her noises fueled him as she begged for more. For harder, faster...begged him to *fuck me, oh my god, yes- Fuck. Me.* Her nails scratching, back arching into him. It was good. It was better than good. But still not enough.

His tongue swept into her mouth and he grabbed her by the hips. He flipped her over onto her stomach and pulled her hips up and into him. He watched Zoey as she readied herself, moving up to her forearms, still panting. Bracing herself for him.

Biting his lip, he dug his fingers into her skin, her hips, and pushed into her. His eyes nearly rolled back with how tight she felt this way. Tight and wet and he could feel everything. He was so deep. And he could tell by the way she grasped at the sheets that she could feel him everywhere.

"Zoey...*fuck*...so good. Oh my god," Jett's whole body was hovering on the edge.

Her back was arched in a steep slope downward and she dug into the bedding, begging for more. She told him how deep he was. That she was full of him.

So close. His eyes closed and he snapped into her. Grunting, growling, fucking so hard. The way she begged for him. However she could get him. The way her body gave into him. He felt like he had complete control like this. Like she was his. He wasn't letting her go.

"Tell me you want me," Jett whispered, slowing his pace, but driving harder into her.

She gasped as he snapped into her and whimpered, "Oh *god*, yes, I want you. Baby, you *know* I want you."

"Tell me," he breathed heavily, closing his eyes and regaining control, "you need me."

"Yes, Jett, I *need* you. So bad, I *crave* you...all the time."

He groaned deeply. "You're mine, baby. *Mine.*"

He held onto her round ass, pulling her toward him and meeting his own thrusts. Wanting to sink his teeth into her. He wanted all of her. To hear her falling apart, gasping and breathless.

"Say it, baby," Jett growled, with a sharp smack to her ass. "Tell me you're mine. Fuck, I need to hear you say it."

Zoey cried out and threw her head back, panting. "I'm yours, Jett. Take me. I'm yours."

Fuck.

Yes...oh...fuck.

Mine...mine...mine.

"Oh God, oh God- yes, yes, *yes!*" Zoey screamed as she began squeezing around him. Panting, screaming, clawing at the comforter.

He let himself go, falling deep into this spell she had him under. Insatiable. Wild. Frenzied. Unbelievably wrecked. All for her.

He shuddered and collapsed on top of her, arms wrapped around her waist, holding her close. He was struggling to catch his breath as he buried his face into the back of her neck, feeling like he was never going to let go. Feeling his heart melt into her. It was hers now. He was at her mercy.

"Zoey, I...love you. It's kind of terrifying, I think, how much I love you."

He could feel her still-heavy breathing with his chest pressed to her back. She rolled in his arms to face him, and he knew his emotions were laid bare across his face. There was nothing he could hold back, even if he wanted to. No way he could protect even the smallest piece of himself. He was all hers and there was no hiding it.

"Terrifying, how?" Zoey asked, her fingers tracing his jaw.

"Like, you could completely ruin me, terrifying."

Again, she stared at him with those expressive hazel eyes. "I wouldn't do that, Jett. I love you, too." She looked intently at him, fingers brushing over his lips. He knew she could see the desperation in his features. That he was holding onto her with everything he had, that he absolutely could not lose her. "You know that, right? I love you, and I'll choose you every time, when it counts."

Jett held her closer, hanging on tight to her, to her words, to this moment, to everything. "Tell me we can make this work."

"We can make this work," she said, bringing his face to hers now. "We will."

He was silent for a few moments before nodding and burying his face back into her, letting himself fall and be completely consumed by her.

They would make it work. One way or another, they just had to.

Zoey woke up with two strong arms wrapped around her, with her back to Jett's chest. She sighed into the familiar comfort of him, the warmth of his body enveloping hers.

And she winced.

Oh God...so sore.

There was a pulsing ache between her thighs, and it wasn't the dull throb of simply being able to feel him hours later. She was sore.

She closed her eyes and thought back to the previous evening. Jett had been completely unhinged and ravenous for her. Now, she wasn't complaining by any means. It was phenomenal, as always. But he'd been hard and fast nearly the entire time. On the counter, in the chair, against the wall, on the floor, in bed. He'd flipped her around and taken her from behind. Surprisingly, they hadn't done it that way before last night. Likely because he knew how big he was and how much more intense that often felt, regardless of size.

There was something about Jett that had seemed desperate. Demanding, like he absolutely needed her to take care of him. To pull him together for once and make him feel like everything was going to be okay. She had felt it in the way he grasped her hips so tight, in the way he kissed her, and especially in the way he'd sunk himself into her.

Tell me you want me...Tell me you need me...Tell me you're mine.

His words echoed in her head and she felt her whole body blush and go warm, melting into him. Her butt was backed up to his lap and she wanted to roll into him, but the ache between her legs reminded her that, at least this morning, morning sex was not an option.

Behind her, Jett groaned and a hand began sliding down her side. He gripped her hips, urging her back into him, and she hissed at the feel of his fingers pressing into her skin.

He stiffened and released his grip. "Are you okay?" His voice was groggy with sleep, but sharp enough to sound alert.

"I'm fine," Zoey replied, stretching. "Just a little sore."

"Sore...here?" Jett brushed his fingers across her hip bone.

"There...everywhere." Her response came out amused, almost a giggle, but Jett didn't seem to find it quite so funny.

He lifted the comforter and looked down at their bodies. Lightly brushing his fingertips across her hip again, he said, "Oh God, I left bruises. Zoey...why didn't you tell me I was hurting you?"

"Jett, it's fine."

"I am so sorry-"

"I'm not," Zoey insisted, now turning to face him. "It's fine. Last night was great. Intense, sure, but amazing. I kind of like you taking charge."

"I wasn't thinking...I knew it would leave a mark, but it seemed sexy last night. Now I just feel like a jerk."

Zoey took Jett's face in her hands and her eyes traveled back and forth between his. "You're overthinking it. I'm fine. You're not a jerk, and last night was well worth it. And it looks like you're not the only one who left a mark." She traced the beginning of a scratch mark on his shoulder that traveled down his back.

Finally his lips pulled up in a smirk. "Fine, but I still ruined the prospect of morning sex."

"You did," she agreed. "But that's okay, because we really don't have time for it anyway. We need to pack."

"Pack?" Jett's eyebrows pulled together.

"If you still want to spend Christmas with my family...our flight leaves in four hours."

CHAPTER 21

They landed at the San Diego International Airport at quarter past one in the afternoon and were greeted by Zoey's dad in the terminal.

"I missed you, Dad," Zoey said, pulling her bear of a father into a tight hug. He smiled warmly and kissed her on the cheek before setting a dark, intimidating gaze on the man behind her. She moved over to Jett's side and put one hand on his arm, the other resting on his chest. "Dad, this is Jett."

Jett's smile was friendly but not overly eager when he extended his hand. "Nice to finally meet you, sir."

Zoey could tell the *sir* had thrown her dad off guard. As a former Marine, he always appreciated the traditional, polite formality of addressing others as *sir* or *ma'am*, but it wasn't something that was heard very often anymore. Lou extended his hand and clasped it with Jett's, both giving a solid, firm shake.

The butterflies in Zoey's stomach danced around a little, excited at the thought that she finally brought home a man her father deemed worthy or man enough for his daughter. Of course Zoey knew this about Jett already, but she was excited for her dad to see how great he was, too.

Jett grabbed their bags and the three of them walked out into the bright sunshine of Southern California in December. The mid-sixty degree weather was a welcome shock to Zoey's system after the bitter cold of Michigan only five hours ago. It was still low for California, but it felt like the middle of summer. She could tell Jett was a little surprised to walk out into the intense sun and warm air and giggled as she saw him eyeing the palm trees blowing in the breeze.

"I promise, they really are real trees."

Jett let out a quiet laugh as they made their way to her dad's 4-Runner. He held the door open for Zoey and she climbed in, then proceeded to load all their bags in the back of the SUV. She noticed her dad watching Jett like a hawk, observing his every move and taking mental notes.

"So, is Ace at home?" Zoey asked her dad cheerfully as Jett got in the back seat.

"Yeah, he was helping Mrs. Riviera with some things next door. She was out there with a ladder this morning. Can you believe that? At her age?" Lou shook his head. "Ace went over and she put him to work. She was bringing him cookies and iced tea when I left. What a rough life that kid has."

"Mrs. Riviera is our neighbor," Zoey explained to Jett. "She's about eighty years old or so and is always trying to do all sorts of projects around her house, so Dad and Ace are constantly over there rescuing her from breaking a hip or something."

"I know how that goes," Jett said. "Last time I was at my grandparents' house, Gramps was out salting the walkway and Grams was in the garage trying to climb the janky ladder into the attic. I couldn't tell you what for, but she thought she needed up there. She's eighty-three. She doesn't need to be climbing a forty-year-old wooden ladder."

"You visit your grandparents a lot?" Lou asked, looking in the rear-view mirror.

"I do, yeah. We're a close family, and I just like to check in. Make sure there's nothing broken or hazardous that they're just letting go because they can't fix it themselves."

Lou nodded and Zoey could tell he was thinking of the next questions to drill him with on their thirty-minute drive back to the house.

Zoey had grown up in Solana Beach, which was about an hour and a half south of Los Angeles, and only a half hour from San Diego. Her dad liked the proximity to the city, but never wanted to live in the heart of it, and it was still close enough to her now that she could visit regularly when she wasn't needed for work.

"Zoey tells me you have siblings?" Lou pressed. "Older? Younger?"

"Yeah, one older brother, and two younger sisters."

The interrogation continued the entire drive north on the I-5 expressway. Lou drilled him about his family, where he went to college, if he played any sports. Why hockey? Does everyone in Michigan play hockey? He asked him about the bar and what kind of place it was and how long it had taken him and Chris to save up to start their own business. What's his favorite football team? What kind of car does he drive? Does he know how to change a flat tire? Can he cook or does he just eat microwave dinners? What does he do when he's not working? Does he have any real hobbies or does he just waste his time playing *'those goddamn video games'* like every other kid these days?

Jett took the interrogation well, answering all the questions promptly and efficiently. He was able to catch Lou's interest in hockey and what it had taken to get the bar up and running. They talked about beer and food, and found they had a shared interest in tacos.

Although Zoey could tell her dad was thoroughly enjoying the conversation, when they arrived at the house, he resumed his stony expression, still not wanting to be impressed just yet.

Lou lived in a small subdivision with mostly single-story stucco houses that had various Mexican and Central-American influences in the architecture. Though small, their house had a back patio that was set to look like a traditional Mexican courtyard, and it's where the family spent most of their time. Their house didn't have an ocean view, but it wasn't a long drive to the beach, and the smell of salt water and ocean air was still everywhere.

Zoey showed Jett where to put their bags and gave him a quick tour of the small house. There was a large kitchen, though no formal dining room, so the dining table took up the middle of the space. The living room wasn't very big, but the large windows on two adjacent walls made it feel much roomier. The walls were a creamy color and the furniture was turquoise, with a colorful area rug beneath the round, wooden coffee table. There were dark wooden beams across the ceiling and a small flatscreen TV mounted over a brick fireplace. Unlike most modern homes, it wasn't an open floor plan, but there were instead many archways that separated one room from the next.

The hallway off the living room led to what were the kids' bedrooms, and on the opposite side of the living room was the door leading to the master bedroom. Zoey, Cassie, and Ace all had smaller rooms. Zoey's was now made into a general guest room that no longer featured her personal touches like the ones that were evident in Jett's childhood bedroom. Ace's room was part-bedroom, part-storage room. There were many totes inside the closet, and all of his swimsuit model posters had been taken down, but his bed was still there for him when he came home from college over winter and summer break.

Cassie's room had been left the same color and still had many of her personal items, but she had only moved out that August. She wasn't sure what her dad would do with it in time, or what he would do with a four-bedroom house once they'd all cycled through college.

"I know it's not a *Hallmark* Christmas movie house, but..." Zoey shrugged, "it's home."

"I love it," Jett said, dropping their bags on the floor of Zoey's old bedroom. "It's bright and colorful and refreshing. It's not a cookie-cutter house like all of the ones on my block."

"I think Dad's starting to like you," she said quietly as she wrapped her arms around him. Looking up into his eyes she smiled. "Don't let the interrogation or the stare-downs fool you."

"It doesn't bother me. Honestly, I think it's exactly what I would do if I had a daughter." He wrapped his arms around her waist and gave her a quick kiss on the cheek. "We'd better get out there though. I don't want him thinking I'm just trying to get you alone in your old room."

Through the large sliding door in the kitchen, they walked out to the courtyard where Lou and Ace were.

Zoey's little brother was tall- *way* taller than her, and a few inches taller than her dad, who was really not a small man. At twenty-one, Ace was just over six feet tall with lean muscle from all his cross-country running. He had the same wavy, dark brown hair as Zoey that he kept long enough that he frequently had to push it out of his eyes.

"So, you're Jett?" Ace asked, giving Jett a sweeping look from head to toe, as though sizing him up. Zoey could have laughed if her brother was going to try intimidating Jett. Even if Ace had an inch of height on him, Jett was thick with muscle and could probably knock him over with a single shove.

"Yeah, you must be Ace?" Jett extended his hand for another firm handshake which Ace returned.

Ace narrowed his eyes at Jett, speculating. "Dad says you're like six years older than Zoey. Can't find any women your own age?"

Jett's face remained calm and friendly as he responded, "Not really. I suppose that means there's something wrong with me."

The corner of Ace's mouth twitched up just the slightest bit. "Probably."

Jett grinned. "This must be what I sound like when my youngest sister introduces me to a new guy."

Ace blinked away his narrow stare and immediately looked more friendly. "You have a little sister, too? Man, I love Cassie, but damn does she need some guidance."

"Sounds like Lizzie. She's great and she means well, but is always falling for the wrong guy. Just anyone who's nice to her and- Bam! She's infatuated. I don't get it, either. She had me and Gavin, and my dad...I don't know why she acts like she has daddy issues."

Ace laughed now. "That's how I feel about Cassie. I mean, sure, we had a rough start, but I turned out fine. Dad's great...and well, you obviously know how obnoxiously responsible Zoey is." Ace shook his head. "I remember one time when Cassie brought this guy home in high school. I couldn't tell you his name, but I just called him Dude-Bro. Because he ended every sentence with *dude* or *bro*."

"You know, I think Lizzie dated him, too," Jett replied. "There was Neck-Tattoo Bieber, Lumber-Jill, the skinny hipster who would be too concerned to break a nail to ever swing an ax for real, and most recently, Brad. Who really doesn't need a nickname."

"Yeah, *Brad* kind of says it all," Ace said with a grin.

Zoey watched as the two men hit it off, even if it was at the expense of their little sisters. She took a seat in one of the patio chairs and they soon followed suit, continuing their discussion of all the horrible decisions their sisters had made and the situations they'd had to free them from.

Lou was sitting back watching the interaction as well and was beginning to look marginally more calm. Zoey hadn't been worried, of course. She knew how amazing Jett was, but was thrilled to see how quickly her dad was accepting him, even if he didn't say it. She could see it in his posture, and the way he almost smiled a few times as he listened to Jett talk about the way his sister always knew she could come to him. That he always had the freezer ready with ice cream, and that she was welcome to hang out and stay as long as she needed.

The plan was to have family dinner together that night as they always did on Christmas Eve. The Nunez family didn't have the typical American Christmas dinner, but instead had combined Lou's Mexican heritage with their mother's American traditions and had an odd smorgasboard of pork tamales, chicken pozole verdes- a stew with shredded chicken, vegetables, in a green chile broth- homemade tortilla chips with guacamole and salsa, as well as roasted turkey, potatoes, and gravy. It was something they'd done since the couple had gotten married and was impossible to discontinue after their mom had died. It was a lot of work, but absolutely worth it every year.

Jett was helping Ace set the table when Zoey brought out the platter of tamales. His eyes went wide as saucers and he looked to her, momentarily speechless.

"You guys eat tacos for Christmas?"

"They're tamales, not tacos. But yes, we combine the foods my mom had growing up and the foods dad grew up with," she replied. "But don't worry, there's also all-you-can-eat chips and salsa."

Jett stared at the massive plate of tamales, still in awe. "I'm never leaving."

"Hm...funny, I was sort of thinking I'd be the one to take my life across the country, but I guess if you want to stay..." Zoey bit back a grin, feeling a little shy being the first to bring this topic up.

His eyes flashed from the food on the table to her. "Really?" The smile slowly tugged up the corner of his lips until it was his fully contagious, beaming smile, laugh lines bracketing his dimples, lighting up his entire face.

She smiled just as brightly back at him and nodded. "Yeah, I think I can make working long distance happen. I'll still have to fly out here sometimes, and that might mean I'm away for a day or two, but I'd get to see my family."

"I might be able to let you go a day or two...here and there...if it meant having you back home full time." Jett's smile still hadn't left his face and Zoey began to lean across the table to give him a kiss.

Ace breezed over to the table and set a giant bowl of warm tortilla chips down. "Shouldn't Cassie be here by now?" He looked from Jett to Zoey and back, registering that he'd interrupted a moment. "Uh...sorry. But seriously, she left to go visit some friends around noon. She's not back yet. Have you heard from her at all, Zo?"

Zoey's eyebrows scrunched together as she wandered to the counter to find her phone. Only three new messages, and all of them were from Quinn. "I don't have anything from her. Which friends was she going to see?"

"No idea." Ace shrugged. "She wouldn't tell me. She's been back and forth between here and her place in LA all winter break, and I honestly don't know if she meant LA friends or friends from home. I tried calling her an hour ago and it just rang until I got her voicemail."

"I don't like that," Zoey muttered. She found Cassie in her favorites and called. The phone rang three times before going to voicemail, but she immediately received a text from her little sister: *Call you in 1 min.*

She showed the message to Ace and they waited quietly for the call to come in. As soon as Cassie's picture lit up the screen, she swiped to answer, "Cassie, what's going on? You should be home by now. It's Christmas Eve."

"I know, I know, I know." Cassie replied, sounding stressed. "Oh God, sis, I screwed up. I am, like, stuck here. I can't leave. I don't know what to do."

"Stuck where? Why can't you leave?" Zoey asked. Jett and Ace gave curious looks and Zoey waved them away from the kitchen and into the hallway, away from her dad so she could put Cassie on speakerphone. "Who are you with? Ace said you were going to meet some friends…"

"I was. I *did*. Okay, we met up to go to Santa Ana earlier today and then ran into these guys from school- from UCLA," Cassie began. Ace already looked annoyed, shaking his head and grinding his teeth, while Jett looked genuinely concerned. "So, they were like 'hey, we're going to Carlsbad to go surfing and then we're going to hang out at this guy's beach house, wanna come?' and we were like hell yeah. So we followed these guys. But they have been drinking non-stop since we got back to the beach house, and the girls don't want to leave, but I'm like…it's Christmas Eve, I'm ready to go. But no one wants to take me home."

"Cassie, why didn't you call sooner?" Zoey tried not to sound too upset or too condescending, but honestly, what was her sister thinking? "We've been here since two o'clock. Someone would've come to get you."

"Well, I don't know. And these guys are, like, trying to get all of us drunk. It's just me, Stacy, and Cameryn, and the guys just keep shoving shots at us. I think Stacy was making out with one of them when I came in here. I'm just, like, really uncomfortable, and I feel like I can't go anywhere."

"Where are you right now? Carlsbad isn't far from here, I'll come get you."

"I'm just hiding out in the bathroom, hoping to avoid another shot glass being shoved in my face."

Cassie relayed the address which Ace typed into his phone, and Zoey assured her she would be there as soon as possible. She told her to stay in the bathroom if she could, and definitely *not* to take any drinks the guys were offering.

"It's only twenty-two minutes from here," Zoey said, looking at the map Ace had brought up on his phone. "I'll be back. Just keep Dad occupied."

"Um, you're not going alone," Ace insisted, blocking her path down the hallway. "We can all go. And Dad's going to figure it out. We don't have to cover for Cassie's stupid mistakes anymore. Following a bunch of dudes to a beach house? Are you kidding me? She'll have to learn one way or another."

"I'm going, too," Jett said. "We have no idea who these guys are or what they're like when they're drunk. And I think we should try to get her friends out of there, too. It doesn't sound like a good situation for any of them to be in."

In the kitchen, Zoey heard her dad talking to someone, then a woman's voice. Good, he'd invited Cindy for dinner, too, which meant he didn't have to sit at home alone while they went off to rescue Cassie, yet again.

Ace grabbed the keys to the 4-Runner off the hook in the kitchen and greeted Cindy before letting their dad know they were going to pick Cassie up.

"Pick her up?" Lou asked, brow furrowed. "She drove to her friend's house, didn't she?"

Ace let out a frustrated sigh. "Yeah, well, she did something stupid, and I'm sure she'll explain it to you when she gets back. But right now we're going to go get her. Hopefully we'll be back in less than an hour."

Lou's face matched Ace's tone, and Zoey recognized the frustration and disappointment setting in. Cassie was always doing stupid stuff like this, but to do it on Christmas Eve might be a new low. Knowing her dad, he would certainly have some words for her little sister once they got her home safely.

CHAPTER 22

Zoey drove with intense concentration as she followed the GPS on her phone to the address of the beach house. Jett could tell she was furious, and also a little worried. He was starting to understand that this was the type of thing Cassie pulled a lot. It wasn't like Lizzie where she just fell for a guy who was nice to her, but instead it seemed as though Cassie would go out of her way to find the wrong guys. The bad boys, the dangerous ones, the guys who had red flags popping up left and right.

Ace sat in the middle seat in the back and Jett could also tell he was fuming. Jett's first impression of Zoey's little brother was that he was an all around good guy. He helped the old neighbor lady, he'd tried to act intimidating for Zoey's sake, and seemed to have a good head on his shoulders. Ace was the type of guy Jett would gladly welcome into his friend circle, even with the nine-year age difference.

After a rather quiet twenty-minute drive, they pulled up to a two-story beach house that was white with dark blue trim. There were lots of windows and a small brick-paved patio that looked like it wrapped around to the back. Loud music boomed from inside the house and Jett noticed most of the curtains on the bottom floor were drawn.

Yeah, he didn't like that one bit.

"You should stay in the car, Zo," Jett said, popping the passenger door open. "I don't want these guys messing with you, too."

"That's a good idea," Ace agreed. "We'll be right back."

Jett and Ace set off for the front door and knocked loudly. There was only a brief delay before the front door was pulled open part of the way, and a tall, fit blond dude peered at them through the crack in the door.

"Can I help you guys? If the music is too loud, we can-"

"We got a call that there are men serving underage girls alcohol here," Jett said. He stood up tall, with his shoulders back and chest out. This guy wasn't just drunk, he was high, too. Not only could Jett smell it, but he could see it in his eyes. Jett may not have a cop uniform, but there was a good chance he could still have this guy feeling like he could be in serious trouble.

"You guys don't look like cops," Blondie said, eyeing them up and down.

"Well, that didn't sound like a *no* to me," Ace said. "Could you step aside, sir?"

"What? Hell no, you're not coming in he-"

That was enough for Jett. He shoved the door open, pushing Blondie aside with it. "Cassie's probably still in the bathroom. Go find her and I'll get the other two."

Jett rounded a small entryway into the living room where a sofa-sectional full of people sat around a coffee table that was loaded with shot glasses, liquor bottles, a bowl, and it even looked like one of the guys had busted out a line of coke. A redhead and a brunette girl looked nervous as they watched the guy get his line straightened out.

"Stacy, Cameryn!" Jett shouted over the noise. Both girls looked up with wide eyes, obviously not recognizing Jett, but somehow they seemed to trust that he was there for them. "Cassie called and said you'd be needing a ride home."

They looked to one another and seemed to agree that, though risky, he seemed like a better option than being pressured into doing lines after however many shots and drugs they'd already taken.

"Whoa, whoa!" A guy with auburn hair stood up and grabbed one of the girls by the arm as she made her way toward Jett. The guy looked at Jett appraisingly. "Who the hell do you think you are? Coming in here and trying to steal our girls from us?"

Jett's eyebrows shot upward and he stepped forward. "Well, I don't think they're *your* girls, and I'm going to tell you right now you've got about two seconds to take your hands off of her."

The dark-haired guy who'd been setting up a line of coke stood and turned to face Jett, too. He wasn't very tall, but Jett suspected all these guys were some sort of athletes at one point. They all had muscles in some form though he figured a lot of it was gym muscle, and not built from practical use. Most definitely not from fighting anyone.

There was a shuffle of feet behind him and he looked around to see Ace with a girl who had to be his sister- the resemblance was obvious. Blondie stood in front of Ace and Cassie and tried to block their way, but Ace wasn't having it. He cocked his fist back and fired right into the center of the guy's face.

Jett hadn't been in a real fight in a long time, but apparently it hadn't been his last.

The auburn-haired guy let go of the girl he'd been holding onto just before Jett's fist came in contact with his jaw.

Sorry, guy, too late.

There were two other men in the room who now wanted to square off with him and he was ready for it. He dodged the first fist that came his way and sent the guy tumbling backward over the sectional. The shorter, dark-haired guy tried to run at Jett, as though making a tackle, and Jett pushed back easily before sending an upper-cut into the guy's stomach.

The two girls were behind him now, next to Ace and Cassie who were standing by the door. Ace's voice cut through the sound of blood rushing in his ears, shouting for him to get going. "Come on, Superman, back to the car! We got 'em!"

Jett turned and saw Ace and the three girls filing out of the front door and backed away from his attackers, not wanting to take his eyes off them in case one of them wanted to get back up. Not likely, given that they were all severely intoxicated and now had been sent to the ground in one way or another.

Once out the door, Jett jogged back to the 4-Runner and hopped into the front seat. Ace and the girls were piled in the back and Ace couldn't seem to stop staring at him with an amused, somewhat awe-struck grin.

"Dude, when did you learn to fight like that?" Ace asked, wide-eyed as though speaking to a lifelong role model.

Jett scratched the side of his jaw. "Uh...well, I played hockey and I got in some fights on the ice. I fought with my brother a lot as a kid. But most of my big fights like that..." he paused, noting the knot twitching in his stomach as the thought hit him. "Most of them I was just backing up Quinn."

There was a silent beat while he and Zoey met eyes for a half-second, then he let it sink in fully.

"So...who the hell brought along Captain America?" Cassie asked, breaking the tense silence.

Zoey laughed quietly. "Cassie, this is Jett, my boyfriend. Feel free to tell him thank you for saving your ass."

They got back to Solana Beach and dropped off Stacy and Cameryn before heading back to Zoey's dad's place.

Lou was an intimidating guy, and although Jett had known and even expected the intimidation when he'd met him earlier that day, he would not want to be on the receiving end of the look he gave his youngest daughter when she walked through the door.

"Cassandra Maria Nunez. Where the hell were you? Are you aware it's Christmas Eve?" Lou boomed through the entire house. "Your brother and sister have been here all day and where were you? Running around with some boys? Getting in trouble with *some boys?* Not only is this the first family dinner we all have had together with Cindy, but Zoey also brought someone from across the country to meet us, and *this* is the first impression you want to make?"

Zoey led Ace and Jett back out to the courtyard while Cassie got a scolding that was making all of them cringe. Not that he could blame

Lou. What his daughter had done was irrefutably stupid, dangerous, and careless.

"Zo, you should've seen your guy in there!" Ace said for at least the seventh time. "Oh my God, he was just like- bam! Hah! Yah!" Ace made various kicking and punching motions in the air and Jett couldn't help laughing.

"It wasn't that cool, I assure you," Jett said to Zoey.

"I'm kinda sad you made me stay in the car."

"Well, that one guy grabbed onto Cameryn's arm and I didn't even know her but I got pissed. If one of them had grabbed you...let's just say your brother would be even more impressed right now. And maybe a little frightened."

"I really didn't know you were such a fighter," she said, wrapping her arms around his waist.

"I'm not. It's your brother's fault really. He threw the first punch and I just followed suit." He shrugged. "Like I said, most of my fights were just backing Quinn up. I didn't always know what we were fighting about, but if he threw a punch, I was in."

Zoey lowered her voice and looked up at him. "You haven't talked to him since the other night at the hospital, have you?"

Jett shook his head no. He hadn't exactly had time to plan ahead or go talk to Quinn before leaving on his flight. He'd had enough time to make sure the bar definitely was closed for Christmas Eve and Christmas Day, and that he wasn't working the day after Christmas so he could fly across the country. He'd made a few phone calls to his family members letting them know he was spending the holiday with Zoey's family and that he'd see them when he got back.

But he hadn't bothered to call Quinn or Rae. He hadn't bothered to send Quinn even a text to apologize for trying to shove him...and blaming Zoey's accident on him. No, he felt the things he needed to say would be better said in person. He'd find Quinn as soon as they got back to Michigan and see if he could sort things out. Talk to him without escalating into a fight.

Finally, after more muffled shouts and scoldings, the three of them were called to come back inside and sit down for dinner. Sitting next to Zoey, Jett made a quick glance across the table at Cassie. He'd expected her to look at least a little humbled, but she only had an air of faint annoyance that moody teenagers so often do.

Okay, so Cassie is not *like Lizzie. That's for sure.*

Jett knew if his dad had chewed Lizzie out the same way Lou just had Cassie, she would be in tears and unable to eat. Cassie...she was stubborn.

Lou said grace over the food before they dug in and started filling their plates.

"Dad!" Ace piped up. "Dad, you should've seen Jett. I've seriously never seen someone fight like that in my life."

Oh great...

"Fight?" Lou's eyebrows pulled together. "There was a fight?"

Ace proceeded to tell the whole story, from the moment they hopped out of the SUV, to Jett shoving in the door, all the way to leaving with all three girls safely in the vehicle. Jett had to admit the way Ace told the story was way cooler than how it had felt, but he didn't mind. Ace's description of Jett's fight with the three idiots in the living room sounded more like something out of *John Wick* than knocking around a few intoxicated douche bags, but again, he'd run with it.

"You started fighting those guys just because my son hit the dumb-ass at the door?" Lou questioned.

"Yeah...I know it was stupid, but-"

"Oh probably," Lou agreed. "Ace doesn't always make the best choices, but he's not a hot-head."

"Thanks, Pops." Ace saluted his dad with his fork.

"But rushing to back someone up in a fight like that...shows some real loyalty."

Jett slowed down chewing on his pork tamale and sat up straighter as he looked back at Lou. He felt a little like he was being X-rayed or like the man was trying to read him like a book. He wondered what he was giving away. Did he look nervous? Satisfied? Proud?

Lou gave him a small nod. "You're all right, Jett."

Jett didn't miss the huge smile that plastered itself to Zoey's face as she kept her eyes down on her plate. He let himself smile too, although not too much. He didn't want to seem smug or like he'd won something.

On the inside, though, he was positively beaming.

The rest of the evening was quite tame compared to how everything started. Lou was more talkative and joking around with Jett, far more friendly and open than he'd been at the airport. The family tried to come up with embarrassing stories about Zoey, but it turned out she had been far too responsible to ever make the stupid choices that led to those good stories most people have by the time they turn twenty-four. Instead the discussion turned into Ace and Cassie's anecdotes on all the times Zoey proved she was the best big sister ever. None of this surprised Jett, and only made him adore her even more.

Lou was walking Cindy home, who only lived a few houses down, leaving the four of them to talk and get to know each other more. They sat out on the back patio until late in the evening, sipping glasses of wine or bottles of beer until everyone was wrapped in sweatshirts and blankets. Cassie took her turn grilling Jett as both Lou and Ace had earlier in the day, but got hung up- as most women do- on how he had grown up with Quinn, played ball with Quinn, and had seen Quinn in locker rooms on countless occasions.

Over the years Jett realized that was one detail he must have seriously taken for granted as a man, as often as he got asked for details on what those particular encounters were like. Frequently he'd skip over any specific details of Quinn and his friends, sweaty and heading to the showers, and instead would entertain people with the tale of The Great Locker Room Fight of '07. Ace, Cassie, and Zoey were all equally enthralled by the story, and they got back to reliving for the fifteenth time that evening Jett's superior fighting skills as told by Ace.

The sky above was dark, a thick haze covering the view of the stars, but the temperature had only dropped to fifty-two degrees, so Jett was plenty comfortable with his extra thick Northern Michigan blood. He and Zoey shared a seat on a bench swing with a blanket wrapped around their shoulders, huddled close together.

"I can't believe you're shivering," Jett said, amused. "It's like spring-time out here."

"You do *want* me to move to Michigan, right?" Zoey replied. "Re-minding me of how bitterly cold it is may not be your best move."

Jett smiled down at her in the low light of the outdoor palm trees- *palm trees-* dressed in white Christmas lights and squeezed her closer. "I'll keep you warm."

Across from them Cassie made a gagging noise and Ace laughed quietly before standing up and stretching. "Not tonight, you won't," he said, making his way around the circle. Jett arched a curious eyebrow as Ace clapped a hand to his shoulder. "Come on, Dad said you were *all right*, but that doesn't mean he's going to let you sleep with his daughter while you're under his roof. You're bunking with me tonight, Cap."

"You're not serious," Zoey said, turning and looking over her shoulder at her bean-pole of a brother.

"I am. Dad's already got the air mattress set up and everything."

"Where does he think I've been staying for the past month and a half?" Zoey argued.

Jett put a comforting hand above her knee and brought her attention to him. "Hey, it's okay. Your dad's house, his rules. I would probably do the same thing if I were him." He kissed her on the cheek before standing and holding his arms out to help her up. "Let's go get ready for bed."

CHAPTER 23

Christmas morning arrived and, as usual, Zoey and her dad got up before everyone else. They went out to the patio and did a short, easy yoga routine together as the sun came up. It was something she had certainly missed since being away, and knew it would be a difficult adjustment once she made the big move- whenever that may be.

She wondered for a beat if she was acting too hastily, telling Jett she was willing to move across the country to be with him, but when she imagined coming back to California and leaving him in Michigan, her heart sank and her stomach lurched and she just knew that wasn't an option.

They always finished with three sun-salutations, and after her final breath out, bringing her arms from over her head, down to her sides, she kept her eyes closed as she spoke. "Dad?" He hummed and she could tell he was also still in mountain pose next to her, just listening to his own breathing. "I know it's only been a little over a month...with me and Jett, I mean, but..." She hesitated, trying to find the right words. Something that wouldn't sound so alarming or life-altering.

"But?" Lou pressed, cutting through the long silence.

"But I...really like him. I mean, I *really* like him. A lot. And I want to give it a real chance. I just don't know if I can do that from...here. You know? From California."

"I can tell you *really* like him. I like him, too, actually," Lou said, and quickly covered, "Don't tell him I said those exact words though. But he's a good one, I can tell. He's the kind of guy who will always take care of you, which I think you could use. Not because you need to be taken care of, but because you've been taking care of people your whole life, and I think it's about time you get a break. He can lighten your load a bit."

Zoey's smile curved up the corners of her mouth, opening her eyes as she turned to face her dad. "That's sort of what I thought. I just...I don't want to leave you guys. I mean, I've always been here to take care of you and Ace and Cassie. What if I pack up and move across the country and something happens?"

"Something happens?" Lou repeated. "Like what? Like Cassie running off with strange boys when she absolutely knows better? Zo, sweetie, she's going to have to grow up eventually. And maybe if you leave she'll have to. Maybe if you're not always here to bail her out, she will finally accept responsibility over her own life." Lou grabbed his water bottle off the small end table next to the bench swing. "Or, and this is far more likely, she'll call Ace to bail her out. But either way, you get a break- a much needed break."

Zoey chewed the inside of her cheek as she considered this. She didn't like the idea of leaving her family, of not being able to see them, not being able to help when she was needed. But it would certainly be nice if her now-adult siblings could learn to take care of themselves. She learned to take care of everyone when she was nine. Surely Cassie and Ace could gain some responsibility now that they were nineteen and twenty-one, right? Ace had already proven how grown up he had become. He really hadn't done anything *that* irresponsible since he was in high school, and that was normal.

What wasn't normal was that Zoey had really never done anything irresponsible. Or selfish. Or made any decisions that were purely based on what she wanted or what was best for her. Right now she knew Jett was what was best for her. No question. Being with him was what she wanted. If it weren't for feeling as though she were leaving her responsibilities and obligations to her family behind, she knew what her choice would be without question.

"Good morning." Jett's voice cleared the fog in Zoey's brain and she blinked over to see him standing in the doorway wearing a plain white t-shirt and maroon basketball shorts. She smiled instantly and her heart felt like a helium balloon in her chest, making her feel like she could float several inches off the ground.

"You're up early," Zoey said.

"Well, it's 10:15 in Michigan, so it's about right."

Zoey padded over to him and wrapped her arms behind his neck. "Merry Christmas." She reached up on her toes and pressed a chaste kiss to his lips.

"Merry Christmas," Jett replied, smiling against her mouth. When Lou cleared his throat, Jett abruptly backed up and scrubbed a hand down the side of his face which was now covered in a thick layer of prickly beard scruff.

"Did you sleep okay in Ace's room?" Zoey asked with a smirk. "I missed you."

"I slept great, actually. Your brother is quite the cuddler."

Zoey's eyebrows pinched together. "But didn't you sleep on an air mattress? He had his own bed."

"Well, the air mattress was pushed right up against his bed and he rolled onto it at some point in the night and big-spooned me."

"Stop, he did not."

"He did. I've never been the little spoon before, but it was kind of nice. I now see why you women enjoy cuddling so much."

Zoey shook her head with a laugh and they walked back inside together into the kitchen. She reached for the coffee canister on the counter and began scooping grounds into the coffee maker. "Well, I was going to say that we could take a trip to LA later and maybe stay at my place tonight, but if you like the current sleeping arrangements, I guess you and Ace can have another night together. I don't want to be selfish."

"I would love to see your place, and I *guess* I could deal with just one night of cuddles from your brother. Wouldn't want too much of a good thing to ruin what we've got," Jett teased, reaching across the table for the plate of homemade donuts Cindy had brought over the previous evening.

"Don't fill up on those," Zoey said. "I still need to make breakfast."

"Since when aren't donuts enough for breakfast?" Jett asked around a large bite of cinnamon-sugared dough.

"I always make fruit crepes for breakfast on Christmas. Strawberry, blueberry, and banana. Every year."

Jett's eyes widened as his chewing slowed. He swallowed. "Lucky for you I'm like a human garbage disposal. I really don't get full." As if to prove a point, he snagged another donut from the center of the table, then made his way over to the counter next to her. "How can I help? I've never made crepes before."

Zoey poured them each a cup of coffee and smiled. "You've made me breakfast at least a dozen times. Just sit over there and look cute. Maybe tell me more stories of your childhood."

Jett grinned mischievously at her over his coffee mug. "I really prefer the way *you* tell stories."

Flashes of the day after they'd had sex for the first time flew through her mind: Jett beneath her on the couch, between her legs, over her with her leg on his shoulder as he pushed deep into her, all while she tried her best to stay on track with each memory, each story she told him.

She could feel redness spreading from her chest, up her neck and into her face, as well as heat beginning low in her belly and slipping further down between her thighs, pulsing with a yearning ache. Jett's sly grin told her he knew exactly what she was thinking, and maybe even feeling.

She bit her lip and sent a gentle shove to his unbearably broad and manly chest. "Just go sit over there and behave."

"Yes, ma'am." His voice was a low growl in her ear before he pressed a lingering kiss to her cheek and found a seat at the table.

Zoey had mostly finished making breakfast, and Jett had helped set the table, when Ace and Cassie finally shuffled out of their bedrooms, yawning and stretching, rubbing the sleep out of their eyes, just as they had done when they were kids. Zoey realized in that moment that she still thought of them that way; as her kid brother and sister who still needed her to make breakfast for them, pack their lunches, and ensure they didn't forget anything for school. But they weren't. Her dad was right. They were both adults now, and it was perfectly okay for them to finally be able to take care of themselves.

"Mornin' Little Spoon!" Ace said loudly, clapping Jett on the back before sitting in the chair adjacent to him.

Zoey brought two bowls of fruit to the table and gave her brother a skeptical glance. "You know, Ace, you calling Jett 'little' anything is really kind of laughable."

"I'm, like, an inch taller. Maybe an inch and a half!" Ace protested.

"Yeah, you're six-one and weigh a hundred and forty pounds."

Ace scoffed. "I'm one-fifty-five! I've been going to the gym all semester at school to lift. I'll get there." He lifted his chin at Jett. "What are you? Like...one...ninety? Two hundred?"

"Two-ten," he corrected, then held up the donut in his hand. "Two-fifteen after this vacation, maybe."

"Damn...I've got a ways to go," Ace muttered, looking down at his skinny arms.

After breakfast, everyone moved into the living room where they opened presents, though there weren't many packages under the tree. Ace and Cassie each got several gift cards for their favorite places to eat while they're away at school, Zoey got a new protective case for her tablet that was almost always in use, as well as a few winter weather accessories. Zoey had bought Jett a set of Red Wings tickets on center ice, which went well with the brand new ice skates that he got for her. They agreed to have more ice skating dates when they got back to Michigan to break them in until she was just as good on the ice as Jett— or kind of close, anyway.

They relaxed for most of the day with constantly full bellies from all the food that was out. Cindy stopped by and brought more treats, putting everyone in a near food coma, not that they were complaining. After an early dinner, they packed their bags and Jett helped Ace put away the air mattress so he could have his full room back. Zoey wanted to take Jett to Los Angeles to see her place, and to catch the sunset at the beach once they arrived she wanted to leave at a precise time. Since Zoey's car was still at her house, Ace let them take his Subaru, and they'd bring it back in the morning before someone gave them a ride back to the airport.

A lot of the drive north had gorgeous ocean-side views, and even Jett couldn't argue the beauty of the Pacific versus his usual view of Lake Michigan- there was no comparison.

Zoey's house was a small gray and white bungalow set in a pleasant, suburban subdivision. Most of the homes that surrounded hers belonged to families, and she was the only single-person home on the block. Most single people in LA lived in apartments, but Zoey had bought her own house after Quinn surprised her with a rather generous *thank you for putting up with my shit for a whole year*-bonus.

The house was more than she needed for just herself, but she absolutely loved it. There were two large front windows, a small covered porch with a porch swing, three bedrooms, two bathrooms, a spacious living room that opened up into a large kitchen that was perfect for entertaining. Everything was done in bright whites and soft blues, with a nautical theme throughout. Though she didn't have an ocean view outside her house, like many places this close to the coast, it wasn't a long drive to get to the beach.

On the porch, Zoey bent to pick up a small Amazon package that she knew hadn't been there very long before unlocking the front door and leading the way into her house. Jett's eyes went wide as he surveyed the space. There was a staircase with a white wood railing that led upstairs, a small buffet table with a dish for keys pushed up against one wall in the entryway beneath a large round mirror. Light gray wood floors stretched through the entryway and into the kitchen and living room. Everything was clean and had an exact place. She wasn't obsessive, necessarily, just organized. It was a necessity from having to keep tabs on everything going on in everyone's lives including her own.

"This is the kind of house I was hoping to find in Traverse," Jett said, eyes still wandering over every detail. "On the water would be awesome, but then you're looking at spending at least four-hundred thousand."

"Waterfront in LA I think starts around a million, so that's not too bad," Zoey said with a shrug. "It's not cheap to live here, but I do okay."

"If you're going to, ya know, come stay with me," Jett hesitated, scratching his jaw, "I'd really like to look into buying a place. Somewhere that's *not* directly above my bar."

"Well, I'm sure my house has gone up in value since buying it. We could take what I earn from selling it and have a lot to put down on a house. Even a waterfront property, if that's what you really want. Somewhere in Rae's neighborhood would be nice."

"Rae's neighborhood?" Jett repeated, then let out a low whistle. "I think she spent at least five or six-hundred thousand on her place."

Zoey bit back a shy grin. "Well, like I said, I do okay. Quinn may be a pain in the ass to work for sometimes, but he pays well."

Jett narrowed his eyes at her for a moment as he considered her statement.

It was always awkward discussing money and earnings with anyone. She wasn't at the top of the earnings pay scale where sports publicists were concerned, but she was very comfortably in the middle, and received generous Christmas and year-end bonuses. The benefit of working directly for an athlete is that he can set whatever salary he sees fit, and the athlete she worked for was working with a hundred and ten- million dollar contract. Sure, he had his fancy house and a few nice cars, but he was otherwise low maintenance compared to most of his teammates, which meant he had a lot of extra money to go around.

"Interesting," Jett said finally, nodding a little. "I had no idea I was getting a sugar momma."

"It doesn't make you feel emasculated, does it?"

Jett shook his head. "Not at all. You go ahead and make money, and I'll just make sure I look cute when you get home."

Zoey took a step toward him, closing the gap and reaching up to kiss him. "Come on, let me show you the rest of the house." She took his hand and pulled him upstairs, directly to her bedroom. She would show him the rest of her house eventually, this was all part of the tour.

Her bedroom was done in the same light, airy tones as the rest of the house. There was a fluffy, white down comforter over her queen size, pillow-top mattress with several large pillows and accent pillows.

She watched as Jett looked around the room briefly before focusing his attention back on her. His eyes dropped to the package she was still holding in her hand and he nodded toward it. "What's that?"

"Oh, I think it's the Christmas present I had sent here for you," Zoey said. She held a finger up to tell him to wait a minute and headed toward the master bathroom. "Let me just make sure that's what it is."

"Sure, sure. I'll pretend it's not some fancy 50,000 volt vibrator," he teased.

Looking over her shoulder before pulling the bathroom door shut, she grinned playfully. "I really don't think there's a vibrator in existence that comes close to what you're packing." That shy but satisfied smile lit up his face and she closed the door behind her.

Tearing open the package, she was pleased to see that it was what she had expected. She pulled out the silky, red, Christmas-themed lingerie and looked it over. It wasn't over the top. There were no giant santa buckles or white fluff. It was just a red silk babydoll-style dress with a short skirt and bow placed where the plunging neckline met in the middle. Simple, but effective. There was also a thick, black silky ribbon that was meant to tie at the waist, but Zoey had other plans for it. If Christmas was Jett's favorite holiday, she was going to give him every reason to love it even more.

She stripped down and dressed quickly, tousling her hair in the mirror, making her dark brown waves fall in a sultry curtain over her shoulders. In the top drawer of the bathroom vanity, there was a selection of lip gloss and lip stain. A subtle, light mauve gave her lips just enough extra color to draw his attention to her mouth, but not take away from the rest of the present.

Once satisfied with her overall look, Zoey slowly opened the bathroom door, peeking around for Jett who was now looking out the large window that overlooked the front yard.

"You might want to pull those curtains shut," Zoey said, her voice coming out as silky and smooth as the fabric she was wearing.

When Jett turned around, his eyes went from pleasantly surprised to deeply yearning in half a second. For a moment, he didn't move or say anything, but simply let his eyes drink her in. Then he half turned, grabbed both sides of the curtains and yanked them over the window before making three long strides across the room and folding her into his arms.

"Dammit, Zo, you look amazing," he breathed huskily into the curve of her neck. Hands already beginning to slide down her sides, to her hips and back up, pulling the short skirt up just slightly before letting it fall back down. His mouth, wet and searching, traveled down her neck to her collarbone and up to her lips, letting his words vibrate into her. "Not still sore, are you?"

She slipped her tongue into his mouth to find his and groaned with relief and a nearly inaudible "Nope." Her hands slipped beneath his shirt and felt his stomach, his ribs, his unbearably firm chest. God, she loved his chest. Hard and unyielding and so perfectly masculine. She dug her nails into his skin and pushed her hips into him.

Jett lifted her, carrying her over to the bed and setting her down on the pillows. He grabbed her hands and held himself over her, holding her hands above her head as he kissed her slowly. Savoring, as his wet, warm tongue dipped back into her mouth. She moaned and couldn't believe her body's immediate response to him. She was ready to wrap her legs around his waist and let him take her, wherever, however he wanted. There was no such thing as too much with him, too far, too fast. It didn't exist. They were right. Perfect. Her body craved anything and everything he had to offer.

"Wait," Zoey mumbled into his mouth, "I almost forgot." She pulled the black silk ribbon off from around her waist, remembering her original plan. Jett looked curiously at the ribbon in her hands as she held it out to him. She bit her lip in a brief moment of shyness, then reminded herself again that there was nothing he could do that would possibly be wrong. "I wanted you to blindfold me."

Again, Jett's eyes widened with surprise before darkening with need, the green of his irises going from stark emerald to dark forest. He rarely gave devilish grins, but he flashed one then that looked almost cocky. "Whatever you want, baby."

Zoey felt herself melt into the mattress with her exhale, shuddering, swooning, hot and wet in all the right places. Jett slipped the ribbon out of her hands and laid it flat to cover her eyes, tying it gently but securely in a bow behind her head.

"I guess you just really want to feel everything, huh?" Jett's voice filled her up and she sighed, concentrating on how sure and steady he sounded.

With her sight taken away, she focused on everything else about the man above her. His voice was low and calm, with just the slightest gravelly tone, and it both eased and excited her. It woke her body up, while simultaneously soothing her. His scent was intoxicating, all earthy musk and sandalwood. He smelled undeniably like man wrapped in clean flannel. The image of Jett wearing an open flannel shirt with faded jeans as he swung an ax permeated her imagination and *God*, she wanted to lick him all over.

Firm hands smoothed up and down her thighs, spreading them to make room for him as he situated himself there. She heard the soft slide and *woosh* of his cotton t-shirt being pulled off and tossed to the side, and with his shirt off, heat radiated from him like the sun.

Her heart was pounding out of her chest. She wanted to reach for him, touch him, feel his hard body with searching hands, but she also wanted to be surprised by him. She wanted the mystery of what she couldn't see, and to discover it simply by feeling what he did to her. To stifle the urge to reach for him, she fisted her pillow in both hands on either side of her head, trying to take steady, calming breaths, telling herself to wait. To be patient.

The familiar touch of his palms skated up her sides again, beneath the skirt of her lingerie, over her ribs and scratching on the way back down. Zoey moaned at the feel of his fingers digging into her skin, catching on her thong and pulling it down her legs. His warm hands felt their way back up, between her thighs, teasing...*teasing*...so close, but not touching where she was hot and aching for him to be. Not yet.

Her ears perked up at the sound of his belt coming undone, the soft rustle of denim being pushed down his legs. She was in the middle of wondering whether or not he'd pushed his boxers off, too, when she felt the hard, warm length of him pressed bare against her thigh. She let in a sharp inhale then bit her lip. Her hips gave an involuntary roll upward into him, begging, pleading for him to go there, but she knew he wouldn't yet.

"You like being teased," Jett growled softly in her ear. "I can see how bad you want me, but every time I don't give you what you want, you get wetter." His soft lips pressed just below her jaw. "Tell me what you want, baby."

Zoey groaned and whimpered. The enormity of that question seemed impossible to tackle. She wanted him everywhere all at once. His fingers, his mouth where she was aching. She wanted to taste him, feel him press into her mouth until she couldn't take him further, she wanted him inside her, thrusting deep as she squeezed around him. She wanted him behind her and ravenous again. She wanted to feel him come inside her, to come on her and feel the wet warmth of it all over her skin.

"Everything," she breathed finally. "I want you so bad, I can feel you in my chest."

This must have been the correct response. Or at least a very, *very* good one. Jett groaned and it reverberated through Zoey's head as she felt the weight shift slightly on the bed. Quiet sounds she recognized as a foil condom wrapper being torn open, then she imagined the pure masculine sight of Jett gripping himself as he rolled his condom on. He'd slide it down his impossibly thick length, run a hand over his balls, and be ready to plunge.

Her legs opened wider for him and she felt the blunt head of his cock as it began pushing into her soft, wet opening. A soft moan turned into a sharp, pleading cry, and she could no longer keep her hands to herself. Her palms felt the way up his shoulders, curling around the back of his neck and plunging into his hair, needing his mouth on her. On her lips, her neck, her breasts. She just needed his talented mouth tasting her, biting and sucking at her skin.

Weight pushed the pillow down on either side of her head and she felt as he shifted his weight to his forearms, elbows anchoring just above her shoulders. His hands tangled in her hair as he held himself there, not allowing her body to move up and away from him as he thrusted into her. His pace was slow to start, sliding his cock all the way in deep, then pulling back before sending another slow thrust, inch by slow, steady inch...*back...in.*

"Oh my God," Zoey breathed, letting her head fall back, exposing the arch of her neck, sending a direct invitation to his mouth.

Jett sucked at the nape of her neck, increasing his pace as she rolled her hips into him. "Zoey...oh God...*so* sexy. Feels *so* good." Removing one hand from her hair, he pulled the straps of the lingerie down low off her shoulders until she felt cool air against her exposed nipples. A hot, wet tongue covered one hard, pointed peak. He sucked her nipple into his mouth, gently scraped his teeth around it, pinching just slightly, making her arch into him.

"More...please, Jett...more."

She felt the suction increase, his teeth dig a little sharper next time, biting just below her nipple and making her cry out. The soft skin of his lips pressed a kiss to the small bite and she wrapped her legs around his waist. *Nothing*, absolutely *nothing* was enough. Nothing was wrong or off limits. Everything with this man was utter perfection.

Jett's mouth shifted its attention to her other breast, repeating the action, sucking and biting, kissing and licking. She cried out again, panting, breath ragged, nails digging into his shoulders. His hips bore into hers in a steady rhythm, and she felt the pressure building deep inside her. Climbing...dizzying...*almost...there.*

Jett resumed his position, anchoring her with his forearms and elbows, thrusting harder. She wanted to look down their bodies and watch the flex of his hips as he pushed into her, filling her. She imagined watching his muscles contract, sweat dripping down his chest between them, that look of concentration he wore when he was putting all his effort into pleasing her.

"Zoey," he whispered. "Zoey, you feel so good. So wet...*goddamn.*" He bit her shoulder and she whimpered, rocking her hips with his, feeling where the base of his cock was rubbing against her clit when he set himself deep- *So. Fucking. Deep.*

Pleasure swirled in her chest and she could feel it getting ready to burst outward, extend to her extremities, curl her toes, and shatter her from the inside out.

His voice and his scent overcame her. His skin against hers, slippery with sweat. His grunts and ragged, heavy breaths, and his weight on top of her were all that existed in the world. He spoke into her neck, encouraging her, praising her.

Fuck, baby, I love those sounds you make.

Oh my God, Zoey, you feel so good.

My dick is so...so fucking hard.

Come for me, Zoey. Come for me, and I'll flip you around and take you from behind. I know you want that, baby.

She did want that. She didn't realize how badly she wanted it until he told her that's what she wanted, but she knew he was right.

"Yes...yes...yes, Jett, oh God, yes!" Whatever he said, she would agree with him. It didn't even matter. She was screaming and he was fucking her hoarse. Dizzy and desperate.

Right.

...There.

Yes!

The spark ignited into a larger flame and it...was...explosive.

She cried out some inaudible words and sounds, and she was spiraling, falling, and it was never ending. She was wrapped tightly around him, squeezing, latching on, legs encircling his waist. Her body shook and quivered and rocked beneath him. She was a wildfire, out of control and growing hotter with every second in this man's presence.

As promised, Jett flipped her over and the sensation was slightly disorienting with the blindfold over her eyes. His hands slid up her sides, over her shoulders and he pulled her up, resting her hands on the headboard which was apparently directly in front of her. Warm, solid palms slid down her back, grasping her ass with a playful squeeze. She had just come and her legs were shaking, but still she was humming with anticipation. Biting her lip, she waited.

Jett slid his hands beneath the smooth silk, pushing it up to expose her ass fully to him. She imagined how she must look: Skin hot, sweaty, and flushed. Red silk skirt pushed up to her ribs, straps pulled down exposing her breasts. Hair wild, and her silky blindfold in place. Well fucked and man-handled. That's probably how she looked right now. Completely disheveled and craving more.

He bent over her and she could feel his large hand next to her significantly smaller one on the headboard. His chest was dripping sweat onto her back, and she had to appreciate the level of exertion he was putting in. His other hand gripped her hips, sinking into those fading bruises from a few nights ago.

Zoey backed into him, eager for more, wanting him now. She tried pushing her hips back again and he stilled her just with the strength of his one hand.

"You'll get it, baby," Jett's calm, gravelly voice assured her. "I'm just admiring the view."

Heat flushed everywhere. Up her thighs, curling like steam into her stomach, up her ribs, chest, and neck, into her face. A thought flashed through her head, wanting him to take a picture of her like this so he could always admire it. So he could keep it with him and always be wild for her.

Whoa, girl. Maybe next time.

Despite the blindfold, she closed her eyes and tried to steady her breathing, slowing it, and once again urging herself to be more patient.

Jett's lips pressed to her shoulder, leaving a trail of kisses across her shoulder and up her neck. Zoey felt the weight shifting on the bed under her knees and she knew he was getting closer, centering himself, before-

"Oh...my...*God*," Zoey moaned, nearly falling apart. She dropped her head between her arms and arched her back, pushing her hips into him again as he dove in again.

"*Fuck*," Jett grunted. It was the only audible word from that point as he began the repeated deep slide of his cock in and out.

This. This is what she wanted. She swore she could feel him everywhere like this. He was inside her, over her, in her head. Deeper than should be physically possible.

Sharp cries and gasps mingled with grunts and guttural moans, primal sounds of pleasure filled the room and they were damn near positive they were the only two beings in existence.

The build was quicker this time, less teasing and playing, but no less intense. Jett's fingers dug into her skin, and his thrusts felt exact. Concentrated. Practiced and perfected as though living out some dirty, recurring daydream.

Zoey gasped when she felt the sudden surge of heat deep between her thighs and she cried out again. Skin flushed and hot, grasping the headboard tight, sure her knuckles had gone white as she came and screamed and panted. Her legs shook and she wasn't sure how long she could hold herself up, now putting most of her weight on the headboard.

Jett's hand moved from her hip and now grasped the red silk around her waist, bunching it and using it to pull her into him. She felt as he came with a drawn out groan, mixed with grunts as he continued thrusting until he let out a hard, shuddering breath and collapsed, chest to back.

They remained still, allowing their bodies to come down from their unbelievable high as they caught their breaths. Finally, Jett tugged the bow behind Zoey's head to untie her blindfold then pulled out, kissing her shoulders again.

Zoey turned around needing to see his face and felt her heart clench when their eyes met. Those bright green eyes looked satisfied, sleepy, and even a little inquisitive. She could see the question in his expression, but cut him off with a kiss before he could ask it.

"That...was amazing," Zoey declared. She smiled and kissed him again, taking his face in her hands and pulling him on top of her as she lay back on the bed again. When their lips parted, she was hit with a sudden wave of exhaustion. Satiated and sleepy. Allowing herself to sink into the pillows with her fingers still tracing his jaw, she gave a satisfied smile and muttered, "I love you."

"I love you too, baby," Jett replied with another soft kiss to her lips. When he sat up to slip off the condom, her eyes were already closed. "Um..." There was a pause and it felt as though it hung heavily between them for those two seconds before he spoke again. "Baby, you might not want to go to sleep just yet."

Zoey's eyebrows pinched together and she hummed in question.

"Unless I was hurting you and you just didn't say anything...I think you started."

Zoey snapped her eyes open and looked curiously up at Jett. "Started?" She looked down and comprehension dawned. "Oh...crap." There was a small spot of blood on her white comforter and she rolled quickly onto her feet, making a beeline for the bathroom.

Well, that answered that question, anyway.

She'd been waiting to start her period ever since the night they had neglected to use protection. The following day had been hectic with Quinn coming back and neither of them had made it to the store to get Plan-B.

Glad she wasn't pregnant at least, she couldn't deny the pang of disappointment that they wouldn't be getting another round while they stayed at her house.

CHAPTER 24

Jett blinked a few times at his surroundings when he woke up. He took in the white nightstand with its small seashell lamp, the sheer white curtains with rays of sun bursting through, the walls such a pale shade of blue they nearly looked white. There were artsy, abstract paintings on one wall, and white shelves with small house plants on another.

Zoey was still wrapped in his arms, her face nestled into his chest as she slept. She had quickly swapped out her white comforter for a light gray one, and rushed to put all the necessary stain removers on the small red spot of the now-soiled comforter before tossing it in the washer and coming back upstairs to remake the bed. It had been early to go to bed, but they were both full from eating all day, and completely satiated from their fiery love-making, so lying in bed together was the absolute perfect option.

In a world where Zoey hadn't started her period, they likely would have fucked long into the night, but Jett was content to hold her, talking and planning what came next. What happened when she left California this time? They'd talked about starting a house-hunt, though for obvious reasons, December and January were not the best months to move in Michigan. No one wants to move a giant U-Haul truck back and forth across town in the snow and slush.

A month and a half. Zoey had come to Michigan a month and half ago, and they were already talking about moving in together. She wanted to move across the country. For him. Because she wanted to really be able to give their relationship a shot. It was crazy, probably, but he wasn't complaining. He was a little worried that she was a planner, an organizer, an everything-in-its-exact placer. And this had most definitely not been part of the plan. He had no idea what would happen if she woke up one morning and just freaked out, knowing that she made the wrong choice, and needed to get her life back on track. Back on a plan, whatever that plan had been before.

Jett sighed into her hair and tried to clear his mind and think of simpler things. Happy things. Last night was a happy thing, that was for damn sure. He thought of the blindfold, of watching her face and body react to every movement, patiently waiting for his touch. Her senses had been heightened and her body had responded to *everything*. Each shift of his weight, each kiss, each word. He wasn't typically much of a talker during sex, but the way her skin blushed and her breath caught whenever he'd spoken the previous night had made him feel like a dirty-talk expert.

Oh...great. And now...my dick is hard.

Zoey wore just a small camisole top and matching pink shorts with white hearts all over them, and he was still naked. He liked to sleep naked anyway. He lived alone, it's something he'd gotten used to. But sleeping with nothing between him and Zoey was the best. Sleeping with a thin, silky layer of cute-yet-sexy pajamas between them wasn't all that bad, either.

She stirred in his arms just slightly, and when she brought her hand up from between them, she unintentionally brushed his cock with the soft palm of her hand. He groaned into the top of her head, knowing there wasn't anything they could do about it right now. Or...well, okay, there was something *she* could do, but he didn't want to be that guy.

"I was thinking," Zoey began, her voice heavy with sleep. Jett wasn't entirely sure if she was talking in her sleep, or if she had simply woken up and her brain whirred into action, ready to tackle each and every item on her always mile-long to-do list. Probably the latter. The girl's mind was a fucking machine. "I was thinking that maybe I could pack an extra bag or two...to take back with us."

Jett immediately perked up. "Really? Like more clothes or...?"

"Just stuff that I like to have with me. A few books, some of my favorite blankets, comfort items. And probably more clothes. I've cycled through the same six or seven outfits a few times by now."

"You always look great to me," Jett mumbled, pressing a kiss to the side of her head. "But I think that's a good idea. And when we get back, we can start looking for houses. Whatever my sugar momma wants."

Her laugh mingled with a sigh and she tilted her head up to him and kissed the underside of his jaw. "Are we crazy?"

Jett's eyes met her gaze and his heart tightened in his chest. He was so unbelievably gone for this girl. He understood what she was saying, that they'd been together less than two months and already they were at this stage. But what felt even crazier to him was the thought that the only other option was to return to life as it was *before*. There was a distinct *Before (BZ)* and *After (AZ)* of Jett's life now, and though his life was nowhere near bad in the *BZ* period, there was absolutely no way he'd be able to function now that he knew what life was like in this new *AZ* time.

"Not at all," he finally replied confidently. "I wouldn't want this to go any other way. We'd be crazy to let this go. That's what I think would be crazy."

She beamed up at him and kissed him softly, then winced. "Ugh...cramps."

"I'm sorry, baby. Do you have any Tylenol or Midol in your bathroom? I'll get it for you." Zoey narrowed her eyes curiously at him and he explained, "Remember, I have two little sisters. I've been sent out for tampon runs as a senior in high school because I had my license and they didn't. I would also be sure to bring home lots of chocolate and ice cream, and I even brought an entire cake one time. I'm a pro."

"Sounds like it," Zoey giggled, then let out a long sigh. "I should probably get up anyway. We've got a long day ahead of us."

And of course, she was right. They found more travel bags in the back of her closet and began packing. Sure, packing and moving absolutely sucked, but Jett was too thrilled that she was actually coming to live with him. They were planning a future together. A month ago he'd been terrified that this would just be a fling he would have to learn to look back at fondly, and be forced to move on or be alone- probably be alone. But they were making it work. It was real, and it was perfect, and she was coming home with him. Everything, again, was so fucking right.

Lou drove Zoey and Jett to the airport, and Ace had happily agreed to come along for the ride. Leaving Cassie alone in the house was apparently a decision that no one felt could be trusted, so she was more or less dragged and thrown into the back seat to make sure she stayed out of trouble for a day. Maybe.

Ace gave Jett a big hug and told him to take care of his sister. This was unnecessary- of course Jett would take care of her- but the sentiment made him that much more fond of Zoey's wiry younger brother. Jett and Lou shook hands, and it was a far different handshake than the one he'd received in that very spot only two days ago.

Cassie was hugging Zoey when she turned and gave Jett a scrutinizing sort of look. "I'm glad you were able to come and throw those shitheads around, but I'm still not happy that you're taking my sister away from me. Who's going to remind me to go to the dentist? Or remind me that I need to send out birthday cards? Who's going to go to the bar with me and make sure strange men stay away from me?"

"Cassie..." Zoey groaned with a shake of her head. "You can do all of those things on your own. And if you need help, call Ace. He's got your back. Always."

Zoey looped her arm through Jett's and he grinned at her sister. "Make better choices, Cassie. I believe in you." Cassie rolled her eyes so hard, she must have seen the inside of her skull.

After their final goodbyes they and their extra bags loaded up onto the plane, leaving sunny and 68 behind for windy and 32.

The late flight put their arrival time in Michigan at a little past 9:30 at night. They'd lost three hours of their day and it was dark, with a clear starry sky, which meant it was bitterly cold. There wasn't much to do the night after Christmas, except lay in bed and watch movies together, discussing just how much nicer the California weather was.

Zoey got out her tablet and snapped her new protective case on it that she'd received for Christmas, and brought up different websites to search for houses. They fell asleep huddled together with her iPad between them, the screen shining bright in the otherwise dark room, a potential dream house on display.

Jett knew when he woke up early that Zoey would be getting to work at some point, and he was scheduled for a night shift- that's what happens when you have three days off in a row, apparently. But he woke up with something important on his agenda. He wanted to go see Quinn. He needed to talk to him about their fight. He wasn't worried about the shoving match; though he and Quinn had never gotten into it quite like that, they both knew that sometimes when words weren't enough, physical aggression won out. They'd both been in fights, they'd both thrown punches and then cooled off almost immediately. What left a sick feeling in Jett's stomach were the words that were said. The things he'd let slip because of anger and defensiveness, and even some possessiveness and jealousy. Not attractive qualities, but he was only human.

Jett pulled into the driveway of Rae's dark blue ranch-style home, with its white trim and wrap-around porch. He trudged up the three front steps and knocked on the front door and waited, feeling his clammy palms start to sweat in his coat pockets. A dozen different possible reactions flew through Jett's mind:

1. Quinn would still be pissed and take this opportunity to shove him back.
2. Quinn would glare and shut the door in his face.

3. Rae would answer and drag him inside to a reluctant Quinn and stand there like a mother forcing her two pouting kids to apologize. And so on...

What he hadn't expected when the oak door swung open, however, was Rae glaring at him with her arms crossed over her chest.

"Jett Michael Miller," Rae said sternly. "What the fuck?"

Jett pinched his eyebrows together in confusion. "Um...I'm sorry?"

"You'd better be!" she snapped. "Alaina Costello? *Alaina fucking Costello?* Are you kidding me?"

It was the wrong reaction, but Jett laughed a little. He couldn't help it. "Seriously, Rae? You still hate her that much?"

"Uh, *yeah.* I do. I can't believe you would hire that bitch," Rae vented, but held the door open for him to come in anyway. "You have blindly hated people for me more than anyone I know. Remember when I came home for the summer after sophomore year and we went to get donuts at Potter's and that woman got the last chocolate frosted one? You hated her with me."

Jett did remember. The woman was probably in her eighties and there was a good chance it was her last ever chocolate frosted donut, but Jett agreed that he would hate the woman, too, because Rae was pissed.

"Remember when we all went to the movies in high school and it was literally the four of us and one other group, and they sat right next to us? That kid chewed his popcorn the entire movie with his mouth open, and we agreed to hate that kid together."

Jett nodded, standing in the entryway, unzipping his winter coat. "That was one of the more reasonable ones. Remember when you told me some dude in a red Malibu cut you off on First street? I mean-mugged and flipped off every guy driving a red Malibu for like three months. And then you pointed out the person you were *so sure* was the guy who did it, and it was a Ford Fusion. I had a vendetta against red Malibu drivers for three months for you, Rae. And it was all for nothing."

"Yes! That's exactly what I'm talking about. Where is that enthusiasm now? You could hate on an eighty-six year old lady, but you can't hate Alaina, the twat-faced homewrecker? What gives?"

Again, Jett laughed quietly, but his smile faded slightly as he caught the sight of Quinn who had materialized behind Rae from somewhere inside the house. Fortunately, Quinn at least halfway grinned at the back of Rae's head. "Come on, Rae, we already talked about this. Give him a break."

Rae whipped around to glare at Quinn, arms still folded across her chest. They were both still in pajamas and Jett realized it was the first time he'd seen his two friends looking so casually domestic together. Despite the fact he was sure Rae picked little fights with Quinn all the time, the image was completely right. They were finally where they were meant to be and Jett truly couldn't be happier for them.

Letting out a huff of defeat, Rae gestured with one hand toward Jett. "Your boyfriend is here to make up with you. I'll let you traitors talk while I go shower. *Without* you." She breezed past Quinn and he watched her walk through the living room until she disappeared down the hall before turning back to Jett.

"Come on in, man," Quinn gestured with his head toward the kitchen and Jett kicked his boots off and followed.

In the large kitchen, Jett took a seat at one of the bar stools around the island while Quinn shuffled around for coffee mugs.

"Coffee?" Quinn asked, holding up a white mug with the words *She's a Catch* next to a small golden snitch across it.

"Sure, black."

There was a long stretch of heavy silence while Quinn poured two cups of black coffee and slid one over to Jett. Quinn didn't sit, but leaned onto his forearms on the marbled countertop. Jett had practiced what he was going to say, or at least had an idea of his apology that he wanted to make, but suddenly all the words jumbled around in his head and he couldn't seem to form a complete sentence. They both looked down into their drinks, silent, neither one of them even taking a sip to help wake up their brains.

"I'm sorry I was such a dick-"

"I shouldn't have been such an ass-"

The words overlapped as Quinn and Jett blurted out at the same time, then they each exhaled a small laugh.

"Yeah, that." Quinn nodded. "I shouldn't have come into your bar like that. I was pissed and shocked and overwhelmed at what we'd come home to. It wasn't your fault or Zoey's. I just..." He shrugged and met Jett's eyes. "I was angry. And I was ready to take it out on whoever was in front of me."

Jett scratched the side of his jaw. "I get it. I know that's always been a sensitive topic with you, and honestly, with how great everything has been going for you the past few years, it's easy for me to forget what your life was like once upon a time. You earned every bit of what you've got now, and that's really awesome."

Quinn chewed the inside of his cheek and ran a hand through his hair, which was a tousled mess, as always. "About what you said...about me being different-"

"Case, no, I was out of line. I don't...I mean, of course you've changed. Who wouldn't? It would be insane for you to still be the same quiet, stressed out, somewhat insecure kid that you used to be. You got out and made something of yourself. Who wouldn't have your confidence after what you've pulled off?"

Jett hesitated, thinking back on that incident in 2006. The first time he had really seen the kind of shit Quinn had to put up with firsthand. He'd known for some time that Quinn's life at home was rough, but he only really knew about his mother being neglectful. He hadn't thought much of it back then. In Jett's naive, adolescent eyes, Quinn was this kid who just sort of was the boss of his own life. He did what he wanted, when he wanted. He could come and go from his house as he pleased and stay wherever he felt like that particular night. He was a kid with no rules. How fucking cool was that?

It wasn't until that night in late October of their sophomore year that he realized just how bad it was. It was more than neglect, and it was more than just a mom with bad habits.

The plan had been for the four of them- Chris, Jett, Rae, and Quinn- to meet up at Jett's house on a rare football-free Friday night. They were just going to hang out, Chris and Quinn were going to spend the night, and Rae would stay as late as Jett's parents would allow him to have a girl over. Yeah, even though it was just Rae, his parents had rules about that stuff. But Quinn hadn't shown up. They'd waited and called his cell, but it rang until it went to voicemail. They were fifteen at the time and only had their learner's permits, but Jett's grandpa was the only one home and had fallen asleep in the chair in the living room. Making a stupid, snap decision as teenagers so often do, the three of them had illegally piled into Jett's grandpa's car and booked it across town to Quinn's house to see what was up.

There were a few cars in the driveway, including Molly's gold Toyota Corolla which had been their main form of transport since September when Quinn turned sixteen and got his license. Rae told them that they would need to go around the back and knock on Quinn's window since there were obviously guests over. It wasn't the first time Jett and Chris had heard this rule, but they hadn't fully understood the reasoning behind it. Regardless, they did as they were instructed.

They found Quinn in his room, sprawled out on the mattress sleeping hard. It wasn't unusual; Quinn always put every bit of himself into football or baseball practice, or a weight training session, and therefore he slept a lot. They woke him and hung out for a few, letting him fully wake up before heading back to Jett's house.

And that's when they heard it. The loud, angry male voice coming from the front of the house. The sound of glass breaking made all four of them sit up straight and wide-eyed.

Quinn stood up and told them they needed to go- *now*. Jett was confused and looked back at Chris as though he could fill in the blanks, but of course he didn't have any answers.

Footsteps were making their way toward the bedroom, stomping and rattling the minimal items Quinn had in his bedroom. Quinn turned and pointed at Rae, telling her to get through the window, telling Jett and Chris to get her out first. This much had at least made sense to Jett- if they were in danger, get Rae out first.

Chris grabbed Rae's forearm and began ushering her toward the window, but she resisted, not wanting to leave Quinn behind. And then it was too late. The bedroom door burst open and a large, yet strangely withered looking man stood in the doorway. He was tall, with dark brown hair and a scruffy beard. He had a cigarette of some kind sticking out of his mouth, and he stared intently at Quinn with frighteningly blank, gray eyes. His skin was dull and dry, and he wore ripped black jeans, and an old black leather jacket.

It was obvious to Jett that Quinn knew who he was, that this wasn't the first time this had happened. The man shouted back at Quinn's mom about the consequences of not being able to pay up, that it wasn't fair her kid had to suffer for her decisions. The man reached for Quinn and Jett immediately came to his defense, shoving the man back before his hand could wrap around Quinn's arm. The man staggered, gathered his bearings, and then stopped, his gaze beyond Jett and Quinn, while a malicious and evil smile- or at least he supposed it was meant to be a smile- curled the corners of his mouth.

The man had spotted Rae, and Jett's stomach churned. Though he had no idea who this man was or what he was capable of, he was sure he could read his mind right then. Again, Quinn shouted for her to get out and charged after the man to throw him off. Jett had wanted to stay next to Quinn and fight with him, but Rae was not leaving and Chris was struggling to hold her back after the man took his first swing and connected with Quinn's jaw. Jett fully understood the importance of getting Rae out, even if she didn't.

Once outside, Jett held Rae in a tight hug, partially to try calming her, but also to keep her from running back inside. Chris called the police and all their parents before running back inside the house to try and help. Charlie DeRose was the first on the scene, soon followed by several cop cars. Molly and the man, presumably her dealer, were arrested and taken away in separate cars. Quinn was treated by paramedics and taken to the hospital for further inspection before being released to stay with the DeRoses' while his mom served her time in the county jail.

And Jett...well, Jett saw his best friend's lack of rules, his anger issues, his "freedom", as he'd been naive enough to think of it, for what it was. But he did his best to never treat him differently for it, to not let it change their friendship, and only serve to solidify their bond.

"You know, that night sophomore year...I couldn't believe I'd known you for four years and had no idea you went through that shit at home," Jett said. "It sucked, because there wasn't a damn thing I could do. So, Chris and I just kind of convinced ourselves that wasn't something that happened much. We couldn't do shit to help you, so it was easier to just make ourselves think it wasn't that bad most of the time. And I think I got so good at telling myself that, that I forgot altogether."

Quinn lifted one shoulder. "Would've been fine by me. I didn't want you guys knowing that shit anyway. I knew as soon as you'd seen that, you'd treat me differently. Maybe pity me or something, and you know how I feel about that."

"We're your best friends, man. You should've been able to tell us and know we wouldn't treat you differently. We understood you a little better, I think, but I don't think anything changed in how we acted around you."

Again, Quinn brushed a hand through his hair, then walked around the island to sit on the stool next to Jett. "You were right about me taking advantage of Zoey. She does way too much for me. She shouldn't have half the workload I put on her, but I guess it was just kind of nice having someone take care of me. Do all the things your parents are supposed to do for you when you're a kid without having to ask. Rae's family did shit for me all the time, and I know after that night your parents and Chris's family stepped in sometimes, too, but it was nice having someone do it *just because.* She didn't know what I'd been through and wasn't doing it out of pity or because she felt bad for me.

It was just something that came naturally for her. Hell, she didn't even like me and she still did it. And I could just fuck around, enjoy life, and make an ass out of myself."

Jett chuckled a little, remembering saying approximately those words to him. "Maybe that's what you needed."

"Did Zoey tell you her new plan?" Quinn asked, arching an eyebrow over his coffee mug as he took a sip. Jett shook his head no. "Apparently she thinks she can make me into a role model. For kids. Maybe kids who had similar shit to go through."

Quinn was grinning as though it were an amusing and completely unrealistic idea, but Jett actually thought it was great. "I could see it," Jett said . "Not all role models have to be perfect. Maybe if kids have someone a little more real, a little rough around the edges that they could still look up to, it would seem more attainable."

Quinn's honey-brown eyes softened for a beat and Jett thought there was going to be a rare, heart-felt, tender moment between them before Quinn smirked. "I'm a little hurt you don't think I'm perfect."

"Far from it, Case," Jett replied, patting his friend on the shoulder. He brought the cup of coffee to his lips and took a drink, then noticed the sound of the shower shutting off. Gesturing with his head in the general direction of Rae's bedroom, he asked, "How long has she been pissed about Alaina working at the bar?"

Quinn let out a sigh-slash-groan and pushed both hands into his hair. "Just last night. We went in to visit because we heard Tyler was going to be there and I hadn't seen him since high school. Alaina was behind the bar and all I did was say 'Hey, Alaina'. I wasn't even overly friendly. I probably sounded confused more than anything, but that was obviously not the correct reaction."

"Of course not," Jett said with a laugh. "You should've shunned her. Doused her in holy water or threatened her with a wooden stake."

"Yeah, well, apparently nothing has changed between those two. Words were exchanged and I was caught in the crossfire. Rae all but called Alaina a whore in front of everyone, and Alaina congratulated me on finding the millions to finally win Rae over. It was a fucking shit show."

Jett tried not to laugh but he was actually kind of upset he'd missed the reunion. "Chris was so sure it would be fine. He was all 'come on, Jett, high school was so long ago. They probably won't even remember why they hated each other so much'. Give me a break. It doesn't matter *why*, they just do."

"About that," Quinn said, and he cleared his throat then set an intense stare on Jett. "How the fuck did Rae find out Alaina was the one I slept with in high school?"

Jett's mouth opened and closed several times before he was able to speak. "Yeah, that's my fault. I let it slip. Sorry, man."

Quinn narrowed his gaze before nodding and taking a sip of his coffee. "I guess that's what I get for being a complete ass and lying to Rae back then anyway. But damn did she slap me in the face with that last night- *'Maybe you should ask her if she's still got her Pontiac and you can revisit the backseat'.* I froze. I had no idea she knew."

Jett scrubbed his hands down his face and laughed again. "Damn, that's brutal."

"I may never get a blow job again."

"She holding out on you now?"

Quinn tilted his head from side to side. "Sort of. We got home and I thought we were going to have rough make-up sex or something, but she just rode it until she got off and then went to bed." Jett let out a low whistle and Quinn added, "It's all right...I mean, clearly she still needs me so she'll come around eventually."

"We all knew Rae could be a piece of work sometimes," said Jett. "Speaking of girls who are a piece of work, have you met Zoey's little sister? Cassie?"

"Briefly," Quinn replied. "Why? What happened?"

"I could've used your help down there. It would've been like old times." Jett filled Quinn in on the events that took place in California, his first meeting with Zoey's dad, the rescue mission for Cassie and her friends, and how he finally won Lou over. He told him about going to see Zoey's house and their plans to start house hunting here in Traverse City.

"Damn, sounds like it's going good then," Quinn said, smiling approvingly. "I guess this means we're going to have to share Zoey somehow between Michigan and California. But if I cut down her workload by doing shit for myself, it shouldn't be too bad. Plus, it'll give you an excuse to come visit us in LA."

"I could probably handle that. Don't know how I feel about *sharing* Zoey, but I'll find a way to deal with it."

"What if I agree to share Rae? She's pretty great. Mean sometimes, but otherwise really cool."

Jett glanced sideways at Quinn. "I'm only talking about sharing Zoey's *time*, Case. That's all."

"Whatever," Quinn said with a shrug. "I mean, if I were going to share Rae with someone, you'd be my first choice."

Jett was giving Quinn another scrutinizing look when Rae entered the kitchen now dressed in blue jeans and a cream-colored sweater, hair still wet from her shower.

"Did I just hear you say something about sharing me?" Rae didn't even spare Quinn a glance as she pulled open the refrigerator door.

"Just with Jett," Quinn said defensively. "You guys could go ice skating and then cuddle afterwards."

Jett laughed and Rae turned to look at Quinn, a small grin tugging up her lips. "It's cute you think you'd be okay with that."

After pouring herself a glass of iced coffee, because even in the winter, Rae can't drink it any other way, she joined them at the island, taking a seat on Quinn's other side. Leaning forward, she got the familiar look on her face that told Jett she was about to spill some juicy gossip. "Did Quinn tell you we went to see Tyler?" Jett nodded and she continued, "You won't believe who he was sitting at the bar with!" She paused for dramatic effect. "Emerson! As in *my* ex Emerson. What a small world, right?"

Jett exhaled. "Oh yeah. He's doing his internship at Emerson's firm."

Quinn and Rae both narrowed their eyes suspiciously at him and Quinn asked how he possibly knew that.

Well fuck.

Jett cleared his throat and rubbed his palms on his jeans. He was sweating now. Why was he drinking hot coffee again? Rae's iced monstrosity looked so much more appealing.

"You know, Emerson did seem a little disappointed you weren't around," Rae said, hedging. "Got a new bromance you want to tell us about?"

Jett stuttered a little. "Oh, that...um, well that's...It's not what it looks like."

"Wow, you must be spending time together. You're even starting to sound like him," Rae remarked, and it earned a snorting sort of laugh from Quinn.

He supposed it was going to have to come out eventually, so Jett explained how Brody had started inviting him to game nights and how Emerson was just always there. He was adamant that he still didn't like Emerson and that he simply tolerated him because he needed a social life when Chris wasn't around. Then he told his friends about Emerson coming into the bar, hitting on Zoey, and how she hadn't let him get to her in the slightest, and how it had prompted Emerson to invite the two of them over to his place for a game night.

"Tyler was there, and he made me promise not to tell Chris about his internship," Jett said. "I felt like I was up to my eyeballs in secrets, but at least this one really didn't seem like my secret to tell. I felt like a shitty friend hiring Alaina, hanging out with Emerson...I'm the guy you always count on to have your back. To be the loyal one, I guess. I hate lying to my friends, especially Chris, because he can see right through it." He looked up from his coffee cup to Quinn. "And then I lost my shit with you at the bar, and again at the hospital. That was all me, I was getting annoyed at Zoey's phone going off every two minutes with people asking about you, and then she'd ask about you and it was like…holy shit, am I ever going to have another conversation with my girlfriend that's not about Quinn?"

Quinn blew out a long stream of air and put his hand on Jett's shoulder. "Shit, man, that's a lot to keep in. I can see why you snapped. And I'm sorry I take up so much of Zoey's time. I mean, she's damn good at her job, but I'll try to be less exciting so it doesn't take up so much of your time together."

Rae got up and walked around to where Jett was sitting on his stool and hugged him from behind with her arms wrapped around his shoulders. "You are literally the best friend anyone could ask for. You don't have to hate Emerson for me anymore. Honestly, I don't even hate him anymore. And you can hire whoever the hell you want for your bar. My issues with Alaina aren't yours, and you don't have to feel bad about any of it, okay?"

Jett smiled and relaxed, giving her arm a gentle squeeze. "Thanks, Rae."

Quinn rounded the island again to the fridge and reached for a small black box, no bigger than a cell phone, and brought it over to Jett. "This is for you."

Jett eyed the box curiously. It wasn't wrapped in gift paper, and only had a gray tag with his name on it. Jett pulled the cover of the box open and saw a black card on top:

I could have sent this in a text, but Rae's making me do this…

Jett laughed, somewhat confused, until he saw what was in the box beneath the card. It was a bottle opener with a distressed leather handle that was engraved. JETT read in bold, capital letters and beneath his name, in smaller lettering were the words *Best Man.*

His smile spread across his whole face and he stood up to face Quinn who was smiling back. They brought it in for a back-slapping hug, doing their best to not be overly emotional, for fear of some God of Man Code smiting them where they stood.

"Thanks, Case. I'll fucking rock the best man thing," Jett said, looking down at the personalized bottle opener in his hand. "Just ask Chris. He picked me over his brother and I fucking crushed it."

"If you pick Chris over me when you and Zoey tie the knot, I'll try not to be too heartbroken, but just know I would rock the shit out of it if you wanted me to," Quinn replied.

"Man, this is going to be fucking epic. I have to start planning your bachelor party. *Holy Shit!* Quinn Casey's bachelor party? It's gotta be huge." Jett already had a million ideas running through his head. This was the kind of thing he was good at. It's what he lived for. He loved doing things for other people, planning the big moments, showing them exactly what they'd be missing in their lives if not for him. Being the best man was like his calling.

Jett and Quinn took their excitement out into the living room where they spent the rest of the morning coming up with bachelor party ideas. After Rae vetoed the first several, they got smart and started writing their ideas down and speaking in code. She still eyed them suspiciously every time she passed through the living room as she got ready to head out to visit Amira.

Before either of them knew it, it was one o'clock and Zoey was walking through the front door with Chris, who had apparently given her a ride over. Their new guests looked particularly pleased that Quinn and Jett were sitting together, hanging out as comfortable and familiar as they had been in high school when they'd alternate between doing homework and watching whatever game was on TV together.

Zoey looked ready to get to work, settling herself next to Jett on the couch and pulling her laptop out of her bag. Catching a glance at the notebook that was lying face-up on the coffee table, she craned her neck to read the notes scribbled on the paper and then paused, her expression absolutely petrified.

"Oh God..." she groaned, as though she'd seen a ghost. "Quinn Casey's bachelor party? This is my nightmare."

CHAPTER 25

The weeks following Zoey and Jett's return from California were some of the easiest, most seamless weeks in the history of anyone who has ever made a gigantic move across the country. Their lives meshed together so well, and they fell into a smooth, comfortable rhythm of living together in Jett's apartment.

Zoey made the spare room into a combination of her work space and his hobby room. His guitars hung on the walls, her desk was pushed against the wall opposite of the guest bed with plenty of space. The closet was perfectly organized with their off-season clothing so that Zoey's and Jett's clothes could fit in the closet in his- *their-* bedroom. She managed to add her own personality to every space of the apartment without taking any of Jett's touch out of it.

They typically spent late nights together, whether Jett worked an evening shift or not, waking up mid-morning. Jett made breakfast while Zoey did her yoga routine in the living room, then they would eat together before Zoey got to work either at her desk or at Quinn and Rae's when Quinn was available for input. Jett went to the gym and came home to shower in time to head downstairs for work, and they found time in between and after to make sweet, toe-curling love to each other. Everything just flowed.

Jett worked the closing shift on New Year's Eve, but the entire bar had been celebrating. Even the bartenders, servers, and cooks got in on the party, lending Jett and Zoey several moments while everyone was blissfully distracted to pull the door shut in the office and have wild, spontaneous sex through the loud cheers of the countdown. Jett was overly pleased with himself when he remarked that he literally fucked her into next year.

Zoey couldn't believe it was the end of January and the weather was actually getting colder. Thirty-two had absolutely nothing on one. *One degree!* How was that even a thing? She tried her best not to even look at the windchill temperatures, because they always seemed to have a small negative symbol in front of them and that was just depressing. She was severely missing the warm weather that her sister was currently enjoying in all of the Snapchat photos she sent every day.

Quinn and Rae had gone back to California the previous week, taking Quinn's mom and her nurse, Sandra, with them. They would be back in a few days, but Zoey couldn't help feeling a little jealous that they were enjoying her sunny home state while she was freezing her toes off.

She tried to focus on the perks of being in Michigan: First and foremost, Jett was here. And he was especially well versed in making her feel all sorts of warmth, letting her forget about the frigid, blustery winds outside their cozy home they'd made together. Second, she was actually making friends here and creating a rather satisfying work-life balance. She started going with Jett to Brody's house for his video game nights and it turned out she and his wife, Amira really got along. The girl was hilarious and over the top, but always fun to be around. Jett's game nights had turned into Zoey's ladies' nights, and occasionally even Chris would come and bring Victoria along. The three of them worked together to mess with Emerson on those nights, finding new ways to make him speechless or feel like maybe he wasn't really the God Among Men that he thought he was.

A third perk of living away from home was that when she received phone calls from her siblings, she was no longer filled with a pending sense of dread that they'd gotten themselves into something and she needed to bail them out. Ace called a few times a week just to talk and let her know how school was going. Almost all of these phone calls resulted in Zoey passing the phone to Jett so they could talk about Ace's dating situation. It was really sweet how close they were getting, and

Zoey was actually appreciative of the distance somehow making her relationship with her little brother even better, too.

Cassie's phone calls were dramatic as always, but that was to be expected. Zoey tried to tell herself not to worry about every little thing her sister got into and to instead just listen to her sister's tales of her life as a college student. *Student* was a very strong word for Cassie. She rarely talked about her classes and when Zoey asked about them she was exceptionally vague, but as Jett frequently reminded her, Cassie would have to learn to figure things out on her own.

It was a Wednesday evening and Jett was working downstairs while Zoey sat at her desk and responded to her emails. She was setting up an event for Quinn at a youth center in Florida where the team would be for spring training. It was a sort of day camp for these kids to play ball with Quinn and some other major league players. These were kids who, like Quinn, didn't have the best lives at home. A lot of them were in and out of foster care or had absent parents and just needed some sort of guidance, and maybe some of the discipline that came with team sports.

She had a FaceTime call scheduled with him that evening- five-thirty California time, eight-thirty Michigan time- to prep him for his third major press interview since deciding to come clean about his past. It was the first major interview that she wasn't practically standing behind him, feeding him his lines, and she was nervous. But Rae was there, and she had this way of calming him. It's like her touch put an invisible, soothing forcefield around him that cleared his head and cooled his near-boiling blood.

Sitting in her desk chair with her legs folded beneath her, she sent the confirmation email for the Florida youth center event and put it in her calendar, then linked it to Quinn's. He now had a calendar that he would have to check from time to time, now that Zoey couldn't barge into his house every day and tell him to get ready. The changes made her anxious at first, like he was going to completely forget and somehow screw up both of their careers, but Jett assured her that was ridiculous. Quinn is a grown man, and perfectly capable of checking his calendar and setting alarms. And if all else failed, Rae knew what was going on.

It was a relief, having some of her workload taken off her shoulders. She was still as focused and organized as ever, but she was actually allowed to have a life of her own. Despite the snowflakes swirling outside her window, she found herself wondering why she hadn't moved to Michigan years ago.

She held a warm mug of black tea and honey in her hands and gazed around the room, imagining all of her and Jett's things in a house. Maybe one like her bungalow in Los Angeles. Jett had a full week of vacation scheduled the first week of March so they could go to California together and work on getting her house ready to sell. It was in great shape, but buying and selling a home took time. She would miss her house, but this life that she'd created in the past few weeks would be worth it. She would find a new house, a home, with Jett and they'd create memories of their own there.

Smiling warmly at the thought, Zoey set down her cup of tea and brought up her saved listings. There were about twelve minutes until her call with Quinn so she didn't feel bad about browsing for a few minutes.

When her phone rang, she sat back in her chair and looked at the time. Six minutes early, way to go, Case. Referring to him by his old nickname that Jett used so frequently had rubbed off on her.

Glancing at her phone, she realized it wasn't a FaceTime invitation, and it wasn't Quinn.

Zoey swiped to answer, "Cassie, it's really not a good time. I have a work call in like five minutes."

"Zoey," Cassie's voice came in a sharp gasp. "Zoey, it's Dad." Cassie was panicked and Zoey could tell she was trying- and failing- to not cry. "You need to come home."

The world stopped as a thousand different scenarios flooded through her head all at once. Luckily, though, this wasn't the first time Zoey had to be calm and collected when she was bursting apart inside.

She knew none of the details, but if Cassie was this upset, she knew it couldn't be good.

"Hey, Cassie," Zoey said in a soothing tone. "Tell me what's wrong. What happened? Where's Dad?"

"He's at home," Cassie explained, her voice thick with restrained sobs. Her next words were choppy phrases, incomplete thoughts. "Cindy called...ambulance...he...he-"

Zoey stood up and yanked open the closet door with urgency, but kept her voice steady. "Okay, Cassie. It's going to be okay. Are you at school?"

"Yes," Cassie sobbed. "I need to...be there."

Her largest travel bag was shoved in the back of the closet and she grabbed it out, laying it open on the spare bed behind her. "Cassie, listen to me. Call Ace. He knows, right?"

"Yeah, he knows," her little sister sobbed and sniffled, and it made her heart ache.

"Find someone- someone *responsible*- who can drive you to the hospital where Dad is staying. Do not drive there on your own, got it?" Cassie made a sort of noise that assured Zoey she understood. "I will call Ace and I'll come home, okay? Find someone who can take you home, and I'll get on the next flight."

After hanging up, Zoey grabbed a bunch of her warm-weather clothes out of the spare closet and packed them into her luggage bag. She rushed around, packing as fast as some sort of *Loony Toons* cartoon character and the panic started to set in. Cassie had been too upset to give her details, so her head was now swimming with different possibilities. A car accident. A house fire. Carbon-monoxide poisoning. Was he helping the neighbor take down her Christmas lights and fell off the ladder?

By the time she finished packing her bag, there were images of her dad lying on the floor or the cement outside with a puddle of blood pooling out from around his head. She was vaguely aware of the text messages she was receiving, her phone dinging every minute or so from the desk where she had left it. Picking it up, she realized she'd missed her FaceTime call and Quinn was asking if everything was okay.

No. Not unless it's okay that my dad is thousands of miles away bleeding out through his head somewhere.

That's not what she texted back, of course. Instead it was far more vague: *Shit, I'm so sorry! Family emergency. Don't worry though, you got this!*

There was a nearly immediate response, but she didn't take the time to read it before shoving her phone into her purse. She wheeled her bag down the hall and into the living room where she found her coat and slipped on her boots.

The front door swung open and Jett slipped in, closing the door behind him. He wore a deep sage henley that was now soaked down the front and was muttering, "Fucking beer kegs. This is one of my good shirts, too," before he looked up and saw Zoey looking like she was making a getaway.

Jett's eyes swept over her appearance where she sat in the chair, zipping up her tall boots. They drifted over the large luggage bag, and then back to her face which she could only imagine was a splotchy, crumpled mess. All the tell-tale signs of ugly crying visible.

"Baby, what's wrong?" Jett strode over to her and knelt in front of her in the chair, one hand cupping the side of her face while the other held her trembling hand.

Zoey sniffled and cleared her throat, not really sure what to tell him. As much as she could, she supposed. "It's Dad. Something happened and he's in the hospital and I don't know all the details but I just know it's bad. I have to go."

"Okay, I'll come with you. We only have a few hours until we close downstairs, I'm sure they can manage without me." Jett swiped the pad of his thumb beneath her eye to stop another tear from falling.

"I need to go now. And maybe I should go on my own," Zoey said. She tried to stand up so she could get around him and leave, but he held her in place.

"Why would that be a good idea? Zoey, you need me right now. Just let me change and I'll-"

"My family needs *me* right now. And I'm here. Thousands of miles away." She shoved her hands into her hair and then shook her head. "I can't be here. I can't...I can't be this far away. They need me."

"Baby, I get that," Jett held her face in his large, warm palm. "You can be there for them, but let me be there for you. We can get the next flight, just let me put on a shirt that's not covered in Oberon." He planted a sweet kiss to her forehead, then stood and headed toward the hallway.

"I mean...I mean, I can't *stay* here, Jett. I can't move across the country. What if...what if something like this happens again? My family has always needed me. My family is everything. I don't know how to be away from them like this. Maybe...maybe there isn't a way to make this work."

Jett's brow furrowed, creating a crease between his eyebrows as he looked back at her. When he turned around fully, she noticed his emerald eyes had a slight gray cast to them. His body was stiff, his arms hung down at his sides as though he didn't know what to do with them and he stared at her like she was speaking a different language.

"Zoey...you don't mean that. You're just...you're just worried, okay? And it's okay to panic, but don't say stuff like that. Don't...don't tell me you have to leave me. We're building a life together, and it's amazing. You're not about to walk away from that. From us."

There was a lump in her throat and she had to look away from his eyes. That sad, pleading look would absolutely break her. But this was it. This was what she had been worried about this whole time. How could they possibly think it could work long-term? All along, this vacation she was on had an expiration date. They'd just fooled themselves into believing they could make it last.

"It has been fun, Jett...it's been wonderful," Zoey's voice was small as she looked down at her hands that were fidgeting with her coat button.

Jett pointed a finger at her. "Don't you do that, Zo. Don't talk about us in past tense like we're something that happened already and you're ready to move onto the next chapter."

Zoey swallowed and looked around the room, trying to avoid Jett's face. His eyes, his soft, kissable lips, the worry and fear written across his expression. She couldn't do what she needed to do if she looked at him. She needed to be with her family. She needed to stay in California. For them. Zoey couldn't make selfish moves and do whatever she wanted. She couldn't leave her family behind. That wasn't how her life worked. That wasn't ever how her life had worked, but she didn't know how to get Jett to understand that.

He was in front of her now, holding onto both her hands, forcing her to look at him. "Zoey, baby. You and me are going to be together. This stuff happens. Life happens, whether you're in California or here. You can't stop it. Don't tell me we can't be together because your family needs you. Your family needs to understand that you need to live your own life. You've said it yourself, your relationships with your siblings are even better with you here."

"I know, but-"

"No. No but. I'm telling you the truth, Zoey. If you're determined to leave it's not because of that. If you leave, it's because you don't want to be with me, but I don't believe that." His breaths were coming in heavier, his shoulders and chest rising with his attempt to control himself. To keep himself together. He swallowed hard, as though a massive lump were constricting his throat as well. "I'm going to go change, and we will go to the airport *together*." He held onto her for a few more moments, for fear that she'd disappear if he let go.

"Jett..." her voice was barely a whisper. "Jett, I need to go home."

His breath shuddered as he exhaled, and she could feel him shaking as he still held her hands, and his jaw clenched with the effort to keep himself in check. To not break down and stay strong in front of her. She closed her eyes and listened to his breathing, then looked up at his face from beneath her eyelashes. He was ducking his head to look at her, to figure out if he could call her bluff or if she was serious.

Honestly, she wasn't sure. She knew she had to get home. She knew her dad and her sister and her brother needed her, that they would always need her. But...she also needed Jett.

It looked like she couldn't have everything. So, once again, she would take the path she was most familiar with.

It took Herculean effort, and she felt like her body had turned to stone momentarily, but she stepped away and out of his grasp. Toward the door.

Jett looked like he wanted to fall apart, but refrained. His eyebrows pinched together, he bit the inside of his cheek, and his face nearly crumpled as he choked out the words, "So, that's it?"

She absolutely hated seeing him like this. His handsome, kind features distorted, tormented, pained. And it was her fault. It was hard to watch him like this, but she didn't want to take her eyes off him either. There wasn't a way to make this work.

Grabbing the handle of her luggage bag with shaky hands, and slinging her purse over her shoulder, the movements were like pushing through mud. She didn't want to go. But she had to. Before turning to leave, she leaned forward, raising on her tip-toes. With one hand, she caressed the side of his face, his strong jaw, memorizing the feel of it, then she kissed him, soft and quick, to his perfect lips that she would miss possibly most of all.

Again, she stepped back, quickly this time. The door pulled open and she took one more painstaking glance back at the most amazing man she had ever met. And then she left.

CHAPTER 26

What just happened?

The phrase was on repeat in Jett's mind as the image of Zoey leaving played on a loop for thirty minutes. Thirty hours, thirty days...who knew?

What just happened?

How did that happen?

Jett sat on the couch, staring back and forth from the blank television screen to the door that Zoey had made her final exit through. He couldn't believe it. Didn't want to believe it. None of this made sense. Zoey loved him and he loved her and they loved each other. So. Fucking. Much. How the hell could she leave?

The beer from the keg that had sprayed all over his shirt was drying, and the smell turned his stomach sour, but he didn't care. He couldn't move. Couldn't think. Couldn't make sense of a goddamn thing.

After what could have been minutes or hours or lightyears, which really wasn't even a measurement of time, but who cared anymore, the door to his apartment slowly opened. Jett knew better than to get his hopes up. Zoey had left. She left with a bag and wasn't coming back.

"Jett, dude...Are you all right, man?" The familiar smooth, rich timbre of Chris's voice cut through the silence of the apartment. Jett stared straight ahead at the blank television screen, unsure if he could voice aloud what had just happened.

The door closed and Chris slowly made his way over, sitting on the edge of the couch next to him. There was a silent pause, and though Jett wasn't looking, he thought he could sense the shifting of Chris's eyes around the place. Chris knew Jett more than anyone. They had been friends since they were in diapers, their mothers having met in some prenatal support group where new mothers and soon-to-be second or third time mothers would coach each other through everything. They'd been born two months apart, and their mothers kept in touch for play dates and helped each other through their future pregnancies.

In high school and again in college when they had girlfriends, or more specifically when they had break ups, they learned how to read each other. They knew how to act, what to say, what not to say, and how to just be there for each other. Jett could practically feel Chris reading the room, the tension...Zoey's absence.

"You don't have to talk about it yet if you don't want to," Chris said after several heavy moments of silence. "You wanna change your shirt though? Oberon isn't meant to be a cologne."

Chris patted Jett's shoulder before standing up and heading down the hall. After some untellable amount of time, Chris came back into the living room with a clean, navy blue long-sleeved shirt and held it out to him.

Robotically, without a word, Jett managed to pull his beer-covered henley off and switch into the clean shirt. Then he sunk back into the couch, brow still furrowed in confusion as he stared ahead, off into space.

His brain wandered to Zoey, wondering where she was. Had she made it to the airport? How was her dad? What had even happened to her dad? Was she safe flying by herself? Taking a cab by herself? Was she crying? Upset? Had she been thinking about leaving for days? Weeks? And she just didn't know how to express it?

He didn't believe that. Not one bit. There was no way the past month had been fake. They were planning a future together. They were saving home listings and making plans to walk through them. He was taking time off in March so they could put her house up for sale and pack up the rest of her things.

She loved him.

He fucking knew she did.

The muscle in his chest squeezed painfully behind his rib cage and his stomach sunk ten feet below the surface.

"Why would she leave?" It was a whisper, and he wasn't actually entirely sure if he'd said it out loud or in his head.

Chris was sitting next to him again and his hand held firm on his shoulder as he let out a heavy sight. "I...don't know, man."

Jett was grateful for Chris being there. He was glad he knew that Jett didn't actually want explanations, he didn't want to dissect everything and figure out where Jett had gone wrong, or what he'd missed. He just wanted someone to be there for him. To agree that this really fucking blew, to let him just feel what he needed to feel.

He barely noticed when Chris got up again until he was setting a bottle of Maker's Mark and two shot glasses on the coffee table in front of them.

"Splurged for the good stuff, huh?" Chris asked as he filled the shot glasses.

Jett's voice came out scratchy and low, "Case got it for me...said I needed to dump the Wild Turkey I had."

"Probably not wrong." Chris passed him a shot, clinked his glass against it, and they tossed them back in unison.

Jett woke the next morning with a pounding headache and winced into the dim light of his room. Yeah, his blackout curtains were drawn, and he was already wincing because it wasn't pitch black. This was going to be a fun day.

He rolled toward Zoey's side of the bed to fling his arm around her, but her space was empty.

Right. Fuck.

His heart throbbed with new intensity at the recognition that she was gone. She left last night. And then he did about ten shots with Chris and passed out. Back in college when one of them had a break up, they'd go shot-for-shot with each other, but Jett was fairly certain

Chris was supposed to close the bar last night, and there's no way he'd have taken ten shots and gotten back to work.

Jett buried his face in Zoey's pillow and inhaled deeply. The scent of her berry and hibiscus shampoo filled his lungs and he didn't want to breathe out.

It was pathetic and stupid and ridiculous, but he lay face down in Zoey's pillow for probably forty-five minutes before convincing himself that he needed to get out of bed. He needed water and Tylenol and a device to remove the memory of the past few months so that he could stop hurting.

Wait, that was whiskey, wasn't it?

Clearly he needed to up his game if he was going to forget how badly he was hurting.

When he rolled back to his side of the bed, he sat up hesitantly, slowly, cautiously, as though his head would physically roll off his shoulders and onto the floor if he moved even remotely faster than a sloth.

He squinted his eyes and groaned, rubbing his head with both hands, then noticed a note on his nightstand. Immediately, he recognized the handwriting as Chris's. Chris always had *pretty* handwriting and was teased endlessly for it. Wispy cursive that curled elegantly and looked like it belonged on wedding invitations. Not what anyone would expect from a guy his size and build, who had been the star quarterback of their football team in high school.

Jett,

Here's some water and extra-strength Tylenol. Get some coffee, take a shower, and take the day off. I already washed the shot glasses from last night so you don't have to smell whiskey ever again if you don't want to. Call me whenever you want.

PS: It really is water. Not vodka like that time in college, you asshole. Love ya, brother.

Jett actually laughed, and then winced at the pain it brought to his head. In college, Chris and Victoria had gotten into a fight and though Jett had known it was Chris's fault, he'd still gone shot-for-shot with him that night and helped him through it. Then he'd filled a water bottle with vodka and left it on Chris's nightstand for him to find in the morning. Drunk Jett thought it was fucking hilarious. Hungover Jett still thought it was funny the next morning, but threw up when Chris had poured him a glass from the same water bottle to go with his breakfast.

Though he trusted that his friend wouldn't pull the same trick on him after such an awful night, he gave the water bottle a cursory sniff before tossing back the Tylenol and taking a swig. The rest of the morning, which there wasn't a whole lot left of, he focused on the directions given in the note. He made some coffee, took a shower, had a second cup of coffee, and collapsed on the couch.

Around noon, he wrapped himself in a blanket from the couch, pulling it over his head like the Sith, and sulked into the spare bedroom to fall onto the bed and stare at the space that had most become theirs. His and Zoey's. Her desk and most of her clothes were still there, though her computer was gone along with the majority of items that covered her desk to make it her own. A framed picture of the two of them sat on one of the shelves and he took it in his hands, studying it.

It was from a little over a week ago when Jett had taken her to an outdoor ice skating rink. She had been getting a lot better on her new skates, and they had asked someone to take a picture of them together. There had been several posed ones that were really nice, but they'd caught this candid of the two of them just smiling at each other.

Jett stared into their faces in the photo and his heart felt as though someone was tightly wrapping fishing line around it, trying to cut off its circulation, he couldn't help the small flutter that recognized their looks as genuine. She wasn't hiding anything, and he knew she didn't want to leave. This had to be a fluke. She wasn't really leaving for good. She couldn't. Zoey had to come back. Her things were here, her new life that he knew she was already loving so much was here. Sure, she complained about the cold, but if she were in California, wouldn't she complain about the heat sometimes? The smog? The occasional earthquakes?

He put the picture back on its shelf and fell onto the bed again, holding the blanket tightly around him. There was no way they could be done. It didn't make sense. But he also couldn't make himself get his hopes up. As he realized weeks ago, he was completely at her mercy. Zoey had the final say here, and if she wanted out, there wasn't a fucking thing he could do about it.

Jett spent his entire Thursday hungover and miserable, wrapped in a blanket, staring at pictures of his and Zoey's time together. He fell asleep on her side of the bed because apparently he was a fourteen-year-old girl who needed to cling to the scent of his lost love in order to get some rest.

Friday morning had an even less promising start when he had the sudden realization that cell phones were a thing. All he had to do was call Zoey and hear her voice and ask or beg or plead with her to come back home. She had called California home, but that was bullshit. Home was with him and he knew it, and so did she.

It was three o'clock in the afternoon when Chris, Quinn, and Rae barged into his apartment. He had his blanket pulled over his head, Sith-style again, nearly covering his eyes. He was shirtless and leaning back into the couch with one hand shoved in his sweatpants and the other holding his phone. The sixty-eighth text message draft that he had typed and would likely delete again was pulled up on his screen.

"Oh, sweetie," Rae pouted in a pitying sort of voice, "dick pics aren't the way to get her back."

"I don't know," Chris muttered. "Have you seen that thing? He might be onto something."

"That's a fair point," Rae conceded.

"I don't think that'll work with Zoey, though. She needs more than a big dick and a charming smile to be wooed," said Quinn. "Believe me, I tried for like a month after I hired her."

"That's sad," Rae replied, shaking her head at her fiancé. "You didn't actually *show* her your penis, did you?"

"No, that would be sexual harassment or something. Jesus, Rae, I can't believe you think I would do that."

"Well, pardon me, Mr. Gentleman. It wasn't long ago you had a dick-pic leak from Snapchat getting passed around the internet like chlamydia at Woodstock's fifty-year reunion."

"Allegedly. It was not my penis."

"Allegedly it wasn't?" Chris questioned. "So...it *was* your penis?"

"Allegedly it was. But it was not. Not my dick. You can take that to the Supreme *fucking* Court."

Jett watched in silence as his best friends bickered back and forth, debating the merits of dick pics, how to correctly woo someone, and what actually counts as sexual harassment. They were talking about him as though he weren't there, and talking about Zoey so freely. As though the very mention of her name didn't shock him into reality over again and slap him in the face with the image of her walking out the door.

Quinn and Rae were supposed to be in California until Sunday, but they were here for some reason. Jett was supposed to work in an hour, but he knew that wasn't happening, even if he hadn't let anyone else in on the memo. And Chris was supposed to be working right now, but he was also here, weighing in on the discussion while Jett stared, eyes shifting from which friend was talking at the time to the next, never moving or bothering to take his hand out of his sweatpants.

Finally they all stopped, then fixed their gazes on Jett.

"Have you eaten anything today?" Chris asked. In response, Jett flicked his gaze to the mug on the coffee table. It wasn't resting on a coaster, even though there was an empty one right next to it. Jett always used coasters, but who cared about coffee rings anymore?

"Is that just coffee? Or is it an Irish coffee?" Chris looked cool and calm as ever, even when Jett didn't respond. He was pretending to be mute. Or he simply forgot how to speak and interact with fellow humans after one day in a cave of heartache and despair.

Chris took Jett's coffee mug off the table and sniffed it. "Is there rum in this?"

Jett lifted one shoulder in a shrug.

"Have you showered today?"

"Showered yesterday," Jett grunted in response as he sunk deeper into the couch cushions.

Quinn and Rae both approached, each taking a seat on one side of him, while Chris sat on the other. Rae put her hand on his arm, then withdrew it. "Jett, can you please take your hand out of your pants?"

Jett grunted unenthusiastically, but did as he was asked. He was a robot now. Robots didn't have emotions or hearts that could be crushed like a grape.

Rae put her hand back on his arm, though was careful to avoid his hand or any part of his forearm that had been inside his sweatpants. "Jett, I know this sucks. This really fucking sucks, and we're all upset for you. We love the shit out of you, and I know you need time to mourn and be miserable, but not tonight."

Jett's eyes narrowed, but he didn't turn to look at Rae just yet.

"We're taking you out," Rae said matter-of-factly.

Slowly, Jett turned his head to look at her. Rae's bright blue eyes were optimistic, her golden blond hair fell long past her shoulders beneath a navy blue winter hat with a giant pom-pom ball on top. It reminded Jett of Zoey's beige one and the knife in his chest twisted.

"Don't wanna go out." Jett resorted to caveman language. Short, monotone phrases. Not even full sentences. That was too much work, and so was leaving his den of despair.

"We thought you might say that," Quinn chimed in. "But I would like to remind you that when I was upset that Rae wouldn't talk to me all summer after graduation, you made me leave my room. You told me I needed to go for a walk or go to the park and hit a ball, go to the gym. Whatever it took to get my mind on something else. You went with me and it helped. A lot."

"And when Lana and I broke up in high school, you dragged me along to a Boyz II Men concert," Chris added. "I thought you were being ridiculous, but it was fun as hell and it got shit off my mind. Even for just a few hours."

"And after Emerson and I called off our engagement," Rae began, and Jett met her eyes intently, "you let me crash in your apartment, but you still made me get out. You took a wine and painting class with me and we made those awful pictures. My lighthouse silhouette looked like a giant black dick, and yours looked like a giant R2D2, which was actually kind of cool. But it definitely wasn't a lighthouse. And you went to the Copy Corner and made those posters of all the reasons women shouldn't date Emerson, and we posted them all around town. You tried to teach me how to bake, and I somehow screwed up chocolate chip cookies."

The corners of Jett's mouth were tugging up just the slightest bit at these memories.

"Basically, what we're saying is that you've always been there for us and made us do what we needed to do, even when we didn't want to," Rae explained. "So, go put some clothes on and probably wash your hands...and then we're going out."

They were right, he absolutely did not want to go out, and Chris and Quinn basically had to pick his clothes out and throw them at him to get dressed, but he did it. He left his cave of loneliness and stepped out into the crisp, fresh winter air. Everything felt different. Nothing really was, and Jett knew it was only that his life had changed and was in all sorts of disrepair, but the world outside his apartment felt just slightly tilted. As though it were wrong that things hadn't turned to chaos and broken down all because his own world had.

They ended up at a small bar on Union street, and when the four of them arrived, there was another small group waiting for them at a corner booth. Brody, Amira, Victoria, Tyler, and even Emerson were already there with drinks in front of them and they scooted down, making room for the rest of them. Quinn grabbed a couple chairs from a nearby table to accommodate everyone. He and Tyler took the chairs, Chris slid in next to his wife while Jett and Rae took the last spaces on the curved booth bench.

A cute waitress with long, caramel-colored hair glided over with a tray filled with shot glasses of clear liquid, each with a lime wedge on the rim.

"Nine shots of Patron with lime," the waitress announced, "and salt." She placed a few extra salt shakers on the table, leaning forward as she did so. Her top was extremely low-cut and Jett felt like she was shoving her tits in his face and had to glance away.

He caught Emerson's unsubtle peek of appreciation down her top before his dark blue eyes slid up to her face. "Thanks, Taylor," Emerson said with a wink. Taylor's cheeks blushed beneath her bronzer as she stood up straight again, and she smiled shyly before asking the table if she could get them anything else.

A few drink orders were placed, and Chris made sure to order a few appetizers, too. Jett felt almost indecent watching the way Emerson and the waitress were practically eye-fucking each other, but found himself grateful to have something else to focus on for a few seconds. Zoey's absence at the table was some kind of sick contradiction in Jett's mind; she wasn't there, and therefore the thoughts of her, the space next to him where he knew she should be, felt that much more tangible. It was like a giant black hole had opened up at his side in the space between him and Chris, and he had to try to avoid looking at what- *who*- wasn't there.

"I honestly can't remember the last time I did tequila shots," Victoria said, hesitantly reaching for one of the shot glasses.

"Who ordered all these?" Rae asked. She snagged one of the salt shakers and was sprinkling it onto the side of her hand where she had already licked so the salt would stick.

"That was me," said Emerson.

Rae looked up, thoughtfully. "You know, this probably won't be the only round of shots we do. Why didn't you just buy the whole bottle? It probably would've been cheaper."

Emerson appeared to be trying to remember something, tapping his chin with two fingers, before replying, "Hold on...wait- oh, that's right. We're not engaged anymore, Rae. You don't get to make that call. If you wanna bicker like an old married couple with someone and tell him how to spend his money, *that* guy's right next to you."

Jett heard the collective sighs and groans around the table. Even Amira's eye roll was nearly audible, but he actually had to stifle his own laugh, turning it into some kind of quiet snort.

"All right, all right," Jett waved his hands, calling off the impending argument before it started. Rae shut her mouth and leaned back, because of course she was about to say something in response, but apparently the fact that Jett was now speaking was worth forgetting whatever retort she had planned.

"I know I'm going to regret these goddamn shots," Jett said, holding his glass up and already wincing at the sight of it. "But I fucking need it. So let's do this."

Everyone at the table held their glasses out in front of them, salt and lime wedge ready. Chris cleared his throat and said a short toast. "To the best guy we know. You've always been there for us, and now it's our turn to pay you back."

"To a night we will soon forget!" Quinn finished. They clinked glasses, sloshing some over the rims.

Salt. Shot. Lime.

The chorus of groans along with wincing faces made Jett smile again. Of course he didn't forget about Zoey. Her face, her lips, her gorgeous hazel eyes swam around in his head throughout the entire evening. He thought about her sleepy, worn out smile the first night he'd taken care of her in her hotel room.

And they ordered another round.

Salt. Shot. Lime.

They laughed, they drank. Their food came out, Emerson flirted shamelessly with the waitress again. Tyler shared stories about the ridiculous, near-hazing that he swore Emerson was putting him through at the office, which got Quinn talking about the hazing he went through his freshman year of college as a new player on the team.

Then Jett's mind wandered off to his first kiss with Zoey on the ice rink. How cute she looked in her hat with the giant pom-pom ball on it. The dinner they devoured together and his taco innuendos.

Quinn ordered the next round of shots, and like a good fiancé, listened to Rae and purchased the whole bottle.

Salt. Shot. Lime.

Amira began the usual game of Never Have I Ever, which Jett could easily see going badly, but between his three shots and his tall glass of Labatt Blue in front of him, he found himself feeling too content and fuzzy to warn against it. Across the table, Brody was starting to feel good, too, and his world famous Conor McGregor persona came out, as he pointed out people throughout the bar that he just knew he could take out. Luckily, Amira and Emerson kept him firmly in the booth and he didn't actually try to fight anyone.

The hockey game Jett took Zoey to for their second date popped into his head. The fights on the ice, telling her about playing hockey. He could tell that she was surprised that he'd ever been a fighter, but even more surprised by the fact that it turned her on.

Tyler, who was usually quiet and reserved, stood up and reached across the table for the bottle of Patron and began filling everyone's glasses up again. He was a giggly drunk, which was a stark contrast to his usual serious, straight-faced personality. Jett got the impression that Tyler didn't drink a whole lot, but was enjoying this side of him nonetheless.

Salt. Shot. Lime.

The night continued like this. They were probably the loudest group in the bar, laughing, shouting, sharing stories, making jokes. Chris was drinking a fruity cocktail with a giant pineapple wedge on the side. Jett had never seen him drink anything other than beer or the occasional gin and tonic, maybe a Tom Collins if he was feeling fancy. Victoria had ordered it- a pineapple mojito- and after one taste-testing sip, Chris called the waitress back to order his own.

After yet another shot, Chris, Quinn, and Rae dragged Jett up onto the small stage of the karaoke bar where they all sang "Ten Rounds of Jose Cuervo" by Tracy Byrd. *Sang* may not be the right term. Giggled, shouted, completely blundered. Those might be more accurate.

Everyone in the bar was singing with them by the end, and Rae was a giggling heap on the floor that Quinn had to pick up and throw over his shoulder to get back to her seat. Not the safest choice since Quinn really wasn't a heavy drinker, and he stumbled quite a bit on the way back to their table.

Jett was laughing, a hard, stomach-muscle clenching, wheezing, hysterical laugh that made his face sore, and he focused on that feeling. He was drunk as hell, but that didn't mean Zoey was anywhere near off his mind. But he was thankful for this night. For his friends and their determination to get him out of his apartment and out of his own head. It's exactly what he would've done for any of them. It made him feel appreciated. Needed.

Tomorrow was going to suck. He might have the hangover to end all hangovers, to stop his casual drinking and make him sell the bar and turn it into an overpriced coffee shop just so he never had to smell alcohol again. His pain and heartache would return in full-force, the twist of the knife in his chest would dig deeper. But tonight was okay, even if all the pieces of his life felt lost and scattered into the wind. Tonight, at least, was a good night.

CHAPTER 27

Zoey wiped the tears out of her eyes for the five-hundredth time before they could fall out onto her cheeks. She breathed in through her nose and out through her mouth, concentrating on her breaths like she did when she was doing yoga. She was standing outside her dad's hospital room and had yet to enter. Still, she had no idea what had happened or what condition he was in. She was bracing herself.

Half the tears spilling out were from this. From the unknown and from what she was about to see on the other side of that door. On the flight, her mind had created a whole new slew of scenarios that could've happened to her dad. From falling and hurting his already-injured knee, to getting hit by a truck. A vicious dog attack, to an armed intruder. On the other side of that door, her dad could be in a cast, or he could be on life support.

The other half of her tears were from the image that just would not go away. Jett's face as she stepped away after kissing him. Confused, desperate, heartbroken.

It wasn't fair. She didn't want to hurt him. She didn't want to leave and had tried imagining what it would have been like if he'd come with her. But in the end, she knew this was the only way. This was the only possible outcome.

With another deep inhale, she let it out and forged ahead into the hospital room.

Cassie and Ace were sitting in the room, having pulled the chairs around the bed. And they were smiling. Laughing even. With their dad.

"Zoey?" Ace looked up, eyebrows pinched together slightly. "What are you doing here?"

"I called her," Cassie piped in. She stood and wrapped her arms around Zoey, pulling her into a tight hug. "You got here fast."

Zoey swallowed, confused. Her dad was in the hospital bed, but he appeared to be fine. He wasn't attached to any wires or tubes or anything. Lou wore a smile that matched her younger siblings' and suddenly she was wondering if she had dreamt that panicked phone call with Cassie.

"You called her because Dad has kidney stones?" Ace asked, incredulous. "Cassie, what the hell?"

"Kidney stones?" Zoey repeated. She was frozen and didn't know how to react. She was waiting for the *and...* because there must be some other reason Cassie would have called her freaking out like she did.

"I didn't know." Cassie shrugged defensively. "Cindy told me she was bringing him here because he was in a lot of pain. He could've been having a heart attack."

"Yeah, in his gut. And he was nauseous," Ace quipped. He smiled and shook his head. "God, Cass, you're such a damn drama queen."

"You're kidding right now." Zoey's voice was cold and hollow and completely disbelieving. The phone call and Cassie's panicked gasps and cries played over again in her head. Then she remembered telling her that she would call Ace as soon as she hung up, but she didn't. She had freaked out and packed a bag. And left Jett.

She had *left* the most amazing man in the entire world. Because her dad...had kidney stones.

"Where's Jett?" Lou asked, his face friendly as he peeked around to see if maybe Jett was standing in the doorway behind her.

Zoey let out a hollow, incredulous laugh and collapsed into one of the chairs. For several moments she just stared at her feet. She was still wearing her winter clothes even though it was sixty-five degrees outside, having been far too anxious to change on the flight. The entire four and a half hour flight she had been crying. Balling her freaking eyes out because she left Jett and she had no idea what was waiting for her at home. She hadn't even cared that people were staring at her like she was insane. Since she was in first class, the attendants tried to be consoling and accommodating, but she had simply apologized to them and continued her public cry-fest.

"Is everything okay, Zo?" Ace asked. Zoey could feel all the eyes in the room on her, but she was still processing. Still trying to make sense of not only her sister's, but her own complete over-reaction.

The door pulled open and Cindy came in with a drink tray of coffees. "Zoey," Cindy acknowledged pleasantly. "I didn't know you were visiting again already. Looks like your dad needs to cut back on the Mountain Dew."

Zoey slowly let her eyes meet Cindy's. The woman had a round face, shoulder-length sandy blond hair, and green eyes. Not the green eyes she needed to see right now.

"Is Jett with you? We really enjoyed getting to know him over Christmas," Cindy said, passing the coffee cups out to her siblings.

"No, Jett's not with me," Zoey stated. She heard the hardness of her voice before she looked at her sister. "Cassie, how the hell could you call me like that? You acted like Dad was dying or something!"

Cassie's eyes went wide and she put her hands up as though telling Zoey to back off. "I already told you, I didn't know what happened. You said you were going to call Ace. I thought you did!"

"This is unbelievable!"

"Why are you so mad?" Cassie raised her voice, "I'm sorry, okay? I'm sorry you had to spend four hours on a plane to find out that everything is fine, but what's the big deal? I know you get practically free flights anyway."

Zoey glared at her sister. She knew it wasn't fair to blame Cassie for how this had turned out. It wasn't right that Zoey had completely overreacted, too, but *ugh!* She wanted to shake her until some kind of lightbulb flicked on in her sister's brain that would make her see how her actions affect others. How Cassie's drama and choices and attitude- everything- had always made Zoey feel like she needed to put her first.

"I left Jett in Michigan," Zoey stated.

"Well, he doesn't exactly need to be here because of Dad's kidney stones," Cassie said with a quick shrug.

"No, I mean I *left* him. I told him it couldn't work out."

"*What?*" Ace and Lou exclaimed at the same time.

"Why would you do that?" Ace shouted. "Zoey, he is literally the coolest guy I have ever met. You have to make it work!"

"Zoey," Lou said, his voice low and firm. He looked around at his kids and at Cindy. "Would you three mind giving us a minute?"

Ace, Cassie, and Cindy all slipped out of the room, leaving Zoey and her dad alone.

Lou sighed, a long, heavy, exhausted sigh. He looked tired, Zoey noticed. He was a huge man, with tough tanned skin and his hair that he'd always worn in the signature Marine Corps high-and-tight cut was more salt-and-pepper than she'd ever realized before now.

"Zoey, why did you really leave Jett?"

Zoey swallowed again and moved over so that she was sitting on the edge of her dad's hospital bed. "I told him...I told him that you guys need me here. And we can't make it work if I need to be here all the time."

"You *don't* need to be here all the time," Lou stated. "We miss you, don't get me wrong, sweets. We miss you, but I think we've actually had more of you in the past couple months than when you were in LA."

Zoey raised a curious brow at him. "What do you mean?"

"Ace told me all about talking to you and Jett on the phone. He says you guys actually talk about things. He says you don't sound weighed down and distracted by your job all the time. And when you visited over Christmas? You were actually present. You didn't have your nose in your phone or eyes glued to your computer. And your job is still doing just fine, right?"

She nodded and looked down at her wringing hands. "I kind of felt that way, too. We talk on the phone more and I feel like I know what's actually going on because I'm listening, instead of just waiting for the next job. The next assignment or problem to tackle. I'm still working a lot, but my life honestly feels more balanced than it ever has."

"So, why leave that?"

She tried to remember the panic and train of thought that led to her decision. What made her feel like she couldn't make it work even though her life was getting along so much better over the past several weeks?

"What if something happens?" She met her dad's gaze. "What if something big happens and I'm not here? I mean, this time it was kidney stones, but what if...what if next time it's bad?"

"All that's going to change is how quickly you'll be able to get here," Lou said. "If I get in a car accident, I get in an accident. You can't stop that from happening. If I fall and sprain my knee again, what's the difference if you're here or not? Are you going to pick up my five-eleven, two-hundred and twenty pounds off the ground and carry me to the car?"

Zoey bit back a smile at the image that invoked in her mind. "Probably not," she admitted. "I guess I'm just so used to being here. I'm used to being the one everyone calls when something happens, when something goes wrong. If I'm not here, you guys will have to find someone else-"

"And that's okay," Lou insisted. "It's okay that we can put our problems on someone else now. You've earned the break. You've done your time- more than your share. I'm sorry for the role that was put on you so young, Zo. You didn't deserve that. I should've been able to do more. I wasn't strong enough for my family back then like I should've been."

"You were heartbroken."

"And you kids weren't? You lost your mother."

Zoey sighed and it came out shaky, on the verge of tears. "I did what I had to do, and I didn't mind. I was sort of a caregiver anyway."

Lou shook his head. "It wasn't right. I know I had a lot going on. My knee was still recovering, I was trying my best not to get addicted to pain pills, which I thankfully never did. I had a lot of demons leftover from the war, things I'd never shared. But I never should've abandoned you. Your mom's death broke me, and I couldn't be the dad you needed. And I'm sorry every day for that. But that's why you need to live your own life now, okay? You need to be happy, and that man...Jett...he loves you. I haven't seen anyone look at someone like that since my own wedding photos. Your mom and I were together for sixteen years. You've been with him for maybe sixteen weeks and he already looks at you like that. You can't give that up."

She was crying again, but she let the tears fall this time. Her dad was right, and she knew it. They'd never really talked much about her mom's death and what had happened afterward. She always tried to not feel resentful or angry that such a huge burden had been placed on her in her mom's absence, and instead focused on ways to make sure everyone else was happy, that everything was taken care of. For the first time she realized that those rare moments when she'd felt like her life was unfair, when she'd wanted to just drop it all and crumble and fall apart, sick of keeping it together for everyone else, were completely justified. Hearing her dad confirm it was like a weight lifted off her shoulders. A tangled, gnarled knot untying in her chest.

Zoey leaned over and gave her dad a hug, laying across his chest and resting there for several moments.

"How do I fix this?" she sniffled and her voice came out mumbled against his shoulder.

"It was a misunderstanding, wasn't it?"

"But I messed up. I hurt him. I can't just show up and say, whoops, sorry, my bad! Hope that doesn't happen again!" Zoey sat up now. "I feel like he needs to know I'm staying. He needs to trust that I'm not going anywhere just because things get tough here."

Lou nodded thoughtfully. "Ahh, yes. You want to grand-gesture him." Zoey smiled a little and he continued, "I do pay attention to those chick flick movies you girls like so much. You and Cassie used to watch *Sweet Home Alabama* and *Legally Blonde...How to Lose a Guy in 10 Days* and *Pretty Woman*, which I can't believe I let you watch."

"A grand gesture," Zoey repeated. "I feel like in all those girly movies it's always when the guy proposes or kisses the girl in the rain. Maybe I can kiss Jett in the snow if there's a blizzard when I get back."

"You'll think of something."

There was a knock on the door and a scrubbed nurse poked her head in the room. "Just checking in. How's the pain, Lou?"

Zoey went out into the hall to let Cindy, Ace, and Cassie know they could come back into the room. When she sat back down in her chair, she reached into her bag and pulled out her tablet, turned it on, and opened up a blank document. She gave the document a heading: Grand Gestures to Win Back Jett Miller.

After the kidney stones passed and Lou was given the green light to go home, they all went back to the house to make sure he was situated. It was already one in the morning, so it didn't take long for every-one to get into bed for the night. Zoey barely slept, turning different ideas over in her head, but found herself distracted. That image of Jett looking so sad and taken aback that she would leave- *Ugh, I'm such an idiot!-* just would not get out of her head. She closed her eyes and tried to think of happier memories andmfocus on the fact that there would be new ones. She would fix this and they would be together.

The next morning, Zoey got up and headed out to the kitchen to make breakfast like she was so used to doing when she stayed in her childhood home. Stretching and yawning as she entered the kitchen, she stopped at the sight of Ace and Cassie scrambling around each other in the small space as they made a huge mess making blueberry pancakes. She smiled at her siblings and tried to join them, but Ace would only let her cut up the fruit and set the table, insisting that he and Cassie could take care of the rest.

That afternoon, Zoey decided she would need to head back to her own house in LA to get a few more things before returning to Michigan. She had no idea what her plan was once she got back, but she didn't want to wait too long. It was Thursday, and though Cassie had classes, she had no intention of making it back to school in time, and Ace decided to take the day off as well. They wanted to help her come up with ideas to show Jett how much he means to her, so they planned a sibling slumber party at Zoey's house for the night and went back to Los Angeles with her.

On the drive, their ideas ranged from Ace's "How about *you* propose to *him!*" and Cassie's "Just show up naked and give him the best sex of his life!"

She told them she would keep thinking.

It was only seven-thirty, but they had all gotten into their pajamas and were preparing bowls and platters of junk food. Popcorn, potato chips, ice cream, and various candy bars cut to look like small hors d'oeuvres. They had each picked out a movie and would play rock-paper-scissors to determine the order they would be watched. It was how they had always done their movie nights, and it usually resulted in quite the eclectic evening of entertainment. Ace picked *John Wick 3*, Cassie chose *Mike and Dave Need Wedding Dates*, and Zoey had gone with the far more classic *Sixteen Candles*.

"What if we come back with you," Ace said, grabbing a giant bowl out of her kitchen cupboard for popcorn. "And then we run into him like it's by accident, but it's totally on purpose, and he'll be like 'Oh my God, what are you guys doing here?' and we'll be like 'Oh, nothing, just helping Zoey move'. And he'll know you're back in Michigan and he won't be able to stay away, right?"

"Where would she be moving to?" Cassie asked. She was sitting on the counter with a pint of Halo Top ice cream that was about halfway gone already.

"Um…" Ace paused, dumping the bag of popcorn into the bowl, "You could…just move all your stuff into his place?"

"You want to help me drive a U-Haul all the way to Michigan and just move my entire house into his two-bedroom apartment?" Zoey replied, one eyebrow raised as if to say *try again, genius*.

"Oh. Maybe not." Ace scratched his head and she could already tell he was moving onto his next big plan. It was adorable how much this meant to him. "Why don't I just call him? Or you could just call him and tell him you overreacted because your little sister's a drama queen and apparently you were channeling her and decided to be one, too."

Cassie grabbed a potato chip out of the bag next to her and threw it at Ace.

"No," Zoey sighed. "I don't want to do this over the phone. You have no idea how hard it is to not call him and tell him it was a mistake or a misunderstanding, but I have to do this in person. He has to know I mean it."

"What if he's all heartbroken right now though and goes out and gets drunk and hooks up with some random chick?" Cassie said with a dramatic gasp. "Zoey! He could be sleeping with someone else right now!"

"He's not sleeping with someone else. He's not that guy," Zoey said. The thought hadn't even crossed her mind, and she knew he wouldn't do that, but the very mention of the possibility made her heart stutter and her blood heat up.

There was a chime from her phone, and she recognized it as an email notification. She had tried to keep her phone out of arm's reach, knowing that she would absolutely text or call Jett and be a blubbering mess and she couldn't imagine it coming out well at all. She wanted to completely avoid that situation and have something planned. She was a planner, after all.

"Oh, I have to check my email really quick," Zoey muttered. She grabbed a tray of chocolates and candy bars and carried it into the living room where they had just about every pillow and blanket in the house thrown over the couch and loveseat to make for comfy movie-watching. She set the tray of treats on the coffee table in the center of the room and grabbed her laptop before plopping down into the sea of cushions and blankets on the couch.

She hadn't been on her laptop since right before her frantic call from Cassie, and when she opened it up, the last page she'd been on flashed bright in front of her. The list of homes she and Jett were planning on checking out. There were four homes on the list that they really wanted to tour, and they'd been in contact with a realtor to show them the homes later that week.

One of the four, however, had really stuck out to them. It was similar to her house now, with light gray siding and white trim along the windows, and gray stone wainscoting along the outside. It had four bedrooms, two and half bathrooms, a large, open kitchen, a formal dining area, and a spacious living room with high ceilings, tall windows, and a gorgeous stone fireplace. It was two stories with a full walk-out basement and a view of the lake, and it was in a nice neighborhood where neighbors were close, but not right on top of each other. There was a decent sized front lawn and a large backyard that gave access to the water. It had a boat dock and a small boat house for winter storage, and at least online, it was absolutely perfect.

The smile began to curve up her lips before the thought had even fully processed in her head. She knew how to get Jett back and make sure he knew she was for real this time. He needed to know that she wasn't a flight risk, and was staying put. After checking her work email and sending a quick response, she came back to the page with her and Jett's dream home and messaged the realtor. It didn't take long to get a phone call back and set up her plan. The earliest the realtor could set up a walk-through was the following afternoon.

Zoey pulled up her trusty travel site and booked a six o'clock flight back to Michigan for the following morning.

CHAPTER 28

Oh...God.

Just kill me now, please.

Jett woke up on his bathroom floor Saturday morning because he'd spent Friday night puking up approximately a thousand tequila shots, along with some mozzarella sticks, wings, and potato skins.

This was it.

This was the end.

He was going to die here in his bathroom. All alone.

"Fuuuuuck," he groaned, putting his hands over his face, palms to his eyes. He remembered thinking to himself that today would suck, but he honestly didn't remember a whole lot else after the fifth round of shots.

His eyes were closed as he tried piecing the night together. Quinn, Rae, and Chris had shown up and dragged him to a bar. They met others there and did a round of sh-

Jett's stomach churned and he gagged at the mere memory of tossing back his first shot.

That's it...I am never drinking again.

After a few more minutes of lying on the floor, soaking up his own misery, he tried pulling himself up to a sitting position, and somehow succeeded. He sat, chest heaving with the effort of it, leaning his back against the edge of the bathtub and letting his eyes adjust to the dim light. He looked down to see that he was wearing plaid boxer shorts that he typically only wore to sleep in. It seemed strange that he would've changed into pajamas if he were that wasted the previous night. The bathroom door was cracked just slightly and he thought he heard the low rumble of another man's voice coming from the living room.

He grunted, then forced himself up and practically stumbled out to the end of the hallway, leaning against the wall for support. Chris, Tyler, and Victoria were all in the living room looking only slightly more alive than he felt.

Squinting into the bright natural light that was shining aggressively through the living room windows, Jett lifted a weak hand in a lame wave as the attention in the room turned to him.

"How ya feelin', buddy?" Chris asked, his voice hoarse.

"Like fuck."

"Same, dude, same," his friend said with a nod. "I'm so glad Mom planned to take Sophia for the night anyway. There's no way I could've gone home to her like this. And no way I'd be able to get up and pretend I didn't drink a whole damn gallon of tequila."

Jett's stomach rumbled again and the nausea quickly made its way up and into his throat. He ran into the kitchen and bent over the sink to throw up, yet again. He let out his final coughs, grabbed a glass out of the dishwasher and filled it with water, rinsing his mouth out.

"Do not *ever* say that word in front of me again," Jett grumbled.

"Still puking?" Quinn's voice traveled down the hallway just before he appeared around the corner, hair sticking in all directions, and wearing a pair of basketball shorts that Jett recognized as his own. Jett could only grunt in response, and glare at the wide, amused grin on his friend's face.

"How the hell are you smiling?" Tyler groaned from the couch. "You drank as much as we did and you threw up on our walk here."

"Puke and rally, man," Quinn replied with a shrug and that stupid grin still on his face. Life was not fair.

"Did you sleep in my bed?" Jett asked, suddenly realizing Quinn obviously hadn't stayed in the living room with the rest of them.

"Nah, spare room. You puked in your bed, remember?"

Jett stared blankly at no one in particular and tried to remember. Nope. That was blank. He shook his head slowly.

"Ah, well, it's okay. Rae took care of it for you. She just switched your sheets over to the dryer so you don't have to get sick trying to clean that up," Quinn explained. "She also helped you change out of your puke-covered clothes."

Jett felt his eyes go from small, squinting slits to wide and alarmed instantly. "She changed my boxers?"

Quinn nodded. "She did. You kept covering yourself so she couldn't see your dick, and then you'd pull your hands away really fast and shout 'Made ya look!' and start giggling."

"You called it Penis Peek-a-boo," Rae said, stretching her arms over her head as she walked past Quinn and into the kitchen. "Lucky for you, I've seen a lot of dicks in my life so I wasn't that fazed." Quinn's obnoxious grin turned into a scowl while everyone else chuckled quietly.

Rae started brewing a large pot of coffee for everyone while they all got comfortable in the living room. Jett was starting to think this was what the day was going to look like. Sitting around being miserable together.

"How is Rae not hungover at all?" Victoria asked. She moved over to make room for Jett and Quinn on the couch. Judging by the placement of blankets and pillows in the room, Jett guessed Tyler had slept in the chair, Victoria on the couch, and Chris had curled up in a pile of blankets on the floor right next to the couch. Or maybe he'd fallen onto the floor and simply hadn't bothered getting back up.

"On our fourth round of shots, Jett looked at me and asked 'you gonna drink that?' so I handed it over to him, and that became the pattern for the remaining...six rounds? I think? I'm pretty sure you literally all took ten shots."

Jett stared across the counter at Rae, now completely horrified. He tried doing the math. He knew it was simple math, but damn his head hurt. "Rae...that's like...I had *seventeen shots?*"

She looked up as though making her own calculations. "Yeah, I guess so. And a beer."

"What the fuck?" Jett whispered. He sunk back into the couch then winced as the high pitched chime of a cell phone went off. "All phones on vibrate. Right now," said Jett, his voice low and threatening.

"Oh!" Quinn looked surprised before quickly covering his mouth. "I mean, oh...shit. I should probably take this."

"Hallway, so I don't have to hear your stupid voice," Jett croaked, pointing to the front door. When Quinn stood up, Jett snatched the throw pillow from the other end of the couch and covered his face with it before toppling onto his side with another drawn out *fuuuuuck.*

"Sweetie, take these..." Rae put two white Tylenol tablets in Jett's hand. "Drink this whole thing, and then drink this." Jett peered up and watched as she held up a pint glass filled with water, then a large coffee mug of black coffee. "Once you finish all of it, take a shower, get more water and then more coffee, okay? And then we'll get you some food."

He nodded and did as she'd instructed, though it took some time. He finished the glass of water, sipped on his coffee until it was gone, and then managed to get himself into the shower. He didn't know how long he spent standing under the hot spray of the water before he started to feel like he could at least move a little faster than a zombie.

It was a miserable morning, and it wasn't until he started feeling marginally better that the pain in his chest made its return. Great, now his head hurt, he was nauseated, *and* he was heartbroken. He tried to focus on the nausea and the ringing in his head. Part of him hoped he would be alone when he got out of the shower so that he could wallow some more, but he couldn't deny how thankful he was for the water and coffee already sitting out for him on the counter while Rae scurried around the kitchen to make brunch.

After staying in his apartment for a little over a week following her and Emerson's break-up, she knew where everything was in his kitchen. Sitting on a barstool, watching her throw together French toast, bacon, and eggs, he recognized with a grateful tug in his chest that she was doing everything for him that he'd done for her in those first days following her heartbreak.

She'd spent most of the nights drinking and the mornings hung-over, and he'd taken care of her. He'd made her iced coffee, shoved glasses of water at her, and always kept a bottle of Tylenol around for mornings. As much as she'd wanted him to drink with her, he made sure to stay sober enough that he could be there for her the next day. Now she was returning the favor.

"Hey," Jett said quietly, but it was enough to get Rae's attention while she flipped over the pieces of Texas toast. She looked up at him with a *hm?* One side of his mouth pulled up into the closest thing to a smile he could manage. "Thank you for the extra shots."

Her blue eyes brightened and her face lit up in a smile. "And thank *you* for never letting me get so drunk you had to change my underwear for me." They both laughed a little before Quinn slid onto the stool next to Jett.

"Got plans today?" Quinn asked, nudging Jett with his elbow.

"Trying not to die, and you?"

"You don't have to work tonight?" Quinn raised a curious eyebrow at him.

"Chris took me off the schedule for a few days. I think I'm supposed to go back tomorrow, though."

"Oh, good. I was thinking about showing you this place tonight for the bachelor party...if we were to do it here in Michigan, anyway," Quinn said. "I feel like we need to do Vegas or something. I'd even fly you all out, but I came across this other place that's not far from here. Supposed to be pretty cool."

"This isn't some ploy to get me into a strip club, is it?" Jett grimaced at the thought. Sure, he'd been to strip clubs in college and a couple other times since, but he wasn't the type to try drowning away Zoey's memory with a bunch of strange women's tits. Right now he felt like seeing other women naked would only make him want to see Zoey naked even more, and he didn't see how that could possibly be helpful.

Quinn laughed. "No, man, I'm not taking you to a strip club." He took a sip of coffee and added, "I can't be seen somewhere like that right now anyway. With this *new image* thing Zoey's pushing-" He stopped dead and met Jett's eyes for half a second before dropping his gaze abruptly.

It was the first time Jett realized he had a relatively permanent tie to Zoey. Even though she'd left the state and left him, she still worked for one of his best friends. Quinn would still have contact with Zoey. Have phone calls and exchange text messages and emails with Zoey. *Fuck.* Life suddenly felt viciously unfair again.

"Sorry, I..." Quinn stumbled over forming his next sentence, and Jett decided to cut him off.

"No, it's okay. She works for you. And we're friends. She's bound to come up occasionally. It's fine. I'll...get used to it, I guess."

"Right," Quinn said, then cleared his throat. "Well, like I said, strip clubs are a no-go right now. But I think you'll really like this place anyway. I sort of want to keep my options open."

"Yeah, of course. We can go check it out."

Jett looked down at the plate Rae had just set in front of him. Any other time, he was sure it would look delicious, but right now he didn't know how he was supposed to eat a bite. The coffee was starting to turn sour in his stomach the more he thought about Zoey and the other night when she'd left. He felt like there was barely an explanation. No closure. It had been so sudden and so unexpected. He still hadn't texted or called her since that night and was beginning to think that was a mistake, so he made up his mind. As soon as his friends left, he would call Zoey.

It was two o'clock in the afternoon before everybody left. He fiddled with his phone for at least a half hour before gathering the courage to press the call button. If she was still in California, it was eleven-thirty in the morning, and she would definitely be up by then. Unfortunately, however, the call rang until it was picked up by her voicemail. Jett collapsed back onto the couch at the sound of Zoey's voice telling him to leave her a message. He couldn't think of what to say, so he hung up.

How soon was too soon to try again? He didn't want to seem desperate, though that's exactly how he felt. Maybe he could text her in a few hours and see if she would be around to call him. All he knew was that he couldn't leave things how they had. He couldn't just move on with no closure, no explanation.

Quinn had told him to be ready to get picked up at five-thirty. He was annoyingly vague about where they were going, but Jett was too hungover, or maybe still too drunk, to care. He went back to bed for a couple hours before getting up, taking another shower because he swore he was sweating tequila out of his pores, and getting dressed in one of his favorite maroon henleys and a pair of dark wash blue jeans. He pulled on a Carhart beanie along with his winter coat, and shoved his feet inside his camel brown Kodiak boots. It wasn't much, but he felt pretty damn dressed up compared to the previous few days of sitting around in sweatpants with a blanket over his head.

At almost exactly five-thirty, Quinn texted that he was there to pick him up.

"So where is this place?" Jett asked as Quinn pulled off of First street and headed toward M-37.

"Not far."

"What kind of place is it?"

"You'll like it, trust me. Stop asking questions," Quinn replied. He pushed a few buttons on the console screen of the new Range Rover Rae had picked out after Zoey's accident and brought up some music on a Spotify playlist.

Jett rolled his eyes and leaned back into the leather seats. "I didn't think the Jeep got totaled."

"It didn't," Quinn said. "The back bumper was dented a little bit."

"So, why the Range Rover?"

Quinn shrugged. "Rae's Jeep was like five years old. We paid to have it fixed and then I ran into one of the kids I coached over the summer. He'd just gotten his license and was saving up for something. I asked him how much he had saved, told Rae about it and we sold it. Then we got this."

Jett smiled. He always thought it would be cool to have a ton of money and be able to do those sorts of charitable acts for people. "How much did the kid have saved?"

"Like three grand. A little more."

Jett shook his head and laughed. "I looked into getting a used Jeep and it was going to be at least fifteen grand. That kid got a hell of a deal."

He looked around at their surroundings and realized they were heading for more residential areas. There were more trees, fewer commercial buildings and businesses, and more homes. Larger homes. Lake homes. The kinds of homes he and Zoey had been looking into before she took off.

They took a smooth S-curve and then drove around another bend before Quinn pulled into a long driveway lined with trees. Jett remembered the pictures from the listing and how he'd thought the trees would give the impression of living in the country, but the location would still have the convenience of being close to town. His heart squeezed itself until it was the size of a raisin in his chest at the memory of looking at homes- *this* home- with Zoey. They'd scrolled through the pictures over and over, and in every room of the house he'd found himself imagining new memories they would make there.

The light gray and stone siding came into view and Jett clenched his jaw tight. "Why did you bring me here?" he asked, voice so low he wasn't sure if Quinn had even heard him.

"Because you're thirty and live above a bar in an apartment that you have completely outgrown," Quinn replied as he unbuckled his seatbelt. "You wouldn't stop talking about this place on our walk back to your apartment last night and I thought you should get to see it."

"I don't want it for just me, Case, you know that," Jett said, his voice still hard, his posture stubborn.

"Well, I drove all the way out here and it looks like there's someone here to show you around, so..." Quinn nodded his head in the direction of the front door as if to say *let's get going!*

Jett sighed heavily like a bull about to run at a red banner, but stiffly unbuckled his seatbelt and stepped out onto the driveway. He knew better than to try seeing who was more stubborn between him and Quinn, and he really didn't feel like going rounds with him again. Quinn walked with him up the wooden boardwalk that led up to the porch, and he cursed himself for admiring how much more he liked the boarded walkway than a regular paved one.

Quinn pulled the door open for him and gestured for him to go inside first, so he did. He looked down at the wood floors that had a white antiqued look to them before his eyes raised to take in the rest of the space.

And then he froze.

Standing in the middle of the large open space between the kitchen and living room was Zoey. She was bundled in a deep purple sweater dress with black tights beneath her open peacoat, along with her tall black boots. Her dark brown hair was in loose waves over her shoulders, and she had a light gray winter hat pulled on.

Jett couldn't stop staring at the sight before him, wondering if she were an illusion and would disappear the second he looked away. Her big hazel eyes brightened in a smile along with her perfect, full lips, and Jett swore the breath was knocked out of his lungs. He shifted his attention to Quinn briefly who hadn't even entered the house all the way and was still standing between the storm door and the inside door.

That slightly less obnoxious, cocky grin was on his face again as he slowly backed out of the entrance. "I'll leave you two lovebirds to it," said Quinn, and he pulled the door shut behind him.

Jett let out a shaky breath that he didn't know he was holding as he looked back at Zoey. She was still smiling, but her eyes were wet with tears that were threatening to spill out.

"Let me just say...I'm *really* sorry," she said, taking a tentative step toward him. "I never should have left without you. I should have listened to you and let you come with me, but I just...I was terrified."

Clearing his throat was an effort as he found himself only able to keep watching her. He wanted to grab her and hold her against his body and never ever let go, but he hesitated. His skin was itching with the need to be near her, to touch her, to bury his face in the perfect curve of her neck, but he was stuck. There were alarm bells going off. Warnings, telling him *not so fast.*

Finally finding his voice, he rasped, "I know you were...I just wanted to be there for you and you wouldn't let me." She took another step toward him and his eyes flitted back and forth between hers. "I know you're used to handling family stuff on your own, but you don't have to. I don't want you to. I *like* your family, Zo. I was worried, too, and you never even texted me to let me know what was wrong."

A sound that was sort of a cough mixed with a laugh escaped and she grinned sheepishly. "Kidney stones." Jett pinched his eyebrows together curiously and she nodded. "Yeah. I was furious with Cassie when I got there and found out that's all it was. I wanted to scream and shake her for overreacting so badly, but...then I realized how badly *I* overreacted."

With one more step, she closed the gap between them and placed a gentle hand on his arm, and her touch warmed him. Just her proximity was all it took to evaporate the cold, hard feeling that had begun to form around his chest.

"Jett, I never wanted to leave you. I felt like I had this obligation to put my family first because I've *always* put them first. But Dad says it's time for me to have my own life now, and that they'll have to figure it out with me at a distance."

It was reassuring to hear that Lou approved of her move to Michigan, but he still wasn't entirely convinced she was no longer a flight risk. He tilted his head. "And what if something happens? What if you get another panicky phone call and feel like you need to leave again?"

"Well, for starters, I told Ace to call you with all family emergencies first. And if we determine that it's more serious than kidney stones or a case of bad gas that Cassie thinks is her appendix rupturing, then we'll go from there. If we have to fly out for something serious, we can, but my being there isn't going to stop those things from happening."

Jett felt the warmth spreading from his chest outward into his extremities as a small smile began to creep onto his face. He stopped it, though, thinking of the past few days. His hangover was still throbbing in his head, although Zoey's presence was admittedly distracting him from any lingering nausea. He knew he looked like hell and had to appreciate that Zoey hadn't said anything about it or even acted remotely like he was the death-warmed-over that he felt like.

"Zo...it absolutely wrecked me when you walked out that door, just like I knew it would." She dropped her gaze when he said this, but he bent his head to meet her eyes again with a finger beneath her chin. "I just didn't think I'd ever have to experience it."

"I know, and I'm so sorry." Her voice was tight with the effort of holding back tears. "That's why I'm here. In this house, I mean. I know we wanted to look at it, and I knew you'd need to be sure that I wasn't going to just take off again. That I was here and staying and all in."

Jett let the smallest bit of a grin tug up the corner of his mouth and glanced around the open room. "Wait...you didn't-? Did you buy it?"

"No," she said quickly. "No, I came back yesterday and looked at it myself, to see if it really was as amazing as it seemed, and...well, it kind of is. So I wanted to show you and see if you agreed."

"Hang on." Jett put a hand up and closed his eyes. "You came back yesterday?"

Zoey bit her lip nervously and nodded.

"Zo, if you would've just come to my apartment you would've saved me from one hell of a hangover."

"You got drunk last night?" Zoey looked panicked as she searched his face.

"Yeah, *really* drunk. Like...seventeen shots of tequila drunk. Threw up all over my bed and slept on the bathroom floor drunk. There are several hours that are not accounted for in my memory and I'm willing to bet I did some really stupid shit."

She seemed to be processing and the look of concern wouldn't leave her face.

"What?" Jett quirked an eyebrow, knowing she was holding back.

"Well, maybe you don't remember, but...you don't think you, like, made out with some random girl, right? Cassie said you could be getting drunk and hooking up-"

"No. I wasn't making out or hooking up with anyone. I'm sure of that."

"How? If you don't remem-"

"My friends were with me the whole time," he assured her.

"Friends? Like...Emerson?"

Jett shrugged. "I mean, he was there, but I do remember even before my first shot that he seemed particularly distracted by the waitress, so I doubt he would've worried about me at all." She seemed to relax just slightly at this, so he added, "According to Case, I wouldn't stop going on about this place and all the plans I had for it. With you..."

She smiled finally and so did Jett. He moved his hand so that he was cradling her neck and kissed her softly on the lips. "Why don't you show me around?"

Her smile widened and her face lit up again as she splayed her hands on his chest and began pushing, backing him up slowly so that they were both in the entryway, looking into the house as though they'd just walked in together.

"So, obviously this is what we see when we walk in. I'm thinking we can put my buffet table there with the mirror like I have at my place in LA. We can get a big rug to put down for everyone to leave their shoes when they come to visit, because I want us to be that house that everyone hangs out at. I like the idea of being a hostess, I guess. And then..." she grabbed his hand and pulled him into the living room. She pointed to the large, high windows and gestured toward the vaulted ceilings. "We could have a twelve-foot Christmas tree if we wanted, and put it right in front of these windows! And the fireplace, I can just imagine our stockings over it. And we'd get a big sectional, a really comfy one with lots of pillows and throw blankets, and a big area rug."

Jett was smiling because he could see it all. Their pictures on the mantel, and even some extra stockings for later down the road.

Zoey pulled him into the kitchen now and showed him how it was perfect for entertaining, because people could hang out in the kitchen and living room and still talk and see each other. Whoever was cooking wouldn't have to feel left out of whatever party was going on, whether it was a Superbowl party or watching the World Series games.

Past the kitchen there was a large screened-in porch that overlooked the yard and the lake. She pointed out the boat dock and shed, saying that they could get a pontoon or a speed boat this summer. Then down the hallway there was a good sized bedroom with two tall windows that had a view of the front yard.

"This could be like our office-slash-hobby room, like the spare room at the apartment. You can put up your guitars here, or! Actually, I might have a better spot for them, and your piano would fit, too, unless you wanted your piano in the living room still, which is totally fine. But anyway, this room could be a lot of different things." Zoey was speaking quickly, but it was with so much excitement that Jett was still rapt with every word.

On the way up the stairway, she pointed out the railing and how they could decorate it with garland for Christmas. The next room was bigger than the previous and she fidgeted slightly, tapping her fingers in Jett's palm that she was holding onto loosely now.

"This room has a lot of natural light and I like that it's up here next to the master bedroom. It's kind of perfect for...I don't know, I just think it would make a good..."

Jett couldn't help grinning at her hesitation, but knew exactly where she was going with it. They hadn't been together long enough to discuss children, but he was glad to know they were on the same page now. "A nursery?" he prompted, smiling down at her and watching her face light up again.

"Yeah," she breathed. "That's what came to mind when I saw it, but I mean-"

"I think it would be perfect, too." He squeezed her hand and pulled her close so he could kiss the top of her head.

Next she showed him another bedroom that was about the same size as the nursery, then the bathroom across the hall before getting to the master bedroom. It took up the majority of the upstairs space and had a large window with a window seat, and Jett could imagine Zoey sitting there, looking over the lake while she finished up her last-minute work emails on her laptop before getting into bed.

There was a huge walk-in closet and what was maybe one of the biggest ensuite bathrooms Jett had ever seen. The shower was fully tiled with glass doors and three shower heads, and there was a separate bathtub that looked like it could comfortably fit two adults at a time. There were two sinks in front of a long mirror with plenty of lights surrounding it and lots of counter space.

"I foresee us spending a lot of time in these two rooms when we first get moved in," Jett said with a slight tick to his eyebrow as he grinned and wrapped an arm around her waist.

"You like it so far?" Zoey beamed.

"Oh yeah, I can see us making lots of good memories in here."

She giggled and nudged him with her hip. "I mean the whole house."

"I was talking about the whole house, Zoey. What did you think I meant?" He winked when she looked up at him and they continued the tour.

The walk-out basement was amazing, and Jett agreed that his guitars would definitely go best down there with the wet bar. He could see the place as a total man cave, but was fine with sharing it as a secondary entertaining area for days on the lake. The sliding glass door led out to the yard with its perfect tree placed close to the lake. He could imagine putting a rope swing on it and showing his future kids how to jump off it and into the water.

They ended up back in the entryway and he held her close, his arms wrapped around her waist and hers wrapped behind his neck.

"So, what do you think?" Zoey asked, smiling because she already knew his answer.

"I think it's fucking perfect. And I'm a little in shock that I might actually be able to afford it somehow."

"Don't you worry about that part," she replied with a sly grin, pressing her smile to his lips.

"Oooh, Sugar Momma's gonna take care of me, huh?" Jett exclaimed in one of his signature voices that always used to send women running the other way. But that's okay. They weren't the right woman anyway.

"I plan on it." She kissed him again, and again, and then he kissed harder, more demanding, and refused to let her break apart so soon.

"Which room do we break in first?" Jett asked, backing her into the kitchen island.

Zoey giggled. "Jett, there's no furniture in here. We don't own it. We can't have sex in someone else's home."

"They took all their stuff out," Jett reasoned. "And I think you and I both know we're getting this house."

"Okay, but that still doesn't change the fact that there's no furniture. No couch or bed or anything."

He dipped his head to her ear and growled. "You've ridden me on the floor before, baby. And I've ridden you."

"Oh…" The sound escaped her like a gasp and a whimper rolled into one.

"So which room?" Jett repeated, now kissing her neck and feeling her chest rise and fall against him.

"Well…the bedrooms have carpet."

With no more prompting necessary, Jett lifted Zoey and she wrapped her legs around him, hooking her ankles behind his back as he carried her up the stairs again. In the master bedroom, he lowered them slowly to the floor and began shedding his clothes as she stripped herself of hers.

It started out hot and heavy, needy and yearning and desperate from their time spent apart, but turned into a slow burn. Jett was on top of Zoey, thrusting slowly into her with long, hard strokes. His lips were on hers, on her neck, on her jaw.

Zoey dug her nails into Jett's shoulders and he knew she was close. Her legs were hugging his hips as he pumped into her, steady, savoring each touch and each moment she was there. Their heads were together as they locked eyes, reveling in each other's presence. They were here. Together. And that wasn't changing.

He saw her body flush as she gasped before letting out a long cry of his name. She tightened around him and shook, grasping his hair and whispering into his ear, "I love you, Jett...I love you so much...so, so much."

"Are you mine, baby?" Jett rasped into the nape of her neck.

"Yes, I'm yours," she panted.

"Always?"

She pulled his attention to her face so they locked eyes again. "Always."

With one more thrust he was done, shuddering and crushing his lips onto hers again. He was claiming her, claiming this room, this house, this memory, and all those that were yet to be made. It felt like a promise to her and to himself that this was it. This was everything.

He wanted nothing more than to be exactly where he was. The perfect home. The perfect girl. The perfect love.

CHAPTER 29

March rolled around and Zoey was struggling to get used to Michigan's temperamental weather. It seemed to tease them with spring for a day, with sunshine and high sixties, and then it would snow. Again. She was beginning to wonder if the snow would ever stop, honestly. But today was at least going to be a good day, because Mother Nature seemed to be feeling rather springy. The sun was out in full force and there wasn't a cloud in the sky, and that was perfect, because today was their house warming party and they were set to have a full house.

They'd closed on their dream home in February and moved everything from Jett's apartment the following weekend. Her own house in Los Angeles had been on the market for less than a week before she received competing offers and accepted one that was far above her asking price. It gave her and Jett a considerable chunk of change to put down on their new house, and finally everything from Los Angeles had been moved there and it all had a place. It was all coming together, not exactly how she had imagined, but even better.

Both her and Jett's families were coming to the party, along with their usual group of friends. Chris and Victoria brought Sophia who was excited to play with Gavin's son, Grant. Jett's sister, Allison, was sporting quite the baby bump now, only three months away from her due date. Her husband, Colin, was like a busy bee, constantly running around to make sure she was situated and comfortable, not needing anything before he went and got himself a beer from the basement bar. Zoey had to smile knowing that growing up with Miller men as her standard, Allison had known exactly what to look for in a man and it looked like she'd found it.

When Zoey's dad showed up with Ace and Cassie, she rushed to the front door and wrapped them all in a big hug, squealing with excitement. She made introductions and gave them the same tour she'd given Jett's family. Most of the guests were congregated downstairs in their second living room, several of the men around the bar area. This tended to be where the tour stopped, and no one seemed too eager to leave when they realized alcohol was available.

Jett pulled Ace into a back-slapping bro hug and offered him a drink before introducing him to the rest of the guys. Chris, Brody, Quinn, and Emerson all greeted him with friendly smiles and welcomed him into their group. Lou made his way over to Jett and as they shook hands, she overheard her dad say something about how nice the place was, and that he was glad he was taking good care of her.

"Hey!" Emerson's low voice was sharp as it cut through the room, "Get out of that fridge. You can have something from the one upstairs." Emerson's little brother, Kolbe, reluctantly closed the beer fridge and sulked over to lean on the bar.

"My birthday was last week. I think I should be able to celebrate," Kolbe muttered. His voice was getting lower, but still had the trademark pitchyness that came with a male voice that hadn't completely changed yet during puberty.

"You can celebrate with some ice cream," Emerson snapped. "You're not getting drunk on my watch, kid."

Raelyn, Amira, and Victoria walked down the steps finally, having taken an extended tour, appreciating the view from the screened in porch-balcony, and made their way over to Zoey and Cassie.

"This house is beautiful," Rae said, pulling Zoey into a hug. "It's so perfect for you guys. Honestly, I wish we could find something more like this in LA than the ultra-modern bachelor pad we live in now."

"It would be hard to beat your view, though," Zoey pointed out. "Maybe you should talk him into remodeling. Make the place feel more like both of yours."

"There we go," Rae said with a smile. "Good thinking. I was looking for ways to spend his money. Maybe if we remodel it, I won't feel like I'm being haunted by the ghosts of one-nighters' past."

Zoey giggled. "You got him to get rid of his old mattress." Victoria gave a curious look while Amira smirked because Rae must have told her this story already. Zoey explained, "I came over on the day Rae was moving in, and they were shouting at each other. I could tell they were upstairs and I couldn't believe they were already fighting and she wasn't even fully moved in yet. I'm walking through to the kitchen, where you can see out onto the pool deck, and all the sudden this mattress comes down and lands in the pool. He literally threw it off the balcony because Rae said she wasn't sleeping in it."

The three of them laughed and Rae continued, "He stomped down the stairs and grabbed his keys and just shouted 'Guess I'm going furniture shopping! Zoey, let the movers know where to put everything!'" She laughed and sighed. "He was so pissed, but when he came back was completely ecstatic about the new bed he'd picked out."

"Daaaamn, girl, you tell him what's up," Cassie said, nodding approvingly. "I don't blame you either. I wouldn't wanna sleep where all the hoes slept that didn't mean shit. You're his queen, he needs to treat you like it."

"Ain't that the truth," Victoria agreed, clinking her rocks glass with Rae's. They both appeared to be drinking either vodka or gin and tonic with a lime. Jett had really gone all out for the bar downstairs, supplying it with professional bar tools, glasses, and stocking the necessary liquors, beers, and mixers.

Zoey noticed Cassie eyeing the mixed drinks and watched as a grin crept onto her face. "Sis, can I have a drink?"

"I'm okay with it if Dad is. You guys are staying here anyway."

Cassie beamed at her sister and dashed toward the bar. She saw her dad nod and then Cassie started searching for her ingredients. She was nineteen, almost twenty. She likely didn't even know what she wanted to drink, and looked like a kid in a candy store, overwhelmed by all the possibilities.

"Damn, Zo, this is a nice place." Quinn approached and glanced around. He held a glass of ice water in his hand and she knew he was heading back to Florida the next day to watch the Spring Training games and run training sessions. "It's amazing what a man's hard-earned money can buy, huh?"

Zoey glared at him, but couldn't help the smile that forced itself onto her lips. He knew she'd been able to buy her house in Los Angeles with that first bonus check he'd given her.

"Hard earned?" Jett called from the bar. "Case, you've been on the injured list for almost a year. Zoey's been the one working hard, putting up with your stubborn ass."

Jett's tone was playful, and Quinn knew it. He smiled again. "All I'm saying is that she's gotta have a really nice, very generous employer. I bet he's good looking, too. Well endowed...a total dreamboat." Quinn winked and Zoey shook her head with a major eye roll.

"*Yeah,* he is," Cassie said suggestively. Quinn turned to look at her and she gave a flirtatious nod and a wink.

He whipped his head back around to face Zoey and the other girls standing in the circle and cringed. "Dammit, I gotta learn to turn off the charm."

"That's not even charm, sweetie," Rae replied. She put a hand on his chest and reached up to kiss him. "You're just overly self-assured. But I still love you."

Over at the bar, Zoey noticed that Emerson was behind it now, mixing up some sort of drink with his own overly self-assured smirk aimed at Cassie.

Oh, hell no.

Alarm bells. Sirens. Flashing lights.

Code red.

Zoey stepped toward them just as she heard Emerson speak. "I'm sorry All-Star's taken, but, uh, you know who isn't?"

Cassie stared at Emerson in shock and her eyes made a slow circuit down his body and back up. Her mouth was partially open as she took in the aggressively handsome specimen before her.

"NO!"

The word echoed through the room as nearly everyone who knew Emerson decided to give their two cents on that particular development.

"No?" Cassie raised a curious eyebrow and looked around at everyone before training her eyes back to Emerson. She smiled and bit her lip, flirtatious as ever, despite the obvious warning.

"Cass…" Jett stepped behind the bar and physically pushed himself between her and Emerson. "I cannot, in good conscience, let you flirt with this man. Besides, he's way too old for you." He snapped his head around and glared harshly at Emerson. "She is *way* too young for you, man!"

The Norse God look-alike shrugged. "She legal?"

Jett seemed to deflate, exasperated. "Please don't make me punch you in front of all these people. We've been doing so well. I actually invited you here. Don't make me regret it."

"Sis can be into older men, so why can't I?" Cassie asked, bringing Jett's attention back to her. She was peeking around Jett's shoulders, sending meaningful and seductive glances toward Emerson.

"Cass, *that* kid, Emerson's thirteen-year-old brother, is closer in age to you than he is," Jett said, pointing at Kolbe. "Emerson has more than a decade on you. Not okay."

Zoey had to laugh at the look on Kolbe's face when he perked up and smirked. It was the same smirk as his brother, and then the same wink. Oh boy. "Actually, I'm fourteen now."

Looking back at Emerson, she saw his eyes go wide as he flicked his gaze between Cassie and Kolbe. He looked thoroughly disgusted with himself.

So, there *was* a line.

He backed away slowly, grabbing another bottle of beer out of the fridge. Brody gave him a consoling pat on the back, and his expression stated that even he thought he might need to reevaluate his life choices.

Turning back to the group, Victoria nudged Raelyn with a teasing, playful smirk. "Remember that time, not so long ago, when you were going to marry him?"

Rae made a face as she looked over at Emerson. "In my defense, he wasn't always quite so...*Emerson.*"

"No?" Zoey questioned. "You think he'll actually settle down one of these days?"

Rae shrugged and Amira offered an evil grin. "I'm not sure he'll ever *settle down,*" Amira said. "But I hope like hell he finds someone who shoves his arrogant ass down a few notches."

Zoey peeked over her shoulder and laughed when she realized Ace was keeping close to Cassie, making sure she didn't hit on or get hit on by anyone else. As nervous as she was knowing that Cassie was across the country getting into God knows what, she was feeling significantly better knowing that Ace was there to be her protector, whether she wanted one or not.

Most of their guests left between seven and eight that evening, though Zoey's family was staying in the house. She showed them to their rooms, letting them have their pick. Lou opted to stay downstairs, saying that Cindy claimed his snoring had gotten really bad and he didn't want to keep anyone up. Ace and Cassie each took one of the spare rooms upstairs. They all stayed up late, sitting out on the screened-in porch, visiting and going over plans for the future.

Zoey was quieter than she normally would be, simply listening to the conversation and enjoying every bit of it, soaking up every ounce of time with her family and Jett. She had loved playing the hostess, and couldn't wait for more gatherings. She could see herself hosting holidays and game nights, even parties for sporting events that Jett liked to watch on TV. Bridal showers, baby showers, birthday parties. She wanted it all. She loved their new home and couldn't wait to start making memories, building a family, and creating traditions.

That night in their bedroom, Zoey was sorting some of their housewarming gifts over on the window seat that people had brought. They hadn't asked for gifts, but most of Jett's family brought various bags or gift-wrapped packages. She grabbed one gift bag that hadn't been opened yet and brought it over to the bed.

Jett came into the room after brushing his teeth and rolled onto the mattress. He eyed the bag curiously. "What's that? Did we miss one?"

"Guess so," she replied. She pushed the blue bag with its gold dots toward him. "Why don't you open it? I did most of the ones earlier."

Jett gasped, exaggerating his excitement, only he probably was actually that excited. "It's like Christmas!" He tore into the bag, pulling out the lighter blue tissue paper until he found what was hidden at the bottom. He slid the tiny green stocking out and let it unroll. Embroidered on the stocking were the words *Baby Miller*. His eyes went wide, then his jaw dropped as he met her gaze. "Is this- are you? Are we-?"

Zoey smiled and felt it in her eyes, her heart, everywhere as she nodded. "Yeah, we're pregnant."

"Oh...Oh my God! Seriously?"

"Seriously."

Jett's smile was huge and contagious and it even made her laugh. He leaned forward and nearly crushed her into a hug, burying his face in her neck. When he pulled back he grabbed her face in his hands and kissed her, soft at first, then slow and deep. He leaned over her, pushing her gently back onto the pillows and his weight came over her.

"You're happy?" Zoey asked.

Jett was kissing her jaw, her neck, and down to her collar bone, pushing her night shirt up and over her head. She could feel his lips still smiling as they made small impressions all over her skin. "Very happy."

Out of habit, he reached for the nightstand and pulled out the box of condoms. She arched one eyebrow at him and he paused, laughing lightly. "Oh, right...guess we won't be needing those anymore." He tossed the box with the flick of his wrist and grinned as he returned every bit of his attention to her.

She felt full with emotion and her heart wanted to reach out and latch onto him for life, claiming him, though she supposed it already had. It was fast- *way* fast- but she wasn't worried. She was blissful and happy, completely in love. She couldn't imagine this life with anyone else.

Zoey flipped the switch on her bedside lamp and let him have her. All of her, every piece of her body, her heart, every ounce of her being was his. They slipped beneath the covers, not a thing between them as he moved over and inside her. Chest to chest, skin against skin, kissing her, loving her, pleasing her. It was what he did best.

She curled her fingers into his hair, straining to stay quiet as he moved into her. Holding on tight to him- her everything- she felt the spark ignite deep inside, shooting outward into each extremity, every nerve and fiber of her being. She clung to him, letting the heat take over as stars flooded her vision and her body shook before melting beneath him.

It wasn't until he'd given her three more toe-curling, blinding orgasms and they were both sweating, panting, and no longer able to keep quiet, that he finally let go. Shuddering and deep, biting her shoulder and fisting the pillow next to her head as he sent those final urgent thrusts into her.

And this was life. *Their* life. It was perfect and messy and things didn't always go as planned, but they had each other. And she knew that was more than enough.

EPILOGUE

Nine months later...

"Merry Christmas, baby." Jett's arm wrapped around Zoey and he pulled her close, leaving a shower of kisses all over her face, neck, and shoulders.

"Merry Christmas," Zoey said through a yawn. She stretched and turned to face him, taking his face in her hands and bringing his mouth to hers. "What time do we have to be at your parents' house?"

"Don't worry about that," he replied. "We have the whole morning to ourselves." Dipping his head to resume their kiss, sliding his tongue between her lips and getting lost in her, Jett's thoughts were cut off by the high pitched wail of the month-old baby in the next room.

"Almost to ourselves," Zoey corrected. She smiled and kissed him again before rolling out of bed. Jett watched as she slouched into a fuzzy robe and wandered out of the room to tend to the new little lady who had his entire heart wrapped in her tiny little hands.

Just a year ago he was falling for Zoey, working out how to make her fit into his life permanently, and now he was at the mercy of another girl with her mother's dark waves and his bright green eyes. She was perfect. He hadn't thought it possible to love Zoey even more than he did, but the day she brought their little girl into his world, into their life, he knew he was a goner. Those two had all of him. They were his world, they completely owned his heart, and he wouldn't have it any other way.

Once out of bed, Jett pulled on a t-shirt and a pair of plaid pajama pants, then made his way into the nursery where Zoey was holding their little girl, Maisie Alexandra.

They'd waited to find out whether they were having a boy or a girl, and as soon as the doctor announced the arrival of their healthy baby girl, they both knew she'd be given the middle name Alexandra after Zoey's mother.

Jett felt his heart squeeze and expand just a little more each day at the sight of them. This life they'd built together was everything he could've asked for and then some. Of course, there was one thing he still intended to change.

After giving his girls each a kiss, Jett wandered downstairs to the kitchen to get coffee started along with some breakfast. When Zoey came down with Maisie in her arms, she sighed into the mug of coffee before offering to help Jett with pancakes.

"I got it, baby," Jett replied. "Sit, relax, feed Maisie...I'll bring breakfast to you."

"Relax and feed Maisie, huh?" Zoey asked with a small smirk. "Have you ever breastfed before?"

Jett paused with his coffee to his lips. "Hm...can't say I have."

"It's a good thing you're cute." Zoey pressed a kiss to his cheek before heading out to the living room and getting situated on the couch.

Once Jett filled two plates with pancakes, he brought them over and set them down on the coffee table. Zoey was looking up at their tall Christmas tree that stood in front of the large windows, just as she'd described before they bought it. A fresh blanket of snow coated the ground outside, and thick snowflakes fell slowly. How had everything in his life turned out so perfectly?

"I talked to Dad last night and he can't wait to come visit next weekend," Zoey said, adjusting Maisie against her chest. "Cindy is coming...I think he might be asking her to move in soon."

"Oh yeah?" Jett asked. His hands were shaking slightly as he poured syrup over their pancakes, and he could feel himself starting to sweat. "You're okay with that?"

"Of course," she replied honestly. "I'm really happy for him. I don't want him to be alone and she takes good care of him. She's not a pushover about his diet and she's actually pretty adventurous. Didn't I tell you about their hiking trip?"

Jett grinned. "Yeah, but wasn't it kind of a disaster?"

"It was! They were supposed to camp out in a tent and it rained in the middle of the night and their tent collapsed. They ended up at a bed and breakfast, which he said was equally horrendous with its floral wallpaper. But the point is, he went hiking."

"And will probably never go again," Jett added, laughing at the image of Lou packing all their camping supplies up in the middle of a rainstorm to find a bed and breakfast.

"At least not overnight, no," Zoey agreed.

She leaned forward and took a small bite of her breakfast, careful not to get any syrup on Maisie. Eyeing Jett, her lips curved in a smile. "You look anxious," she said. "I know you're like a little kid on Christmas, but you look like you're about to jump out of your seat if I don't let you start opening presents soon."

Jett's smile widened. "But the nice thing about being the adult is that I can open presents whenever I want."

"Okay, why don't you get started then?" She pointed to a larger, square-shaped package under the tree. "That one is yours from me and Maisie."

Jett shook his head. "I'll wait until you're done. Breakfast first, then presents. Gotta teach the little one patience."

Once all three of them had finished their breakfasts, they moved down to the floor in front of the Christmas tree. Zoey began handing him packages that were either labeled from her or Maisie or from Santa. Jett waited patiently until all the presents were passed out, Maisie's pile being the largest, before standing up and finding one last small present that was on the fireplace mantel.

"You forgot one," he said, sitting back down in front of her, where she sat with their daughter in her lap. "Maisie and I worked hard to pick this one out." Jett handed Zoey the tiny square package and her expression froze, lips parted slightly. "Why don't you open it first..."

Zoey looked for a moment like her breath was caught. It wasn't exactly a secret that it was a jewelry box. It was tiny, square, and had a simple red bow around the green and gold wrapping paper. Her fingers shook as she gently opened it, and her eyes went wide and she gasped when she flipped open the black, velvety ring box.

A vintage-style, pear-shaped diamond sat in a halo of smaller diamonds. The intricate band was cut and carved to resemble the same ring her mother had been buried with. Zoey's beautiful hazel eyes flashed up to Jett, welling with happy tears.

Jett reached over and plucked the ring out of its cushion and held it out to her as he maneuvered himself onto one knee. "Zoey...it was a year ago when I first told you that I loved you. That may not seem like a lot of time, but when I said those words, I knew what they meant. I knew it meant I wanted you and no one else for the rest of my life. I knew that only you would make me feel so alive, so free, so complete. I knew it meant that one day we'd have a family and we would sit side by side and watch it grow. I knew you were the one I would want by my side until I was old and gray, and that even then I would look at you and see the most wonderful, perfect, beautiful person in the world and still wonder how I got so lucky..."

The tears in Zoey's eyes spilled over now and she smiled, holding onto their little girl in her lap.

"And then a little over a month ago you gave me a little girl, and every day I wonder how I could love you even more, and every day you still find ways to make me fall in love all over again. Watching you with Maisie, listening to you sing to her as you rock her to sleep...I know I'm not the only one lucky that you're in my life. I love you so much and I will never stop loving you, I will never stop showing you how much I love you. I will always be here to comfort you, to take care of you, to hold your hand when you need it, be strong when you need it- and even when you don't."

Amazed that he'd made it all the way through his speech, he held the ring out again, taking Zoey's hand in his, and he smiled. "Zoey, will you please marry me?"

Zoey nodded vigorously and she sniffled and tried wiping her tears away with the back of her hand. "Yes! Yes, Jett, I will marry you."

Jett beamed as he slid the ring onto her finger and leaned forward, covering her mouth with his and feeling her lips curve into a smile. He kissed her and let it consume him, tangling his fingers in her hair as he pulled her close, slipping his tongue between her lips and feeling her relax against him.

Then a small mumbling sound came between them and he parted their lips, looking down at his daughter who was still in Zoey's lap. He dipped his head and placed a kiss on top of Maisie's little head of dark waves.

"Same goes for you, little one," he said. "I will never stop showing you how much I love you. Even when your fourth or fifth sibling is here, I promise there will still be enough love to go around."

Zoey half-laughed, half-snorted. "Fourth or fifth sibling? When were you going to clue me in on this plan?"

Jett lifted his head and met Zoey's gaze again. "Oh, we're going to have lots of children. A big family. It'll be great."

Raising a skeptical eyebrow, Zoey asked, "Not trying to compete with anyone, are you?"

"What? It's not like I'm asking for a whole baseball team or anything. That would be ridiculous."

"And how many hockey players do you need on the ice at a time?"

Jett shrugged, turning into his shoulder, and mumbled, "Six." Zoey fixed him with a stare. "But that's irrelevant. I just thought we'd have a big family."

Shaking her head with a laugh, Zoey leaned forward and kissed him again. "We'll talk about this later."

"That's not a no." Jett grinned proudly.

"Just finish opening your presents," Zoey said, rolling her eyes but still laughing. "Not that any of them are going to top this one." She looked down at the new, shiny addition to her left ring finger.

"I love you, Future Mrs. Miller," Jett said. He kissed her again. "I can't wait for you to be my wife."

"And I can't wait for Maisie to be ready for a nap." Zoey's eyes glinted mischievously and Jett smirked.

"Baby number two, here we come."

He was kidding, of course. Kind of. This life of theirs was everything he could have hoped for and more, and he wasn't in a rush to change it any time soon. He knew whether they had two more kids or ten, there wasn't a single soul he'd rather live their crazy, perfect, chaotic life with than the woman right in front of him.

Right now he was happy. *They* were happy. Soon she would be his wife, and as long as he had Zoey at his side, he knew things would only keep getting better.

Thank you all for reading Crowd Pleaser. I hope you really enjoyed Jett and Zoey's story and didn't mind how sappy we got there at the end. Now get ready for a complete 180 in the third installment of this series: *Game Changer.* I know we all can't wait for the handsome, charming, yet arrogant Emerson Yates to meet his match!